# Trace the Edges

by

Laura Cacace

This is a work of fiction. Names, characters, organizations, places, events, and incidents are either products of the author's imagination or are used factiously. Any resemblance to actual persons, living or dead, or actual events is purely coincidental.


ISBN-10: 1981883096
ISBN-13: 9781981883097
ASIN: B075X4CHQZ

eBook published by Kindle Press 2018.

Cover designed by Alyssa Perfetto.
Edited by Bryony Magee.

For Nana and Grandma—

Two strong women who inspired a little girl every day she was lucky enough to know them.

## *Year Four*

She turned her face toward the light, determined to find the glittering outline of the golden orb pressed against a blue sky. Her eyes watered, so she squeezed them shut, just for a moment, before blinking them open and searching again.

"Charley Worth." Nana's hand closed around her granddaughter's. "I'm starting to think you *want* to blind yourself."

Nana tugged little Charlotte along, distracting her from her goal for the moment, but not deterring her in the least.

Charlotte Worth looked through hazel eyes to find a world in vibrant color, thrumming with endless possibility. She found herself forever looking for a sparkle in the dust, a free toy in her cereal box, or bubble gum at the center of a lollipop. She felt it all the time, somewhere deep within her—a need to look for that bit of silver, the small burst of light beaming through the dark clouds that sometimes hovered over life. Her unfailing curiosity was something that her parents never quite understood. But she was a little girl, her mind free from the knowledge of what the world was really like, and her mother and father planned to do everything they could to keep it that way. With Nana Rosie's help, they were sure to succeed.

"Charley," she'd say, using the nickname Charlotte's parents hated because of its masculine counterpart. "We've got the whole day ahead of us, and the world at the tips of our toes. What would you like to do?"

Charlotte's answers varied: the park, the mall, the library, but most often her answer was the train station. She would cling to Nana's wrinkled hand as they made their first stop at the deli for sandwiches. For Nana, pastrami on rye bread, and for Charlotte, ham and cheese on a roll, hold the mayo. When they were back in Nana's red Buick, Charlotte watched as her grandmother covered her eyes with large, rose-tinted sunglasses, and slowly reversed out of the spot. The pair sang together, tunes Nana knew from church, or their favorite, 'The Sun Will Come Out Tomorrow', from Annie. Nana's voice was always off-key, raspy with age and years of smoking, but Charlotte never noticed, only sang along with her.

When they got close enough to hear the sharp whistle of trains pulling into the station, Charlotte jumped up and down in the red velvet seat of the car, the sound going right through her limbs, leaving her flailing in excitement. Nana parked, and they took their untouched sandwiches to the northbound platform and sat down on a bench where they could watch the trains come and go as they ate, Charlotte delighting in the stories Nana made up for the people coming and going.

"He's in a hurry," Nana said. Charlotte clutched her sandwich as the well-dressed man raced past them, forgetting to chew in her interest. "He's rushing home to his wife, who just went into labor. The baby will be here *very* soon."

Charlotte turned all the way around in her seat to watch the man jump into his car and peel out of his parking spot. "Is he going to make it there in time?"

"Looks like it," Nana replied. "Just in time to kiss both his wife and his brand new baby girl."

"How do you know it's a girl?" Charlotte asked, staring up at her grandmother as if she really did hold all the secrets of the world.

Nana met her eye, staring into the hazel depths that were so like her own, and smiled. "I have a knack for these things, Charley. When you're as old as I am, the world doesn't seem so unpredictable."

Charlotte believed her, accepted the answer (even if it didn't make much sense), and faced forward in her seat again, content in the knowledge that her grandmother was special, and hoping that meant she was special, too.

After finishing their sandwiches and their game, Nana took Charlotte's hand and led her back to the car.

"Well, Charley. Another day is under our belts. And you know what?" Nana looked down at Charlotte then, her kind eyes and wide smile surrounded by soft wrinkles, and her drooping cheeks a shade of pink, all framed by a head of light silver curls.

"What?" Charlotte asked.

"I bet the sun will shine even brighter tomorrow."

## *Chapter One*

The rain should be a comforting sight. I've grown so used to it over the past few months—the feel of it on my face, the cold, sometimes warm *plop, plop, plop* of it on my shoulders, soaking my hair, the feel of puddles under my feet with my wellies on—it's stranger if it *isn't* raining. But the steady downpour is pooling in the lush grass of my front yard, not the bustling streets of London, and a day that should be an exciting one—seeing my best friend for the first time since my return—feels more like it's mocking me instead.

"Here's the same gray sky," it seems to say. "The same dark, gloomy clouds, and the same incessant rain, but Charlotte Worth, you are still three thousand miles from where you want to be."

I down the rest of my coffee, my only solace on this ironically dreary day.

"Charlotte, you ready to go?" my father asks, slinging his suit jacket across his shoulders and sliding his arms into the sleeves.

"As I'll ever be," I mutter, lifting my heavy bag from its place on the kitchen chair and dragging it (maybe too) dramatically to the front door.

"Cheer up, buttercup. You're going to have fun today," Dad says, with a chuckle I can't help but resent as he locks the front door behind us.

"I'd rather have fun in London," I say with a pout, before running to the car through the downpour and tugging on the handle of the passenger side door, only to find it locked. *Of course*. "Dad!"

"Go ahead," he calls, mercifully clicking open the locks as he makes his way around the car to the driver's side. I slide into the front seat and swipe at the raindrops on my forehead and bare arms.

Dad starts the car and grins over at me. "I wouldn't say that last part to Andrea if I were you."

"Good thing you're not me, then," I say with a smirk.

Andrea. My best friend since high school. The only real friend I've ever had. From the moment we met in freshman year art class at Lincoln High, she understood me, mainly because she was just like me. I'll never forget the way she leaned over, breathing Skittles breath onto my shoulder as she watched me sketch, and said, too loudly, "Wow, that's really good!"

I'd smiled, the sketch of my hand almost as lifelike as the real thing.

"Thanks," I'd said, and glanced over at hers to repay the compliment. But the sight of the dark lines, the deformed thumb—*Was it a thumb?*—and too long middle finger had me saying, "Yours, um… yours really *isn't* good."

Too late, I'd realized that I should've padded that with something positive, something constructive, and braced myself for her to yell, glare, insult me, or all of the above. But the smiling girl with the dark skin and large brown eyes had just laughed—cackled, even—agreeing with me before introducing herself.

She called me last night to ask about today—to see if I would mind meeting her in Manhattan. Which didn't make much sense, considering she only lived about ten minutes away here in Westchester.

"For what?" I asked, already dreading the journey downtown. "Why can't we just meet somewhere around here?"

"*Because…*" she said, pausing long enough to make me think her emphasis on the one word should've explained it all.

"Because…?"

“Because I’d rather explain it to you in person! And there’s something I want to show you. Now, are you willing to meet me downtown, or not?”

The impatience in her voice made me smirk.

“One question first…”

Andrea didn't have to make a single noise for me to know that she was probably hating me at that moment.

“I’ve been home for two days, I’m still pretty seriously jet-lagged… shouldn’t our first time seeing each other in nearly four months be on my terms?” I asked.

There was a silence on the line then that made me wonder whether or not the call had been dropped, but then Andrea said, “Meet me in Washington Square Park tomorrow morning at eleven. Drink as much coffee as you need to, but you better be there.”

“Can we meet earlier?” I asked, knowing that the battle was already lost. “My dad’s got a class at nine, and I won’t have a ride to the train.”

“Fine. We’ll meet at ten.”

I blew out a resigned breath. “Sounds good.”

“Good,” she said. “And Charlotte?”

“Hm?”

She was smiling for the next part. I could tell. “I can't wait to see you.”

I smiled, then, realizing in that moment just how much I’d missed my best friend. “Me too.”

Now, Dad doesn’t try to talk on our ride to the train station, somehow understanding that speaking in a civilized manner is not something my brain’s up for this early on a summer morning. I spend the five-minute ride staring outside, watching the town I grew up in fly by, but its familiarity no longer holds the same kind of comfort it used to. And I wonder if it was worth it—the choice to leave home for so long, spending months on my own with only my new friends to rely on, and falling in love with a city an ocean away from everything I know.

Yes. Yes, it was.

The reality of being back still sucks, and the fact that people expect me to be *happy* about being back—when I know

I've learned so much more about myself, not to mention the world, in the four months I spent in England, as opposed to my first twenty years here—is pure torture.

"Alright," Dad says as he puts the car in park. "Text me and let me know what time to pick you up."

I nod. "Thanks."

With my bag—filled with tickets, receipts, and other bits of my trip that I didn't have the heart to throw out—weighing down the whole right side of my body, I open my umbrella, get out of the car into the pouring rain, and rush towards the entrance of the station. But I don't get far before Dad's voice stops me.

I blink through the downpour, the rain like white noise all around me, but I find his wide smile—the one that causes his hazel eyes to sparkle just like hers used to.

"The world's at the tips of your toes, kiddo."

The words fly towards me at a rate of ninety miles per hour, like a baseball whizzing across home plate, my chest the catcher's glove. The rain drowns the sound of the impact.

*Strike three*, no one shouts.

She's the glint in his eyes; a shadow who trails his steps; the honesty in his smile. Swallowing over the lump in my throat, I force a smile and nod once before turning back towards the entrance and joining the steady flow of people heading inside, all of us entirely unaffected by the sharp whistle of a train pulling into the station.

***

On any other day, my commute into New York City would be routine, completed on auto-pilot. But today, having been out of my schedule for an entire semester, I can't help but notice everything anew: the rain pelting the East River as we cross over it, gray meeting gray with a splash of white, the blur of Harlem streaking past the windows, and the dry, dark tunnel leading into Grand Central Terminal. It's all familiar, but more like something from a distant memory; fuzzy around the edges, the sharp clarity of it left behind three months ago.

The faces around me are the same, too: solemn, tired, bored—people so complacent in their lives and the rush of each day that they don't even realize how sad they look as they file out of the train like ants marching out of a hole, off to do the same tedious work they do each redundant day. And as we all follow the leader into the main terminal, then scatter in different directions, I realize with a sick knot in my stomach that I'm one of them again.

After a jolting ride on the subway, I arrive at the West 4th Street station and follow another stream of different, but similarly unamused-looking people back out onto the damp city streets. It's stopped raining at least, and as I head down the gum-spattered sidewalks, avoiding dirty puddles and other people, I realize this is where it feels most like London; where I can be just another anonymous face in the crowd. Here, right in the mix of it all in Manhattan, I try to pretend that I'm still there, that I can hear the lilt of British accents all around me.

But even my imagination can't hide the arch of Washington Square Park, can't make it something it's not, can't bend it into the shape of the Shaftesbury Memorial Fountain in the middle of Piccadilly Circus, or mold and point it skyward like Nelson's Column in Trafalgar Square.

If I can't be there, the arch, I suppose, is the next best thing.

That's part of the joy of living so close to New York City--the trek down from Westchester can feel endless, but there's never a lack of things to do, or things to see once you're here. In that way, it's a lot more like London than I give it credit for.

Settling onto the driest bench I can find, I study the arch, the artwork etched into its sides and release a sigh. The familiarity in this moment *is* comforting, and it dulls the ache for London just the smallest bit. I have to believe that more adventures will present themselves. Have to believe that I haven't peaked at twenty years old. Have to believe that my life now will hold more for me, in every sense it hasn't before.

The air stirs around me as two joggers race by. I watch both of them for a moment—two men donning gym shorts and sweaty t-shirts—and imagine they're training for a marathon, maybe a triathlon, judging by the fit looks of them. When one gives the other a shove, and the "shove-ee" smiles and shoves back the "shove-er", I know they've known each other a long time—maybe since elementary school, when one (Kyle) picked the smaller one (Andrew) for his team in a game of kickball on the playground. No one ever really liked or picked Andrew because he was too uncoordinated to be of any use, but Kyle saw the potential in him—his speed. They've been best friends ever since. Now that they've both grown and are on more equal footing, they push each other to reach their potential.

When Kyle and Andrew disappear from sight, I pull my sketchpad from my bag, flipping through the pages slowly, seeing everything again in my mind, and I wish there was some way I'd been able to capture it for real. Art may imitate life, but there's no way it could ever be the same thing. I trace the edges of Tower Bridge in my sketch, blurring the lines of the pencil just a bit with the tip of my finger. I'll have to go over it again, but right now I pretend I'm there, as if just touching my rendering of the beautiful bridge can bring me back, and I see it in my mind's eye.

Until a familiar voice interrupts my memories.

"Well, if it isn't my favorite wannabe Brit, back stateside and absolutely *thrilled* to find her best friend exactly where she left her."

I whip my head around to find Andrea smiling at me as she nears the bench.

"Was that supposed to be a British accent?" I ask, standing as she sets her bag down. "You should know it could use some work."

She hugs me then, and I breathe in the smell of coconut, as familiar to me as the strong arms wrapped around my waist. Andrea is several inches shorter than me, and our hugs always went this way—her arms around my waist, her head tucked under my chin, her frizzy, black 'fro tickling my nose. But she'd never squeezed so tightly, never held on for this long, and I realize how much I missed her.

"I've missed you, girl," she says as we pull away, and grips my hands in hers. "You look *great*."

"Oh, are we being nice to each other today?" I grin. "In that case, so do you."

Andrea smirks. "I figured I'd at least try to get through the first five minutes without any snark, but since you already went there…" She sits down on the bench, and I sit beside her, both of us turned so that we can look right at the other. "How does it feel to see me after so long? What's changed? Do I still have an air of authority and a wing so sharp, men bow down before me in fear?"

I stare at the perfect, sharp wings of the black eyeliner she's referring to, and smirk.

"Don't give yourself too much credit," I say. "I may've come all the way down here to see you, but the real draw is that the city is more like London than my house is. And yes, to all of the above. And it's *really* good to see you."

"I knew you had ulterior motives," she says. "And I'm proud of you. That almost sounded genuine."

After another moment, we both drop the act and giggle.

Andrea reaches into her bag, pulls out her sunglasses and puts them on. "So. What was your favorite thing about it?"

She may be a little bit of a thing, but the volume at which she speaks would make anyone who wasn't looking think she's much larger. Andrea demands attention. She always has, even when she looks as cute and innocent as she does today, with her high-waist black shorts and black-and-white striped top, her hair a somewhat contained 'fro atop her head.

Before I have the chance to respond to her impossible question (I loved all of it too much to pick *one* favorite thing), she asks, "Did you meet Prince Harry and tell him I love him?"

"He was unavailable every time I tried to get in touch. Strange, really."

"Probably for the best," she says, turning to look out at the people milling around us for a moment. "He couldn't handle me, anyway."

I nudge my prescription glasses further up onto the bridge of my nose. "True. Even I can't, and I've known you for six years."

She smiles. "I take a twisted sense of pride in that. But seriously, how was the land of the royals? Everything you hoped it would be?"

"In all seriousness…" I look away from her towards the fountain. "I wish I'd never left."

As soon as the words are out of my mouth I realize how they could be taken, and I glance at Andrea, ready to put a more positive spin on them, but she beats me to it.

"Thanks a lot."

"Andi, you know I didn't mean it *that* way, I just—"

"Don't you think I know you well enough by now to know what you mean?" She shakes her head, grinning at me. "You and that mouth, Charlotte. Consider yourself lucky you have such an understanding friend who puts up with both of you."

"Oh, please." I sit back and cross my arms. "You're even worse than I am. At least I *attempt* to sound apologetic afterwards."

Andrea presses her lips together, sucking them between her teeth for a moment, before saying, "I can't even deny it," and screeching a laugh.

I've almost forgotten how contagious her laughter is, but the sound of it now has me giggling along with her.

When we're both breathless, giddy just from being together after so long apart, she pats my knee several times. "Okay…before I hear more about the trip—and I intend to hear everything," she says, eyeing me with a smile. She's practically bouncing out of her seat now. "There's something I want to ask you, and it has to do with why I wanted to meet so early."

I gasp and hold a hand up to my wounded heart. "You mean you *didn't* just miss me?"

Andrea's smile doesn't falter. "I had a meeting this morning with the people at the community theater…"

I nod after a moment, watching the excitement form on her face, in her grin, in her eyes as they crinkle up.

Andrea's done plays for as long as I've known her. I remember the first one I saw our freshman year. She was the Queen of Hearts in Alice in Wonderland, which couldn't have been a more perfect role for her. Her normally loud voice so simply turned maniacal, and as the kind of person who enjoys any kind of attention, she had the whole audience completely captivated. She's been doing shows with the community theater on the Lower East Side ever since graduation, and only getting better with each new role.

"I've been trying to get them to allow me the time and space to do a play, and…they finally said yes! I'm directing my first play in a *real* theater!"

"Oh, my God, Andi! That's amazing!"

She slaps at my hands in her excitement, and squeals loudly enough to attract the attention of passers-by. I smile at the strangers in apology, but Andrea doesn't even seem to notice.

"I *know*," she says, oblivious to the confused stares of the general public. "I get a full eight weeks of rehearsal time, and then a whole weekend for shows!"

"That's incredible, Andi. I—"

"You know how long I've wanted this, Charlotte, probably better than anyone. And as much as I love acting, I need to try this. I *know* I'll be good at it."

"Of course you will," I say, able to cut in this time. "You're *great* at telling people what to do."

"I know!" she agrees, not catching my joke, or just choosing to ignore it. "I've done enough plays now. Directing one should come pretty naturally to me. And I get to cast it and everything. They're basically giving me total freedom." She digs into her purse and pulls out a pack of cigarettes, smacking the bottom of the container.

"Who'd you have to accost for full freedom?"

She giggles as she puts a cigarette between her lips, and then plunges her hand back into the bag for a lighter. "You know me too well, girl." She removes the cigarette from her mouth with two fingers, her other hand still in the depths of her bag. "But no one, actually. After the success of the last play—when I stepped in for Nora after she got sick on opening day—I guess they just trust me."

She pulls a lighter out and puts the cigarette back between her lips. "And they should," she says over it. "I've done, like, six plays with them at this point."

Andrea flicks the lighter and puffs, smoke swirling quickly around her and meandering over to me.

I cover my nose. "Smoking kills, you know."

Andrea blows a puff straight out in front of her. "So does nagging, but I don't see you stopping."

"It takes much longer," I say through my fingers. "And besides, I do it out of love." I make a show of sliding all the way to the other side of the bench. "I'd like to have you around for a while."

"Well I'm glad you feel that way, Charlotte…" Andrea releases another long breath of smoke with a devilish grin. "Because I have a proposition for you."

"Uh oh," I say, my hands dropping away so that she can see my already-excited grin. "I'm in for it, aren't I?"

## *Year Five*

"Nana!" Charlotte called from across the sandbox.

Nana always sat on the same bench in the park. The one closest to the exit. Charlotte darted between other children towards her grandmother, oblivious to their curious young eyes as they trailed her. "Nana, are you watching?"

"Of course I'm watching," Nana Rosie said, smiling as her granddaughter skidded to a halt right before hitting the pavement, sending sand flying everywhere.

"I'm following a trail to a magic temple," Charlotte said, and brushed away the hair that had fallen in her face. But it fell right back into her eyes, so Nana reached over to curl it behind her ear. "And I found these clues to help me."

She held up fistfuls of sandy garbage—bottle caps, a broken toy soldier, a few rocks, and a gum wrapper.

"Ah," Nana said, leaning over to eye Charlotte's hoard. "Let me know when you find it. I hear there's a lonely princess inside, looking for a friend."

Charlotte's eyes lit up, looking more green than brown in the sunlight, and with a promise to find the princess she was off, running past the other children playing together, on an adventure of her own creation.

Charlotte's parents weren't around much. They each worked odd jobs to keep up with the rent of their two-bedroom apartment in the suburbs of New York. But when they did spend time with her, she demanded their attention. Not in the way a spoiled child might, by screaming and carrying on to get his or her way, but in a way that confused, and even sometimes frightened them. Charlotte was fearless from the moment she put her hands and knees to the green carpet of Nana Rosie's living room and crawled. Even putting a finger in an electrical socket didn't scare her away from doing it again. Even a twenty-five foot drop to the ground didn't stop her from climbing a tree just to see the view. Even the chatter of classmates, whispering about the strange girl with a mane of red curls, didn't stop her from going off on her own. Mr. and Mrs. Worth, like all parents, feared for their daughter. But their fear was rooted in the way she didn't need them; the way she didn't rely on anyone but herself. Their only comfort, the only certainty they had that Charlotte's recklessness wouldn't get the best of her, was Nana Rosie.

Nana took up the slack, keeping an eye on Charlotte in her own home, and at the library where Nana had worked as a librarian since long before Charlotte was born. Unlike Charlotte's parents, Nana understood her granddaughter and took pride in the way Charlotte kept herself busy in the library, pulling books from the shelves at random and reading them aloud on the floor, giving the characters different voices, as if she were reading to an audience. She loved when Charlotte played by herself in the park, singing to herself or making up little games as she wandered around picking up bottle caps and broken plastic toys long forgotten in the sand. She saw the way young mothers eyed Charlotte, with a mix of tenderness and wariness as they pulled their own children closer to their chests. She saw the genuine surprise in their eyes when little Charley nudged her glasses up her nose and asked them if she could borrow their shovel for her mission. And Nana felt only pride. She felt like she was witnessing a miracle each time her granddaughter surprised her somehow, and saw Charlotte's independence as a special gift, rather than a dangerous trait.

"Charley is a leader," Nana would say when her son and daughter-in-law complained that she was too strong-willed, too much a detriment to her own well-being. "She'll never do what you hope she will, and forcing her won't do anyone any good. Support who she is instead of worrying about who she isn't."

Luckily, Charlotte didn't often feel weighed down by her parents' concerns, but Nana did. She didn't know if they *couldn't* understand, or simply wouldn't take the time to. Charlotte might not sense their fear, but just in case she ever did, Nana had a plan.

"Charley," Nana said, looking up from her book at the dining room table while her granddaughter sketched in her first ever sketchpad—a birthday present from one artist to another. Charlotte looked up. "Hold onto your curiosity. Let it keep you moving. You never know when or where you'll come across something extraordinary."

As any five-year-old might, Charlotte took her grandmother's words literally, and decided that if she were to discover something extraordinary, she wanted to discover it quickly. From then on, she did everything at a light jog, running anywhere and everywhere—across her room, the living room, in the halls of school, on the playground at recess, even in the library. She'd gotten in trouble for it many times, and her parents and teachers tried to slow her down, but Charlotte was determined—so determined that she found herself in the emergency room with a broken ankle after skidding across the hardwood floors in their apartment and falling over, her foot twisted at an odd angle. She and her parents deduced that Nana Rosie probably didn't mean for her to start sprinting *everywhere* with her advice.

Charlotte slowed down after that. She didn't stop moving, but hoped that extraordinary things wouldn't mind waiting for her to discover them.

## *Chapter Two*

I can already feel the cigarette smoke clinging to me—my hair, my clothes, and my lungs.

Andrea ignores my snide remark, and from the look she gives me, I know it's not the right time for banter.

"I'm listening," I say.

She flicks ash to the ground, letting the cigarette dangle from her fingers and burn red for a moment. "Okay, so, *of course* I'm thrilled about this opportunity. I've wanted to do this for too long not to be."

I nod.

"But…and this is only for your ears, Charlotte Worth. You cannot tell a soul."

"Who the hell do you think I'd tell? The only person I talk to apart from my dad is you."

"Right, I know. This is just—well…it's embarrassing. It's hard for me to even say this to you, and you're my best friend." Her eyebrows are drawn together, and she stares at the ground as she takes another long pull from her cigarette.

"Spit it out, Andi."

She whips her head around, eyes round with something I don't often see in them…fear.

"I'm scared I'm going to screw it up," she finally admits, taking another long drag before tossing the cigarette. It blinks red before dimming a little way away; smoke curling up and toward the sky. "I know I won't, but I have this…" She gestures to her stomach. "This feeling that it's not going to be what I expect. And don't get me wrong—I know it'll be a challenge. But I want to take it on, and I think it'll really help to have someone I trust wholeheartedly on board."

She looks straight at me then, and I nod, waiting for her to continue.

When all we do is stare at each other, her eyebrows shoot up. "So? Will you?"

"Will I wha—? Oh."

"Will you help me?" Andrea asks. "You're the only person I could think of. You're my best friend, Charlotte, and I know I can count on you."

"But…" I'm a little taken aback, not just because she's asking me to help her with a play, but because she's asking for help at all. Andrea's the proudest, most independent person I know, and she'd never admit to this kind of thing unless she was being totally serious. "But, the last time I was in a play, or even involved in one, I was *six.*"

"That's okay," she's quick to say. "You've *seen* lots of plays, and it won't be hard. Besides, it's not like I'm giving you full control or anything. I'd just like to have that extra pair of eyes and ears, and someone creative to help with set design, and—"

"Set design?" I ask, perking up a bit.

Andrea smiles. "See? There's something in this for everyone. I also hoped you might be interested in creating the artwork for the program, and ads and stuff. We wouldn't need that for a while, but if you're at rehearsals, or at least some of them, I'm sure you'll have plenty of inspiration."

It sounds like a pretty good deal, despite my nerves. The fact that I've never worked on a play is the only thing making me think twice about it. But this is Andrea, and if I were to work on a play with anyone, I'd want it to be with her. At the same time, this is *Andrea*. I know Andrea, and with her, something that's supposed to be fun could quickly turn into a whole lot of *not* fun. She takes her work and her ideas so seriously, and if other people's ideas don't gel with hers—it would be an understatement to say that she doesn't take it well.

"*If* I were to accept," I say, and I pause, looking right at her so she knows I'm serious. "What else might this entail?"

"Nothing." Andrea's eager now, and the word comes out too quickly, too high-pitched. "Just your artistic abilities, of which there are *many*." I resist the urge to roll my eyes. "And, perhaps more importantly, to offer moral support."

I know I'm going to say yes. It's not like I've got anything else going on. Just passing the time until school starts at the end of August, and wallowing in self-pity. This is too exciting an opportunity to pass up. But, at the same time, there's an ebb of doubt in the current of my certainty, whispering reasons why I couldn't, *shouldn't* do this.

*No experience.*

*Liking plays doesn't mean you should be part of one.*

*Can I really handle something of this magnitude?*

And I let all of it wade there, antagonizing me, knowing that it's prevented me from doing things with its talk before. But it's not there long before I let my excitement drown it out with a big SCREW YOU.

"Okay," I say, smiling at Andrea.

With a shriek of what I hope is happiness, she throws her arms around me, thanking me repeatedly with stale cigarette breath.

"Alright, alright get off me. You stink."

"I'm too excited to insult you right now." She's actually clapping her hands.

"No need to." I smile. "Thank you for asking me."

"Oh." She clucks her tongue. "Girl, I wish I could say I did it for you, but…" She shrugs. "I asked you for mostly selfish reasons."

"I accepted for mostly selfish reasons, so I guess we're even."

We giggle a little more before I think to ask, "So, what play is it?"

Andrea pulls one leg up onto the bench and tucks it under the other. "It's called 'What Was Lost' by a Canadian playwright. His name's André Caron." She pauses, reading the look on my face. "The name was a total coincidence."

"Sure it was," I say with a smile.

"Anyway, it's about this guy who's kind of pathetic, but in an endearing sort of way, and he finds out his wife's been cheating on him, and that's how the play starts. Just him, alone in their kitchen waiting for her. But he doesn't have the courage to say anything, and basically—"

"Okay, Andi. Why don't you just send me the script?" I ask, afraid she's about to dive into the whole plot.

"Say no more," she says, a gleam in her eye as she reaches into her bag. She pulls out a bundle of pages. "I printed a copy for you."

I take the stack from her and stare down at it, feeling its weight in my hands. "How'd you know I'd say yes?"

"I didn't," she says with a shrug. "But I planned to badger you about it until you did."

"Practical," I say with a nod of approval as I flip through the pages.

"I thought so. If you can't read the whole thing before auditions, don't worry about it."

"When are auditions?"

"This weekend. Friday and Saturday. Sunday, too, if necessary. One to four each day."

"I can't do this weekend," I say with a sigh. "I'm…going to my mother's." I grumble the last part, hating the decision to go even more now. "But maybe I could—"

"No worries. That's more important." She winks at me, to which I respond with a roll of my eyes. Andrea knows the situation with my mother well, and she also knows that's exactly what I *don't* want to hear. "I'm planning to film all the auditions anyway, unless someone objects. So, we'll just go through all of them next week when you're around."

Seeing no way out of my weekend plans, I suck in a long breath. "That sounds…reasonable."

"It does, doesn't it? Now, about the set…" Andrea slides another cigarette out of the pack. "I was thinking—"

"Seriously?" I eye the culprit in her hand, then stare up at her. "It's been five minutes. You can wait at least half an hour."

With a long sigh, she slides the cigarette behind her ear. "Happy?"

"I'd say 'content' is a better word for how I'm feeling." I smile sweetly.

"As I was saying," Andrea says, giving me the side-eye. "I was thinking a wall…" She holds her hands straight out in front of her, fingers parallel to her face.

I hold back laughter. "A wall?"

"Yes. One wall, cutting the stage into two halves." She looks over at me, expectant, and my giggle comes out with a snort.

"Are the cigarettes the only thing you're smoking, or…?"

"Laugh it up, Charlotte Worth." Her voice is even louder over the sound of my laughter. "Remember who's giving you the creative space to frolic in!"

"Right, right." I collect myself as best I can. "I think the last thing you said had to do with a *wall.*"

Andrea only stares at me, unamused as I choke back more laughter.

"You know what?" she says, gathering her bag close to her and slinging the strap over her shoulder. "You'll get it when you read the script."

She stands, then, and I follow, scrambling to grab my bag and catch up to her. "Wait. Where are you going?"

"I'm going to show you the theater space, so maybe you'll be able to picture what I'm talking about."

I take long strides to keep up with her, and almost make a comment about how fast her little legs can take her, but the words stop short on my tongue when she removes the cigarette from behind her ear.

"Hey—"

"Ah!" Andrea holds up a finger, the cigarette dangling from her lips. "Not a word."

I pretend to zip my lips, staying silent for the moment, but coughing emphatically when the smoke drifts toward me.

"If I develop lung cancer from secondhand smoke," I say, "it's on you. I hope you can live with that."

"Everyone's got to go out somehow, right?"

We stop at the corner of the street, waiting on the light, and she stares at me as she takes another hearty drag and lets the rank smoke creep out the side of her mouth.

"If anyone's going to be responsible for my death, call me crazy, but I'd prefer it be me."

"Well, this conversation's certainly taken a turn."

We step around the opposite stream of people-traffic as we cross the street.

"Leave it to us to go from discussing decorative walls to causes of death in two minutes flat," I say, turning to smile down at her.

"I said nothing about it being decorative!" she says, eyes wide and voice rising an octave with outrage.

"Well, what was I left to assume? The only thing you said you pictured was a wall. What's the point of having me on for my artistic abilities if all we have to design is a *wall*? Of course I'd think it's going to be decorated."

Andrea shakes her head, a smile tugging at the corner of her lips. "I love you, Charlotte, but sometimes…" She pauses to take a puff and releases it just as quickly. "Being friends with you feels like work."

I smile, throwing an arm around her shoulders despite the smoke. "Now you know what it feels like to be friends with *you.*"

Laughter bubbles up and past her lips. "Touché."

"And…" I lean down and press a firm, loud kiss to her smooth cheek. "I love you, too."

She throws the nub that's left to the ground and releases the last stream of smoke with a smile. "I missed you, girl."

The words bring back London, the wet sidewalks, the crowds of strangers, the pangs of missing a place I don't know if, or when I'll ever see again.

"Missed you, too." I mean it, but keep to myself the part about missing London more.

We round a corner, the street quieter than the last one we were on, and Andrea speeds up. "It's just at the end of the block."

I smile, her excitement almost tangible. "I know. I've been here before, remember?"

But she's not really listening.

I've seen all her plays, sometimes multiple times a run. And she was amazing in each one. But this… This is big. Directing is her real dream, and she's choosing to make me a part of it. Her nerves are now my nerves.

This is what I wanted. An opportunity. An adventure. Maybe it'll help with the post-London depression. Maybe it will lessen the ache. But right now, staring at my new adventure, thinking about my old one, all I want is to go back. My memories of it dangle at the front of my mind, taunting me with the freedom, the independence, the sense of novelty in everything I did there.

"The world's at the tips of my toes," I mutter.

"What?" Andrea glances over. We're in front of the theater now.

"Nothing," I say, staring at the pretty brick facade, wishing desperately I could believe those words again.

# *Year Six*

"You're lying," said one of the little girls surrounding Charlotte.

"I'm *not,*" Charlotte insisted.

Surprised, Nana leaned in closer to listen.

The girls turned to eye Nana, who was acting as a lunch monitor at Charlotte's school. They stood around Charlotte, and if Nana didn't know better, she'd think that Charlotte was the sun of their little universe. But Charlotte didn't need to be their sun, and never waited for anyone to orbit around her. So, the fact that she was with them at all was a little surprising.

All the other children were running around them on the playground, but the little girls stood still, staring at Nana, their young eyes alert with suspicion. Nana turned her confused attention to Charlotte, whose little brows were drawn together beneath her glasses, and smiled, hoping her granddaughter would smile back.

She did.

The little girls leaned in closer to Charlotte, whispering things Nana couldn't hear, but she kept her eye on them, wondering what this was all about. Charlotte never expressed a desire to make friends—she didn't seem to mind being alone on the playground—but that didn't mean she didn't want to, somewhere deep down. And Nana wanted that for her if that was what she wanted.

After a few more moments, the group of girls turned to face Nana with Charlotte standing at the back. One stepped forward, pushed her long, dark hair behind her ear, and looked up at Nana with large brown eyes. "Excuse me, Charlotte's grandma?" she said.

"Yes?"

"Are you a witch?"

Nana laughed, taken by surprise, but the girls looked completely serious, and when she glanced at Charlotte, she noted the worried crease of her granddaughter's light brows.

"Depends on the day, really," Nana said, still smiling.

"But can you do magic?" the same little girl pressed, even more eager now.

They all looked eager. They wanted to know the truth, but Nana could see it in their eyes—they wanted even more to believe whatever Charlotte had told them.

Rather than affirm or deny the question, Nana asked, "How much has Charley told you?"

"She said that you're a witch, but the good kind. Like Glinda from The Wizard of Oz. And she said that you only use your magic for good things, like helping people and stuff."

"Well—"

"And she said that she's a witch, too. And she doesn't have her magic yet, but she'll get it when she gets older. And no one knows about you guys being witches except you and her. But I don't believe her."

Nana was staring at Charlotte, whose eyes were pleading with her grandmother to confirm the story, and Nana had to fight back a smile. Not only was Charlotte always prone to making up stories—it was another one of the things her parents tried to "correct" about their daughter—but she had these girls hanging on her every word. She could see in their eyes the desire to believe, the desire to trust that this strange girl, with her auburn curls flowing wildly around her face, her now-green eyes large and bright, and a look in those eyes that hinted at something wild and uninhibited inside, was telling the truth. Their disbelief was rooted in an adult skepticism, as if they could hear in their minds what their parents would say if they were to relay Charlotte's story.

Nana was an adult in most senses of the word. The wrinkles on her face and her hands would say as much to six-year-old girls. They turned to her because they wanted her to deny all of what Charlotte had told them. But they didn't know Nana Rosie Worth well enough.

"Do you trust these girls, Charley?" she asked, looking only at her granddaughter.

The little girls swiveled to eye Charlotte, who looked surprised, but nodded.

Nana sighed dramatically. "Well, then I guess it's okay that you told them."

A collective gasp rolled over the few girls, and Charlotte smiled at the back of the lot.

"But I have to be sure you won't tell anyone. Not your parents, or your friends, or cousins, whoever. You can't breathe a word of this to anyone," Nana said, looking each little girl in the eye.

"What happens if we tell?" one of the little girls asked, eyes wide, a piece of her short brown hair in her mouth.

Nana waited a moment. "You don't want to know."

They were all quiet for a moment, then the first little girl who spoke piped up again. "Wow! You *weren't* lying!" she said to Charlotte.

"Told ya," Charlotte said, pride coloring her voice.

They chattered together for several moments before taking off at a run towards the other end of the playground, with little Charlotte at the front now.

Nana smiled, remembering all the times Charlotte had tried to get herself out of trouble with her colorful stories. It was almost like it was a game to her, one that required not only creativity, but follow-through and determination. And she was *good* at it.

Charlotte had always loved the smell of coffee grounds, and whenever her mother found a container knocked over in the cupboard, black grounds everywhere, Charlotte was prepared.

"It was a ghost," she'd said once. "He was an old man with glasses and a grumpy look on his face, and he misses coffee the most about being on Earth, so he was trying to make some, and then it spilled, but because he's a ghost, he can't pick it up, and—"

"Charlotte," her mother would say, impatience all over the word, "telling lies is not an attractive quality. Clean this up."

Nana Rosie had never seen Charlotte's story-telling as anything other than creativity. It wasn't her fault she was an imaginative little girl with a penchant for minor destruction. Besides, the trouble she caused was never so bad that it couldn't be fixed. The worst of her offenses included sticking her father's favorite tie into a paper shredder just to see what would happen. But he had plenty of other ties. And even though she'd flushed her mother's wedding band down the toilet (her excuse had been that she'd stuck a tracker to it so that she could follow its movement—see which ocean it ended up in), and her mother cried for two hours afterwards, things could have been worse.

At least she was healthy. At least she was intelligent and kind and happy.

To Nana Rosie, that was what mattered: that Charlotte grew up happy and healthy, her talents honed and supported by her family's love. If she caused a little mischief along the way, so be it.

When the bell rang signaling the end of recess, Charlotte ran toward her grandmother while the rest of the children lined up. Nana Rosie grunted from the force at which Charlotte threw herself into Nana's arms.

"Oof, Charley," she said, pulling her granddaughter close.

"Thank you," Charlotte said, smiling up at Nana. "For not telling them the truth."

Nana sighed, understanding Charlotte's need to relate to the other children and the world around her. She appreciated that Charlotte's way of relating to the world veered a little left of what might be considered normal. But she also knew that Charlotte was straddling the fine line between being imaginative and flat-out lying.

And she'd sucked Nana right into the middle of it.

Nana Rosie knew her granddaughter, and she knew that Charley would never intentionally hurt anyone. She'd just grown so comfortable living in the worlds she created for herself, she had trouble understanding how things worked here in reality.

"Charley," Nana sighed, watching the little girls laugh across the yard, eyes wide with the secret they were given. "You know, making things up is your way of having fun, and that's fine, but not everyone likes lying. It doesn't feel good when someone lies to you."

"But, I thought—"

"Now, I know you didn't mean anything by it, but what happens when those girls find out the truth?"

Charlotte hung her head, and stayed silent.

"I'm not saying this to hurt you, I just want you to be careful. Pretending something is real when it's not, while fun, is still a lie. And now I'm lying for you, too. I don't like to lie, Charlotte, and you shouldn't either." Nana paused to curl Charlotte's hair behind her ear, and smiled. "Besides…there's a lot less to remember when you tell the truth."

"But they like me now," she said, and Nana's heart cracked along a seam.

"If they're real friends," Nana said, leaning down to look her granddaughter in the eye, "they'll like you no matter what."

Charlotte turned her head, watching her new friends for a moment. "You're not going to tell them the truth, are you?"

Nana shook her head. "I was hoping you would do that. When you're ready."

Charlotte sighed, but nodded, and when the classes began heading back into the building, she gave her grandmother one last hug before running off to join them.

Nana watched Charlotte run right to her new friends, who smiled and accepted her without a second thought. Nana knew she shouldn't have lied, knew she should have led by example, but seeing her granddaughter smile that way made it all worth it.

Charlotte already dreaded having to tell Maddie, Jaclyn, and Eileen the truth, afraid that when they found out there was nothing special about her, they wouldn't want to be friends with her anymore. Now that she had them, she didn't want to lose them.

So, she thought, smiling and laughing along with them as they walked into the lunchroom, if she could just keep this one secret—keep this one lie—she promised herself she would never tell another one again.

## *Chapter Three*

"What do you mean you went to a strip club?" Dad's voice is panicked, and his fork hangs suspended halfway between his open mouth and his nearly clean plate. A piece of pasta falls off the end as he stares.

Andrea slaps a hand over her mouth too late, and her bark of laughter has me snickering. Dad's eyes, round with shock and embarrassment, are doing nothing to slow the mounting sense of hilarity in this kitchen.

"We didn't *mean* to," I say through giggles. "We had semi-good intentions for the night. 'The Flying Dutchman' looked like your classic British pub from the outside. It had wooden siding and the lettering was all black and fancy—it looked really normal." I glance across the table at Andrea, whose hand is still over her smiling mouth, and smirk. "It was only *after* we went inside that we realized the 'Dutchman' was flying high on something a little more primal than alcohol could afford him."

Andrea narrowly avoids spewing water all over the table, and I can't control my own laughter any longer. Dad looks between us, horrified into silence, but smiles when we can't stop laughing. Finally, he shakes his head, stabbing at the pasta on his plate with more force than necessary.

"I thought I wanted to hear more about your trip," he says. "I guess I was wrong."

"So, I guess now *wouldn't* be the time to tell you that after we left, I let the homeless man outside of McDonald's steal my virtue."

Andrea crumples in a fit of loud giggles, and Dad smirks over at me, swallowing before saying, "Charlotte Worth, you are going to be the death of me."

"Nah, that's a little too ambitious." I pop some pasta into my mouth, and talk over it. "I'm really just aiming for a full head of gray hair."

Dad smiles at me, and shakes his head in disbelief before looking to his other side at Andrea. "Why are you friends with her?"

She wipes under her eyes, still smiling. "Cause she's no worse than I am. In fact, this is mild compared to me."

Dad looks between the two of us for a moment, then drops his wrinkled napkin onto his clean plate. "Well, if you don't mind, I'm getting out of here before it gets any worse."

"Thank you for dinner, Mr. Worth," Andrea says from her seat. "It was great."

"Really?" He pulls the red apron over his head, leaving him in his suit, the tie he loosened around his neck, and his sleeves rolled to his elbows.

"I think you've finally perfected it." I smile at him, taking another bite to prove my point.

"Yeah?" Dad smiles, his hazel eyes more brown in the dim light of our kitchen. He grabs my forearm and gives it a squeeze before folding his apron. "Thanks, kiddo."

Since Mom left, Dad and I have taken turns cooking dinner, typically switching off every other night. Neither of us knew how to cook when we started, but I picked it up quickly, starting with pasta and sauce before expanding my horizons and working with meats and vegetables. Dad, however, really only feels comfortable with pasta dishes. It wasn't pretty at first. Too bland, too salty, pasta too soft, too hard. But now, with over a year's worth of practice, it finally tastes just right.

I raise my water to my lips and mutter, "I'm lucky I survived the process, but at least we made it here."

Dad rolls his eyes, but Andrea comes to his defense. "I don't believe her for a second, Mr. Worth. This was just too good."

"Thank you, Andi," Dad says. "At least *someone* appreciates my hard work."

I huff a little, but don't say any more. Dad kisses my head, leaving me abruptly grateful for him despite my making fun.

When my mother left us a little more than a year ago, we floundered, neither of us sure which way to swim to reach the surface of our grief, and neither of us sure how to relate to the other. Dad was too used to his job being his main focus, and it felt like I didn't know him well enough to reveal just how much my mother's abandonment hurt—especially because he was a victim of it, too.

My parents were still teenagers when they had me—both seventeen, both scared and excited when they got married, and neither really ready for what they had gotten themselves into. But they did love each other. At least, that's what Nana told me.

But having a child so young meant that neither of them was able to pursue their dreams. Dad wanted to go to college, then write for a newspaper and eventually pen a best-selling novel, but found himself in the local grocery store full-time, working to support Mom and me, putting college off indefinitely. Mom dreamed in color, her hope of becoming a designer put on hold so she could stay home, forgoing her education to take care of me.

Dad somehow found the time to return to school when I was four years old, but Mom never found the time, or the desire. As Dad tells it, Nana was around. The library allowed her to bring me into work on the couple of days a week she was there. But Mom felt alone nonetheless, and resented Dad for getting out of the house each day, leaving her with their baby—leaving her with *me*.

Even then, I sensed it. Her disdain, her resentment, even if I didn't know it was the direct result of me. Those were the bad days, as I've come to call them. The days where she barely looked at me, and when she did, it was always with a frown. The good days were only marginally better, but her smiles on those days were strained, never quite reaching her brown eyes.

Nana Rosie days were my favorite days. Her touch on my cheek was a gentle reassurance when I was sad, her eyes were always intent when she listened to me talk, and her laughter was always a pleasant reward. Her love was always tangible, and the knowledge of its presence, a comfort in its consistency.

I rarely felt that much love with Mom. Somewhere deep inside, I'd always understood that I was a chore to her, an obstacle to be overcome. Maybe it was her ever-present frown, her exasperated sighs when I made a mess in the living room, or how her eyes never strayed from her magazines when she took me to the park.

Whatever it was, her abandonment a year ago had only confirmed everything I already knew.

"Alright," Dad says. "I'm off to save the world. Have fun, you two."

"Is he going to sleep?" Andrea asks after he leaves the kitchen, glancing at her watch. "It's only 7:30."

I hear my father's footsteps on the stairs. "No, he's going up to write."

Dad's a professor at a local college now. Teaching students about writing seemed like a good way to pair his passion and financial needs until he could finish his book.

Which *still* hasn't happened.

He's been working on this particular novel for years, never finding it "good enough" or "ready" to be sent out for potential publication. So, he sits with it every night after dinner and nitpicks, changing a character's hair color, adding a twist in the plot that has lovers pulled away from one another, then put back together, only to be torn apart again. If only life could be tweaked to such perfection.

There are nights I can tell he goes without sleep because his brown hair is a tangled mess in the morning, and there are dark purple circles under his eyes. My dad's a handsome guy. At thirty-eight years old, he looks about thirty, all of his hair still there and still brown, hazel eyes bright, and a smile at the ready for any and everyone. Even on those mornings following his sleepless nights, he's kind and gentle, if a little distracted. But he still stands at the kitchen counter and packs our lunches, gulping hot black coffee like it's a milkshake and smiling like it's been years since he's seen me when I finally make my way downstairs.

"Well, *he* may not want to hear all the dirty details," Andrea says, pushing her clean plate forward on the table and propping her elbows up. "But I sure as hell do."

"Dirty details?" I ask. "Is that what you think of me?"

"Any guys?" she asks, point-blank.

I know I won't be able to wiggle my way out of answering. Not with Andrea. But that doesn't mean I can't deflect for as long as possible.

"There were some." I take a sip of water with what I hope is a look of disinterest.

"And?" she presses. "Did anything happen with any of them?"

"Well," I say, consolidating our dirty dishes by stacking them up and placing our used utensils on top. "My friend Mason and I had daily sing-alongs to show tunes. Wicked and Billy Elliot were our favorites."

Andrea rolls her eyes. "Did you hook up with anyone or not?"

I don't meet her eye. "Maybe."

"I *knew* it!" she exclaims, smiling wide. I feel abruptly shy. "Was he British? Are you guys still talking?" Her eyes widen with her next loud intake of breath. "Did you have *sex* with him?"

"No, no, and a resounding no."

"He wasn't British? That's kind of disappointing, then."

"Sorry?" I say, not meaning it at all.

I'm afraid to even shift in my seat, let alone stand, hoping that will be the end of our discussion about it, knowing full well that if we delve any further I'll be on the receiving end of a lot of well-meaning, but firm, criticism.

The next few moments of quiet are like the glimmer of hope at the end of writing a long paper; the winding down of words and explanations where the final period is in full sight.

"So…" Andrea says, drawing the word out and prolonging the completion of that paper with another loaded question.

I only stare at the dirty plates in front of me.

Her frustrated sigh is enough to let me know I'm not going to like where this is going. "Charlotte, you are the only person I know who literally always has something to say, except when it comes to your relationships. Or, should I say, near-misses?"

"The second one is probably a little more accurate," I say, fighting back a smile when she glares at me. "Alright, well, if you *really* want to know…"

She rolls her eyes, but I don't let that stop me. If I stop for anything, I might not go through with the explanation.

"His name is Michael, he lives out in California. He was in London with his school and staying in the same student accommodation we were in, and I saw him around a lot."

We met in the laundry room about a week into the three months I was spending there. He caught my attention just because he'd dumped a whole bag of clothes—darks *and* whites—into the washer machine right next to the one I was using.

"You know you're supposed to separate them, right?" I'd said, unable to help myself.

He turned toward me, and he was so tall he had to look down. His eyes were the lightest shade of blue. Then he smiled, and my heart stuttered. When he looked back into the front-loader machine, his grin grew even wider. "I *knew* I should've just bought more underwear to avoid all this," he said.

And I laughed.

"Ew," Andrea says, her nose wrinkled in distaste. "What about the rest of his clothes?"

"That's what *I* said!"

We kept running into each other after that, and finally, when we'd run into each other at eight in the morning in line for coffee at the cafe down the street, we decided to hang out. Only, we didn't stop. It didn't matter that we each had our own groups of friends, or our own schoolwork to worry about. Most days after that, we wandered around the city together, taking in the magnificence of Big Ben, the surreal history in every inch of places like the Tower of London and Westminster Abbey, the brilliance of plays on the West End, and the world-renowned pub culture. We adjusted to life in London together, and I woke up every morning looking forward to seeing him.

My relationship with Michael escalated in a way that threw me for a loop. He was a friend. A *good* friend. He made me laugh with his sarcasm, his wit, and intelligence. With his shaggy blonde head of hair, blue eyes and freckles, he wasn't too bad to look at either. And as time passed, the natural twists and turns of our conversations were peppered with natural touches—a hand on his forearm, his hands on my shoulders, our legs pressed together when we sat close on the Tube. Then, at the top of St. Paul's Cathedral, he kissed me, both of us breathless for reasons other than the five-hundred steps we'd just climbed.

"So…"

There it is again. That two-letter word with so much meaning and ambiguity behind it, I find myself contemplating ways to eliminate it from the English language.

Andrea leans forward. "Why didn't you guys, you know…?"

"Andrea Rollins!" I say after a dramatic gasp. "I am appalled at your lack of propriety. Where does it end? I simply can't believe you would come out with such a rude and impertinent question!"

Her eyes don't move from my face, and there's a small smile at the edge of her pursed lips.

I shrug, thoroughly uncomfortable. "We just didn't." She doesn't look appeased, so I continue. "We made out a lot. And we spent a lot of time together, but I didn't like him *that* much."

"Of course not," she says. "You never do." I choose not to dignify that statement with a response. "So, he lives in California."

"He, uh…he's actually from New York. He's out in California for school."

"Wait… Is he home?"

I purse my lips. "For the summer, yeah."

Her eyes widen, and she stutters a bit. But I know what she'll say. What she'll ask. *Why* haven't we already seen each other?

"Have you heard from him?" she asks instead.

I look down at my lap, trying to figure out a way to avoid the next chapter of our story, but find none. Grabbing the plates in front of me, I stand up, thinking it might be easier to explain without having to stare directly across the table at her.

"You, uh…" I put the plates in the sink. "You don't remember what I said before I launched into my grand tale of adventure and romance, do you?"

The floor groans as she pushes her chair back, and her footsteps sound next. She sets the water glasses down on the counter next to the sink. I'm already scrubbing away at a pot when she slaps my arm.

"Ow!" I exclaim, yanking my hands out of the water and soaking the front of my shirt in my surprise. "What the hell?!"

She ignores me. "You didn't answer him, did you?"

I busy myself tending to my wounded arm rather than willingly falling victim to the shame her disappointed eyes will induce. Her scolding is going to accomplish that well enough on its own. Out of the corner of my eye, I see her cross her arms.

She already knows that I haven't, so why bother affirming it with words?

My silence earns a scoff. But then she sighs. "Charlotte," she says, and her voice is softer than I anticipated. "Why do you always do this?"

My cheeks are flaming now. Pity is so much worse than anger and frustration. I toss the towel I was using to dry my shirt onto the counter. "Do what?"

"You *know* what."

I meet her eye. "Do you mean my pathetic inability to allow myself to get close to any guy I've ever deemed worthy of my fleeting affections?"

Andrea has this way of looking at me sometimes that makes me feel completely transparent. Her eyes, usually so warm, feel like lasers on my skin, intent on searching until they find what they're looking for.

She's doing it now.

"Okay, look," I say, holding up a hand in defense. "Before you get all pissy on me, hear me out. I really thought that this guy had some potential. So much so, that I actually told him I had feelings for him."

"This isn't news, Charlotte. You *always* tell them you have feelings for them."

"Right, but that wasn't my only point. He told me he felt the same way, yada-yada-yada. We kissed a lot, whatever. He was an okay kisser—a little overeager, but I could've gotten past that eventually."

Andrea quirks a brow, totally unimpressed with my explanation thus far. But she doesn't interrupt.

"But then, on my last night, a big group of us were hanging out in one of the game rooms, trying to spend every last second with one another, and he told me he wanted to talk in private. So, I go with him, right? And he leads me into this staircase that no one ever used because it contained heat like I imagine the pits of Hell would, and he just full-on starts making out with me."

Andrea's eyebrows are drawn together now, and I take that as my cue to keep going.

"Like I said, okay kisser, a little too eager, but bearable. Then, he pulls away and starts telling me how I've 'changed his life' and he's 'never felt so close to anyone before', and it's going to be 'unbearable' not seeing me every day."

I can't help but cringe, even now, recalling the next part of our conversation. I need to fully emphasize the gravity of it. "And Andrea, I swear to you, there were actual *tears* in his eyes as he said it."

Shuddering at the intense discomfort of the memory, I take in Andrea's thoughtful expression and decide my point needs one more detail to depict the true horror of Michael's weepy confession. "We weren't even *drunk*. Like, this guy was crying as he told me how he felt, in the middle of a mediocre make-out, and expected me to what? Tear up about the fact that yeah, we wouldn't be seeing each other every day, and our incredible trip was ending, but we both live in New York and had already planned to hang out whenever possible? I don't think so." She just stares at me. "I mean, come on, Andi. If anyone's going to understand the turn-off to overly emotional people, it's you."

If I were feeling braver, I might've revealed that this explanation is only part of a much larger, longer, more embarrassing one.

Though I wouldn't trade my experience in London for anything, I would, without a millisecond of hesitation, trade in the way my relationship with Michael was all anyone could talk about by the end of the trip. We were just having fun, enjoying our time spent together, but my group of friends was too invested in it—more invested than they had any right to be. If the girls had it their way, Michael and I would have eloped in London and come back to New York to start our life together, having an indefinite amount of children and getting through all of the problems we'd face by relying on our endless love. All so that they could swoon over the idea of a classic romance taking place under their watchful eyes—a twisted way to reassure themselves that if it was possible for me, it was possible for them.

And, well, I just wasn't having any of that.

It wasn't any of their business. I appreciated the excitement over the potential for our relationship, and the warped sense of support they felt they were giving me with their barrage of questions and advice. But the encouraging looks, waggling their eyebrows in our direction so that only I could see, forming hearts with their hands and holding them our way, and let's not forget their oh-so-subtle insistence that we *always* sit together, and staring knowingly at us when he so much as put a hand on my shoulder—it only served to turn me off to the whole thing faster than it would have happened naturally.

Because that's how these things work, and I consider myself lucky to understand it all without having had any bad experiences or heartbreak myself.

Andrea releases a deep breath through her nose, and leans against the counter beside me. "Alright. So, that probably wasn't the best plan of action on his part, but—"

"Andi," I say to interrupt, staring at her wide-eyed. There's no way she could really make what he did sound better than it was.

She winces. "Okay. That's pretty bad."

"*Thank* you." I cross my arms, satisfied, and lean back beside her.

"But, in his defense," she says, holding a finger straight up in the air. "There's no doubt in my mind that you led him on."

And there's no doubt in my mind that she's right. I'm all too aware of my tendency to get ahead of myself in these situations, only to pull away just when I've fully hooked the poor soul who's gotten himself tangled in Charlotte Worth's feelers. And it's not something I take pride in. The guilt about this particular situation still makes me sick to my stomach. I don't like knowing that I feed on the hearts and lap up the emotions of young men on more than one continent. But I don't know how to change the way I feel when it reaches that make-or-break point.

So, I take comfort in the fact that I don't enter into these things with the *intention* of leading guys on, only to leave them to wallow in what I'm sure is a heap of self-doubt and pity.

It just sort of happens.

Kind of like when you pick a book from a shelf because the cover looks interesting. You start reading with all these grand hopes and expectations, only to find that it isn't thrilling you the way you wanted it to—whether that's because of the story itself, or your own expectations, is up for debate.

I do exactly what the well-known saying heeds against: judge books by their covers. And I've tried to change it, as each "near-miss" relationship goes to show. But they still all end with the same result.

"Well," I finally say in response to Andrea's statement. "What's done is done, right?" I turn back to the sink full of dishes. "I'm just going to move forward, not think about it anymore. I know I made the right decision."

Andrea comes back over with the empty bowl of pasta and sets it on the counter beside the water glasses.

"Besides…" I eye her with a grin. "I've got a play to focus on now. I don't need any distractions."

I don't know who I'm trying to convince more—Andrea, or myself.

Andrea smiles back, though. "Well, in that case, I absolutely agree. It was the right choice."

"Glad you approve."

The play isn't going to change the fact that I'm no longer in London, or the fact that I've hurt someone I care about and have since avoided facing the consequences. But I have to keep moving, keep running toward new horizons. I'll drag the doubts and uncertainties along with me if I have to, but of one thing I can't be more certain:

It's been two days since I've been home, and a new adventure is already long overdue.

## *Year Eight*

"That meatloaf looks like dog shit," Jaclyn said, the word sending a thrill of excitement and fear through Charlotte all at once with its abrupt appearance.

The other girls laughed, all agreeing with Jaclyn's sentiment, but Charlotte was more uncertain, nodding along half-heartedly. The giggle she knew was supposed to come out was stuck somewhere in her throat.

As Charlotte grew older, her sometimes brutal honesty came less often, as she found that weighing her words before speaking them often ended with better results. Her desire to be alone went away, replaced instead with a need to be accepted. She stopped playing the strange games she'd made up, and stopped talking to the imaginary characters in those games. She hadn't found a lost treasure, or a lonely princess, or had a new top-secret mission in a while. But she did play jump rope and tag, and she did make fun of the boys in her class for having cooties, particularly James Sawyer, who smelled funny and ran with his hands straight out behind him like he was some kind of superhero.

She had real-life friends, girls who wanted to spend time with her, and real people to talk to. All she wanted now was to be liked.

But she'd never been so deliberately disobedient. She may have upset her parents too many times over the years, gotten into trouble for silly things she'd done in the house like breaking things, messing up the living room with her games, or flooding the bathroom by sticking too many toys down the toilet (to set them free into the world, of course). But she hadn't gone into any of that with the intention of getting herself into trouble.

Cursing, even under the swell of sound in the lunchroom, was too risky. Teachers hovered too close, kicking up a breeze that could carry the words up, and into their adult ears, and Charlotte didn't want those words to be heard coming from her lips.

She also didn't want her friends to think she was lame. She tried to turn the conversation in other directions, throw out a word or the name of a TV show and see which way it went from there. But it didn't matter which way it was pointed, her friends still managed to include the words in whatever they were saying. It was like they were testing out sour candies, rolling them around on their tongues until the eye-watering tartness subsided, until they were sweet like candy should be. And they popped one, after another, after another.

Charlotte tried to bring herself to say a curse—any curse—just to *do* it. Get it over with, and move on. Wince through the sour taste to get to the good part. But she only became more frustrated with herself when she couldn't.

Nana Rosie could sense that something was off about Charlotte on the playground that afternoon. A year ago, it wouldn't have been unusual for Charlotte to go off on her own. A younger Charley Worth preferred it that way. But since she'd begun spending time with friends, she didn't seem to want to be alone anymore.

So, Nana made her way to Charlotte, who was sitting on a ledge with her sketchpad in her lap, dragging a pencil across the page. Her friends were across the playground playing jump rope.

"Charley," Nana said, eyeing the other little girls before looking back at her granddaughter, whose curly hair was gathered high in a pony-tail on her head. Charlotte didn't look up. "What are you drawing?"

Charlotte sighed, and her pencil stopped moving. "I didn't get to finish it in art class." She held up a picture of a cartoon character, but one Nana couldn't recall ever seeing before. It had long, gangly legs, with knobby knees, almost like a flamingo. But it had arms instead of wings—short arms that looked more suited to a baby than an adult, attached to a small, round torso. Its face, with a button nose and large, round eyes, was smiling.

Nana thought it was one of the strangest looking things she'd ever seen, but she couldn't deny that it was also well drawn. Charlotte's lines were clear, the shapes precise, and as she had been so many times before, Nana found herself surprised and impressed by Charlotte's talent.

"We had to come up with our own cartoon characters," Charlotte said, staring at the picture. "I'm calling him George, and he has really skinny legs that don't hold him up all the time. But he still smiles, because he thinks falling is funny."

Nana smiled. "That seems like a special kind of superpower."

"I guess," Charlotte said, putting the notebook back in her lap and staring at it. "I'm going to color him in next."

"You should give him, uh…oh, what do they call those things?" Charlotte stared at Nana, watching her squeeze her eyes shut as she thought, waiting for her to continue. "You know, what you wear when you ride a bicycle. On your arms."

"Elbow pads?"

"Yes! Elbow pads. And some for the knees, too."

"Yeah," Charlotte said, eyes lighting up. "And a helmet!"

Nana laughed. "That's it. If he's always falling, he's got to protect himself somehow."

Charlotte agreed, and lifted her pencil to add the new parts of George's appearance. Nana leaned on the ledge beside her, watching her hand so easily create the necessary shapes, forming them into items so lifelike, Nana stared at Charlotte—at the lip tucked between her teeth—in wonder.

"Is everything alright, Charley?"

Charlotte looked up. "What?"

"Why aren't you playing with your friends?"

Charlotte shrugged. "I wanted to finish this."

Nana waited for more that didn't come. "Is that all?"

Charlotte's eyes flicked up to the girls across the schoolyard, stayed there for only a moment, then returned to the page in front of her.

"I just don't like what they're doing," she said, her voice soft.

"What are they doing?" Nana asked.

Charlotte kept her eyes cast down. "I'd rather not say."

Charlotte may not have been comfortable with the new things her friends were choosing to say and do, but that didn't mean she wanted to get them into trouble.

Nana thought about her response for a moment, wondering what those little girls were up to that Charlotte no longer wanted to be part of it. But studying them playing jump rope didn't give anything away, so she lay a hand on Charlotte's knee and waited until she looked up, hazel eyes green in the sunlight beneath heavy, worried brows.

"I'm proud of you," Nana said. Charlotte's eyebrows crinkled together. "Whatever it is, I'm glad you're brave enough to choose not to do it. A lot of grown-ups don't even know that—that you always have a choice. But you do, Charley. You always do."

Charlotte was trying to understand; trying to believe that Nana wasn't just saying all this to make her feel better.

"There's no sense in making a decision just for the sake of making a choice. As you get older, it's going to be harder and harder to do, but try to remember that."

Charlotte didn't completely understand what that meant either, but she knew it was important. And she knew that Nana was telling her it was okay to feel whatever she was feeling. That it was okay to separate herself if she wasn't comfortable. But it didn't *feel* okay. It felt more like she was sneaking away from her friends in silent shame, her head hung low as she wondered what was wrong with her, why speaking words—they were just stupid *words*—was so difficult.

But even then, Charlotte Worth didn't like the idea of doing something for the sake of doing it.

She still doesn't.

Plus, she never liked sour candies.

## *Chapter Four*

The subway jerks to a stop, and the guy I stumble into huffs louder than necessary. I glance at him as I steady myself, but don't apologize. My thoughts are otherwise occupied.

When Dad asked if I was sure I wanted to spend the weekend at Mom's, I said yes, I'd be fine. It wasn't *exactly* a lie. She is my mother, and it's been a long time since I've seen her. Did I relish the thought of seeing her in her brand-new apartment with the man she'd left us for, living the life she had chosen over the one she had with me and Dad?

No. But I didn't say that. It was easier on Dad if I was agreeable, and easier for me to just get it all over with so that I could go back to avoiding her.

With each step, each one bringing me closer and closer to having to face all of it, my thoughts shift like images in those old toy stereoscopes—the ones that you put up to your eyes like binoculars and look through as you manually click a wheel of different pictures into view. And my thoughts are clicking *fast*. Images of my mother kissing me goodnight when I was little; pouring herself coffee in the morning; smiling and snapping pictures at my high school graduation; and flipping through the mail when she got home from work.

Then, her closed bathroom door, through which I could hear her choked sobs over the sound of running water; her excited smile when she got a job with an interior designer; and the back of her navy blazer and curled ponytail as she walked out the front door of our house for the final time, without her usual obligatory "goodbye" tossed over her shoulder.

I squeeze my eyes shut for a moment while I wait to cross the street, willing the memories away, but only succeed in digging up more details of that day. I'd gone to school thinking my life was as normal as it could be, and returned home to find our house exactly as I'd left it. Mom's decorative touches were everywhere—the bright yellow walls of the kitchen, the fake plants meticulously placed on surfaces throughout the main floor, her floor-to-ceiling bookcase shelved with books that only Dad had read, the grape and wine theme of our kitchen and the abstract paintings hung up on too many of the walls.

She was supposed to be home at five, but she was late that day. After about an hour of unanswered calls and texts, I decided to start dinner, the anxiety a small knot in the center of my chest. After two hours, uneaten food, and several more calls to her cell and office with still no word from her, Dad and I were freaking out. Coming up on hour three, I was left to imagine what had happened to her. And I considered each and every horrendous possibility.

She'd fallen onto the subway tracks and gotten hit by a train. She'd been kidnapped. (Could parents be "kidnapped"?) She was beaten and raped, left for dead. She lost her bag with her phone in it, and was wandering the streets of Manhattan trying to make her way back to us when she slipped, fell and hit her head, and she was in the hospital having fallen into a coma, and she didn't have her bag or even her phone, so the hospital had no way of identifying her…

But Dad was strangely solemn after that third hour had passed. While my anxiety felt like a bowling ball pressing against my ribcage from the inside, Dad's seemed nonexistent. Through my tears and shouts, insisting that we had to *do* something—go find her, or call the police, *anything*—Dad remained silent, eyes fixed on the hardwood floor of our living room, the phone clutched in his hands.

When he stood without a word and made his way upstairs, I followed, and when he paused in front of her closet door, breathing deeply as if he were bracing himself, the anxiety in my chest deflated a bit, making room for sickening certainty. He pulled the closet door open in the same way you might rip off a Band-Aid. I remember feeling like I couldn't breathe when I saw it empty from over his shoulder. My frantic tears came to a confused halt, and my anxiety dissipated almost completely, leaving nothing in its wake.

All of the images clicked into place in my mind, going round and round for a full, cohesive explanation.

Empty closet. *CLICK.* Wedding ring on the dresser. *CLICK.* Dad's grip on the ring, knuckles white, closed fist pressed firmly to his lips. *CLICK.* His shoulders, normally broad and strong, slumped and small with the weight of our discovery as he turned away from me. *CLICK.* The slam of the bathroom door in my face. *CLICK.*

Mom. Gone.

*CLICK.*

Mom lives just a couple of blocks from the station, and standing outside her Upper West Side apartment building, I can't help wishing the walk had taken longer. But I make my way up to the twelfth floor, and find myself standing outside her door—*their* door.

My feet ache to run, my mouth opens to scream, but I clamp it shut, breathe deeply while my arms tremble at my sides, wanting to punch, scratch, inflict pain. But my feet remain planted on the *Welcome!* mat, my mouth stays pressed into a tight line, and my hands bury themselves deep in the pockets of my shorts.

With a few deep breaths, I raise a shaky, unreliable hand and knock twice, recoiling as if the door is a poisonous snake I've just poked with a stick.

There are quick footsteps, the sound of heels clacking on the floor, and then she's there in front of me, her smile wide, brown eyes surrounded by a ring of dark eyeliner and smoky eyeshadow. She's still dressed for work—a charcoal pantsuit with her hair pulled back into a low bun at the base of her neck, curled tendrils of the auburn strands framing her face. For a moment, I'm taken aback by how much I resemble her. We have the same slight overlap in our two front teeth, the same small, rounded nose, and the same fair skin that allows so much to be revealed in particularly emotional moments…like this one.

My cheeks feel just as red as hers look, and her hesitation is written in the way her whole body leans towards me, hands slightly outstretched, but remains on her side of the door.

"Hello, Charlotte," she says, her voice quiet, her eyes unsure. It's been so long since we've seen one another, but it's been even longer since we've felt truly comfortable around each other.

"Hi," I say, hiking my bag further onto my shoulder for lack of anything better to do with my hands.

"You—you look beautiful," Mom says next, her fingers tangling in front of her, voice small and breathy.

I glance down at my black shorts, white tank top and jean jacket, and bite back a scoff when I note the coffee stain on my shirt. "Uh, thanks."

"Come on in." She smiles, moving to the side and gesturing to the modern-looking apartment with a small sweep of her hand.

My first step over the threshold onto the dark wood floor feels wrong. And as I move further into the apartment, taking in the pristine white walls and black furniture, decorated with accents of the same colors, I feel like a traitor. My being here means I've betrayed my father, and myself. It means I've accepted her new life, and her decision to leave us the way she did.

I have to fight the urge to run back out, get on the subway, and head home where I belong. And when I successfully stifle that urge, I choke down another scream.

"Is this all you brought?" Mom asks, interrupting my outlandish plots to remove myself from the situation. Obviously, turning around and sprinting out the door might not go over well, but a fainting spell could work, or offering to cook dinner and making sure to give myself raw meat, or scaling down the fire escape in the dead of night—give my mother a taste of her own shitty meds.

All I say is, "Yep, this is it."

Mom smiles and offers to take my small duffel while I slide my purse off my shoulder. She sets the two bags down next to the couch. "Hope you don't mind, but this is where you'll be sleeping." She motions to the black leather sofa. "We only have the one bedroom—Upper West Side rent is a little steep."

I want to say something like, "*Could've found a two-bedroom in the Bronx for a lot less,*" or, "*Guess that's the price you have to pay when you choose luxury over your much less glamorous husband and daughter in the suburbs, who have since removed your pretentious art and decorative pieces from our humble abode.*"

But all I manage to say is, "That's fine."

We sit on the couch that will be my bed, as far from each other as we can get. I try to make myself as small as possible in the corner, tucking myself in like a blanket, a checkered pillow clutched to my chest. She sits at the very edge of the cushion, back straight, hands folded too deliberately on her lap.

We're both quiet, uncomfortably so, and I use the awkward silence to take in the rest of the apartment. To my left is the kitchen with its sparkling black granite countertops and stainless steel appliances. Across from where we're sitting is an oversized entertainment system taking up practically the whole wall. The flat-screen TV is smack in the middle, flanked by what looks like a stereo, a DVD and a Blu-ray player, and I don't even know what else. To my right sits a bookcase, set up in the same imperfectly perfect way Mom organized ours all those years ago.

"So," she says. "How are you, Charlotte? How was London?"

"Good. I'm good." I cross and uncross my legs. "London was great. I, uh, wish I could go back."

Now would be the perfect time, actually.

"I'm so glad you had the chance to do it," she says with a smile. It almost looks genuine.

Too bad I know the truth. She and Dad argued about me going from the get-go. He made the argument that I should, but she didn't want to cover part of the cost. At least, that's what I gathered from listening outside Dad's bedroom door while they were on the phone for their monthly call. I was usually the only topic of conversation.

"So, where's Richard?" I ask, deciding it best not to mention all of that.

"He, uh…" Mom stands and walks into the kitchen. "He should be on his way home from work. He said he'd stop and pick up dinner." She rummages around in the fridge. "Want something to drink?"

"No thanks."

She closes the door with nothing in her hands, and plants both of them on the countertop, her eyes cast downward. After a moment, she looks up. "Any plans for the summer?"

"Actually…yeah. I'm helping Andi out with her play. She's directing it."

"Oh, that's nice." She smiles. "What play?"

"It's, uh, not very well-known, but it's called 'What Was Lost'." She looks clueless. I can't even blame her. "It's by some Canadian guy."

"Hm. Well, I'm sure it'll be fun." She grabs a dishtowel from the handle of the oven door. "You always did like plays." And then, more quietly, as if she's not sure she should say it, she says, "Just like your father."

I don't say anything more as she wipes down the already sparkling counters, just try to discern the underlying tone of that statement. Sadness? Shame? Regret? Guilt?

From the way she buffs the gleaming granite, rubbing at nothing like Lady Macbeth trying to clean her blood-stained hands, I imagine it's a combination of all of the above.

"How *is* your dad?" She's a little breathless from her exertions.

"He's good." *No thanks to you,* I add in my head.

"Good." Her voice is too high, too bright. She hangs the towel back in its place and gathers plates from the cabinets.

"Let me help you," I say, and move towards her. She tries to get me to sit, but I can't anymore. Sitting still is only making my anxiety worse.

We're quiet as we set the table, a task that takes no more than two minutes to complete. Not nearly long enough.

"He should be here any minute, now," Mom says, straightening the utensils next to each of the three plates. When they're even more perfect than they were before, she sighs. "I'm just going to use the bathroom. I'll only be a minute."

I nod as she moves down the hallway, hoping that Richard won't arrive while I'm out here by myself. But there's a good possibility that he will, because that's my luck, so I make myself look busy, comfortable, like I belong here on the couch in his black-and-white living room. I pull my phone out of my pocket and text Dad to let him know that I'm here, then just browse the Internet.

A door opens minutes later, and I can't see from my spot on the couch if it's the front door or the bathroom door. But when Richard's tall, lanky frame rounds the corner from the foyer, I do my best to blend in with the black leather couch.

"Hey, Charlotte!" He sets all the bags he's holding down on the kitchen counter before reaching me in two strides. I stand and tentatively return the hug, his gray tweed jacket scratchy beneath my bare arms.

"How are you?" He pulls away, and gives me a big smile, his blue eyes magnified by his thick, frame-less glasses. "It's been so long since we've seen you. How was London?"

"I know, uh…" I watch, flustered and uncomfortable, as he loosens his tie, then removes his jacket, his smile never wavering. "It was good. Really good."

I sit down again, feeling too exposed standing up. He pushes his glasses further onto his nose and rubs his clean-shaven face as he looks at me again. "I want to hear all about it over dinner." He pulls white cartons out of the paper bags he brought with him. "Your mom said you like spicy chicken and broccoli. Hope that's okay."

"Yep." I don't move from my spot on the couch. "Thanks."

"No problem." He gives me another grin, and I hate that he's always been kind to me. Granted, I've only been around him once before, four months after Mom left. He took us out to some fancy restaurant for a dinner filled with small talk and awkward silences, then surprised us with tickets to one of my favorite plays, Phantom of the Opera.

I knew he was trying too hard, but even with that knowledge I found it hard to hate him like I wanted to. I still can't seem to. This man, with his warm blue eyes and kind smile that crinkles the edges around those eyes, is the reason my family is broken. He's the button that got sucked into our vacuum cleaner. The shard of glass in our deflated tires. The metaphorical wrench that stopped the continuously winding wheels of our life together. And yet, I can't quite reconcile the two versions of him in my head. I want—*need* him to prove himself as the evil villain in the story of my life. But when I'm around him, he seems more like a lost puppy that we took into our home. A puppy that's proceeded to urinate and defecate on everything I love, but licks my face afterward with big, soulful eyes for inevitable forgiveness.

Mom comes out, then, wearing sweats and a t-shirt. I look away while they greet each other with a kiss, overwhelmed with the desire to go home. But we sit down at the dinner table like the family we're pretending to be, and the two converse briefly about work before turning their attention to me.

I smile politely, feeling like my face is going to crack into two halves, and answer their questions about London and the classes I took there, all while trying not to stare at their joined hands resting on the table. I pick at my food, anger filling my stomach in place of an appetite. Chinese food has always been one of my favorite dinners, but sitting with them in their apartment pretending everything's okay—I let it go to waste for the first time in my life.

## *Year Twelve*

"Charlotte?"

Mrs. Worth closed the front door behind her and waited for Charlotte's answer. She dropped her bag on the floor, kicked her shoes off, and sighed when she didn't receive one.

It was a balmy June evening the summer Charlotte would turn thirteen. Charlotte had spent the day with Nana Rosie, and Mrs. Worth had experienced a miserable day at work—her receptionist position in a doctor's office. The air conditioning unit had been sputtering for days, but on that particular day it stopped working entirely. The heat made all the patients testy, and all day they complained about the wait with no air conditioning. Mrs. Worth, just as hot and surly because of it, was responsible for placating them even as sweat trickled down the dip of her spine and beaded at her hairline. It was almost blissful to walk into her air-conditioned home after five o'clock, but her frustration resurfaced when she called Charlotte's name once more, and still didn't receive an answer.

After a quick check of Charlotte's room and a sweep of the rest of the house, Mrs. Worth determined Charlotte was not there. Not panicking yet, she called Nana Rosie, sure that Charlotte simply hadn't left yet.

"She's not home?" Nana asked, and panic spiked in Mrs. Worth's chest.

"She's not with you?"

"Charlotte left to walk home a little over an hour ago." Nana's raspy voice held an undercurrent of concern now, too.

A walk from Nana's house should've taken no more than fifteen minutes. Dread overtook Mrs. Worth the way an intruder might, wrapping its arms tight around her chest and locking everything in place.

There were a few moments of silence on the line before Nana spoke. "Alright, don't worry yet, Lindsay. You know Charley—she probably met with a friend and forgot to call." Mrs. Worth didn't respond, her mind turning over other, more frightening possibilities, so Nana said, "Why don't you call Ben and see if he's heard from her?"

But Mrs. Worth somehow knew that Charlotte wouldn't have called her father. When she called her husband anyway, he confirmed her assumption, and, like Nana, he didn't seem to understand Mrs. Worth's growing concern.

"Linds, don't worry. You know Charlotte. I'm sure she'll be home soon." What he said next was not directed at her, but someone else. "Just a minute…thanks."

Mrs. Worth wanted to scream, make him choke on the fact that their daughter was missing. She was only twelve, she hadn't called anyone, and they had no idea where she could be. How could he *not* be concerned?

These thoughts flew through her head, building onto her already monumental anxiety and now sparking her anger. She *should've* screamed, but stayed silent, hoping her anger was evident in the seething gasps of air she sucked through gritted teeth.

"Linds?" he asked then. She bit her lip. "Alright, look, I'm not sure, but maybe she went to the park my mom used to take her to when she was a kid."

"She's *still* a kid, Ben."

Mrs. Worth could see the playground in her mind's eye, with its blue jungle gym and green swings planted in the middle of a huge sandbox, and she swallowed the urge to remind him that she had taken Charlotte there, too.

He released a long sigh right into the phone. "You know what I meant. I think she still likes to go there. Why don't you drive by and see if you spot her? If not, call me and we'll figure this out."

Mrs. Worth nodded, though her husband couldn't see her. The fear felt like a fist in her chest, clenching harder with each passing moment that Charlotte didn't walk through the front door.

"Lindsay?"

"Yeah?" She was fighting back tears.

"She's fine. I'm sure of it." He paused. "We'll find her. I promise."

Mrs. Worth didn't return his "I love you" before hanging up and grabbing her keys. As she got to the car, started it, and pulled out of the driveway and down the street, the most horrifying thoughts and images clouded her vision.

Charlotte passed out on the sidewalk, having inexplicably lost consciousness.

Charlotte, auburn hair so like her own, splayed around her bloodied head after a fall.

Charlotte lying face down in a scarlet pool, her small, bruised body mangled on the street after the fatal impact of a speeding car.

Charlotte, hazel eyes full of fear, cheeks red and blotchy, bound at the hands and feet, with tape over her mouth, in the possession of the ugliest, biggest captors Mrs. Worth could imagine, their nameless, nondescript van hauling the helpless little girl far away for their own evil purposes.

Tears leaked from the corners of her eyes, but her body was wound tight with sobs that she refused to let wrack her. Why hadn't she told Charlotte she loved her today? Why didn't she appreciate her daughter's independent spirit, instead of scolding her for it? Why didn't she see that Charlotte was special—*so* special that she was almost impossible to understand? Why didn't Mrs. Worth try harder?

The effort to keep her tears at bay was too much, and pathetic squeaks of fear between shuddering, gasping breaths filled the interior of their Subaru. Mrs. Worth clutched the steering wheel until her knuckles were white, jerking it from side to side as she made the necessary turns to get herself to the park.

She *had* to be there.

*Charlotte had to be there.*

Mrs. Worth pulled into the parking lot adjacent to the park after the longest five-minute drive of her life. She threw the door open and scrambled out of the car, her eyes sweeping the expanse of the playground. The fist in her chest—her heart—pounded in time with the quick dribble of the basketball in the court when she caught a glint of red in the slant of light from the setting sun.

Mrs. Worth jogged around the car, holding her breath, praying it wasn't a trick of the light, that the bright red head of hair coming into view—the one that shimmered redder in the sunlight—was real. And as she took in the freckled face tilted up and back against the bark of a tree, the rest of her small body sat against it, the fist in Mrs. Worth's chest let go, allowing her heart to thump faster and lighter than it had moments before as she made her way into the park.

## *Chapter Five*

The rest of my weekend spent with Mom and Dick (it's just too easy) consisted of them pretending that the way we had all ultimately found ourselves together hadn't happened, and me trying not to enjoy our activities too much. Dick didn't make my task an easy one, to his credit. We went to two museums, the Met and the Guggenheim, on Saturday, and a matinee showing of Les Miserables on Sunday.

How could my will to remain bored and disinterested compete with that?

What's even worse is the fact that I knew I was being bribed into complacency. Mom's raised eyebrows and wide smile each time Dick revealed the next bullet on our itinerary were dead giveaways. But I found myself having fun despite the nagging voice in my head reminding me of their indiscretions. Not only were we doing and seeing some of my favorite things (in and of itself, another giveaway)—I was *enjoying* it.

My mother is still a stranger to me, but I discovered that I liked the person I was getting to know. It seemed every day with Dick was a good one. She smiled more in the past two days than I've seen her smile in the last five years. She laughed more freely, too—not the stiff, inhibited, polite laugh that I was used to; the one that didn't touch her eyes. Now it was louder, more carefree, a sound I'd never heard. It made me want to laugh along with her, ignore the fact that her laughter was in response to something her new boyfriend had said, and focus on the mother I'd never gotten to know.

Was she always hidden beneath the somber looks, the loud silences, and the anger and impatience I'd known for the better part of my life? Had she chosen to stay hidden, or had she wanted to come out all along? Had the woman in front of me this weekend felt so stifled that the mother I knew was drowning under the weight of her own life? Was she only able to free herself when she met *him*?

I knew my mother had bouts of depression; that sometimes getting through the day was too much for her. And I knew that on those days, when she holed herself up in her room, it was better if I left her alone. But it killed me to think that neither I nor my father had ever made her laugh like Dick could.

Dick—lanky, goofy Richard—was just what she needed. Dick, with his smoothly combed brown hair, stupid, thick glasses and endless supply of tweed jackets, made her smile in a way that I'd never seen. And I understood why—or I tried to. He was smart, personable and kind. He seemed genuinely interested in my life. He wanted to know about London, school, my interest in theater and art, and didn't push me in one direction or the other when I admitted that I still wasn't sure what I would like to pursue for a career. He didn't scoff at my majoring in English, or urge me to go into a field with more job security. He told us stories of his own experiences growing up—his fishing trips in Jersey with his father, and his mother's constant support of his artistic abilities despite his father's steady insistence that he work towards a trade if he didn't want to be serious about school.

"She's the reason I'm an architect. She's the reason I've realized my dream," he said, taking a sip of wine at dinner on Sunday.

My mother held a hand to her heart as he finished his story, and tangled the other with his from her seat next to him at the table. She would never be that woman to me, I realized. She would never be the mother who was my reason for achieving anything. And that realization felt like a slow but steady stream of ice water flooding my vessels. Looking from her to him, I knew that he was the reason why—the quake that had caused the final crack of the chasm that separated my family.

For all my wishing that he would just like act like the dick I wanted him to be, he didn't. But I had to remember that he was, even if, in any given moment, I couldn't see that side of him. He was a home-wrecker regardless of how well he could play nice. What I didn't—*couldn't*—let myself consider was the fact that the woman who shared her DNA with me, the woman I called my mother, had just as much a part in the rumbling creation of the rift as he did.

So, while the two days spent with Mom and Dick went as well as they could've, the nights spent on their black leather couch left me with nothing but my hot, simmering fury. I was sure it would boil over sooner rather than later, so my plan was to try and keep it on the lowest heat possible until I figured out what to do about it.

"Alright, well…" my mother said the first night. She stood watching Richard as he lifted his jacket off one of the bar stools, before looking right at me. "Are you going to be okay out here?"

I didn't ask if I had a choice. "Yeah, I'm fine."

"Are you sure?"

"Positive."

Richard wished me a good night, eyeing my mother before heading down the hallway. The light from their bedroom went on, creating shadows in the darkness, and only when the door closed, shutting out that light, did my mother speak again.

"Well," she said, releasing a deep breath. "You know where the bathroom is, and if you need anything, uh… you know where our room is."

I nodded, not wanting to think any more about *their* room.

"Do you need anything? Toothbrush? Pajamas?"

"I'm good," I said from my seat on the couch, already wanting this to be over.

"Okay, well…" She looked uncertain, like she wanted to leave, but she didn't know how. "Good night."

I tried to smile. "Night."

She forced one too, her lips remaining closed, before glancing around the room and making her way down the hallway after Richard, her heels clacking all the way.

Getting ready for bed may have kept my hands busy, but it was not enough of a distraction for my mind. I brushed my teeth thinking about what they might be talking about in there, if they were talking about me like I was a problem that needed to be solved. A child they felt sorry for that needed to be placated.

I washed my face wondering what she wore to bed, if she still wore a baggy t-shirt and pajama pants. Something told me she didn't. I put my pajamas on and remembered the way she used to pull my comforter up over me and kiss my forehead before saying goodnight, the way she would sometimes smile at me as she pulled my bedroom door closed.

I'd been so little then. It was before the real depression set in, and even though the memories were fuzzy, blurred around the edges, the feelings were sharp and clear, and I didn't want to, but I wished I could feel them again. For real.

Then I lay down on the couch, pulled my blanket up and over myself, and that was when the anger boiled over.

Both nights, closing my eyes only meant seeing my mother wrapped up in the arms of a man who was not my father in the bedroom. So, to distract myself, I read the script for the play once through the first night, and again on the second night.

And it was totally depressing. Funny, but a huge let-down.

The main characters are a young couple who have fallen out of love with one another for reasons unbeknownst to the audience. The husband finds out that she's been cheating on him in the very first scene, and spends the length of the play devising ways to make her fall for him again. I spent the entire time hoping with every cell in my body that he'd succeed, that he'd get her back. That they'd live happily ever after.

It was hard to imagine how a love that seemed so right in its early stages could turn out to be so wrong—why such bad things happen to good people. The audience would question all of that if we were able to pull it off correctly. It made me all the more eager to get started with the whole process. Plus, there was a hot, almost-sex scene at the height of the play that was unexpected, but left me *very* pleasantly surprised. Not only was the intensity of the scene steamy enough to heat up the theater, but the raw emotion there served to be the turning point for the whole play—the couple's game-changer. And let's just say, I knew how it would end before I flipped to the final page of the script.

After ruminating on the possibilities for the staging, as well as what the actors who would play out this intense, heavy scenario would need for the entire weekend, it's almost a relief to finally get into the theater the following Wednesday.

"Hey, girl." Andrea barely glances up from her seat behind a desk, its surface cluttered with papers. In the middle, she's got her laptop open, and it casts a white glow over her face in the otherwise dimly lit room.

I drop my bag beside the desk. "Did a bomb go off in here, or something?"

Andrea's oblivious, totally engrossed in what she's watching on her computer screen.

"I'll take that as a no," I say, and sit beside her, eyeing the screen. It's a girl standing on the stage in front of us now, and Andrea's voice sounds over the computer, feeding the girl the lines she's supposed to react and respond to.

"How's it going?" I ask after a few moments, sitting far back in my chair so as not to further disrupt the mess of papers she's got scattered across the desk.

Andrea sighs, and pauses the video. "It's going. Twenty-seven people auditioned, so it was a pretty good turnout." She shuffles some papers around before pulling a stack from the corner of the desk. "These are the people I've cast."

She hands me the small stack of papers and I flip through them, the words blurring on the page because I'm not wearing my glasses. As I reach inside my bag for them, the only thing I can really make out is a fuzzy, large asterisk at the bottom of the first page.

"So, those are the audition sheets. The actors and actresses filled out the top part with their names, numbers, and availability over the coming weeks. And the bottom was for my own notes and thoughts," she explains. She leans over to see which one I'm looking at. "That guy was incredible. He's our Nick."

I flick through the rest of the papers, making sense of nothing but that large asterisk at the bottom of each one as it comes into and out of focus. Eight characters, eight pages, and eight actors: the main couple, of course, Nick and Olivia, then Nick's brother Jonathan, Olivia's best friend/co-worker Maggie, Olivia's parents, the waiter for their first date, and lastly, Olivia's nameless lover.

"So, if you've already cast them," I say, straightening the papers out against the desk before setting them down and lifting my bag onto my lap. "Why are you still watching the audition videos?"

Andrea sighs, and closes several tabs on her computer. "Because I'm obsessive and want to be sure I cast the right people."

I stare at her, and open my mouth to say something, but she holds up a hand. "Don't," she says. "I'm crazy, I know." She closes her laptop and rifles through the dozens of papers. "Did you have a chance to read the script?"

"I did. Can't say I loved it in its entirety. Obviously, I wanted it to end differently, but it made me emotional, which, you know, is hard to do—because I have the emotional range of gnat." She presses her lips together in a smile, and I shove aside the mess of garbage in my bag, feeling around for the firm square of my glasses case. "But all in all, I enjoyed it."

"They're on your head, Charlotte," she says without looking up, pulling the sheet she was looking for from the rubble.

Only mildly embarrassed, I yank my glasses down from my hair, snagging a strand in the corner where the arm meets the frame.

"And I'm glad you liked it, but didn't like it," she says, scribbling in the corner of the piece of paper. "That's the whole point. I was a little wary of choosing to do this particular play cause of all the heavy material. And there's the whole thing with, like, the sex scene and stuff, which should be interesting to work on—having to direct people to make out with each other might be a little weird. But it was funny in a lot of ways, too. And you know I never shy away from a challenge."

"That, I do," I say, and pick up the audition sheets again, leafing through them with working eyes.

"Oh! And this is the cover of the book version of the play," Andrea says, shifting papers to pull a slim book from the depths. "Thought it might give you some inspiration."

The glossy maroon cover is definitely not much help. It's plain, aside from the gold script etching the title smack in the middle of the page. "Hm, okay, I'm thinking we keep the color scheme, slant the text a bit more, and we're good to go."

"That is not what I hired you for," Andrea says.

"I was unaware you 'hired' me. We haven't discussed my pay."

"Anyway," she says, ignoring me. "I just thought it might help to see it."

"Thanks, but no thanks." I hand the book back to her. "I've already got some ideas in the works."

"Ooh," Andrea says with a smile. "Do tell."

"Nope." Her eyebrows crinkle at the center, and her bottom lip juts out in a pout. "You can see the finished product, but my first attempt isn't quite done yet."

"Fine," she says, and leans forward. "But I'll have to see it eventually. It might help to make sure you're on the right track."

"Or…you'll just use it as an opportunity to dictate how I should go about it."

She purses her lips. "Yeah, I've got enough on my plate. Just show it to me when you're done."

She says it as if it were her idea, and I laugh. "Glad we can agree."

I reach a hand down and touch my bag, reassuring myself that my sketchpad is still in there. It's always been hard for me to share my artwork, mostly because a lot of what I draw is a direct depiction of how I'm feeling in any given moment. Of course, something like this is purely professional, not emotionally driven, but it still feels wrong. Like I'm sharing a part of myself that usually lays deep inside, hidden from view. I can't help feeling like it should stay that way, even in a situation like this.

"Alright, now that that's settled…" Andrea stands, and pushes her chair back. "Help me get everything ready." She heads up the stairs and onto the stage.

"Ready for what?" I ask, following her anyway.

She keeps moving, disappearing behind the curtain side stage as she calls back, "The cast will be here in fifteen minutes."

"What?" I ask, totally taken off guard.

Andrea drags a chair out, holding another one aloft in front of her. "Didn't I tell you? First cast meeting is today. Now,"—she thrusts a chair into my arms—"help me make a circle with these."

"Some warning would've been nice," I say, though I don't know why. It's not like I have any real active part in all of this.

Andrea shrugs, setting the chair down a couple feet from mine. "What's the difference? You're here now, anyway."

I follow her as she heads back to the side of the stage. "Just for moral support, right?"

"Yeah," she says, not meeting my eye before lifting a chair off a stack of chairs. "And for your own inspiration. And you've got to meet the actors at some point, right? Might as well be now."

"Right," I say, lifting another chair from the stack.

It's ridiculous to be nervous. I'm not even in the play, so it's not like there's anything I have to do. No one I have to impress. But the bundle of nerves is there, lodged in my chest, and they're coiling in on themselves to form a nice little knot. This is all new—something I've never done before—and my anxiety rears it's big-ass head. So, when we finish setting up, I pull out my sketchpad, hoping to relieve the senseless quaking inside of me, and make room for the excitement that should be trying to break through.

Andrea arranges and rearranges the chairs, so I know I'm not the only one trying to dispel some nervous energy. I smile as she shifts one just a couple of inches to the left, stares at the circle for a beat, and moves the same chair the same couple of inches back to the right.

"Hey," I say from my seat in the circle. Her eyebrows are drawn together when she tears her gaze away from the chairs to look at me. "You've got this, girl."

Andrea smiles a little, and lets out a breath with the movement of her lips. "This is why I need you."

Only a moment later the door creaks open behind us, and a girl starts down the aisle toward the stage.

"Well," Andrea mutters, straightening her spine and sliding her hands down the front of her shirt. "Here goes nothing."

## *Year Twelve*

Mrs. Worth didn't recognize the sound at first, the wild gasp of relief that came from somewhere deep in her stomach as she moved towards her daughter, tears still blurring her line of sight. Rounding the chain link fence, her gasps turned into laughter; into a kind of relief she didn't know existed. As she grew closer, Charlotte opened her eyes and saw her. They were green in the sunlight, just like her father's, and her brows furrowed in confusion for only a moment before she pushed her mess of curls aside and stood.

Mrs. Worth pulled her daughter into a long, tight embrace, tears still streaming down her cheeks. Charlotte hugged her back, bewildered as to why her mother was holding onto her as if she might never get the chance again, but happy to be held nonetheless. The two stood there, wrapped up, neither wanting to let go—Mrs. Worth because, minutes before, she had convinced herself she would never get to hold her daughter again, and Charlotte because she wasn't sure when she would get another chance to hug her mother. So, they held on, like straight lines intersecting, the moment forever imprinted in their minds and hearts, but somehow ending just as quickly as it came.

Mrs. Worth kept a hand on Charlotte's back as she leaned down to pick up her sketchpad and her book bag. And she kept an arm wrapped around Charlotte's narrow shoulders as they walked to the car. She even planted a kiss on her daughter's forehead before opening the passenger door, making good on the promise she made to herself ten minutes ago—to never take her daughter for granted again.

Charlotte was more excited than she let on, happy to finally be getting the attention she had always wanted from her mother. She didn't care that she didn't understand why. She just stayed quiet as she buckled her seatbelt, letting herself enjoy the way she was feeling, afraid that speaking would only remind her mother of the way their relationship usually worked.

"What were you doing here, Charlotte?" Mrs. Worth was still calm as she backed the car out of the parking spot.

Charlotte hesitated for only a moment. "I didn't really feel like heading home after Nana's, so I thought I'd come here and read for a little while."

Mrs. Worth glanced at her daughter, perplexed, but she tried to remain patient. "Well, why didn't you tell Nana that you were coming here?"

"I didn't make up my mind until I had already left her house," said Charlotte.

Mrs. Worth glanced over at her daughter, now unable to hide her impatience. "You could've called one of us to let us know. Me, or your father…I was worried sick."

Charlotte found it hard to hide her impatience as well. "You mean with the cell phone you won't buy me?"

Mrs. Worth scoffed, feeling the relief morph into frustration. How could she be so thoughtless? So careless? So inconsiderate? Didn't she realize what could've happened? That she could've gotten hurt, or kidnapped, or *worse*? Didn't she realize that no one knew where she was; that if anything had happened, no one would've known where to find her?

"Besides," Charlotte continued, looking out the window. "I'm not a little kid anymore. I can go to the park by myself."

"You are twelve years old, Charlotte. Nowhere near old enough to make decisions without asking your parents. What if something had happened, what if—?"

"Mom, it's really not a big deal. Nothing happened, so just drop it, okay?" They'd pulled into their driveway, and Charlotte didn't wait for her mother's response before getting out of the car and slamming the door behind her.

Mrs. Worth watched Charlotte march to the front door, her pale skin exposed by her jean shorts and tank top, her body stick straight—the body of a child, no matter how she liked to think otherwise. Mrs. Worth followed her, noting that her husband's car was not parked in front of the house.

"Charlotte…" She tossed her keys onto the table in the foyer. When she got no answer, she moved toward the kitchen. "Charlotte?"

Charlotte was pulling a bottle of water from the fridge when Mrs. Worth rounded the corner.

"So, are you just going to ignore me now?"

Charlotte took a long pull from the bottle.

"Fine, then you can listen." Mrs. Worth planted her feet and clenched her fists, finding she needed the stability more than she cared to admit. "You need to start thinking about people other than yourself. You can't just—"

"What is *that* supposed to mean?" Charlotte was incredulous.

"It means…" Mrs. Worth's voice was considerably louder. "That you only ever think of *yourself*. Exactly as I said. You had me and your father and Nana scared to death today. I thought you'd been kidnapped…or killed, or *both*, for God's sake! You can't just decide to go somewhere and not tell anyone. You're still a child, you—"

"I'm *not* a child anymore, Mom!" Charlotte yelled, her voice louder than her mother's for the moment.

"Yes, you are!" Mrs. Worth yelled, matching her daughter in volume.

But that was the thing neither of them understood. The harder they screamed, the more their words were lost in translation.

Charlotte knew her mother would never understand.

Mrs. Worth didn't know what it would take for her daughter to listen.

And when it was clear neither would do or say what the other wanted, Charlotte stormed off to her parents' room—the only one with a lock on the door—and Mrs. Worth crumpled into a chair at the kitchen table. The distance they forever kept between them, loud and too expansive to properly hear each other over the gaping hole in the middle, widened once more.

Sniffling, Charlotte picked up the phone in her parents' room, dialing the number of the one person who always made her feel better.

"Charley, is that you?"

"Yeah." Charlotte hoped Nana couldn't hear her stuffed nose. "I'm sorry for not telling you where I was going."

"Don't apologize, Charley, just do better next time." Nana could hear that Charlotte was upset. "I'm glad you're okay. You had your mother pretty worried."

"She's mad at me," was all Charlotte said, feeling the sting of the truth bring more unwanted tears to her eyes. "She thinks I'm too young to go to the park by myself. But I'm not a little kid anymore. She doesn't need to worry about things like that."

"She's your mother, Charley. She's always going to worry. And she wasn't mad at you, she was just scared. She came home from work and didn't know where you were."

"I know, but I'm fine! I go there all the time by myself. Just because she chooses not to pay attention doesn't mean I don't have a life. Nothing bad happened. I'm okay. She got so angry for absolutely no reason." Nana was quiet. And Charlotte felt the need to explain more. "I just went to the park to read. What's so wrong with that?"

"It's not what you did that was wrong, Charlotte, it's what you didn't do. You should have told me, or at least gone home to call your Mom or Dad to tell them. We were all worried something had happened to you."

Charlotte lay down on her parents' bed. Nana's words poked holes in all her anger, and she felt regret seep in in its place.

"I just didn't think about it," she admitted.

"I know, Charley." Nana felt for Charlotte. She understood that her granddaughter was scatterbrained and independent, which usually made for an interesting combination. But there were times, like this one, when it let her down. "Do better next time," Nana repeated. "Now, go talk to your mom. Straighten all this out."

"Okay," Charlotte said, even though she had no intention of talking with her mother.

"And Charley?"

"Yeah?"

"Turn that frown upside down."

## *Chapter Six*

"Amanda! Hey! How are you?" Andrea smiles widely at the girl walking down the aisle.

"Hi, I'm good." She smiles, tucking a piece of her long brown hair behind her ear as she looks around. "I thought I was running late, but looks like I'm the first one here."

"You're right on time," Andrea says, beckoning her onstage. "Amanda, this is my good friend Charlotte. She's going to be helping out a lot."

I'm sure my smile falters for a moment when I snap my gaze to Andrea.

A *lot?*

"Charlotte," Andrea says, raising her brows at me. I stand to greet the new girl, taking Andrea's cue. "This is Amanda, she'll be our Liv."

It's obvious that she's much younger than Olivia should be—she's petite, and her blue eyes gleam with an almost childlike enthusiasm as she smiles up at me. But if she's going to be playing Olivia—broken, beautiful, angry, weary Liv—she must be pretty good.

"Nice to meet you." I shake Amanda's small hand. "And congratulations."

"Thank you," she says, and glances between us like she isn't sure who to smile at first. "I can't wait to get started!"

Andrea offers her a seat, and I resume my own. But before I can even get my sketchpad out of my bag, the door opens again, and a remarkably tall guy strides down the aisle. Each of his steps looks like the length of two of mine.

"I've arrived," he announces, his voice loud and expressive as he lifts a long arm up, and holds his palm open toward the ceiling.

Andrea starts to laugh. "With a flourish, of course."

"Is there any other way?" he says, and flips the long hair he *doesn't* have over his shoulder. He goes right to Andrea and kisses her cheek, his broad shoulders completely blocking her from my view.

"Max, this is Amanda. She's playing Liv, and this is my best friend Charlotte."

"Hey!" Max says, his round brown eyes falling on the two of us. He cracks a wide, crooked smile. "Nice to meet you both. Looking forward to working with you."

"Oh, I'm not…" Max stares at me, and I pause. "I mean, I'm not in the play. I won't really be working with you, just—"

"Charlotte," Andrea says, cutting me off, "will be helping me for the most part. And she'll be doing the design for the program and stuff."

"Oh, you're the artistic friend Andi's always talking about," Max says, folding himself into the chair next to Amanda. His limbs are so long, they take up much of the circle, and he takes a moment to position each of them just so.

"Max and I have done a couple plays together," Andrea says.

"Yeah. And I'm a little concerned for us all now that you're directing," Max says, grinning up at her.

"You're the first one on the shit list," Andrea says, and I finally sit again, laughing along with both of them. Amanda looks a little worried, the smile wilting on her lips as she stares at the three of us, but before I can say anything reassuring, the door opens again.

Another guy is making his way down the aisle towards us. He's tall too, but narrower, and a bit more proportionate than Max. He gives his head of dark brown curls a shake before flicking his brown eyes up, and he nods at Andrea by way of hello. Only when he's onstage do his eyes sweep over the rest of us, finding an empty chair as far away as he can get from the three of us already sitting.

But before he can sit down, the door opens again, and our attention is turned to the four people now walking down the aisle.

The new group comes in talking, and as soon as they make it up onto the stage, Andrea's trying to get their attention. I pull my sketchpad from my bag, ready to continue the drawing I'd started earlier today.

"Alright, guys…" Andrea is shouting now, and I bite back a smile, watching as everyone continues talking for a solid twenty seconds. "Hi, over here. Hey!" She smiles when she finally gets their attention. "So, I think we're only waiting on one more person, but…"

The door slams open, and a girl runs in. "I'm here!" she shouts, the sound of her feet smacking the concrete floor echoing off the walls. "I'm sorry, the subway was— And then I was stuck— And then I ran, but…" She looks around the circle of chairs at each of us. "Hi."

"Have a seat," Andrea says, and I know she's bothered by this girl's tardiness but she does a good job hiding it. "Okay! Now that we're all here, let's get started. Charlotte, would you mind passing out the scripts?"

I look up at Andrea, surprised to have been addressed so early on and a little nervous to have nine sets of eyes on me, but when she only looks at me, expectant, all I can do is get up and do as she says.

"Great." Andrea claps her hands together and sits, crossing her legs. "First off, congratulations to all of you, and welcome to the cast of 'What Was Lost'. When you get your script, please take a look at the rehearsal schedule I've put together to see if there are any dates or times that won't work for you. It's better if we get that out of the way now."

I hand Max the last script, and he smiles excessively and thanks me. I sit back down and pick up my sketch pad again just as Andrea goes into what she'll expect from them. And as I touch up the lines of the mirror, the shading of the hair, the downcast eyes of the girl, and the straight line of the man's mouth, Andrea goes on about needing one hundred and ten percent from each of them, about how memorization will be key, about how this is an emotional rollercoaster of a play, and it's their responsibility to get that emotion across to the audience. I fight a smile the whole time, but especially when she threatens to kick them out of the play if they don't have their lines memorized by the "off-book" date. It's an empty threat. She'll need them more than they'll need her, and I'm sure they know it.

Well, from the wide-eyed look of fear on Amanda's face, not *all* of them know it. But I don't say anything. Just continue sketching.

"Now, a little about myself…" Andrea clears her throat. "This is the first play I'm directing, but I've been an actress pretty much my entire life. I've done upwards of twenty plays, including a national tour of Annie when I was nine. Otherwise, I enjoy yoga, knitting, and yelling at people who look at me funny."

Everyone snickers at that, but only I know how true it really is, and I continue working on my sketch with a smile on my face, rounding out the woman's reflection in the mirror.

"Charlotte," Andrea's voice replaces the sound of everyone's laughter. "You're up."

She pats my leg, and my stomach feels like it flips over when I look up to find everyone's eyes on me again. My burning red cheeks probably detract a little from the menacing glare I send Andrea's way.

"Er, hi. My name's Charlotte Worth. I'm, uh…" I sit straighter, and fold my arms over my drawing. "Here to help out. And, uh… Andrea is a good friend of mine. She asked me to help with artwork, and the set and stuff. And I can attest to the fact that she does enjoy yelling at people." I catch Andrea smile out of the corner of my eye. "Namely, me," I say, and Max laughs unabashedly from his seat on my other side. Now

I'm smiling. "I don't have nearly as much experience in theater as her, but I *was* a sheep in Aesop's Funny Fables in the first grade, and I did some pretty badass grazing, so I wouldn't say I'm totally useless." Everyone chuckles a little more. "And, uh, I'm excited to work with you all. But don't ask me to protect you from Andi."

More chuckles sound, and I sit back in my seat, twisting my fingers together so that no one will see them shaking.

"Hi, guys, I'm Amanda Ferrara. I'm playing Olivia." She curls her long hair behind her ears, and keeps her blue eyes trained to the floor. "I'm twenty-one. I've been acting since I was in elementary school." She looks right at me then. "I was actually Nana the dog in Peter Pan when I was in seventh grade, so I feel you on the animal roles. But my favorite role was definitely Juliet. That was when I was in high school."

"Why?" Max asks. "Was Romeo hot?"

Amanda's cheeks flame while the rest of us laugh. "Yeah, he was, actually." Her shoulders rise to meet her ears. "But that wasn't the only reason."

"Of course it wasn't," Max says, giving her a wink. When Amanda doesn't continue, he sits up. "Oh, is it my turn?" He doesn't wait for anyone else to jump in. "What's up, guys, I'm Max, otherwise known as Maximilian. But you don't *have* to call me that." I cover my mouth with my hand to keep from laughing too loudly. "I'm playing Nick's brother Jonathan. I've been into theater since I was about thirteen, but I've been gay as long as I can remember. No direct correlation between the two."

Andrea's infectious giggle echoes in the expanse of the theater, and we're all off again, growing comfortable with one another the longer we go on.

There's Lou, who's new to theater, and he's playing Olivia's father. Jane, the girl who showed up five minutes late, is the oldest of the group at twenty-six, and she has a three-year-old daughter back home. She'll be Olivia's mother. Then Cameron, who's soft-spoken and rather meek, but cute, with a strong jaw and bright smile. He admits to obsessing over poetry—poets like Keats and Whitman and Hughes, so he's automatically okay in my book. He's playing Liv's lover. Then

Mark, who looks like he still belongs in high school and has long blonde hair that touches beneath his shoulders. He's playing the waiter at Nick and Liv's first date, and for whatever reason, he admits to wetting the bed until he was ten years old. We all laugh, but we laugh even harder when Max holds up a hand and says, "I was eleven."

By the time we reach Tanya, I find myself totally caught up in these people, smiling at their stories, forgetting my own self-consciousness and the sketchpad in my lap.

"Tanya Moore," she says, and sits up a little straighter, smoothing out the skirt of her floral dress. "I'm twenty-two, and I'll be playing Jenna. Let's see, uh, I went to modeling school when I was a kid, and that's actually how I started acting. I did some commercials, and some work as an extra in various movies."

"Ooh," Max says, his arms crossed, his long legs extended so that they rest in the middle of the circle. "Anything we'd know?"

"No, only because I don't want you looking it up. It's embarrassing."

"I'll take that as a challenge," Max says, smiling at her.

Tanya smiles right back. "Good luck. You're not getting it out of me. Anyway, I'm thoroughly devoted to theater now. It's so much more fun than film work."

"*Totally*," Max says, and the sarcasm I'm starting to love about him is evident once more.

Tanya giggles. "Okay, okay, enough about me. Moving on, please."

It's quiet again as we all turn our attention to the last person. Leather jacket guy, as I've come to call him in my head. It's only weird that he's wearing one because it's over eighty degrees outside, so I thought it strange as soon as he walked in. Then again, I'm getting chilly in here, so maybe he's the smart one. He's certainly the only one who hasn't let himself laugh this whole time. The only one who's barely cracked a smile.

The only one I find myself eager to get to.

"Graham Hudson," he says, and his voice is not as deep as I thought it would be. "I'm playing Nick." He leans forward then, his leather jacket squeaking as his elbows come to rest on his knees. "Grew up in a lot of places, and I started acting towards the end of middle school, and…" He holds his hands up in between his knees. "That's really it."

It's quiet for a few moments, and he doesn't look up at us, only at his hands where they're folded together between his knees. But I stare at him, watching his dark eyes flick back and forth as he waits for some kind of response. Then his tongue pokes out between his lips, and I notice the silver hoop at the corner of his bottom lip for the first time.

"Has anyone ever called you 'Graham Cracker'?"

I hear the question, decipher its meaning, smile as everyone laughs—but can't believe that I was the one to voice it, especially when I feel the heat of Graham's dark-eyed glare. It could melt paint off a wall, so it's no surprise that my cheeks feel like they're going to drip off my face.

The laughter quiets quickly because he's still glaring at me. His eyes never leave mine, and a smile doesn't tilt his lips, not even for a moment.

"*No.*" He practically spits the word. "You're the *first* person to come up with it. Do you feel special now?"

It sounds like he's being sarcastic, but there's no mistaking the venom that poisons any sense of ease I may have had; that pierces the small bubble of comfort we created. But as embarrassed and regretful as I feel for not filtering my thoughts before voicing them, I'm also so angry I can barely see straight.

"Actually," I say with a forced smile. "I always do."

If an apology is what he expected—and from the way those nearly black eyes stare at me, never blinking, he did—he's got another thing coming. I stare right back, daring him to snap at me again.

Someone clears their throat what feels like five minutes later, but has probably only been a few moments. It takes me a second to realize it was Andrea. "Okay. So…um, now that we've kind of gotten to know each other, we can get into the real nitty-gritty."

I don't hear the next part—can only focus on the burning in my cheeks, in my chest, the tremble in my fingers knotted on my drawing, and Graham's black stare still boring into me. I look away first. I have to. But even staring at Andrea, I can't focus on what she's saying.

Embarrassment and anger are writhing around in my torso like snakes on a bed of hot coals, heat taking up too much space in my body. I breathe deeply through my nose, keep my eyes locked on Andrea, and with each intake of breath, each exhale, my body—tensed in defense from the moment he said "*no*"—begins to unwind, relax, and I slump back in my chair.

"I put your names on the days you'll have to be here, so Graham, Amanda, that's most days for you," Andrea's saying when I can finally somewhat focus again. "The rest of you, look for your names each day. But, come tech week at the end of July, everyone will have to be at every rehearsal. Obviously, let me know if you have another obligation, but I need to know as soon as possible to work around it. Otherwise, I really need everyone during those last two weeks. Do everything you can to be here."

I can't look at him again. Not yet. But I want to. Not for any other reason than the fact that he needs to know I'm fine. Unaffected. That he didn't scare me. That he *can't* scare me. And I won't be spoken to that way again.

"Obviously, this is where we'll be doing the show," Andrea says. "And this is where all rehearsals will be held."

It's easier to listen now, and my pounding heart has slowed, but I still need another moment before I do it—before I look over. I uncross my arms, allowing the stiff muscles to soften as blood rushes through them.

"When do you expect us to be off-book?" Max asks. I can only assume "off-book" means to have their lines memorized.

"We'll say in about a month for now. At that point, you'll still be able to call for a line and all that. Week six is when I'll want you to be solid."

In the next few moments of silence, I almost look over.

"Oh, and another thing," Andrea says, hugging her script to her chest. "We'll start blocking each scene next week, so, when you're practicing, think about what might seem natural for each situation."

I have no idea what "blocking" means, but everyone else is nodding, so I keep quiet.

"Now, I thought it would be a good idea to read through once today, just to give you guys a feel for your lines."

Everyone opens their scripts, so I follow suit.

"Don't worry about acting right now. We're just reading the lines out loud so you each get a sense of your character and his or her place in the story." Andrea opens her script then, resting it on her crossed legs.

I flip to the first page, and look up again when Andrea leans over to me. "Could you read the stage directions? Just for context's sake."

It feels like my voice has disappeared, scared out of being used again. I clear my throat to yank it back, and speak as clearly and as loudly as I can. "Yeah, sure."

There's a paragraph of stage directions that preempt the lines on the first page, and I hope my voice doesn't quake as I begin. "A young man sits at the kitchen table. He's wearing a suit and tie, which hangs loose around his neck. The table is set, but he's not eating. He glances at the clock and sighs in frustration. A woman enters."

Graham picks up then, voice smooth and hard as buffed granite, and I allow myself to finally look up; to finally eye him again. His script is propped open in one large hand, and those dark eyes sweep back and forth across the page as he speaks.

It's a shame I can't focus on the dialogue, but I find myself too caught up watching him, the way he fiddles with his lip ring between lines, and glances up to look at Amanda as she feeds Olivia's lines back to him.

Andrea pokes me when I miss my cue, and I stutter through a block of stage directions, keeping my eyes downcast as Graham and Max take off with a scene. If I don't look at him, I can believe he's the too-nice guy he's portraying. The sincere sadness and contagious hopefulness all sound so real, so believable, and I wonder how someone who comes off so cold, who has no problem making someone else feel two inches tall, could sound even remotely likable, let alone genuine.

But he does it. And I don't want to be as intrigued as I am.

I keep up enough to read the stage directions that open the next scene, and Amanda and Tanya begin, firing their lines off at one another.

That's when I feel it—the heat in my cheeks, a tightness in my chest.

I match Graham's stare over the top of our scripts. His is still propped open in his large hand. The other hand rubs at his dark scruff, and he doesn't look away.

Neither do I.

After a few more seconds, I smile, just a little, hoping to let him know that I'm unaffected, that I'm more than fine, that I'm already over it. Whatever weird thing "it" was. Only then does he focus on his script again.

Feeling like I've somehow won, I continue smiling as I return my attention to the script in my lap, deciding that I won't let myself care about his words, what he might think of me, or anything he might say in the coming weeks.

But I can already feel it, that familiar itching in my fingers—the one that tells me to pick up a pencil, to put on paper what I can't get out of my head.

I stop myself. I leave my sketchpad firmly beneath my script. Because I won't draw it, that minuscule amount of light I saw in the depth of those dark eyes.

I refuse.

## *Year Twelve going on Thirteen*

He was looking again. And Charlotte, while she didn't want to be obvious, couldn't help but glance back.

Charlotte graduated from elementary school without honors, but with an award in English Language Arts. She knew she wouldn't stay friends with the girls in her class, and definitely not with any of the boys, but she was okay with that. Being with them felt like wearing clothes that never fit right—too tight in the armpits, too loose around her hips, and too long in the leg. She supposed she could get them fitted, or adjust herself to make them fit, but she didn't feel they were worth the effort.

That summer, Charlotte spent her time split between Nana's house and the park. Both her parents worked all day, so when they didn't drop her off at Nana's she was left to her own devices. With a book bag chock full of books and pencils, she'd stroll through the tall, wrought iron gates of the park and remember when they used to look twenty feet tall. After a spin around the sandbox, watching the children jump around and giggle and scream in their play, she'd take a seat under a tree at the far end—what she liked to think was her own personal spot. It wasn't lost on her that no one ever sat there. She'd read or draw, looking up occasionally to eye a child who strayed too close, or a couple of mothers walking by chatting, or she'd glance into the basketball court directly across from her spot, eyeing the group of boys playing in secret wonderment.

She wrapped herself up in her little world like a mother swaddling a child—no room for too much movement, or any unwanted cool air to get inside. But one day at the end of July, she looked up in terrified surprise when the basketball hit the chain link fence between the court and the playground with such force, Charlotte was sure the whole thing would come toppling down. She didn't attempt to hide her annoyance with the boys, who were all looking her way in amusement or indifference. All but one, who had picked up the ball when it bounced back their way.

"Sorry!" he called to her. The rest of the boys looked ready to resume their game, bored with what lay on the other side of the fence, but not him. He stood still, smiling at her, his blue eyes squinting through the sunlight to see her, and she felt tingles shoot through her stomach when he turned away.

After a week, Charlotte learned to expect the glances, and to look forward to them. She'd gotten braver, not averting her gaze as quickly now, holding the stare and smiling when he smiled. But each day he left without saying a word. She watched him go, stared at the dark gray patch of sweat on the back of his light gray t-shirt, and her disappointment spilled over any sense of hope she might have had like black ink, blotting out the fact that he'd looked at her and smiled at her at all.

She wasn't interested in boys anyway, and told herself to forget the whole thing ever happened.

But how could she when he was always there, scrubbing away the ink with lingering glances and shy smiles? Charlotte found herself recalling every bit of him in her imagination when she left. He was tall and skinny, but there were noticeable dips in his thin arms; the suggestion of muscle. She already loved the way his shaggy brown hair darkened and curled at the ends when he was sweating, and she'd seen enough of his narrow stomach when he pulled the bottom of his shirt over his face to wipe his sweaty brow to recall it with almost perfect clarity.

She had never considered the idea that boys could be beautiful, but this boy, with his knowing smile and bright blue eyes—beautiful was the only word that fit him.

Three weeks, and he still looked over. And Charlotte still waited for those eyes to meet hers.

But this time, when Charlotte glanced up, he strode toward her.

Charlotte wondered if girls her age could have heart attacks, because surely the pace at which her heart was thumping couldn't be healthy. Then he was standing in front of her, close enough to touch, blocking out the sunlight, casting her in shadow, and she thought that if it were going to happen—if she were going to die—it would have happened already.

"Hi," was all he said. Charlotte couldn't help but think his blue eyes—so light they were nearly transparent—looked like they held a secret, one she felt a nearly desperate need to uncover.

"Uh…" She cleared her throat. "Hi." She smiled, clutching her book to her chest, sure that he would see the outline of her heart pounding without the cover.

"I'm Adam." He didn't hold his hand out or anything, for which Charlotte was grateful. Her palms were slick with sweat.

"I'm Charlotte," she said, the words coming out on a wisp of breath.

"I noticed you sit here a lot, and, uh…" Adam rubbed his hands on his shorts. "I was wondering if I could sit with you today."

He was looking right at her, a small smile on his face, as if he already knew what her answer would be. Charlotte's heart lurched pleasantly at his request, and before she could really consider his question, she nearly shouted, "Yes."

Adam took a seat next to her, leaving more space than she would've liked between them, but she was too afraid to chance moving closer. She scrambled for something to say, but everything sounded stupid in her head, so she stayed quiet. So did he. She was all too aware of the fact that she had never dated anyone—a fact that was a crippling embarrassment to her, even though he had no idea.

She chanced a peek at him from the side. He had his thin arms propped up on his bent knees, and he kept twisting his fingers together, his eyes on the basketball game going on without him. It was strange and exhilarating looking at him this close, like seeing someone you've seen on TV in real life. She'd watched him for so long and was sure she knew what he looked like. But, up close, she could better see the strands of gold in his brown hair. There was a beauty mark on his cheekbone, the shadow of a mustache on his upper lip, and tiny blonde hairs on his tan arms. His eyelashes were long, and curled up, making those blue eyes even more captivating. And she'd thought that he was beautiful *before*. With him this close, it was harder to get a good breath, as if her cells were stunned too, no longer soaking up the oxygen they needed.

She looked away when he caught her staring, and took off her glasses, making a show of polishing them.

"Are you going to put them back on?" he asked then.

Charlotte stared at the purples frames in her hand, surprised he'd asked. "Why?"

Adam smiled, looking like he was caught, like he'd said something he shouldn't have. "I like them."

Charlotte's insides went white hot, and she was sure they were liquefying right there under that tree. Soon, she'd be just a warm puddle of goo and a pair of purple glasses sitting next to the most beautiful boy she'd ever seen. Her embarrassment shone on her cheeks as she slid the frames back on, the world around her coming into clearer focus as she looked anywhere but at Adam.

There were a few more beats of silence before he asked, "What are you reading?"

That was all it took.

Charlotte told him that it was the third book in the Harry Potter series, surprised to find he had no idea what that was. So, she went on to explain what it was about, how the wizarding world worked, and how Hermione Granger was her favorite character. Adam interrupted to ask questions about the characters, which may have annoyed her if he were anyone else, and told her he wasn't really into reading but the books sounded good. Charlotte told him English was her best subject in school, and he told her science was his. He asked how old she was, told her he had just turned fourteen. He played basketball, baseball and soccer. Charlotte told him she was always bad at sports. She described Nana Rosie, and told him a little about her parents. He had two older sisters who wanted nothing to do with him, and his dad always took him to his games. His mom often brought snacks for the team, and he tried not to be embarrassed about it.

They didn't notice that his friends were leaving until one of them called out to Adam. Charlotte, having completely forgotten about anything but Adam for the past however many hours, told him that she should leave, too, and they stood.

He surprised her by leaning in for a hug, but she was more surprised by how warm, and strong, and *good* his arms felt around her. She hoped he didn't hear her suck in a big breath when her cheek pressed against his chest. His heart was beating just as fast as hers. It was a quick hug, and they agreed to meet in two days since Charlotte knew she had to go to Nana's the next day.

But it was already, Charlotte thought as she walked home, two days too long.

## *Chapter Seven*

The head of curls is taking a while to perfect, and I tell myself this is only a rough draft; that Andrea hasn't even seen it to confirm whether or not she likes it—but, for whatever reason, I have to be sure they're right. My pencil moves over each twist and curve, filling in the blank spaces with meticulous precision. Then, I follow the rounded curves of his shoulders, sure that I can capture the strength in them with the right shading; that I can feel the tension in the muscle beneath my fingertips if I draw it well enough.

I snap my book closed when his voice, too close, says, "Okay, and then get up, right?"

When I look up, he's standing not five feet from me, taking a long pull from his water bottle, staring not at me, but at Andrea. I make myself look back down, relief filling the place where only startled nerves had been a moment ago. I take a deep breath, staring at the doodles on the cover of my sketchpad.

"Right as she walks in, yeah," Andrea says, and Graham puts the cap back on his water bottle and leaves it on the floor before heading back over to her and Amanda.

"Amanda, you'll enter from over here, stage left," Andrea says, walking through the motions herself. Graham sits down in his chair, jangling the keys dangling on the belt loop of his black jeans as she walks towards him. We've already pulled a desk onto the left side of the stage to act as the kitchen table, and he's sitting in a chair behind it, hydrated and ready to run the first scene.

"And you'll set your bag here, at the end of the table, then walk to the fridge. Don't look at Graham at all."

Amanda nods, clutching her script, and then waits as Andrea instructs Graham.

"And you'll just sit here, doing different things to express your stress. So…" She motions for Graham to stand, then sits in the seat herself. "You could drum your fingers, or twirl a fork—when it's here, obviously." She twirls a pen instead. "Whatever feels right to you, and it could be something different every time."

Andrea is so upbeat, so invested in what she's saying, and Graham just looks bored.

"Okay, let's run it and see how it looks." After clapping a few times for no apparent reason, Andrea prances over and sits on the stage floor next to me. I crack open my sketchpad again, sure that I'll remember the movements—what I learned is called "blocking" in theater terminology— to jot them down in a minute. I continue shading in the shirt on his chest, flicking my eyes up as Amanda walks onstage, her expression solemn. Graham turns to watch her, his crinkled brow softening when he sees her.

"Try it one more time, Amanda," Andrea says, causing both of them to look over. "I want you to count to ten-Mississippi in your head. Give Graham a chance to anticipate you."

With a nod, Amanda heads back side-stage, and Graham looks down at his lap. My pencil pauses, hovering over the page. He stays like that for a few moments before lifting his head up, and his eyebrows are drawn together again. His knee bobs up and down under the desk, and after another moment he glances up at the spot where Andrea intends to place a clock. His leg is still shaking.

Amanda walks in with a blank expression. Graham whips his head around to stare at her, dark eyes wide. But she doesn't look at him. She lets her bag fall off her shoulder and hit the ground, then walks behind Graham to where-would-stand the fridge and pretends to peer inside. Graham stands then, watching her back before she turns to face him.

They're just about to launch into their lines when Andrea stops them. "Good. Okay, let's try this now. Graham, you stood at a good time, but look a little more uncomfortable. Like you're not sure how to handle this situation at all."

Andrea stands and walks over to them, and I close my sketchpad, already eager to continue it later. I should be watching them anyway, not just because I should pay attention to what I need to be writing down, but because I have the real, breathing subject right in front of me, and I want to study him while I can.

For inspiration, of course.

Graham mumbles something that I can't hear, but Andrea replies, "Think of it this way… your wife has just shown up two hours late. She didn't call, didn't text, and then she doesn't say a word when she finally arrives. You're pissed, you're confused, you're hurt, but most of all, you don't know what to do or say because you don't want to fight with her. All you do is fight."

As I scribble everything down, I can't help but think that's a lot to portray in a short amount of time, for one person, with one face. Graham is supposed to be angry, but he has to be uncomfortable with that anger, and scared to say anything to his wife (who he's pissed at) because he doesn't want to fight—which he knows is inevitable because it's happened so many times in the past. I'm exhausted just thinking about it.

I eye him as he studies his script, wondering what he'll do, how he'll pull it off. From the little bit of rehearsal I've seen, I know he's a great actor—perfect for Nick. I also know he rakes his fingers through his hair when he's getting ready to go into character, and he rubs his fingers over his scruffy chin when he's listening to Andrea, and he prods his lip ring every so often with his tongue…

"Charlotte."

Andrea's staring at me.

"Did you get all that?"

I hope so.

"Yep," I say instead.

When we run through it again (and again), so much is written in Graham's body language—nerves in the shaking leg before Amanda enters, anticipation in the way he stands too quickly when she arrives, and impatience in the way he clenches and unclenches his fists when she ignores him. Confusion and hurt are colored in the expression on his face—the furrow of his dark brows, the wide set of his eyes, the way he opens and closes his mouth as she moves around the room, trying but failing to speak the words he needs to say. And fear plays in the quake of his voice when he finally does talk, choosing to remind her of the time.

I wonder if I can read all of that because I know it's what he's supposed to be expressing. But from the way goose bumps rise on my arms, I don't think it really matters.

After a few more run-throughs of the scene, adding and removing movements as we go, Andrea declares it time for a ten-minute break. Amanda and Graham don't say anything as Andrea walks back over to me, but they don't leave either.

"What do you think so far?" Andrea asks in a low voice as she sits beside me. I eye Graham and Amanda, surprised to see Graham smiling as he speaks with her.

"I think it's looking great," I say, still watching them. "And they're perfect together, just the right amount of chemistry to act like they have no chemistry."

"I know, right?" Andrea lowers her voice even more. "How am I doing? Too demanding? Not demanding enough?"

"Just the right amount of demanding." I smile at her, kind of enjoying the fact that she's unsure for once in her life.

"Right. Okay, good. Thanks." Andrea looks down at the script in my lap. "How's the recording going?"

"See for yourself." I hand her the script, eyeing my scribbled stage movements over her shoulder, hoping I've been doing it right. She scans the pages, flipping through several before handing it back to me.

"Looks good. Just remember to write stage left or right. That's always important."

"Yes, ma'am."

"And could you do it in pencil from now on? The scribbles are off-putting."

"It's my script," I say, a little offended.

"I know, but I have to look at it, too," Andrea looks over at me, and I wait for her to tell me she's joking. She doesn't.

I sigh more loudly than I need to and turn to my bag, rummaging through it for a pencil. Luckily, I never leave the house without one. "I thought I was supposed to be here for moral support. And artistic inspiration. Now you have me writing down stage movements."

"Blocking," Andrea says. "It's called blocking. And I know, but I couldn't find a stage manager that I could trust."

"So, I'm stage manager by default?" I ask, putting one pencil back in favor of a sharper one.

Andrea flashes me a grin. "Don't you feel honored?"

"Honored. Sure. Let's go with that."

Andrea giggles a little, but her laughter is so loud Graham and Amanda look over at us. "I owe you big time, Charlotte."

"Mhm," I mumble, trying to yank myself away from her arms, now wrapped around my shoulders. "At least I have time to think about how I'll make this worth my while."

"Whatever you want."

"Whatever?" I ask, making sure she hears herself.

She's got a small crease between her brows now, and I know she's no longer listening. "What do you really think of them? Be honest."

She asks as if I *wasn't* honest with her a few minutes ago.

Graham is sitting at the table again, running his fingers over his chin as he studies his script. Amanda's pacing back and forth beside him, her mouth moving soundlessly as she says her lines to herself.

"So far so good, I think." I know that won't be enough for Andrea. "They both seem to take direction well, and, uh…" I glance at them again for some ideas. "They're good heights for each other."

If Andrea was actually listening, she probably would have rolled her eyes at me, made a snide remark—something to indicate how inane my point was. But she isn't, and I almost laugh when she turns to stare at them, making a low "mmm" noise in agreement with my assessment.

"Alright." She claps twice a moment later. Graham and Amanda both look up. "Let's get going again. From the top."

I have a bit of a break from scribbling down Andrea's directions because she has them run the same thirty seconds' worth of movements over and over again, and my eyes find their way to Graham more than I want them to. He listens to everything Andrea says with a blank expression, nodding so that she knows he's listening. But he's much more expressive in scene. Every emotion and thought is written on his face, revealing a depth I wouldn't have otherwise though him capable of; an understanding I would've thought he didn't have.

Amanda is incredible, too. The energy and enthusiasm from that first day has disappeared, shut up tight somewhere inside her as she inhabits Olivia. But I return to him again and again, studying him like he's a painting I'll never understand.

I'm already too invested to care if I never do.

Graham runs his fingers through his hair when Nick's exasperated, and I find the point of a widow's peak under the spill of curls on his forehead. And when Andrea stops them again, his tongue pokes out, prodding at his lip ring.

He barely glances at me the entirety of the rehearsal, but when he does meet my eye, I'm immediately reminded why I shouldn't care if he does or doesn't. I didn't know a stare as cold as his could heat me the way it does. I tell myself it's residual anger flaring up, and try to believe it.

Graham lifts his arms up over his head to stretch, and his pale gray t-shirt rides up a bit, revealing a toned stomach that I make myself look away from. He certainly has the whole "bad boy" thing going for him with the black jeans, plain t-shirt, leather jacket thing. I mean, it's summer time. Who wears that kind of stuff during the summer? And there's no denying he's attractive in that I-know-he's-no-good-for-me way. But his personality stamps a seal on the whole package—a seal that I have no desire to crack.

"Alright, let's call it a day," Andrea says, her voice resounding in the otherwise empty theater. "Great job, you guys. Keep practicing your lines with the blocking in mind, and if you can work it out to go over it together, even better."

Amanda's nodding along to every word, the bun on her head wobbling with each movement. She glances at Graham. He looks back at her, his lips forming a small smile.

"But if you feel like you need extra time with it, text me or Charlotte. Our numbers are on the schedule, and one of us will figure something out to help you guys."

I whip my head around to stare at her the moment she says my name, but she doesn't look at me.

"So, we'll see you tomorrow, Amanda. Graham, we'll see you Friday with Max."

The two of them turn toward each other, Amanda with a smile, and Graham with a quick raise of his thick brows.

"Now I'm available to run lines?" I say through clenched teeth when Andrea is close enough.

She gives me a grin. "Didn't I mention that?"

She doesn't wait for me to answer, just walks down the stage steps to the front row of seats where she left her bag.

"As a matter of fact," I start to say, following her down the steps, "*no.*"

Andrea shrugs. "Well, it's not a big deal." She tucks her script into her bag. "I figured I won't be available all the time, but between the two of us, we should be able to cover everyone."

Typical Andrea. Making plans for me and only letting me in on them when it's too late. "What if I don't want to?" The thought of Graham asking for help with lines—while laughable because of the way he reacted to me last week and hasn't spoken to me at all since—is intimidating nonetheless.

"They won't get in touch with you, anyway," Andrea says, before smiling at Graham and Amanda as they walk by us, up the aisle. "Get home safe, you guys!"

I roll my eyes, arms crossed as Amanda says too sweetly over her shoulder, "You too!"

When they're out of earshot, I say, "So, why bother offering if you know they won't?"

Andrea sighs. "Look, Charlotte. It's all about building trust and communication at this point." She lifts her bag onto her shoulder. "The best directors I've had were readily available to us, eager to answer our questions. I want to be that way for them, and I want them to know we're available to them."

"*We?*"

It's Andrea's turn to roll her eyes. "I guess I thought you'd be a little more invested." She walks past me, heading up the aisle.

I feel guilty, but this always happens with her. She drags me into something under some kind of pretense, and before I know it, I'm in way over my head. Like the time she talked me into trying out for the swim team just so that we could get into the off-limits pool area in our high school. But I made the team and she didn't, and my parents and Nana were so happy, so surprised I was interested in swimming and so excited to share it with me, I didn't know how to get out of doing it. So, I woke up at six a.m. every Saturday morning for six months to get ready for our weekly meets at eight. And cursed Andrea every time my alarm clock went off.

It was a good metaphor for our friendship, really. Meeting her had seemed like a good thing at the time. She was fun and loud and brutally honest, and didn't care what anyone else thought. We had that in common. But my life hasn't been the same since.

Most of the time I'm fine with it, and though I'm upset now, I remind myself that she'd be just as invested in one of my hair-brained schemes as she is in her own. All I'd have to do is ask, and she'd be down for whatever. Besides, the only thing I have planned for the summer is wallowing over London, and how much I miss it there. And I have to admit, in the week or so I've been working on this with her, the ache of missing it has lessened considerably.

"Wait," I call, releasing a long breath before grabbing my bag and running to catch up with her. I hook my arm through hers when I reach her, and all of my defenses leak right out of me. "I don't have to help Graham, do I?"

Andrea giggles, and her hand comes up to hold mine in place. "Nah, girl. I deal better with assholes like him."

I smile, relieved to have at least that off my mind. If being there for Andrea means being there for the entire cast, then so be it. She's currently the only person in my life who's there for me, who knows about all I've had to deal with in the last few years. I need her. And now, she needs me. But if I can avoid working with Graham apart from regular rehearsals, I will.

I like to think everyone deserves a chance, and sometimes even a second chance. Graham is capable of tenderness. I saw it in the scenes we ran today. But I won't let myself be fooled, either. Graham's an incredible actor, and that tenderness is an incredible act. And as Andrea and I lock up the theater, I promise myself to suppress the confusing, already overwhelming desire to have him look at me with any degree of tenderness, real or not.

## *Year Thirteen*

Charlotte was on a mission—a mission to find out what Nana was hiding. A mission to learn more about her grandmother's past. A mission to know what made Nana Rosie Worth the tough woman she knew.

It had to be something amazing, like growing up in the jungle, where she and her parents lived amongst animals, protecting each other from all the predators like lions and cheetahs and panthers. Or, on the off-chance that wasn't realistic, maybe Nana's family moved a lot because her father was a really important person who had to travel the world, and Nana had to be tough to say goodbye to all of her friends in each place. Or maybe her parents didn't like Charlotte's grandfather, and insisted that Nana end things with him. But Nana was in love with him and chose to run away with him instead, somewhere far away from her home and her parents so that they could get married and start a family.

But if it was anything like that, Charlotte didn't know why Nana wouldn't tell her.

So, she asked. But it couldn't be just any question. It had to be one that would garner the most information.

"Nana," she said, sitting in the front seat of Nana's car as they drove to the store. "Why don't you ever talk about my grandpa?"

It was quiet for a few moments before Nana answered. "He died a long time ago, Charley."

"How?" Charlotte pressed, voice quiet, afraid being too loud might dissuade her grandmother. Nana's mouth was closed, but Charlotte watched her jaw tense and release, then tense again, and knew that she had asked the wrong question—that this was not something Nana wanted to discuss.

"Did you love him?" Charlotte asked, hoping that her grandmother would at least answer that.

Nana clenched her hands around the steering wheel. Her whole body had tensed, Charlotte noticed, like Charlotte's did when she knew she was getting a shot at the doctor's. Like Nana was bracing for something painful.

Or, Charlotte thought, her stomach jolting uncomfortably as Nana's jaw tightened, because she was already in pain.

"Yes," Nana finally said, her chest rising with a deep breath. "I did."

Charlotte sensed that she should stop. She had a feeling she should've left it there. But Nana had loved her grandfather. And maybe she was sad that he wasn't around anymore, but surely there were happy parts to their love story. Otherwise, Nana wouldn't have loved him.

Charlotte was desperate to know the happy parts. "How did you meet?"

Nana never got angry with Charlotte. She'd never even raised her voice around her granddaughter. But in that moment, when she stepped—too hard—on the brakes at a red light, Charlotte was afraid Nana might be angry.

"His name was Henry," Nana said, her body still stiff. "I was thirty-four years old when I met him. We were married a year later, and I had your father the same year."

That wasn't really what Charlotte had asked, but she wasn't about to say so. And once more, she knew she should stop; knew from the tight look on Nana's face that this was not something she wanted to talk about. But Charlotte was still thinking about the good parts, still eager to know the man who had made her grandmother fall in love, still desperate to understand why Nana couldn't talk about him. “How did he die?”

Nana sighed loudly. “Let’s just say, he never knew how to help himself.” She stepped on the gas. “Now...what do you want for dinner?”

Charlotte knew that was the end of their conversation. But she answered Nana and turned to look out the window, even though she had even more questions. The cryptic reply made Charlotte all the more curious about what her grandfather was like, and why talking about him caused Nana to hide things from her. Nana never hid anything from her Charley. And Charlotte didn’t want to make her feel more uncomfortable by pushing her for answers. But she *had* to know. So, for now, she stayed quiet, and promised herself that when she got home, she would pose her questions to the only other person on Earth who could supply her with information regarding Henry Worth.

## *Chapter Eight*

I almost fall walking through the front door, not just because I'm exhausted, but because the house is darker than it is outside, leaving me to wonder—not for the first time—if my dad is some kind of nocturnal creature. Shrugging my bag off my shoulder and letting it hit the ground with a thud, I squint through the darkness to get to the kitchen, and flip on the light.

I poke my head into the fridge, my mind still mulling over the scene Amanda and Tanya practiced earlier, and I smile remembering the way neither of them could keep a straight face in the midst of their "argument".

It's almost like I can breathe easier, smile more fully, and be more of myself when the oppressive presence of a certain Graham Hudson is missing. I haven't spoken directly to him, one on one, since that first day, and I plan to keep it that way for as long as possible. But his presence on that stage, in that room, was like a force I couldn't hide from; an awareness I couldn't shake. He was like a black hole, all my energy swirling toward him, weighing me down even when I wasn't looking at him, or him at me. I had to be every bit the actor he was, pretending what happened between us never had, working my face into a smile and speaking loudly to hide the way my voice shook when I addressed him along with the other cast members. My skin still prickled uncomfortably when I called to mind the heat of his glare, but he could never know that.

While it was a relief not to have him at rehearsal, there was a part of me—a minuscule, negligible part—that *wanted* to get pulled in; to turn and find his heavy, dark stare looking my way, even if he only scowled as I soon as I matched it. It was the same part that, somehow, for whatever reason, almost kind of *liked* the way his presence made me hyperaware of myself, my actions, and that prickling heat crawling across the surface of my skin.

But, like I said, all that—negligible.

"Thought I heard you down here," a voice says, startling me out of the fridge. The scream that works its way up my throat doesn't sound, but my heart is racing all the same.

"Jeez, Dad." He laughs as I close the fridge, clutching my chest with the other hand. "You sure you're not a bat?"

"Last I checked, no," he says, patting his chest and sides for effect, still grinning. "There's leftover pizza in there if you're hungry."

In my fear, I momentarily forgot my hunger, but as my heart rate slows, my stomach rumbles more insistently. I open the fridge again and scan its contents, finding the triangle-shaped aluminum foil.

"How was your day?" Dad sits at the round kitchen table, one elbow on its surface as he watches me.

"Long," I say, watching the red lights of the convection oven grow brighter. "How was yours?"

"Good," he says, voice quiet. "I missed you, though."

My heart thumps uncomfortably at his words. "I missed you, too."

As much as I'm enjoying working on the play, it does hurt not to see my dad for more than a total of an hour a day. I missed him while I was in London. He was the only constant in my life anymore, and not seeing him made me feel like something was wrong…off. I try not to think about it, and I don't want to spend the little time I have with him upset that I can't see him *more*, so I try to lighten the mood.

"But I can see you're managing without me." I tilt my head towards the bubbling cheese pizza, the lights in the oven now dimming.

Dad smirks. "It's been a struggle."

"I'm sure." I hiss when I burn a finger on the metal grate of the oven, but grab my pizza and walk over to him, too hungry to prolong it anymore.

"How was rehearsal?" he asks.

"It went well. It was just the two girls tonight, and we're still trying to figure out the blocking for this one scene." I take a bite of my pizza.

"That's the movement and stuff, right?"

"Mhm." I'm still chewing when I say, "We're still working out a few little things, but it's looking good."

He's smiling at me, an amused look in his eyes.

"What?" I ask, swallowing my food before taking another large bite.

He chuckles, his eyes crinkling at the corners. "You're just so delicate, Charlotte Worth."

I smack his arm, knowing that's anything but a compliment. "I'm starving! I haven't eaten anything since, like, four o'clock, and it's now—" I glance at the clock hanging over the fridge, "—10:37."

"I'm only joking, kiddo." He's still smiling as he reaches over, rubbing my arm softly. "I'm glad to hear everything is coming together."

I make sure to swallow before I speak this time. "Me too."

We're quiet for a few moments, and all the amusement in Dad's face washes away. He runs his hands over his eyes, nose, then his mouth.

"Your mom called today," he says through his fingers.

The monthly phone call.

"What did she have to say?" I tear my crust apart and pop a piece into my mouth.

"Not much." He sighs. "She wanted to know when you were free to see her again."

Now, I sigh. "Not for a while." I can't keep the bitter taste in my mouth from making itself known, and Dad hears it.

I can tell by the way he's looking at me—like I'm a child who doesn't want to eat her vegetables. "I told her you were really busy with the play, but that I'd ask anyway."

"I don't want to go again." I'm not eating anymore, just picking apart what's left of my pizza crust.

"I thought you had fun last time?"

I scoff, but the thing is, he's right. I did have fun. But it wasn't fun because I was with Mom and Richard. It was fun because we spent the weekend in museums, seeing Broadway shows, and eating delicious food. All of it was their way of bribing my acceptance of the situation, but that knowledge only allowed me to enjoy everything for what it was. And all of our activities gave me the chance to avoid too much conversation. I wandered away from them in the museums, was able to completely forget their presence at the show, and only spoke when asked a direct question at dinner. So, just because I had fun didn't mean I was in any rush to go back.

"I did. Sort of. But it wasn't fun because I was with Mom and Dick twenty-four-seven."

"Charlotte, don't use that word." He rubs his eyes again, his voice holding none of the resolve the demand requires.

"For your information…'Dick' is a nickname for Richard. I don't make the rules, Dad."

He's fighting back a smile now, but successfully beats it, arranging his mouth into a straight line. "Well…I don't like it, and I don't want to hear you use it again."

"Fine," I say. He won't *hear* it again.

"Have you…?" He folds his hands together on the table, looking abruptly uncomfortable. "Have you talked with your mother about everything?"

I debate lying, telling him what he wants to hear, what I wish I could say is the truth, but end up shaking my head. "Have you?"

He nods once. "Yeah. Over the course of the year, we've discussed most of it." I stay quiet. "You should talk to her, too."

"Why?" All the anger is right there, brimming over the surface now. It's always there, just beneath everything else. I've pushed it down again and again for the last year, keeping it locked up in its cage. But it's ramming against the bars now, clamoring for escape. "Why should I be the one to talk to her? She's the one who left, shouldn't *she* be the one to talk to *me?*"

"You're not wrong, kiddo, but—"

"*She's* the one who owes me an explanation, and she hasn't even tried to broach the subject despite the chances I've given her. She's only rubbed it all in my face—her new life, her new boyfriend, her new home. Why should I go out of my way for her at this point?"

He shrugs, and he's staring down at his hands folded on the table. "Because you're the bigger person, Charlotte. You always have been."

"That's not going to work, Dad. She's lucky she's gotten what she has." My fists are clenched, eyes full and wet despite myself. "When she realizes that, then maybe we can talk."

After what feels like an endless, tense silence, he says, "It's up to you, kiddo. I just want you to be happy, you know that."

Dad pushes his chair back, but doesn't stand right away. There's an element of guilt in the mix of my emotions for unleashing my anger on him. He has every reason to be just as mad as I am, if not even *more* pissed than I am. But rage doesn't wait for the right person to target, it only knows impulse, and mine convulses at the mere mention of her name. I only hope I can keep the cage sealed until I'm brave enough to take it out on the person who deserves it most.

But as I look at Dad still sitting here in front of me, I realize that he doesn't seem to be as angry as I am. Not nearly. Not anymore.

I swallow and breathe deeply, steadying my voice, but it sounds small without the edge in it. "Have you forgiven her?"

Dad laughs, but it's obvious he doesn't think my question is very funny.

"Forgiveness." He says the word like he doesn't even recognize it. "It's a funny thing. Everyone thinks of it as this one-time deal, you know? As if saying the words—*I forgive you*—wipes away all the ways you've been wronged from your mind. But I have to do it every day. There's this…this sense of *wrongness* that comes with forgiving someone who's hurt you—a fear that they'll do it again. Each day I wake up and remember what your mother did, and I have to choose to look past it all over again."

"But why? How can you look past it?" I ask, tamping down the fear that I'll never be able to get to that point.

Dad shrugs. "It's not easy. Some days it feels impossible. But I choose not to live my life holding onto my anger—not for her, but for me. And for you. I don't want to live my life hating her."

I look into his eyes, more brown than green in the dim light of the kitchen, and wonder if mine look the same. Wonder if I'm capable of the same kind of strength—knowing full well that right here, in this moment, I'm not.

"Wow," I say, breathless as I lean forward, towards him. "Are you, like, a writer, or something?"

I smile when the crinkles appear beside his eyes and around his grin.

"Writer, philosopher…Dad extraordinaire." His eyes sparkle just like Nana's.

"Impressive." I stand, taking my plate and napkin, happy to twist the cap closed on that conversation. He stands beside me when I put my dirty plate in the sink.

"Just… think about what I said, okay?" Turning to face him, I lean back against the counter, and nod even though I don't want to. "I'm heading up to bed."

"Okay," I say, not moving from the sink, knowing he'll probably write for at least another hour.

Dad's at the door to the hall when he turns around to look at me again. "By the way, I'm thinking I'll go see Nana soon. Probably in the next couple of days." He lifts a hand toward me, then lets it drop. "You should come if you have time."

I nod before he leaves the kitchen—another lie.

Nana isn't there anymore, and I can't pretend that she is like he does. Can't pretend that the woman I love is still there. Can't delude myself into a false sense of comfort like he can. And as I run the water over my plate, it's hard to think that

Dad's strength in this instance is anything more than that: a delusion.

## *Year Thirteen*

"Dad?" Charlotte asked, entering the dining room where he was writing. It had only been a day since her conversation with Nana about her grandfather.

"Yeah?" He didn't look up from his computer right away. He was typing out the rest of a thought. When he did look at her, he smiled. "What's up, kiddo?"

Charlotte was careful as she walked toward him, fearing that one wrong move would render him unwilling to reveal the secret of her grandfather.

"I just…" She sat next to him, but didn't meet his eye. "I wanted to know a little bit about my grandpa."

Mr. Worth's eyes widened, surprised that Charlotte had thought about his father at all considering neither he nor his mother had ever spoken of him. That he knew of, anyway.

"Oh." He took his glasses off and rubbed his eyes. "Okay, uh, what do you want to know?"

Charlotte's excitement felt like small bubbles rising and popping in her chest. But she contained her smile, knowing full well that her father could still shut her down if she didn't tread carefully. There were so many things she wanted to know, and she didn't know what to ask about first. What did Henry Worth look like? How had he and Nana met? What did he do for work? Why was Nana so unwilling to discuss anything to do with him?

"How did he die?" She looked up at her father, hoping this particular question would not earn the same kind of evasive response Nana gave her.

He sighed and rubbed his eyes again. "Did you ask Nana about this?"

"She wouldn't talk about it." Charlotte readied herself for a let-down, sure that he wouldn't tell her the truth because Nana hadn't.

Mr. Worth nodded. "She doesn't like to think about it, let alone talk about it." Charlotte stared down at her lap, trying to hide how upset she really was, but then her father continued. "But I think you deserve to know a little about your grandfather. You're old enough now."

Charlotte had to tone down her excitement once again so that he wouldn't change his mind. She folded her hands in her lap and sat a little straighter, giving him her undivided attention, as if to remind him that she *was* mature enough to hear it. All of it.

Mr. Worth sat back in his chair and laced his fingers together on his stomach. "His name was Henry. He and Nana met at her brother's restaurant. My Uncle Frank. He lives in Florida now." He paused. "Anyway, they were both older when they got married. Nana was already in her thirties, and your grandpa was a few years older than her. He had been married once, and as far as I know, it didn't end well. Nana had never been married. She was a career woman." He smiled. "She was always ahead of her time."

"Did she work at the library then, too?" Charlotte asked, hoping she already knew something about her grandparents' story.

"Yep, a different library, though. She grew up in Brooklyn, and her parents made sure she got an education. She worked at one of the libraries there. But anyway, she told me she never loved anyone before your grandpa. He was charming, and handsome, and funny, and smart. And his family had a lot of money to boot. He loved her, too. They were married less than a year after they met. And they had me the year after that."

"Wow." Charlotte smiled, but wondered why Nana didn't want to talk about this. It was so romantic.

"Yeah. They were head over heels for each other. I remember growing up…my dad would start dancing with her out of nowhere, even if there was no music playing. He just grabbed her and swung her around in his arms. And if he was really feeling frisky, he would dip her. She always yelled at him, or smacked him with a dishtowel because he was usually interrupting her cooking or cleaning, or something like that, and she was worried he'd dirty her work clothes." Mr. Worth paused to laugh. "But I knew she wasn't actually angry. She was always smiling when he did it."

Charlotte was sitting at the very edge of her seat, her elbows on her knees and her head in her hands. Mr. Worth felt a wave of affection watching her, and ruffled her curls. She wrinkled her nose and swatted his hand away.

"What else?" she insisted.

He wanted to shield her from the next part. The part where everything—his mother's happiness, and his own, tumbled like a landslide into a broken heap of tainted memories. He wanted to shield her the way a father should. *His* father had been the rumble beneath the ground, the one that forever changed the way he and his mother were built. Mr. Worth had promised himself the day Lindsay told him she was pregnant that he would never be that rumble. He would be the soft breeze swishing through the trees, forever moving them, forever changing them for the better.

But Charlotte was looking up at him, her honey brown eyes wide with curiosity. His mother and father were her family too, and he didn't want to be the kind of father who hid things from his child.

"Well, my dad—your grandpa—he had a drinking problem. Alcohol," he clarified, not sure how much she knew about it and hoping she'd understand, "it makes you do things differently than you normally would when you drink too much of it."

Charlotte understood more than he thought. She'd learned about the effects of alcohol in school, and heard whispers in the hallways about it—whose parents had a cabinet full, or who had tried drinking it—that kind of stuff. All of it left her with a vague curiosity about alcohol in general, but not enough to get her thinking about trying it. She didn't say any of this to her father, though, just waited for him to continue, her fearful need to know what happened to her grandfather outweighing her need to boast her knowledge on the subject.

"Like I said, his family was pretty wealthy and he worked as part of their company. They were in the oil business. But when I was five or six, he and Nana started fighting a lot about money. She'd yell that she didn't make enough to support a family on her own, and demanded to know what he did with his income. Looking back, she had to have known." He paused when Charlotte looked confused, her light red brows furrowed. "He spent his money on alcohol. And other things, I'm sure," he said, more to himself than to his daughter.

"Like what?" she asked.

Mr. Worth gave her a tight smile. "It doesn't really matter. Anyway, the fighting went on for a while. Sometimes, he didn't come home for days, and I remember being afraid of the way he stumbled and broke things when he did. The fights got much worse." He recalled the loud bangs of pots and pans in the kitchen, the yelps of pain from his mother, all dulled by the closed wooden door of his room.

"But then they got divorced when I was seven. I stayed with Nana and we moved out of the house into a small apartment here in Westchester. My dad visited every so often for a while, but then he stopped coming." Mr. Worth couldn't look at Charlotte for the next part. "I hadn't seen him for about five years when I found out he died."

"How?" she asked. And he knew he had to say it.

"He was drunk, and got hit by a car."

Charlotte gasped, and he looked at her. Her eyes were glistening with tears, and Mr. Worth was momentarily amazed. He was sure not many thirteen-year-olds would be so affected by a story like his, or even understand it for that matter. He reached out a hand and brushed a tear away before it could get too far down her cheek. "Nana took care of me by herself all those years. And it was much later when I found out that when the court tried to force my dad to give her a percentage of his money, she said no. She refused it."

Charlotte was shocked. "Why?"

Mr. Worth shrugged. "Nana was never the kind of person who liked to ask for help. And he had broken her heart. She wanted nothing to do with him anymore, and that included his charity. She only let him visit for my sake, so that I could see my dad." Charlotte's eyes were red, but she looked thoughtful again, considering each of his words and what all of it meant about Nana. Mr. Worth held her hand. "She used to tell me that the only person you can ever really rely on is yourself, but that was never true for me. I always relied on her. Still do. She's the strongest person I know."

It made sense now why Nana never spoke of him. Why she never spoke of the past at all. Why she didn't want to talk about it, even when Charlotte asked. Why Charlotte had always known her Nana was special, but couldn't ever put a finger on exactly why. She'd been through so much, and had never spoken a word of it, never complained. Not even to her son.

Charlotte wished she hadn't asked in the first place. Wished she didn't know that her grandfather was a drunk. Wished she didn't know that he chose his addiction over his wife and son. Wished all of it didn't make her hate him, even though she'd never met him.

As if he read her thoughts, Mr. Worth said, "He was a good man who made a lot of bad choices, Charlotte. And his addiction ended up killing him."

She nodded. But she didn't want to know anymore, and cursed herself for being so desperate to know in the first place.

"Nana never liked to talk about him. Even with me. So, don't feel bad that she didn't tell you. But if there's ever any more you'd like to know, you can always ask me," Mr. Worth said, and Charlotte nodded, knowing she should. He continued looking at her, finding all that was familiar about her, and smiled. "You're a lot like her, you know… You have the same spirit. The same kind of strength."

Charlotte didn't know what to say to that. This story made her look and think about Nana in a different way—one that, if possible, put Nana on an even higher pedestal in her mind. And hearing that she was just like her…

She had never wanted to be like Nana more.

Mr. Worth tugged on one of her curls a few moments later. "You still there, Charlotte?"

She smiled. "Think so. Thanks for telling me, Dad."

"Any time, kiddo." Charlotte stood, and left him with a quick kiss on the cheek. Mr. Worth picked up his glasses and watched her walk toward the living room, wondering if it was possible that she stood taller than she had ten minutes before. "Charlotte?"

She turned, her curls whipping over her shoulder, eyes wide and expectant beneath her glasses.

"No boys any time soon, okay?" He smirked, pulling his glasses on again.

Charlotte grinned, a blush staining her freckled cheeks. "No promises, Daddy."

With that, she skipped out of the room, her giggles echoing through the house.

"Charlotte Rose Worth…" he exclaimed, amused by her response.

"Just kidding!" she called back.

# *Chapter Nine*

"Remember that time we got lost upstate?" Graham looks so comfortable, so happy in his seat in the middle of the stage, right next to where Andrea's wall will stand when we finally bring it in.

Amanda grins over at him from her seat on the cot we're using as Nick and Olivia's bed. "And you had to pee so badly that you ran into the woods? And the raccoons scared the hell out of you?"

"Their eyes were *glowing* out of the bushes. It was terrifying!" Graham exclaims, sending them both into a fit of laughter.

He's the happiest I've seen him in the few weeks we've been rehearsing. And it isn't even his happiness—it's Nick's. This is the scene right before the turning point, the scene when Nick and Olivia have a civil, comfortable, even happy conversation. And Graham and Amanda are acting the crap out of it.

"The view from the house was incredible," Amanda says, her legs folded up on the bed. "I loved waking up to the lake every day."

"I could've gotten used to that." Graham glances down at the script in his lap. After a healthy pause, he looks up again, with no trace of a smile left. "We always said we'd go back."

She looks away, appearing unsure what to say, so he goes on, "We said we'd do a lot of things."

Graham stares down at the floor between his knees when she still doesn't answer, and Amanda takes the opportunity to scan him, studying him with furrowed brows for several moments before her forehead softens. "A lot has changed since then," she says softly, causing Graham to lift his eyes and match her stare.

It's in these moments of silence, the moments where Nick and Olivia simply watch each other, that the chemistry between Graham and Amanda sizzles, crackling loud in the air between them like a science experiment gone right. I wonder, purely out of interest, if they've found time to rehearse together. And, if they have, where they went, what they talked about…and if they've practiced the kissing scene at all.

"Alright," Andrea's voice slices through the air with a loud *whoosh*, and the crackling stops. "It's looking really good, guys. Let's call it a night."

I snap my script shut, hoping no one noticed that I zoned out for the rest of the scene.

"Before we go, though…" Andrea stands, and I follow suit. "Next rehearsal we'll be working on the bedroom scene." She pauses, and Amanda and Graham eye each other, shy smiles on their faces. I decide they have *definitely* rehearsed outside of the space, and hate the way the realization sits in my stomach like a parasite, gnawing at my insides.

"Obviously, it won't be the most comfortable of scenes to practice, so I think it'll really help if you guys can spend some time together outside of rehearsals. You know, to chat, and run lines, and basically just get more comfortable with one another."

Amanda nods, covering her mouth with her script, her cheeks tinged a pretty pink. Graham stands still, hands shoved into his pockets, his expression blank.

"So far," Andrea continues. "You're both doing great, and the chemistry is just right. But the bedroom scene is the pinnacle of the play, and it's definitely the most emotionally driven—which says a lot, cause the whole play is pretty emotional. I just want it to be perfect. And you two are totally capable." Andrea bends to pick up her script from the floor, and smiles when I hand it to her, having already grabbed it. "But that's it for tonight, so feel free to head out. We'll see you guys tomorrow."

Andrea sighs as she turns to me, her voice much softer and less professional than it was moments before. "I really hate to do this to you, but would you mind cleaning up tonight? I'm supposed to be out in Jersey in twenty minutes for my aunt's birthday and my mother is going to kill me already, but maybe she won't be as mad if I'm only, like, half an hour late versus an hour, and—"

"Andi," I say, interrupting her before she stops breathing. "Go, it's fine."

"You sure?" she asks, already slinging her bag onto her shoulder.

"Positive," I say with a laugh. "I've got it, don't worry."

"I love you, you're the best, thank you!" she calls, already running offstage past Graham and Amanda, who are engaged in conversation while packing up.

I look away, annoyed with the parasitic grip in my stomach.

We set everything up tonight—the "kitchen table", all the chairs (meant to be couches), the cot, and some papers that are now scattered on the floor from one of the argument scenes. With a sigh, I tuck my script into my bag and push my glasses on top of my head, grateful that we haven't created the wall that will separate the "kitchen" and "bedroom" yet.

When I've gathered all the papers and set them on the desk, I pull two of the chairs offstage (the side Graham and Amanda *aren't* chatting on), letting the feet drag on the wooden floor with a long, drawn-out screech. Allowing myself ample time to stack the chairs, I hope that they'll be gone when I walk back out. But I stop short when the only person I see is Graham—just Graham—kneeling down where he and Amanda were just talking, tying up the laces on one of his sneakers, his leather jacket laid out on the floor beside him. With a deep breath and a quick prayer that I can do the rest of the cleanup silently—or that he'll leave—I move to the cot, the prop sitting furthest away from him.

Shifting so that my back is to him, I try to focus on folding the damn thing up, and try to forget the fact that Graham is still behind me. But his presence brings about that awareness of myself I thought I liked; that swirling of energy, spinning around and around and sucking everything in the room toward him. Heat tears through my nerve endings and leaves them frayed, and the effort to keep my eyes on the cot leaves me stressed. Frustrated, I grab one end of it and push it up, confused when the legs don't fold in. But a little more pushing has them nestled against the bottom of the frame, so I move to do the same thing to the other side.

He hasn't left—I'd know if he left—but I tell myself it doesn't matter, and lift the other end of the cot, eager to get this over with and get the hell out of here.

But, to my horror, the first side of the cot goes crashing down when I lift the second, hitting the floor with a loud *BANG*. I wince, eyes screwed shut even when the echoes of the sound quiet. When I peel one eye open, Graham's there on the other side of the bed, lifting the half that's just fallen. My brain doesn't catch on right away, and I stare at him, jaw ajar for a moment, waiting for him to look up and yell at me, scold me, tell me I wouldn't know the proper way to fold up a cot if I took a class on it, or something.

But he just looks at me and waits.

I lift my side.

When we've got both halves up, I latch the two together in the middle, wondering if he'll talk, wondering if he expects me to, wondering if this is his way of reaching out—of apologizing. I feel his eyes on my face the entire time. Neither of us says a word before I wheel the cot offstage and put it right next to the stack of chairs. When it's in place as precisely as I can manage, I stare at it for a moment and breathe, taking in deep lungfuls of air that aren't weighted down by the vortex around him.

Then, feigning confidence, I strut back onstage. He's shrugging his jacket on over his red plaid shirt, and glances up when I stop. The urge to break through the silence, to fill it with words no matter how meaningless, is so strong I have to bite my lip. He's not smiling, and he doesn't look like he's about to, so we just stand there, waiting for something, but waiting for nothing. I fist my hands, hitting them repeatedly against my leg as I move towards the desk still sitting in the middle of the stage.

It's so quiet I can hear the soft soles of his sneakers as they touch the floor, and I know without having to look that he's behind me, following me. But I reach the desk without acknowledging him and pause, deliberating, slightly overwhelmed by its size. It's a teacher's desk, its surface about the size of a regular kitchen table, and it's pretty obvious I can't lift it by myself. But, after a few moments of consideration, I move to the far end of it, grip the edge and push, the heavy feet grinding against the floor in protest.

"Need some help?" Graham asks over the noise, and moves closer to the desk before I can answer.

Even more flustered now, I manage to say, "No, I got it," and shove again, using the balls of my feet for purchase against the floor. The groaning sounds of metal on wood echo throughout the theater once more.

"So, you're gonna drag this, too?" Graham yells over the screeching, causing me to stop again.

For the first time, I detect amusement in his dark eyes. Then, so quickly I can't be sure I'm not imagining it, his lips quirk at the edges, his silver ring glinting under the stage lights.

"I'm not dragging it," I say between breaths, my voice steadier than I thought it would be. "I'm pushing it." I shove with renewed fervor. At this point, I'm just trying to get out of here—away from him.

But he steps directly in front of the desk and grips the other side, surprising me by lifting it, cutting off the groaning noise completely. He grins when I stumble, exposing slightly crooked teeth behind his lips.

"Lift," is all he says.

And I listen.

Together, we carry the stupid thing across the stage. His curls shift as he glances over his shoulder every few feet, and the fact that he's walking backwards gives me the opportunity to study him a bit more. It's ludicrous that he's wearing a leather jacket again. It may get cooler at night, but it's still summer time. "Cool" is low seventies—at best, high sixties. But I can't say I mind the look. The sleeves of the jacket have risen high enough up his arms that I can see the muscles straining in his wrists. As we slide between the red curtains, my eyes travel up and over the broad expanse of his chest and shoulders, covered in plaid. There's no way he wasn't suffocating in the eighty-something degree heat today.

But that just makes me think about what he looks like sweaty.

"Careful," he says, yanking me out of my own thoughts. He's looking at the corner in my right hand, which I didn't notice is dragging one of the curtains along with us. I elbow it impatiently, almost losing my hold on the desk, which, thankfully, he doesn't seem to notice.

"Where does this go?" He's looking at me again, and it's more unsettling than I'd like it to be.

"There." I flick my eyes to the spot behind him on his left, next to the cot. His head swivels to see where I've indicated, and he keeps it turned when he moves us forward (or, in his case, backward) again, giving me the chance to examine the strong cords of his neck, the higher part littered with dark scruff.

When he turns his head back to face me, I quickly look away. We fit the desk against the wall and set it down. My hands sting a bit, the impressions of the edge of the desk red on my palms. I swipe them against my jeans, unsure what to do or say now.

Graham doesn't look at me right away, but I notice the corners of his mouth turn up and realize I'm staring. "Kitchen table will be a lot lighter," he says.

I avert my gaze, but smile without thinking. "Yeah," I say, confused by the change in our relationship, but more pleased by the shift than anything else. "Thank you. For your help."

"No problem." He moves towards me and I feel my pulse thump hard in my throat, but then he skirts around me, and I hate myself for being disappointed.

My eyes stay on his back as I follow him onstage. I'm not exactly sure what to make of the change in him, and I probably shouldn't push him any more tonight, but my name is Charlotte Worth, and I enjoy pushing the envelope even when I shouldn't.

"So…what was that about? At the first rehearsal?" I pick my bag up from the floor, eyeing Graham as he stops and turns around several feet in front of me, his bag on his shoulder. I'm embarrassed to think that he was about to leave without waiting for me, and only stopped because I continued talking.

But he almost smiles. He's fighting it. "Why don't you tell me?"

I blink. "What?"

He doesn't take a step backward, or glance away. His eyes stay locked on mine. "Do you always ask people awkward, invasive questions upon first meeting them? Or was I just lucky?"

My defenses snap up. "Do you always verbally abuse people who ask you about yourself upon first meeting them?"

Graham smiles now, but it holds no joy, no happiness—only annoyed amusement. "Only when they ask stupid questions."

It's infuriating, really, to watch him watch me looking all calm and collected while I feel like my blood is about to boil over.

"Regardless…" I'm frustrated, and stumbling, and he's just standing there, a quiet vortex that, instead of sucking *everything* in, only pulls more and more meaningless words from me. "Didn't your parents teach you if you have nothing nice to say, not to say anything at all?"

He's still grinning. "You mean that wasn't just a suggestion?"

He's joking with me. And he's doing it to piss me off. And it's working.

"Oh, so you *do* understand jokes, then?"

"Sure," he says, matter-of-factly. "When they're funny."

"If I can recall, everyone was laughing until you went all ape-shit."

"Well, I didn't think it was funny."

"Clearly."

We're just staring at each other again, and Graham's smile is slowly growing, like he's realizing I'm not going to let him walk all over me, and he kind of...*likes* it.

If I wasn't nervous before, I certainly am now.

"Look," I finally say, and take a few steps toward him—toward the stage steps behind him. "We don't have to be friends, or even talk outside of rehearsals. But we do have to work together. So, I just want you to know—no hard feelings."

Graham crosses his arms, that grin working its way back up the corners of his mouth, tugging on the lip ring. "That's a pretty sucky apology."

Now, I let myself laugh. Because the fact that he thinks I would apologize, when I have nothing to be sorry for, *is* funny. "Probably because it's not. If anything, you should be the one apologizing to me."

"How do you figure?" Graham asks, like he's inquiring about the weather.

I'm starting to think he just enjoys the banter, and to be honest, I don't have time for it. And if that's not the case, if he really can't see why I deserved an apology, I'm not about to waste my breath explaining it.

"You know what…?" My arms fall to my sides, and I can't remember when I lifted them. "Never mind. See you tomorrow."

I try to walk past him, head down the stairs and out of the theater. At this point, I just want to be away from him; away from the way I notice everything about him, and about myself when he's around—it's exhausting.

But he turns when I get close, facing the same direction I am.

"What are you doing?" I've stopped in my tracks, and glance up at him over my shoulder, momentarily overwhelmed by how far up I have to look to meet his eye.

I'm even more overwhelmed when those eyes light up from somewhere within with his grin.

"There's only one exit, Charlotte."

I try to maintain whatever dignity I have left as I walk quickly—but not too quickly—up the aisle ahead of him. Not speaking helps. But I don't have time to hide my surprise when he reaches out in front of me to grab the door and pull it open.

"After you," he says, totally smug. I hold on tightly to the small shred of dignity I have left as I walk through it.

Graham Hudson is a strange character. That much is obvious. After he calls his goodbye to me, heading in the opposite direction down the street, I can't help but feel like he's blindfolded me, spun me around a dozen times, and set me loose, unsure when or from where the next blow is coming—if it's coming at all.

But even stranger is the way my hands are reacting to him—the familiar twinge in my fingers that has me curling them up and unfurling them in quick succession, a vain attempt to relieve the itch until I can sit on the train.

The pinprick of light in his eyes, surrounded by all that darkness—it's too good, and my hands are already mapping them out in my mind, already shaping, shading and rubbing, for no other reason than me wanting to memorialize that light on the page. Not for Andrea, not for the play—just for me.

Perhaps strangest of all is the way I take out my sketchpad when I'm finally on the train, and let them.

## *Year Thirteen (and a half)*

She watched them carefully from the corner of her eye: the way the girl swung her fake blonde hair over her shoulder; the way he laughed at something she said; the way she touched his arm before walking away, down the hall in the other direction.

He followed.

Jealousy was not an emotion Charlotte was used to feeling. Though she'd seen what it could do to people on television, and in the books she read, she, herself, didn't have much experience with it. She was an only child. She didn't ever have to share her toys, or worry about anyone else receiving attention from Nana Rosie or her parents. She was the axis of their universe, and that was the way she liked it.

So, when Adam had come along, she expected much of the same from him. But instead, he quickly became the axis of *her* universe. And now he was off-kilter, and she didn't know what to do to knock him back in place. That unfamiliar emotion hit her like an eighteen-wheeler on a highway—there was no stopping it, no slowing down the intensity of it, and no way of disarming it.

She had experienced so many "firsts" with Adam. Her first day of high school, which she might have been nervous about under normal circumstances, but she had him—a sophomore, her first boyfriend, her first kiss, her first (she was sure) love. She couldn't imagine having a relationship with anyone else. No one else would laugh at her jokes like Adam, or ask about her Nana like Adam, or buy her ice cream and kiss away any remnants of it on her lips like Adam.

So why did it seem like he could imagine all of that with someone other than her?

Adam stopped, talking to another blonde (at least her highlights looked natural), and when he leaned in close, staring over her shoulder at a notebook she held open for him, the gnawing in Charlotte's stomach ramped up. It felt like something was moving around in there, taking giant chunks out of her guts with its teeth.

Head held high, Charlotte stood and marched in their direction, eyeing the way the girl spoke to him, searching for any hint of flirtation in her smile. Charlotte willed him to see her, to look up as she passed, to forget about the girl, grab her hand, and walk her to Algebra. But as she got closer, she ducked behind a small group of students heading in the same direction, cursing herself for her cowardice.

"Nana," she said later that day in Nana's kitchen. She was sitting on the counter, snapping the ends off some green beans for their dinner. "How do you make a boy fall back in love with you?"

Nana kicked the oven door closed and wiped her hands on a dish towel. "What?"

"You know," Charlotte said, swinging her feet back and forth. But she lowered her voice for the next part, afraid her father had already heard from his spot in front of the TV in the living room. "Adam. He's being stupid."

"Boys are always stupid, Charlotte. The sooner you learn that, the better."

"But he wasn't stupid before we started school. He *loved* me then, and…" Charlotte threw a green bean into the colander beside her. "I don't think he does anymore."

Nana had one hand on the counter, another on her hip. She nudged her glasses further up onto her nose. "Tuck that lip back in, Charley Worth." Charlotte looked down, embarrassed to realize she had, in fact, been pouting. "Why do you think that?"

Charlotte sighed. "He barely talks to me in school, but has plenty of time to talk to his friends. I see him all the time in the hallway talking to these...*girls*." She wrinkled her nose in distaste. "He doesn't even notice me anymore."

Nana was watching her in such a way that Charlotte felt like she needed to add more, give her more details. "And then," she exclaimed, "he acts totally normal when we *do* talk outside of school—like absolutely nothing's wrong. Like he hasn't been talking to other girls and acting as if I don't exist."

"Maybe there *isn't* anything wrong," Nana suggested.

Charlotte tilted her head to the side, and pressed her lips into a straight line, staring at Nana as if to say, *You're kidding, right?*

"Maybe this Arthur's just got a lot of friends."

"His name's Adam, Nana."

Nana waved a hand. "Same difference."

Charlotte couldn't help but laugh, even though Nana was wrong—so wrong, Charlotte almost couldn't believe it. Nana was always right. "You haven't seen these girls. There's no way he doesn't like one of them. They're all so *pretty*."

Nana clucked her tongue. "Not as pretty as you. Are you finished with those green beans?"

Charlotte glanced at the bag beside her. "Only a few more."

"Finish up, I want to get those going before your mom gets here."

"Are you even listening to me?" Charlotte asked, snapping another green bean at both ends.

"I'm listening, Charley, and I think you're being silly."

"But you haven't *seen* them, Nana! They're all...*made* up, and they have these well-manicured nails, and pretty clothes, and fixed-up hair. How am I supposed to stand a chance?"

Nana looked right at her granddaughter, at the auburn curls tied up in a large bun on top of her head, at the combination of a purple plaid shirt and black-and-white striped pants, at the glasses tucked into her hair instead of on her nose where they should've been.

"You've got more personality in your little pinky finger than those girls have in their whole bodies, Charley. If Aaron can't see that, you don't need him anyway."

Charlotte suppressed a smile, but didn't even correct her this time. "You don't know that."

"Don't tell me what I know," Nana said, taking the colander out from under Charlotte's arm, but not before Charlotte could shoot the last green bean into it. "I know my granddaughter. And I know that you are more beautiful than you even realize. Inside and out."

The front door opened, and the sound of Mrs. Worth setting her keys and bag down on the front table echoed down the hallway.

"Please don't tell them!" Charlotte said, afraid Nana would reveal her well-kept secret to her parents. They didn't have a clue about Adam.

"I've kept it this long, haven't I?" Nana said, stirring the string beans into the heated oil and garlic in a pan on the stove.

"Hey," Charlotte's mother said as she walked into the kitchen. "Need any help?"

Charlotte looked at Nana, who was looking at her mother. "You could put the salad together."

Mrs. Worth grabbed an apron, and didn't even glance at her daughter.

Nana put a lid on the pan and turned to face Charlotte again. "You're the moon, Charley."

Mrs. Worth looked between the two of them, lettuce in hand as she moved to the counter. "What?" she asked, eyeing Nana.

Charlotte didn't look away from her grandmother.

"Just reminding Charlotte who she is," Nana said to Mrs. Worth, who looked confused by the response. "She's the moon in a sky full of stars. And she'd do well to remember it, don't you think?"

Mrs. Worth glanced at her daughter, something else mixed in with the confusion in her eyes—something Charlotte couldn't identify. All her mother did was nod.

“Smells good in here,” came Mr. Worth’s voice from the doorway leading into the dining room. But when he looked at each of them, his eyebrows drew together. “Everything alright?”

Mrs. Worth cut into the lettuce, a loud crunch breaking through the silence. Charlotte stared at her grandmother, who stirred the now-steaming string beans and smiled at her son as she said, “Just fine.”

## *Chapter Ten*

"Okay, Amanda. When he grabs your waist, I want you to jump up and wrap your legs around him," Andrea says.

I jot down the direction, pressing my pencil to the page harder than necessary.

Amanda approaches Graham slowly, her eyes shooting from him to the floor like she's maneuvering a tight rope. But when Graham grabs her by the waist, her legs swing up and around him as if they've done this a hundred times.

"Good," Andrea chirps, unable to contain her joy. "Now…" She pauses, circling them, analyzing their position from every angle as they look anywhere but at each other.

"Does this…?" Andrea brings a hand to her mouth, pensive for a moment before swinging a finger between them. "Does this work for both of you?"

When they finally look from each other back to Andrea, they're both smiling.

"I'm good." Amanda giggles, causing Graham to grin.

Andrea is totally serious. "Graham?"

"Good," Graham says, looking as comfortable as if he were holding nothing at all.

"Charlotte?" Andrea calls, forcing me to tear my eyes away from the placement of Graham's hands on Amanda's backside.

"Hm?"

"What do you think?" Andrea asks, staring at her actors in their rather compromising position. Graham and Amanda are looking at me, though, and I'm far too aware of the fact that it's the first time in the hour and a half we've been rehearsing that Graham's *really* looked at me.

"Um, it's good." I stand, taking my script with me, and adjust my glasses on my nose. "But I think it could be better."

Andrea is already nodding. "You're right. You're so right." She's studying the two of them, her eyes roaming up and down their bodies, searching for where she went wrong. "What do you have in mind?"

My eyes dart over to Graham when Amanda's feet hit the ground with a soft thump. He shoves his hands into the pockets of his dark jeans, and the lines of his forearm are taut, like he's clenching his fists. His eyes are fixed on his shoes as he shifts from one foot to the other. It occurs to me that he could be annoyed with my suggesting something different from what they've already agreed worked.

But Amanda is looking up at me with wide eyes. Next to me, she's short; next to Graham, her small stature is almost comical. It's her stare, full of interest, and respect, and patience, that helps me drum up my courage again.

"I just think we can draw all this out a bit more," I say looking at Andrea again. "You know…really have a slow, steady burn before it all goes up in hot, sexy flames."

Andrea laughs, Amanda blushes, and Graham crosses his arms.

"Yes!" Andrea is still snickering, and she moves beside me so we can analyze the actors together. "What do you suggest?"

With a quick smile at Amanda, I look right at Graham. "What if we have Graham walk over to Amanda instead? You know, while she's saying her lines about how they've changed, and how they have nothing in common anymore? But as he gets closer, like, with each step, she becomes more uncertain about what she's saying because after all this time, the physical attraction is still there."

Andrea's nodding, holding a hand to her mouth, eyes moving slowly across the stage as she pictures it.

"We can still have the whole jumping into his arms bit," I continue when she doesn't say anything. "But it'll be even steamier because he'll have her back against the wall when they finally start making out."

Andrea's still quiet, still thinking, her lips now pursed as she stares at her actors. Amanda is looking between the two of us, waiting for a directive. Graham is staring right at me, brows furrowed low over his eyes, and it's that look—dark, heavy, and full of judgment—that makes me feel self-conscious.

"Not that I've thought extensively about it."

Andrea laughs, and Amanda covers her mouth as she giggles. My heart flutters like a frightened bird's wings when I catch Graham lick his lips, his cheeks working to suppress the smile that's tugging at the corners of his mouth.

"I love it," Andrea finally says, her loud laugh quieting as she looks at Graham and Amanda. "You guys okay with it?"

"I love it, too," Amanda says with a smile.

I'm waiting for his answer though, trying to see his thoughts in the depths of those shadowed eyes. He meets my gaze, and there's still amusement in them.

"Yep," Graham says, eyes moving from me to Andrea. "Let's do it."

"Great." Andrea claps like she's trying to rally a team together, and everything inside me warms and liquefies while I pretend I'm unaffected by Graham's agreement. "Let's take it from the beginning of the scene. Graham, you start over here." Andrea waits for Graham to take his place by the bed. "Amanda, you'll be over here for the beginning, then slowly move upstage, keeping your back to the wall. Do what feels natural in terms of when you want to move, and we'll work out the kinks as we go, alright?" Andrea smiles, claps once more, walks over to me and sits. "Ready?"

Amanda keeps her eyes down on the floor, and Graham shakes out his arms while stretching his neck. It's one of those things you have to see to believe, watching an actor—a good one, like these two—slip into character. Amanda looks up, and it's like she's flipped a switch somewhere inside of her, going from light to dark, turning off all that's warm, innocent and childlike about her. The small, pretty, mild-mannered girl watches Graham like a predator stalking its prey, her eyes following his every move, ready to attack.

When Andrea calls, "*Action!*" Olivia tears Nick apart, finally releasing all of the pent-up emotion she's held back for too long in one explosive monologue. Each word strikes Nick like a blow, crumpling him like a piece of wasted paper. Olivia paces the length of the wall where it stands perpendicular to the audience, never moving closer to Nick as she shatters every bit of hope he's scrounged up for their future together. Even when he sits on the bed, back to the audience, head in his hands, clearly unable to take much more, Olivia pummels him, blaming him for their relationship going wrong, and leaving her to deal with the miscarriage by herself, and, worst of all, not being emotionally or physically available when she needed him.

Nick falls apart like a card castle taking the brunt of a soft breeze. But there's nothing soft about Olivia in this scene, and as soon as she has fully and totally defeated him, he begins picking himself back up.

"You're wrong," Graham mumbles, still sitting on the bed, back to the audience.

"What?" Amanda demands, frustration evident in everything—the tone of her voice, the lines in her forehead, her deep, panting breaths, and the way she stands, feet apart, closed fists planted firmly on her hips.

"I said," Graham says through gritted teeth, before standing and looking her square in the eye. To my utter astonishment, his dark eyes are red-rimmed and watery, but his voice shows no sign of the tears. It's low and deep, a current of anger thrumming just beneath the surface when he says, "You're *wrong*."

Amanda shakes her head, still breathing heavily, and crosses her arms.

"Not about all of it. I should have done more about the job. My ego was wounded, but that's no excuse. I should've realized the kind of pressure it was putting on you." It's as if the words are choking him, and getting them out is the only way to loosen their grip. "But you're wrong about the baby. I *was* there. And maybe I should've tried harder to get to you, but the more I pushed, the harder you pulled." Graham shakes his head, his face scrunched up with anger, sadness, and frustration. "So, I let you."

There's a quiet moment between them, but Amanda keeps staring at him, listening to what he has to say for the first time in a year. Graham looks up from his script.

"I was dealing with it, too." He glares at her. "*I was grieving, too*." He brings a hand up to his eyes, covers them while he lets himself feel the weight of his grief. When he pulls it away, sniffling loudly, he drags it over his mouth. "Maybe I should've been more present for you. But Liv, you can't be present for someone who's not there anymore." His fists curl at his sides. "Someone who was all too willing to jump into bed with the next guy who looked her way."

Amanda's jaw goes slack, and her eyes widen. "Fuck you, Nick." She doesn't yell, just spits the words out, her clenched fists crinkling her script. "*This* is why we're so damn dysfunctional!" Like we planned, Graham takes a tentative step toward her. "We go for the jugular every time and I'm *sick* of it." He waits, watching her. "I know you want to make things work, but…" He steps forward again. "I just don't think I have it in me anymore. We're just…" She gulps when he takes another step. "We're so different now. And…" He's near enough that she has to look up at him, and her breaths come quick and shallow. "You just…you make me *hate* you sometimes. Like…" There's less than a foot of space between them, and Amanda breathes the next words. "Right now."

Graham reaches out slowly, like he's savoring every second as he takes her by the hips, his long fingers curling around towards her back. "You hate me," he says softly, ignoring her gasp of surprise, and stares down between them, at her heaving chest. "Right now?"

She's staring at his mouth when she nods, then lets out a breathy, "Yes." He pulls her against him, his hands traveling up her sides. He's totally in control, lips slightly, teasingly parted. She swallows. "So much."

He's quiet as he leans closer, shrinking down almost to her height. I know what happens next, and I'm sure Andrea will stop them with a new thought, with a note about what could be done differently or better. But her hand clamps down on my arm, and I don't have time to prepare myself before Amanda reaches up, yanking Graham's lips down to hers in a fierce, desperate kiss, her fingers twisting into his dark curls.

He doesn't hesitate, just leans down and lifts her, never detaching his lips from hers. She wraps her legs around his waist, finally matching his height, and I wait for Andrea to stop them with each distressing, passing second—when their lips pull away, and reconnect over, and over again—but she doesn't. Their heads turn from side to side, their lips never parting for more than a moment at a time, only to let out wild gasps of air. Amanda slides her hands over the scruff on his jaw, holds his face, and I swear his arms tighten around her.

Discomfort would make sense. It's awkward to watch any two people kiss in front of you for any amount of time, let alone for this long. And I'm definitely uncomfortable.

But there's something else going on; a clawing feeling in the pit of my stomach that I can't shake. It's so insistent, so distracting, so infuriating, and it has no reason to be. We *told* them to do this. They *have* to do this.

When he presses her back into the wall, I consider leaving—just getting up and walking out—anything for relief. Not only am I so jealous I can barely see straight, but I *facilitated* all of this. It's my fault it's as passionate as it is, and the hatred for myself burns hotter than the jealousy, tearing through me and leaving my body flaming red from the inside out.

With no end in sight, I consider pretending to faint, or yelling at them to stop, or knocking the podium off the stage from where it stands mere feet away from me. But Graham saves me the trouble when he detaches himself from Amanda's lips.

"Uh, sorry, but…" His mouth is red and swollen, his eyes impossibly dark as he smiles shyly at Andrea. "You didn't tell us what to do next."

"Oh," Andrea laughs, pretending to smack herself in the forehead. "Sorry, um, just got caught up, I guess."

I want to kill her.

Andrea laughs again, and Graham sets Amanda down, still looking directly at Andrea. Amanda clears her throat, eyes wide and glassy, then touches her lips. My insides flare up again.

"I was actually thinking," Andrea says as she stands. "You could just turn around, and walk over to the bed." She acts it out as she speaks. "Then set her down, and, um…would you be comfortable taking off your shirt?"

It's official. My best friend is trying to kill me. Cause of death: incineration from the inside out.

"Yeah," Graham responds without a moment's hesitation. "That's fine."

Even Amanda whips her head around to stare at him. I can't blame her. She was just kissed senseless by him, and not only will she have to kiss him again, she's now hearing that clothes will be removed in the process. She returns her attention to her script and scans the page, cheeks still flushed.

"Great," Andrea says, serious and focused once again. "So, Amanda, you'll take off his shirt, then Graham, you'll climb over her on the bed, and kiss her again. We'll blackout then, but at that point the audience will know what's going on."

"Right, okay," Graham says, running his hands through his already mussed-up hair before giving Amanda a wicked grin. She smiles back, her cheeks reddening even more.

"Charlotte, what do you think?"

Andrea is still standing by the bed, but Graham's eyes slide over to meet mine when she says my name, holding none of their usual darkness, notwithstanding the dark color, and all signs of judgment are gone. They seem unsure now, questioning—but what they could be asking remains a mystery. My cheeks warm, not so much in anger this time, but embarrassment, because I shouldn't be so affected.

I don't *want* to be this affected.

"Good," is all I can get out. I make myself smile because I know he's watching me. Sure enough, when I chance a glance back at him, he lowers his eyes slowly, bringing a hand to the back of his neck to rub it swiftly before turning around.

For the next run-through, I busy myself jotting down all of the movements we've put in place, trying not to picture them as I write. I retrace the words each time Graham and Amanda go back in for the kiss, trying to understand how I've gotten here—to this state; this unprecedented jealousy over kissing someone I barely know, and don't even really like.

At least…I didn't *think* I did.

But the truth is overwhelming each of the several times their lips meet, every time her hands tangle in his curls, or slide over his shoulders, or scrape down his bare back; it's all feeding and stoking a raging, internal fire.

"Alright," Andrea calls as she stands. "Looking *hot*, guys. It's almost there. And the only way to make the whole scene more comfortable for the two of you will be more practice. So, we'll keep running it."

R.I.P. Charlotte Worth.

"But let's take a breather now." Andrea grins. "No pun intended."

Graham's lips quirk up, and Amanda blushes. They're both still breathing heavily, and I try to avert my eyes from the quick rise and fall of Graham's bare chest, the shallow dips in the flat expanse of his stomach, the shadowed trail of hair from his belly button down…

"Max and Tanya will be here in about ten minutes," Andrea says, with a glance at her watch. "So, we'll just wait for them to get here before continuing at this point."

I stand, maybe too quickly, hoping to appear nonchalant—as if I *haven't* just been scanning Graham's naked half for beauty marks, scars, or birth marks.

Andrea walks with me over to my bag where it sits several feet away on the floor. "Oh, my God," she gushes. "That turned out *way* better than I expected!"

Glancing over my shoulder, I catch Graham smile at Amanda before throwing his white t-shirt back over his head, and try to sound happy when I say, "Yeah, it was great."

"I mean…" Andrea lowers her voice even more. "Amanda looked a little shell-shocked, but I guess I can't blame her. It was only the first run-through, and Graham is, uh…overwhelming, to say the least."

The flames in my belly flicker hot when I hear Amanda laugh.

Andrea barely takes a breath. "I was a little worried that this scene might be a problem, but after watching *that*, I'm pretty sure we don't have anything to worry about. And to think this was just *rehearsal*. The *first* rehearsal."

Biting my lip, I nod, keeping my eyes on her when I say, "Yeah, you definitely don't have anything to worry about. It's all, uh…looking great."

"I know! And it's all thanks to you! Never doubted you for a second," she says with a wink.

I feel like I'm being smothered, contained while the heat eats me alive, and all I want to do is squirm away, find a corner, and cower. "Just part of the job description, right?"

Andrea's joy disappears, replaced by a look of worry as she searches my face. "Everything okay? You seem a little…stiff."

"Oh." I scramble, then notice my phone still clutched in one hand. "Yeah, it's just, uh—my mom texted asking me to call her. And I *really* don't want to." I laugh, hoping she won't see through that, too. But Andrea knows about my mother, and I shamelessly use her sympathy to my advantage. "But I should, so I'm just going to go outside to deal with this."

"Okay," Andrea says, her concern easing just a bit. She grips my arm and says, "Remember, don't let her walk all over you. Let me know how it goes."

And I walk out of the theater, guilt pooling in the pit of my stomach like hot lava.

The air is thick with moisture outside, and loud with the whooshing sounds of cars speeding by and more than occasional honks. I suck in a deep breath, hoping to regain some reason with lungfuls of the tainted New York City air. I shove my glasses up into my hair, rubbing my eyes, hoping to clear the images of him kissing her, pressing into her, leaning over her from my mind. But they're there to stay, flooding my mind like spilled paint, blurring out everything else.

I know I'm being unreasonable. I don't *really* want him. I deserve better than someone who *sometimes* speaks to me. Better than someone who doesn't acknowledge my existence unless someone else addresses me first. Better than someone who looks at me with the fires of Hell in his eyes when I pose a simple (maybe somewhat, potentially offensive) question.

Now if only my unchecked hormones could catch up with my impressively reasonable mind.

I jump when the door opens next to me, and can't help my sharp gasp when a head of dark curls appears out of it. Before he can turn around, I snap the hand holding my phone up to my ear.

"Mhm," I mumble, eyeing him as he turns and looks at me, letting the door fall closed behind him. "Really?" I say into the phone, avoiding his eyes and trying to sound interested in what no one on the other end is saying.

Graham walks past me, and I let my eyes follow his black Converse sneakers from where I'm standing with my back against the wall. He stops a few feet away, and mirrors my position—back on the wall, arms crossed, looking out into the street. With my phone pressed to my ear, I can better hear my pulse as it thuds faster and faster.

"Right, yeah," I say, struggling to vary my responses, and feeling stupider by the moment. Graham's watching a woman and her dog as they walk along the sidewalk. The black Labrador stops to sniff around a tree. "Listen, I have to get going," I say. "Yeah, I've got to get back to rehearsal." I wait. "Yep, alright. Bye."

Pretending to end the call, I tap the screen and shove the phone into the pocket of my jeans, feeling my face, which had cooled since coming outside, redden anew.

"Who was that?" Graham asks. He says it clearly, calmly, but something in his tone, in the *way* he asked, makes me feel like he knows there was no one on the other end of the line.

I look right at him. "I don't think that's any of your business."

Graham smiles, and my stomach gives a pleasant, unexpected jolt. "Fair enough."

Silence sets in, disturbed only by shouts, laughter, the screeching of tires halting on the street, the zoom of cabs speeding through the intersection, and the honks when someone cuts them off—all sounds of the city on a Saturday afternoon, sprinkled with snippets of conversation that come and go with passersby on the sidewalk. For a few brief seconds, I marvel at the way he seems so comfortable in the gaping chasm of awkward quiet between us. His feet are crossed at the ankles, his arms crossed over his chest, and his eyes follow the movements of two men in suits talking as they walk by, coffees clutched in their hands.

Not able to stand it any longer, I say, "Why are you out here?"

Graham meets my eye with a smirk. "Do you not want me to be?"

That's not it. That's not it at all.

"No." His eyebrows shoot up, and he looks more smug than he has any right to be. "I mean…I don't care one way or the other, I was just…curious."

Graham doesn't move, doesn't look away, but I do, afraid he can see right through my transparent answer. I try to keep calm, hoping he won't poke holes in it just for fun.

"I needed some fresh air," he says after another moment. "Change of scenery." I feel comfortable enough to look at him again, and he leans a little closer to me, an easy smile on his face. "It's not easy pretending to be someone else, you know?"

"You're really good at it," I find myself saying, surprised when his smile widens, but is somehow shyer than it was before. "That sounds weird," I say with a nervous laugh. "But it's true."

For the first time since I laid eyes on him, he looks uncomfortable. He runs his hand through his hair to try and hide it. "Thanks," he says, looking forward again.

I'm not sure why I say it—maybe because I'm enjoying seeing him look unhinged for once, or maybe because I like the fact that he's finally reacting to me more than I should, or maybe simply because I'm a glutton for punishment.

"You looked like you knew what you were doing," I say, not tempering my smile. I cross my arms and grip my elbows. "In that last scene, I mean."

"I'll take that as a compliment," he says with a breathy laugh before meeting my gaze again. His eyelashes are long and just as dark as his eyes, and I'm glad to have the wall behind me for support.

I shuffle my feet, shifting my weight. "You and Amanda have great chemistry."

He's looking down at the ground, but a small, close-mouthed smile plays at his lips. He says nothing.

"It helps that you're both great actors, I guess. Especially when you have to do scenes like those. I mean, you barely know each other, right? But it looks so real when you're—" I break off, stop myself from saying exactly *what* they were doing. "When you're in the moment like that. That intensity would be pretty hard to fabricate, I bet."

I don't know what I'm trying to get at, and Graham still isn't looking at me, but he's still smiling, and still very silent.

After a nine-months-pregnant pause, I can't stop myself from saying, "Jump in anytime, here."

Graham chuckles, his smile wider now, the light in his eyes flickering like a flame when he finally meets my eye again. "What would you like me to say?"

There's no hiding my annoyance because it's the only cover I have for my embarrassment. "Anything that involves words would be good. That's typically what people do when they hold a conversation. It's not usually a one-person deal. If it is, it typically means something's wrong."

"You're kidding," he breathes, a shit-eating grin gracing his lips. "And here you were doing so well."

"Glad you're amused. It's a nice change from the detached, emotionless look on your face. If the acting thing doesn't work out for you, you'd be a shoo-in for a job at a department store. I hear they're in desperate need of mannequins these days."

"Huh," he says, leaning on one shoulder to turn fully towards me. "I hadn't heard about the mannequin shortage."

Graham smiles. And despite the fact that I just insinuated he'd make a great *mannequin*, I let myself laugh and shake my head, my heart thumping hard against my ribcage. I'll take the banter over his aloofness any day.

"Thank you," he says a few moments later, breaking the not-as-awkward silence that resettled between us. "For all the things you said. Truth is, that kind of chemistry doesn't always happen. And when it does—it's just luck. So, I guess we're lucky to have it."

His eyes are on the street, and I'm able to watch unashamed as the tip of his tongue touches his ring, shifting it back and forth where it clings to his lip. Then all I can think is that Amanda got to feel it against her mouth, and heat surges through me again, not because I'm jealous, but because he's so close—his *mouth* is so close. I blink, tearing my gaze from the silver hoop, and take a deep breath.

"We'd better get back," Graham says, only small traces of his smile left. But his eyes are still light, not full with the storm I usually see.

"Yeah." My voice is almost a whisper, so I keep quiet as I turn to grab the door handle.

Awareness of him slips down my spine like a pulse. I wait for him to say something else as we walk back down the sloping aisle between the seats and back onto the stage—but he says nothing. Just smiles at Amanda and grabs his script without even glancing my way again, and I wonder why, feeling stupid for it, I expected anything more.

## *Year Thirteen (and three quarters)*

"But Mom..." Charlotte watched her mother stir a pot of tomato sauce on the stove. "I *have* to go."

"Charlotte, I said no when you asked me last week, I said no when you asked me the other night, *and* last night, and I'm saying no now." Mrs. Worth didn't look at her daughter, just continued stirring, but her voice held a distinct note of warning.

"Mom, *everyone* else is going." Despite the fact her mother seemed wedded to her decision, Charlotte hadn't given up yet. Knowing just what was at stake—knowing that Adam would be there and needed to see her there, too, she *couldn't* give up yet. But of course, she couldn't say that to her mother either. Her mom didn't even know about Adam in the first place, and Charlotte had a feeling bringing him up now wouldn't help her argument.

She glanced over at Nana, waiting for her to chime in and bolster Charlotte's case with a reassuring word. But Nana sat quietly at the table across from her, lips pursed and glasses perched low on her nose as she filled in a crossword puzzle.

"Since when have you cared about what everyone else is doing?" Mrs. Worth asked, turning to look at Charlotte.

She didn't. Adam was the only person Charlotte cared about—and she was going to get a reaction out of him.

"Since now. Besides, Dad already said I could go."

Mrs. Worth frowned, and with an exasperated sigh, she dipped her wooden spoon back into the pot, knuckles white around the handle. "You're too young, Charlotte. Your father should know better."

"These are all kids *my* age, Mom! Plus, there will be parents there."

It was a flat-out lie. One she'd used every time they'd had this argument, to no avail. She had no idea if there would be parents there, and she also knew that some sophomores and juniors would be in attendance as well. "I'm almost fourteen. I'm old enough to go to a party. I *promise* not to do anything stupid."

Mrs. Worth looked at her again, and Charlotte could see her mother's will wavering, the conflict in her tired brown eyes.

Nana, who Charlotte hadn't been sure was even listening, coughed, but didn't look up from her crossword puzzle, just put her pen to the page and scribbled.

"I really won't, Mom," Charlotte prodded, looking her mother squarely in the eye. "You can trust me."

Mrs. Worth sighed and leaned back against the counter, glancing at Nana just as Charlotte had. She sounded weary when she said, "It's not a matter of trusting you, Charlotte."

"Then what is a matter of?" Charlotte asked, her voice rising again despite herself. She hadn't missed the fact that her mother hadn't exactly said that she *did* trust her, either.

"Do not raise your voice to me," Mrs. Worth said, eyes flaring, her shields going up again.

Charlotte huffed, even more annoyed. But she knew if she was going to win this, she had to dial her frustration back. "You're right, I'm sorry. But you can trust me, Mom. I'm un-peer-pressurable."

It got her mother to smile, and Charlotte's stomach gave an excited jolt.

"Nobody's un-peer-pressurable," was her mother's response. But she was still smiling.

Charlotte smiled too, sensing her mother's defenses toppling, so she fought the urge to defend herself again, and didn't say anything more, just waited for the go-ahead she was sure was coming her way.

The two stared at each other, neither wanting to admit defeat, and neither one wanting to give the other what they wanted.

Mrs. Worth pressed her lips into a thin line, as if keeping her mouth tightly closed was her last-ditch effort to prevent the words from spilling out between them. But her lips broke apart with a puff of air a moment later. "Fine. You can go."

Charlotte shrieked and jumped from her seat to hug her mother. Mrs. Worth didn't hug her back, only spouted off directives as Charlotte squeezed her. "But you *have* to be home by ten. And I don't want you drinking. *At all.* And no driving with anyone who's been drinking. Or driving with anyone at all, actually. Your father or I will pick you up. And no going into any rooms alone with a boy. And absolutely no smoking. And don't—"

"Okay, Mom. Okay." Charlotte was about to let go of her mother when she felt Mrs. Worth's arms wrap around her in return. Charlotte breathed her in—she smelled of garlic and her strawberries and cream shampoo—and noticed Nana smile over her mother's shoulder.

"Thank you," Charlotte said when she finally stepped away.

"Don't make me regret this." Her mother gripped her shoulders, squeezing for a moment, and she was suppressing a smile when she turned back to the stove. "You better have fun at this thing."

# *Chapter Eleven*

"*This* is him?!" Andrea exclaims, staring at my phone with a combination of awe and disbelief on her face.

We've just finished painting the wall for the set—the kitchen side a pale yellow, the bedroom side a slate blue. Water bottles in hand, we sat in the front row of seats, and the layer of sweat beading on my skin dried quickly in the air-conditioned theater. And because it's been on my mind, I'm showing Andrea the picture I've been thinking about since I saw it.

Michael posted a picture of the two of us in front of Big Ben, and all my guilt came rushing back this morning as soon as I laid eyes on it.

"That's him." I take my phone back. "Can you keep it at a decibel that won't deafen me? Please and thank you."

"I would've been *all* over that if I was there," Andrea says with a grin.

I stuff my phone back into my bag so that I won't have to see those blue eyes staring up at me, see the way his arm curled around my shoulders, or the way his head tilted towards mine so that his chin was pressed against my temple.

"I'm sure Calvin would love to hear that."

Calvin is Andrea's friend. Very good-looking, very tall, very *close* friend.

Andrea rolls her eyes. "Calvin and I are not exclusive. Not even close."

"You would be if you wanted to be. You have to know he's in love with you."

"I don't *have* to know anything. Besides, I made it clear from the very beginning that I'm not looking for a relationship and he's fine with it. We have fun together. That's all that matters." Andrea eyes me again. "Now, back to you…"

I sigh.

"You *really* don't like him?"

"It's not that," I say, too defensive. I rein my voice in a little bit. "I just don't—I'm just not *attracted* to him."

"You looked pretty cozy with him in that picture." Andrea closes her script. "Just saying."

She's not telling me anything I haven't already considered. I did enjoy spending time with Michael in London. I thought he was nice, and funny, and cute, and kind, and everything a guy should be. I enjoyed kissing him, too, loved feeling wanted—feeling special. But it was wrong to use him the way I did. I knew it then, and I know it now. He made me feel good, and I didn't let myself linger in thoughts of where it would go when we got back, or how long I'd want to be with him. I let myself want him in the moment; let myself be with him because the end was always in full sight.

"Can we move on now that you've gotten that out of your system?"

"One more question." Andrea turns in her seat, pulling her foot up underneath her. "You said he's going to be a doctor, right?"

"Andrea…" I say in warning.

"I mean, they can make a *lot* of money…"

"Seriously?"

But she just laughs at my outrage. "I'm kidding, girl, I'm kidding. Look, I don't care one way or the other. You say you're not into him, you're not into him. Fine by me. I just know you have a tendency to sabotage things before they can really begin."

"No, I don't," I say.

She pats my leg. "Save yourself the effort. We both know the truth on that front, so I'm not going to argue with you about it. But, as long as that's not what you've done here, I don't care."

I sigh again, sure that this is different. "It wouldn't work. I don't like him enough to keep up a long-distance relationship."

"I'm not saying you have to. Just don't be mean."

"I haven't been!"

"Have you gotten in touch with him yet? It's been over a month since you got home."

I stay quiet.

"That's cold, Charlotte."

"Colder than you actively having a 'friends with benefits'-type situation with Calvin and telling him, and yourself, that you don't want a relationship?"

Andrea glares at me. "It's not the same thing. I've been upfront with him right from the start."

"But you're still going to sit here and pretend you don't realize what you're doing is hurting him, and judge me for what I've done or haven't done with a guy I had much less of a fling with, three thousand miles away from home? Nice."

"I'm not judging you, Charlotte. But it sure sounds like you're judging me."

I don't mean to get so defensive that I end up going on the offensive. I don't mean to pick on her relationship with a guy she's been seeing for six months. It's her business. I don't want her to think I'm judging her for it. But I can't stop myself. Not when she's making me out to seem like some bitch who only used Michael for my own twisted purposes.

"I'm just pointing out that we're both pretty fucked up when it comes to this stuff. So, I'd appreciate it if you kept your advice to yourself, unless I ask for it," I say.

Maybe it's harsh. Maybe it's just because I'm angry, and embarrassed, and feeling guilty for the way I've handled—or *haven't* handled—the situation with Michael. But if anyone's going to understand brutal honesty, if anyone's going to respect what I'm asking despite the way I'm asking it, it's Andrea.

"You've got a point," she says, and smiles at me. "You know I don't know how to keep my mouth shut."

"And you know I love you for it."

We're both quiet for a few moments, and a memory flickers into focus in my mind. Her voice, her floral perfume, her bony hand in mine…

"He isn't worth this, Charley," Nana said while I cried in her arms about Adam. "You are, and always will be worth so much more than what you're feeling right now, you hear me?"

Aside from a few sniffles, I stayed quiet.

"Nod so I know you understand what I'm saying."

I understood her, but I didn't believe her.

I'd nodded anyway.

"Know what Nana used to say?" I ask before I can stop myself.

Andrea looks up, her eyes meeting mine.

"She'd say, 'Charley, you're too smart for men. You don't need them.'"

Andrea laughs, rubbing her nose a bit like she always does when she's amused, but she doesn't cackle. "She was right. We don't."

We smile at each other, and I feel something well up fast in my chest. Something hot and hard and immoveable. I take a deep breath to push it back down.

"But it's nice to have one around every once in a while, isn't it?" Andrea asks.

Andrea's the only person, aside from Nana Rosie, who could always see right through my bullshit. And, like Nana, she didn't judge me for it—she just called me out on it. We're one and the same—have been right since the beginning. Two brutally honest souls just trying to get by. I've learned how to tone it down, how to refrain from saying exactly what I'm thinking or feeling, because I know that my kind of honesty can be hurtful. Andrea just doesn't care. What you see is what you get. And if you don't like it, screw you.

"Anyway," Andrea says when I don't reply. "You said you had a few ideas sketched out for the programs, right?"

"Oh, um…" I pull my bag onto my lap, happy for a change of subject. "Yeah, just a few rough ideas. But I figured I'd show you now just to get a better idea of what you're looking for."

Andrea eyes each one as I turn the pages of my sketchpad, and when she reaches for it, I let her take it, the knots in my stomach tightening every time she flips the page. I don't know if I'll ever get to a point when it *won't* be hard to let people see my work—a point when it won't be hard to hear them say what they like or don't like, or how it makes them feel. And with this particular situation, I have no doubt Andrea will be vocal about what she *doesn't* like.

"I have other ideas," I say when she flips back and forth between two pages, pursing her lips as she considers them. "I know these are probably not exactly what you're looking for, but I had to get myself started, and—"

She flips one page too far, a page that features a set of eyes I'd rather her *not* recognize.

"Look!" I say, too loudly. "What about this one?" I land on the drawing of a single table looking lonely by itself on the page just beneath the title. "I was thinking a more minimalist approach might be the way to go, and—"

"No," she says, wrinkling her nose as she stares at the sketch. "Definitely not minimalist. These are great, Charlotte, but…I need more. I want to see the angst on the page, you know? It doesn't have to be dark, but I would like it to be…*raw,* somehow. Tension. Find the tension."

"Now you sound like one of my art professors."

"I just… I want to feel more from it. These are good, but none of them are giving me that feeling. None of them are hinting at what's to come."

And here I thought I was prepared for the criticism.

"That's a lot to ask when this tense, angst-filled, hint-at-what's-to-come design needs to share the small bit of a page with the title and director's name."

"You can do it," she says, yanking on a stray curl that's made an escape from my ponytail. "That's why I asked you."

I sigh and close my sketchpad.

"Come on, let's get out of here." Andrea stands, blue paint all over her fingers and jeans. "If I stay any longer, I'll think of things to do, and I have work in an hour and I'm absolutely going to be late already."

"How have you not been fired yet?" I say with a laugh as I stand. Andrea works part-time in a restaurant near her house, only twenty or so minutes from mine. She's been working there for well over five years, but every time we talk about it, she's running late.

"Let's not tempt fate, shall we?" Bag slung over her shoulder, Andrea starts up the aisle, and I follow close behind.

It's sweltering outside, the air heavy with moisture, and we both groan when we step into it, locking all the cool air behind us in the theater. Andrea immediately pulls out her pack of cigarettes, lighting up just as we reach the sidewalk.

"I'll see you tomorrow, okay?" Andrea says as she hugs me, her breath stale as she quickly releases the smoke over my shoulder. She's already speed-walking in the direction of the subway before I can make a remark about her lungs lasting that long.

I head in the opposite direction, where I spotted a food cart earlier. Even though it's hot and sweat is trickling down the small of my back, between my breasts, and along my hairline, I don't want to go home. Not yet.

Only two people are ahead of me in line: an older gentlemen with a newspaper tucked under his arm, and a girl, probably around my age, with her nose in a book.

I wait, staring up at the way the Chrysler Building seems to poke a hole in the web of white, billowing clouds around it, piercing through to the blue of the sky. My fingers itch to capture the image. Even though I've drawn the building—many of the buildings in Manhattan—several times already, and even though it's never changed shape or color, the sky behind it always does. The way the sunlight hits it, and where the little pockets of shadows settle, is always different.

"Looks like great minds think alike." The voice startles me out of my own head, and I don't have to turn around to know who it belongs to, but I do. Because I *want* to.

He's wearing blue jeans today. And a white t-shirt. And a crooked smile.

"Aren't you hot?" I ask.

Graham chuckles, glancing down at his jeans. "A bit." His eyes move over my face, and somehow, for whatever reason, they don't seem as dark today. "So, uh…" His gaze flicks down to my body and back up to my eyes. "What have you been up to?"

It's only now that I remember I'm covered in paint, and it's the first time all day I feel embarrassed about it. "Andi and I were working on the set. The wall's painted."

Graham eyes me up and down once more, head to toe, and I feel every already-sweaty inch of me heat for an entirely different reason.

"Wow," he says. "I'm surprised you had enough left."

I try *really* hard not to smile. "Very funny."

"Next!" the man in the cart calls.

"Hi," I say. "Could I have a small iced-coffee, cream, no sugar, please?"

The man pulls a clear cup from a stack next to him.

"Do you hate puppies and sunshine, too?" Graham asks, stepping up beside me. "Make that two, please. One with sugar, and lots of it." He reaches into his pocket, and pulls out his wallet.

"What are you doing?"

Graham pulls a ten-dollar bill out before glancing up at me. "Buying you coffee."

"What? No. Why?"

Graham releases a few chuckled breaths. "Because I want to."

I watch him hand over the bill, too stunned to say anything to stop him, and too stunned to thank him when he hands me my coffee.

"You didn't have to do that." I pull the wrapper off my straw, still not sure what to make of all this.

"I know," he says, shrugging his shoulder as he takes a sip. He grins right at me, thoroughly pleased with himself.

I stir the straw around, the ice clanking softly against the plastic cup. "Thank you," I manage to say before taking a sip of my own.

"You're welcome," he says at the same time I ask, "What are you doing here, anyway?"

If I didn't feel awkward and sweaty with his eyes on me before, I certainly do now. They crinkle a little at the sides when his lips lift at the corners, his lip ring glinting in the sunlight.

"Andrea said I could come run lines with her today, so…" He holds out his hands. "Here I am."

I consider that for a moment. "Andi left."

His grin falters. And I find it more endearing than I should.

"What?"

"A few minutes ago. She's got to be at work in less than an hour."

Typical Andrea. The girl is constantly overbooking herself.

"Damn." He looks genuinely disappointed. "She told me any time today, she'd be here."

"Yeah. She should definitely start writing things down," I joke. It doesn't quite hit its target. Graham's lips don't lift as high as they did before. "Sorry you had to come all the way here."

After a moment, Graham shrugs, and lifts his straw to his lips. "At least it wasn't a total loss."

He smiles and takes another sip of his coffee. He doesn't turn and head in the other direction, doesn't say goodbye, doesn't say anything more—just stares at me, smiling. I try to breathe as un-obviously as possible, but with him this close, looking at me the way he is, I'm nervous. And uncomfortable. But not in a bad way.

"Maybe," I find myself saying, "if you want… I could help."

Graham looks at me like he was expecting me to say exactly that. "Really? You don't mind?"

"Not if you don't."

"Why would I mind?"

"I don't know," I say, flustered now, remembering the way he helped me with the clean-up last week. The way he didn't wait for me to ask, or didn't offer and wait for me to answer. He just did it. "But we can't use the theater. Andi locked up, and she's the only one who has a key."

"That's alright. We can find somewhere else."

Nervous and excited for reasons I don't want to admit to myself, I wrack my brain for somewhere we can go. Somewhere we can sit for a while, where they won't make us leave after an hour.

"Okay, um, coffee shops are out." I hold up my full cup like an idiot. "Maybe the park? It's hot, but it's only a few blocks away and no one will kick us out."

Graham shrugs again, and swallows a sip of coffee. "I'll go wherever you want to go."

I try not to take that any other way than literally.

## *Year Thirteen (and three quarters)*

Remembering her reassurances to her mother, Charlotte scoffed at her own stupidity. There was nothing reassuring about her current situation.

The couple making out next to her were complete strangers, and the majority of the others were people she'd only seen in the hallways at school. The members of the basketball team—all still wearing their sweaty red jerseys—were the only people with whom she was somewhat familiar. And that was mostly because of the way Adam used to talk about them.

Charlotte tried to look like she was having a good time. She nodded her head along to the pounding bass rhythm blasting through the speaker behind her, smiled when she made eye contact with someone (only to have them look away as if she didn't exist), and tried to keep her expression generally pleasant despite the way her insides felt—like they were crumbling into tiny, unfixable shards, tearing at her chest as they fell.

She'd never felt so out of place. Girls her age were wearing so much makeup, Charlotte wondered how they could see anything but flecks of glitter. Too many people were holding plastic cups filled with who-knows-what, sipping the liquid between laughing and dancing. The boys, in all their gangly awkwardness, waited for girls to approach them, and took that as the go-ahead to touch wherever and however they liked while they were dancing. Charlotte wondered if this was what all high school parties were like, but decided she didn't care enough to find out.

As much as what was going on made her uncomfortable, Charlotte was content to sit on that couch and have no part in it. Content to be in her good pair of jeans and her favorite blue sweater, as opposed to the tiny skirts and plunging necklines her peers had chosen. Content to have no one touch her. Content to be invisible there in that room, rather than to be the life of that kind of party. On some level, despite feeling like a fish in a desert storm, Charlotte was content to be in her skin.

That was before Adam walked into the room, looking every bit as attractive as he had all those days she'd watched him in the park, and she tried to ignore the stab of regret she still felt at what she'd done, how she had ended it between them—in the hallway right after school, when she knew she could make a clean escape.

When Adam's blue eyes swept over the room, his smile lifting his cheeks, all of Charlotte's self-confidence slipped away like sand through a sieve, leaving only the pebbles of her hope behind. She'd planned this—she would smile at him anyway, so that he would see her having a good time; so he would see that she could fit into his world; so that he would realize he shouldn't have let her go.

She was still drumming up her courage when Adam's eyes fell on her, but she didn't have time to smile anyway. They passed over her so quickly, it seemed like he didn't see her there at all. She couldn't breathe, couldn't think, could only feel the pain of his disinterest, the shocking strength of it on her chest, like an elephant using her ribcage as a stepping stool.

Somehow, she stood and moved through the crowd. Elbowing her way through the mass of teenage hormones felt like swimming in the deepest depths of the sea, the pressure of it working against every limb. But she made it to the kitchen and the sliding glass door leading out to the backyard in one piece.

Walking into the cold night air was like breaking the surface of the water and taking that first deep, gasping lungful of air. Here, with only a few party-goers at the far edge of the yard, Charlotte clamped a hand to her mouth and let her tears spill over in silence, steady and hot against her cheeks. She hated everyone—Adam, the basketball team—everyone, including her biggest disappointment: herself. She pulled her new cell phone from her pocket, too upset to be excited about the prospect of having a reason to use it, and was again disgusted, this time by the fact that it was just nine o'clock. She'd barely made it an hour into the stupid party.

Forgetting her pride, she dialed a number, hating to be wrong, but knowing that admitting her mistake was the better option of her two.

She couldn't go back in there.

"Charlotte?" her mother answered. Charlotte bit her lip, tasted the salt of her tears. "Charlotte, are you alright?"

"Mom." Her nose was stuffed. "Can you come get me?"

Her mother sighed, not even attempting to hide her annoyance. "I'll be there in ten."

## *Chapter Twelve*

"Damn it." Graham rubs his eyes. "What *is* it with this scene?"

"It's alright. You'll get it," I say. "Let's run through it again."

"Could we just…take a break? I'm getting everything mixed up at this point."

"Oh. Um…" I close my script. "Sure."

Graham sighs, and I stare out at Washington Square park, at the people walking around, telling myself to focus on them, to notice them. But with him sitting this close, all I can focus on is the few inches between our knees, the way he runs the palms of his hands up and down on the tops of his legs, the dark hair on his arms…

"So, Charlotte…"

I swirl the ice around the bottom of my now empty cup, and take a long, slurping sip of the watery coffee at the bottom.

"What's your story?" he asks.

I let myself look at him. "My story?"

He brings a foot up and crosses his legs, holding onto his ankle where it rests on his knee. "Yeah."

"Why the sudden interest?"

"Would you rather sit in silence for another five minutes? Cause we can totally do that, if you want."

I narrow my eyes at him. "Alright, smartass. How about you start us off. What's *your* story?"

Graham smiles, shifting to place his arm on the back of the bench we're sitting on—just inches from the back of my neck. "Guess sitting in silence it is, then."

I cluck my tongue and, feeling braver, shift around to face him. "Oh, come on. Were you really going to make me do all the talking?"

"That was the plan, yes. Besides…you're so good at it."

I can't help but laugh. "I'm going to pretend I didn't hear that, and make you a deal." He quirks a thick brow. "I'll answer a question of yours for each one you answer of mine. Sound fair?"

"Can we negotiate a two-for-one deal?"

"Just ask me something," I say, already exasperated, but enjoying it nonetheless.

"One more thing…"

I let out a sigh. "I think at this point I'd prefer the silence."

"We have to be honest," Graham says, prodding at his lip ring with his tongue. I try not to stare.

"That won't be a problem," I say with a smile.

"Okay. Hm…" Graham makes a show of thinking up a question, rubbing his chin with the hand that isn't around my shoulders.

"Any time would be good," I say after several moments, glancing at him from the corner of my eye.

His face swivels in my direction, his hand dropping from his chin. "Are you like this with everyone?"

"Is that all you could come up with?"

"No, I'm serious," he says, eyes never leaving mine.

So, I glance away. "Like what?"

"So…combative."

"I am *not* combative."

"Really? Would you like to argue me on it some more?"

There are no pleasant jolts in my stomach now, only the insistent prods of annoyance and the corrosive heat of embarrassment. "If anyone here is combative, it's you. You lashed out at me day one, minute one."

His easy grin is slipping away. "I thought we went over this…"

"I don't remember receiving an apology."

His lips are forcing a smile now, the edges shoving back against the middle. "I don't recall needing to give one."

As annoyed as I am, as confused and muddled as my mind feels—a mixture of anger, and remnants of hurt battling the swirl of unwanted attraction towards him—I don't want him to become Day One Graham again.

"You are…" I shake my head, trying to come up with words. When I can't, I look out at the park again, all of its movements a blur of nothing in my eyes, which can only see him, and already long to take him in again. "You're just…*infuriating.*"

I can see his smile from the corner of my eye, and suppress one of my own when he says, "That makes two of us."

*Two of us.*

I stare at the empty cup in my lap, feeling a lot like the ice turned water at the bottom: completely liquefied.

"Your turn," Graham says, one of his fingers prodding my shoulder from its position behind me.

I glance at him, feeling my cheeks heat despite myself, and scramble for something to say that isn't, "*That was the first time you touched me.*"

"Um…" I close my eyes, scrunching my brows together, and take a deep breath. "Are you in school?"

"Graduated. Last semester. My turn—what's your favorite thing to do in the whole world?"

I want to know more. Want to know if he did well or not, or if he had a lot of friends, or if he dormed or lived at home. But all I manage to say is, "What?"

"If you could be doing one thing at any given moment—one thing that makes you happy—what would it be?"

Even with Graham's dark eyes on me, I don't have to think about it. "Draw."

"Draw? You mean, like, sketch?"

I nod.

"Why?"

I meet his eye again, and smile when I can see how seriously he's asking. "Nothing else quiets my mind, or…focuses my energy the same way. I get things—images—stuck in my head, and, I don't know, I just…*have* to get them down on a page. And I always feel better afterwards. Calmer, somehow."

Graham's smiling. "Can I see something?"

"What? No. And that's already two more questions than you're allotted."

He's still grinning, but holds his hands up in surrender. "Fair. Your turn."

I shift more fully towards him, feeling one of his fingers brush against my shoulder as I move. "What's *your* favorite thing to do?"

Those dark eyes, somehow light with his smile before, narrow. "Pass."

"*What?* You can't pass."

"We never said we couldn't pass."

"We never said we *could*, either."

"My turn. Can I see some of your drawings?"

We've only been playing for maybe five minutes, but I'm completely exhausted. "No."

"Come on." Graham's gaze moves to my feet, where my bag is resting. "I *know* you have your sketchbook in there."

"No, I don't," I say, hoping I don't sound too panicked.

Graham breathes a laugh. "Yes, you do. You're always doodling in it during rehearsal. And I'd be willing to bet you don't leave the house without it."

I stare right at him, noting the flash of realization in his eyes when he processes what he's said; what he's just given away. It's gone just as quickly as it appeared.

"Tell me what your favorite thing to do is, and then I'll show you a drawing."

"Two drawings."

"Is this how you get through life? Just bargaining for everything?"

Graham gives me a devilish grin. "I'm good at it, right?"

I roll my eyes. "Do we have a deal?"

He considers it for a moment, staring right into my eyes, and I can see the amusement dancing there. "Fine."

"Good. You go first while I get out my sketchpad."

Graham sighs, and I look purposefully down at my bag, wondering what it could be and why it's so hard to tell me.

Finally, he says, "Cooking."

I sit up, my sketchpad in hand, and try to temper my surprise. "That wasn't so hard, was it?"

Graham smiles, but it looks pained, tight; it doesn't reach his eyes—they flick down to the book in my hands. "A deal's a deal," he says, the sides of his mouth easing a bit more, stretching a bit wider.

I'm already fearful of what he'll think, already afraid of revealing this part of myself, but at the same time I *like* that he's so eager to see, so eager to know this side of me. And he already uncovered a part of himself that he clearly would've preferred to keep hidden, a realization that makes my heart leap up into my throat.

Fully aware of the eyes I've drawn too many times watching my face now, I angle the book away from him and flip to something safe, something I'm proud of, something that won't lead to too many invasive questions.

I hand him the sketchpad when I find it, watch his eyebrows draw together a bit, creating a little crease between them just begging to be captured by pencil and paper. His arm leaves the back of the bench, as if he needs both hands to appreciate what I'm sharing with him.

"Wow," he says, continuing to study it, the ghost of a smile on his lips. "This is—"

"It's Big Ben," I say, nervous as I stare at the lines of the building with him, feeling the warmth of his arm where it's pressed against mine.

"I was going to say incredible," Graham says, a smirk lifting the pierced corner of his lip as he glances over at me. "I can see that it's Big Ben."

"Right," I say, releasing a shaky breath of laughter. "Wait, really?"

"Yeah, it's pretty obvious," he says, his smile growing wider.

"No." There's a nervous fluttering in my chest now. "I mean…about the other thing you said."

Graham's not looking at the drawing anymore. "It's *incredible*, Charlotte."

My heart is trying to stage an escape, break free from its prison inside my ribcage.

"The amount of detail is just…amazing." He shakes his head, his eyes scanning the sketch again. "Did you draw this from life?"

I'm feeling shy now, like I want to curl up and fold in on myself, keep all of these feelings locked up tight inside. But they're escaping through my shallow breaths, through my smile as it widens, through the crazy racing of my heart. I feel like I'm expanding with every breath I take.

I nod, nudging my glasses further up my nose. "I spent the semester in London this past spring, so I had a lot of time to get it right."

"Did you like it?"

He's staring at me with only interest in his eyes, as if he somehow knows this is all I really want to talk about anymore, but I'm still a little self-conscious saying, "It was the best four months of my life."

"Why?" he asks.

I try to temper my surprise, my excitement, and shrug. "It was just…"

But how am I supposed to put it into words? I've spent weeks missing it, missing the life I had while I was there, thinking about all of the sights and places I still long to see throughout my days—Big Ben, the Thames, Covent Garden, the hustle and bustle of King's Cross, even the Tube—thinking about the sheer sense of freedom being there gave me. I don't know how to word any of it; how to express all of it without diminishing just how much it meant.

"It was perfect," I finally say. "The city is beautiful, brimming with life—in a way that's somehow just like New

York, but entirely different at the same time. And…I don't know. Being there, I just felt…free."

It still isn't enough. More thoughts are making themselves known, but I'm already embarrassed of what I've said, and how I've said it.

"In what way?" Graham asks, and I snap my gaze back to him, cheeks heating as I smile.

I shrug again. "It just… I don't know." But I *do* know. "I think, sometimes…it's easier to be yourself in a place where no one knows you. No one has any expectations. You can totally reinvent yourself and they wouldn't know the difference, you know? You can't disappoint them."

When I meet his eye again, my embarrassment spikes. Hard. A big, sharp block of it in my chest. "Okay, that sounded way more depressing than I wanted it to…"

"No, no." His hand rests on my knee for just a moment, but I can't think of anything else for the next several, can't focus on anything but the heat he left behind on my skin. "I—I get it. That's, uh, it's actually why I love acting. Granted, it's a little different, and definitely a little weirder, but I never feel more like myself than when I'm not myself at all. When I'm someone else, living their story and their problems, somehow, I'm more at ease with who I am. Sometimes, being someone totally different is just…easier."

Only a few short weeks ago, it was hard to imagine even talking to Graham Hudson. But here I am, feeling completely exposed in front of him, surprised to find that what he's just revealed, the exposed part of himself he's just shared, matches mine almost perfectly.

He's quiet now, and maybe I should have said something after his revelation, but it almost seems too late. Instead, I watch as his gaze returns to my drawing, the way he runs his fingers gently over the lines, tracing the edges like he might be able to feel the real thing; see and understand exactly what I've seen.

I clear my throat, dislodging the well of emotions that started bubbling there, and nudge his shoulder with mine. "So…cooking, huh?"

Graham nods, still focused on my sketch. "Cooking."

"Wouldn't have guessed that."

"Why?"

I shrug, not entirely sure myself. "I don't know. You just don't seem like you'd have the patience for it."

Graham's lips twist up at the sides a little. "It's actually one of the few things I do have patience for. That's why I like it."

Nodding, I say, "When can I expect a four-course meal?"

Graham chuckles, and sits back. "You're funny."

"That's not fair. I showed you a sketch."

"Not only is that not the same thing, but me cooking for you wasn't part of our deal."

"In the interest of sharing our favorite things, it is. And maybe it would've been if you'd just told me your favorite thing to do without me having to make a deal with you to find out."

Graham sighs and runs a hand through his hair, smiling despite himself.

"I won't tell anyone," I say, leaning a little closer, trying to catch his eye. "You can still be tough, impatient, nothing-fazes-me Graham Hudson even after you cook for me."

Graham's lips want to smile, but he doesn't let them. "Maybe."

And just like that, I know that's all I'm going to get. "I'll take it. For now." I reach out, pluck my sketchpad from his hands, and smile at him. "We should get back to it."

Graham smiles down at me as he opens his script. "You're like a drill sergeant."

I sit up, my sketchpad safe in my bag again, and smile. "Oh, this is nothing." I push my glasses up into my hair. "My Nana didn't even take breaths when she tested me on stuff for school. I swear, she was like one of those auctioneers—one long string of words that I had to decipher before even beginning to think about the answer. And before I could get the answer fully out, she was on to the next question."

Graham's eyes are bright, and his scruffy cheeks lift with a big smile. "What did she do if you were wrong?"

"She usually didn't catch it," I say. "She thought the faster I got the answers out, the more I knew. Accuracy didn't matter." I laugh, remembering how intent she'd be reading my study questions through her thick glasses. "She wasn't the best person to study with, but she was the most fun. My dad would always have to go over it with me again later, though."

Graham chuckles, a sound that sends my pulse racing, pounding hard in my throat. "She sounds like a real character."

Realizing how close I've come to more questions, how I've practically been inviting him to ask more, I nod, swallow, and change the subject. "Any of those in your family?"

"What?"

"Characters. You know, personalities too big for one person in the best way possible?"

Graham doesn't hesitate. "My grandpa. He died when I was twelve, but—" his arm comes around my shoulders again, and already I can feel warmth radiating from it, "—he was just the greatest guy. A big prankster. Loved making people laugh."

He's looking at an older couple walking their Golden Retriever, but I can tell he's seeing something else, and I'm surprised by how much I want to see it, too.

"He used to take us to a park near his house," Graham says. "Me and my brother—and we'd take a loaf of bread and go to the lake and feed the ducks. But they were really *brazen* ducks. They'd walk right up to you and quack, demanding the food. And even though we wouldn't admit it, Joey and I were pretty scared of them. So, my grandpa decided he'd really get us, right?" He holds up his thumb and index finger like pincers. "He used his fingers to nip at the backs of our ankles when we weren't looking." He starts to laugh, and I can't help it: I giggle along. "Joey got so scared once, he fell headfirst into the lake. That was the last time my grandpa did it. He felt really bad."

"You must miss him," I say a few moments later when we both catch our breath.

Graham's still smiling, his eyes on the ground, his fingers curling and uncurling the corner of his script. "Yeah, I do. My brother has so much of his personality, though. Sometimes, it's like he's still here."

"How old is your brother?" I tuck one leg under the other on the bench, fully facing him now.

"Seventeen. In his senior year, which is crazy." He plucks a thread from the frayed end of his jeans. "He's a great kid."

Graham's dark eyes are alight with a different emotion—one I haven't seen from him yet, and it takes me a moment to pin it down. "You seem proud of him."

Graham nods, the pride flashing in his eyes as they meet mine. "I am."

"That's so nice. I wish I had an older sibling like you." Realizing how my words could be misconstrued, that he might think I see him as something akin to a sibling, I clarify. "Or a younger sibling, or any siblings, really. It would have been nice to have the company all those years."

"Don't get me wrong. It's not *always* fun having him around all the time."

"Yeah, but I'm sure it's better than long stretches with no one around." I want to sound joking, light, like I don't really care, but the words leave a bitter taste behind.

When I look up, Graham isn't really smiling anymore, and I feel my own smile droop, the corners melting like the sides of an ice cream cone. His gaze doesn't falter though. If anything, it steadies, as if he's trying to find something more in my eyes. Without warning, images of my mother walking out of the house that fateful morning play like a video reel in my mind, and I look down, afraid he might see.

"That was definitely more than five minutes," I say, cracking open my script with a smile that takes too much effort.

While I'm afraid of delving any deeper, afraid of what I might say, and how it might make me feel, I'm more afraid of the way I want to continue; the way I want him to press me for more so that I have an excuse to tell him everything.

"More than five minutes well spent."

I grin over at him. "You definitely asked me more questions than I asked you."

Graham opens his script as well, his heavily marked and highlighted. His lips ease into a smile when he glances up. "We'll just have to do this again, then."

My stomach feels like it's flipped over, but I pull my glasses back down on my nose and try to act nonchalant despite the smile working its way from my lips up to my eyes. "Guess we will."

I let myself stare at him when he looks down at his script, watching the way he licks his lips, running his tongue over the silver ring in the one corner. "Alright, Sarge." He looks at me with a smirk. "Where are we taking it from?"

I giggle, glancing down at the page I've opened to in my lap. "You tell me, soldier. I'll follow your lead."

Graham continues to play with his lip ring, his tongue moving it back and forth over his smiling lips. "Let's go from the scene at work with Johnny. The second one."

I nod, eager to escape into the world of the play, another place where I don't feel weighed down by my life. And this time, I'm going there with him. "Forward…march."

## *Year Fifteen*

Charlotte twisted this way and that in Nana's dusty attic, getting a view of herself in a long, free-standing mirror from as many angles as she could, admiring the way Nana's old black-and-white polka dot dress fell, too loose, off her shoulders and around her bust. The black heels nearly fit her, and the long string of costume pearls and matching earrings were Charlotte's to keep now. She bent and lifted the handle of an old-fashioned suitcase—a hard shell lined with coarse blue fabric. It was empty, of course, but Charlotte imagined the weight of it full of clothes, and pretended she was going away, leaving her family behind—all the fighting, and all the tense silences in between—to travel the world.

She spun around, watching as the light, pleated fabric of the skirt lifted, rippling out through the air. Maybe, she thought, if she spun hard enough, fast enough, she could take flight. But she stumbled, her ankle twisting painfully when she came down wrong on Nana's heel.

Pretending, if only for a few moments, was its own beautiful escape.

"Charley," Nana called. "Come look at this."

Charlotte stomped toward the stairs, only a slight sting left in her right ankle, the too-big heels clomping against the floor as they flopped off the back of her feet. Nana Rosie was standing in the middle of the staircase between the landing of the attic and the door at the bottom of the stairs, which opened into Mr. Worth's old bedroom. She was looking at the built-in bookcase that spanned the wall of the stairwell, the one filled with old books that Charlotte always trailed her fingers over on her way up to the attic.

Nana glanced up as Charlotte came to the top of the stairs, and used a finger to push up her glasses. "Well, don't you look lovely," she said with a smile.

Charlotte returned it and curtsied, still feeling elegant in Nana's dress.

"Come here," Nana said. "Come look at this." She reached a wrinkled hand up and slid a book out from between the others.

Charlotte gripped the railing for support as she maneuvered the steep steps in her pumps. "What is it?"

The book was an ugly, muddy brown color, made worse by a thick layer of dust that had settled onto the cover. A flurry of it rose up like a cloud when Nana flipped through the yellowed pages. Charlotte could see that some of them had been bent in the corners, and markings were scribbled underneath and next to some of the text. The binding was also badly cracked, as if someone had left it open, facedown, and settled an unabridged dictionary onto it.

"This," Nana said, a small smile lifting her soft cheeks, "was my favorite book when I was young." She closed it then, and ran her fingers over the cover, wiping the caked-on dust away to reveal scripted gold lettering.

"Little Women," Charlotte murmured as she read. "By Louisa May Alcott."

"It's a wonderful story." Nana flipped through the pages again. "All about young girls— sisters—and their family. My mother read it to me when I was little, much younger than you are now, but I loved it. I always thought Jo and I would've been great friends if she were real. I was too headstrong as a girl, much like her." She looked pointedly at Charlotte. "Much like you *still* are."

Charlotte didn't know who Jo was, but from the fond look in Nana's eyes, she was happy to be like her. "How old is it?" she asked, eyeing the frail-looking cover and binding, afraid to touch it for fear it might disintegrate in her hands.

Nana's eyes widened as she nodded. "Pretty old. It was my mother's before she gave it to me." She was caught up on one page, running her fingers over the words. "It may be old and dusty, and it may have ripped pages and dog-eared corners, and too many markings to actually read it properly." She closed it again. "And it's certainly not the prettiest thing. But that doesn't mean it doesn't have something to say." She looked up at her granddaughter, who was still eyeing the filthy book with a mix of curiosity and mild disgust in her eyes. "Kind of like me," she finished with a chuckle.

With that, she held the book out toward Charlotte.

"For me?" Charlotte asked.

Nana shrugged as Charlotte took the book from her. "It seems only right that you should have it now. Make your own markings, dog-ear your own pages."

Despite the layer of grime Charlotte felt under the pads of her fingers, she hugged the book to her chest. "Thank you."

"You're welcome." Nana smiled. "Shall we head on up now?"

"Yes," Charlotte said, eager to have Nana up there with her, in a place that she'd so often enjoyed by herself. It was almost as if the attic, filled with all of Nana's old belongings, all the things that made up her past, had become Charlotte's. And as much as she enjoyed the thought of having some piece of Nana's past all to herself, she was happy to share her space with Nana, and excited to hear how all these things were part of her grandmother's life.

Charlotte clambered the rest of the way up the stairs and kicked off the pumps, having had enough of trying to maneuver in them. By the time Nana reached the last step, she was breathing heavily, so Charlotte gripped her by the elbow to steady her.

The room was filled with cardboard boxes stacked against the slanted blue walls. One small window on the opposite wall was the only source of the room's dim light, and just next to it stood a rack of Nana's old dresses, where Charlotte had found today's ensemble. Nana looked at it all in a kind of awe, a distant look causing her eyes to glaze over behind her glasses.

Nana's gaze settled on each box, some with scrawled lettering across the side, others stacked haphazardly with no indication of what they held within, as if she were remembering the precise moment she had placed it there.

"Here." Charlotte motioned to a chair nearby. "Sit down."

Nana turned to look at the high-backed armchair Charlotte was referring to, with its pale pink upholstery and dark wooden frame, and sat in it with a long, slow sigh, running her knotted fingers over the arms. "This was my grandmother's. We took it after she died. My mother used to sit in it and read, or just look out the window, watching all the goings-on of the neighborhood. She was nosy, my mother. She just loved to know what was going on with everyone."

Eager to hear more about Nana's family, Charlotte grabbed a box and sat cross-legged in front of Nana on the floor, the box between them. "This is my favorite one. It's got all of these odds and ends in it. See?" She held up a small statue of a woman dancing, her dull purple skirt swinging around her.

"Oh," Nana exclaimed, reaching for it. "This was my mother's, too. She loved to collect all these knick-knack kinds of things." Nana turned the figurine around and around in her hand and let out a laugh. "My father hated them, though. He didn't like clutter, and would've preferred it if we'd kept the house bare of decorations. But he loved her, so the figurines stayed."

Charlotte smiled, imagining Nana's parents, and Nana as a little girl in a home full of little statues. She pulled another figurine from the box, a rotund man with red cheeks and an overflowing beer in his hand. Nana laughed in earnest, explaining that her father had found this one at a flea market and brought it home as a joke, hoping his wife wouldn't like the ugly thing.

"She displayed it smack dab in the middle of the mantel," Nana finished, still chuckling at the memory.

Charlotte and Nana Rosie stayed like that in the attic for what felt like hours, and Charlotte listened intently as her grandmother spoke of her childhood. When Charlotte was younger, she'd created stories for the little figurines, giving each of them a part to play in a never-ending game, never once imagining that long before she was around, they lived and played many other parts. The idea of it captivated her.

"Mom? Charlotte?" a voice called, interrupting Nana's story about a little sailor.

"Up here!" Charlotte called back, recognizing her father's voice.

Nana stayed quiet as Charlotte turned toward the staircase, the sound of footfalls vibrating through the room, sending dust particles whizzing in all directions in the now steady stream of light coming through the window. Mr. Worth's head of brown hair came into view first, and Charlotte smiled at him from her seat on the floor when his hazel eyes met hers.

"What are you two—?"

The sound of glass shattering cut him off.

## *Chapter Thirteen*

When I was seven, I went to my first sleepover at my friend Nicole's house. The only reason I didn't pack every single toy I owned was because my mother wouldn't let me, but I did take my favorite stuffed animal—a pig wearing a scarf I'd named Pinky—and my purple Aladdin nightgown. I was eager for a night of independence, fun, staying up late eating chocolate, and watching movies.

But Nicole's mother had us in bed by nine, television off, lights out, and Nicole seemed to nod off as soon as her head hit the pillow. I stared at her with a nervous quiver in my stomach, accompanied by a sharp pang in my chest—the one I usually felt when I was about to cry. All I could think about was my own room, my own Pocahontas sheets, not her bright pink Barbie bedspread. Her breathing had evened out next to me but mine came in shorter pants, my fear of the strange room made worse by the way it seemed to darken as I stared into it. I squeezed my eyes shut then and burrowed under the covers, the longing ache for my home locked in my chest until sleep found me.

Sleepovers hadn't been my thing for a long time after that. The echoes of that longing, that ache for my home, had stayed with me, flaring up if I so much as thought about sleeping away. I never imagined that I could feel those pangs for anywhere other than my house and family, but I've been homesick for my flat in London ever since I got back—even the tiny bathroom with the shower that always overflowed. I miss the Tube every time the subway is late (and even when it isn't), and find myself desperate to hear a British accent in my daily commute. But most of all, there's an ache in my chest for the freedom from responsibility, the freedom to come and go at my own discretion, and the freedom from nagging questions and incessant phone calls.

The freedom from my mother.

"I called a few times, but I kept getting your voicemail," Mom says after an awkward exchange of small talk.

Folding myself into a seat at the back of the auditorium, I watch Andrea open the cot onstage, feeling that familiar ache bloom deep in the center of my chest—that longing for London; for a place that, in some ways, felt more like home to me than mine ever did.

"I've been busy." I keep my voice low, but I can feel my temper rise when she speaks again.

"Too busy to even call me back?" Mom's voice isn't tight with anger, but it does hold a perceptible note of *something*, and it isn't something I can remember hearing from her before.

"I've been really tired."

The auditorium door opens to my left, and Amanda walks in, a wide smile on her pretty, heart-shaped face.

"Right. Of course you are." The admission of defeat in my mother's voice is one I recognize because it's something I have, for so many years, felt myself when she brushed me aside. Hearing it now, I can't help feeling a bit of satisfaction. It sucks not being a priority for someone you care about. Especially someone who, biologically, is supposed to care about you more than anything else in the world.

Graham walks in just behind Amanda, a small, amused smile playing at his lips. My heartbeat quickens at the sight, and then thuds in a hot, unsteady rhythm as he falls into step beside her, his hand finding the small of her back as they head toward the stage.

"Charlotte?" My teeth clench together. "Do you think you'll be able to come this weekend?"

The hope in her voice is lost on me. I can't think. All I can do is feel the heat of the anger bubbling in my chest, searing away the ache I was feeling only moments ago as it courses through my blood like a runaway blaze.

"No." It's a low sound that comes straight from the back of my throat.

"Oh. Okay, well. Maybe the weekend after—"

"No, Mom. That's not going to work for me either." My words are sharp, their severity cutting through the tension like the edge of a blade. But so did the way she left us, and I'm still recovering from that festering wound. She'll get over this.

"What? Why—?"

"I don't want to come spend the weekend with you and Richard." *Dick,* I add in my head. Aware of the high, echoing walls around me, I do my best to keep my voice low, but there's no hiding my animosity. Not anymore.

"But," she stammers. "I thought—"

"I can't keep pretending what you did never happened, that it never changed anything. Maybe *you* can. You certainly never gave a shit about me for most of my life. Maybe it's easy for you, but not for me. Not anymore. I'm done."

Maybe I'm being harsh. Maybe I'm letting my emotions get the best of me. Or maybe this is what she deserved all along.

"Charlotte." She's gasping. "I—"

I hang up on her.

It wasn't as difficult as I thought it would be. She was never one to get too emotional, so I know she'll get over it. As the anger ebbs, I feel lighter. The conversation I've feared for the better part of a year, and the expression of emotions I've kept pent up for much longer, is now behind me. Exhaustion—the relaxed, drowsy kind—settles into my bones in exquisite relief.

In a daze, I make it up onto the stage, taking up my script and settling myself in a chair while the relief lingers like a drug.

"You okay?" The voice is close to me, and I glance up to find Andrea's big brown eyes boring into mine.

"Yeah." I smile. "I'm good."

"You sure?" She's smiling a bit, too, but the concern is still there in her eyes. She knew I was on the phone with my mother—it rang as soon as the two of us walked into the theater.

And it's that concerned look that tugs at the well of emotions, a mix of relief, gratitude for Andrea's concern, and (I'll admit it) sadness all thrashing around inside me, but I push them back, afraid if they get too close to the surface, I'll break.

"I'm fine," I say. "Promise."

Andrea smiles, and holds my arm for a moment before sitting down next to me. I stare down at my open script, pretending to study the few notes I made for this particular scene. It's one of Nick's daydreams, a flashback to his first kiss with Olivia. It's the only scene we haven't looked at since the few initial read-throughs.

"Alright, guys," Andrea calls, demanding the attention of a giggling Amanda and a smirking Graham. "Let's get to work."

After taking a bit of time to map out and firm up choreography, Andrea sits with me again as I scribble the last of her direction next to the text. "And," Andrea says, "Action!"

Graham looks more vulnerable and nervous than I've ever seen him when he reaches for Amanda's hand just as she opens the door that leads into her "apartment". Amanda turns back to him in breathless surprise, and Graham drops her hand as if it burned him.

Amanda's features morph from disappointment when Graham buries his hands in his pockets, to amusement as he rambles on about how much fun he had with her and how great he thinks she is, a noticeable tumble of desire and terror in his eyes. That's when Olivia puts Nick out of his misery, and I look away, waiting for the scene to be over.

"Okay, cut." Only when Andrea stands do I look up, still too quickly. Amanda's leaning in to Graham, her hands resting flat against his broad chest. He's holding her gently at the elbows, and they're still so close, their noses are almost touching. Graham smiles when she mutters something only he can hear, his lips spreading impossibly wider as she giggles. I force myself to look down at my script again.

"You're just not awkward enough here. You've got to go that bit further." Andrea is halfway between me and them, yelling even though she's the only one speaking. "We'll run it a few more times, but I think the set-up is good. And the lighting will probably be pretty low, cause its Nick's dream, so we want to differentiate it from reality." She nods, mostly to herself, eyes searching the floor as she thinks of more to say. "Just, up the stakes. I see lots of energy, which is good. But it's got to be more nervous. More like they're both jumping from a ledge without a parachute. Got it?"

Both Graham and Amanda nod.

"Charlotte, do you like it?" Andrea asks, turning to face me.

"Mhm." I want the mumble to sound positive, but don't dare look at Amanda or Graham, afraid their stares will shatter my resolve.

"Great," Andrea says after a brief pause. "Okay, let's run it again. Feel free to take some more liberties if you'd like, now that we've got a blueprint for the scene. And remember, up the energy. Panic if you have to."

Neither Graham nor Amanda change much the second time through, apart from intonation here and there. The distance between them lessens as the scene goes on, and the excited energy sparks between them as they move together—all signs of a first date gone right. The audience will know how the relationship ultimately fizzles, but this is a scene meant to provide that bittersweet hope. It may be bad now, but things used to be so good, so beautiful, in the beginning.

The ending would break their hearts.

Before Andrea has them run it through again, she touches on a few more things she thinks might work: Amanda can keep in mind that not only is she into Graham, and endeared by his nerves, but she also wants to encourage him because she's feeling the same way he is, like a shaken soda bottle ready to burst at the slightest twist of the cap. Graham—though the kissing scene was tender, with just the right amount of wanting—could cup her jaw instead of holding her waist, a small difference that might better communicate the uncertainty and desire in Nick and Olivia's first kiss.

With these things in mind, they run through it again.

And again—with only subtle nuances between each take.

The more it goes on, the longer the jumble of emotions builds inside me. I don't regret what transpired between my mom and me. I've wanted to say those things for a long time. But something doesn't feel quite right about it. The satisfaction is gone too soon.

I try to put it out of my mind, focus on the task at hand. But watching Graham and Amanda is only making matters worse. Right over that layer of sadness sits an uncomfortable, stifling desire to be in Amanda's place. Each time they start the scene over, the blistering heat of it sears deeper, licking at the sadness and residual anger till I'm left with a sick, unsettled feeling in my stomach.

"Great job, guys," Andrea calls from next to me, clapping her hands for no real reason again. It's like I'm slammed back into my seat, into the moment, as if the warped pull of my thoughts spits me back out, and my body tenses from the impact.

"Next week is tech week. We've got full-cast rehearsals on Saturday and Sunday, and I'll expect you to have your lines completely memorized. You have a break tomorrow—no rehearsal, so I expect you to practice. Together, if you can."

I look sideways at Andrea, upset enough over the undeniable attraction between Graham and Amanda that has nothing do with their characters. Andrea smiles. "Yes, that means work on the intimate scenes as much as possible."

Amanda and Graham don't even try to hide their grins, and when Graham chuckles—that sound that still surprises me with a pleasant jolt in my chest—my eyes swivel to find the source without my permission. He's looking right at me—the second person I want nothing do with today, so I promptly avert my own gaze, refocusing on Andrea.

"Work on those lines, and I'll see you both Saturday." Andrea claps her hands and stands. I follow suit, and turn my back to Amanda and Graham as they start to talk.

"Charlotte." Andrea's hand finds my shoulder, and my muscles tense even more at her gentle touch. "Hey," she says softly, removing her hand. "You're not alright, are you?"

She steps closer to me, and I push my glasses up into my hair, rubbing my eyes of their tears before meeting her gaze.

"Just tired." I attempt a smile and hope she doesn't notice it wobble.

She presses her lips together, and stares until I have to look away. "You know you can talk to me about anything. Right?"

Unable to speak for fear of breaking down, I nod. The current has grown stronger, whipping around all throughout rehearsal. But now I can feel it pulling back, back, back, gathering enough momentum to crash with the force of a tidal wave. It's just a matter of time, and I don't want to be here when it happens.

As if she's read my thoughts, Andrea says, "Why don't you just head out? I've got the clean-up tonight."

I try to hide how grateful I am. "Are you sure? I feel bad."

"Go, I've got it. Maybe you'll catch an earlier train."

"Okay. Let me just—"

"Charlotte." She grabs my arm and gives me a small smile. "Just go, okay? Text me when you get home. Call if you feel like talking."

The current gives a sharp pull.

"Okay," I reply quietly. "Thanks."

I leave Andrea with a closed-mouth smile, afraid anything more might reveal too much. Grabbing my bag, I head for the stairs, aware of Graham and Amanda gathering their things to my right. She's saying something, her sweet voice high and cheery, but Graham is silent—listening, I suppose. I'm more aware of his silence than I am of her voice. I risk a glance their way, feeling somewhat cheated of my lingering, appreciative stares despite my treacherous mix of emotions.

His dark stare feels like a touch, one that causes me to suck in a quiet breath. His expression is the same as always—blank at first glance. But, as I look deeper, I can see the question in his eyes, and look away before he has the chance to discover any answers in mine.

There's a part of me that longs to turn around, run to him, and give any and all of the answers he might want. That same part of me feels tethered to him somehow, and the connection will relax only if I stay near him. But with each step I take, it stretches, the tension increasing more and more the farther away I get, the pull of it a constant reminder of the presence on the other end.

There's another part of me that can't shake the jealousy; that hates the looks and the conversations he shares with Amanda. It refuses to dismiss the dislike he had for me when we first spoke. It reminds me that I'm nothing more than a person to run lines with when he needs help. That part stands by with a large pair of scissors, anxious to snip the cord tethering me to him when she has the chance.

The train ride home is shorter than usual. Andrea was right: I was able to catch the earlier express. But I feel so strung out, so eager to be home, I can't draw, or read, or even listen to music. Instead, I stare out the window into the night, the lights of buildings and neighborhoods streaming by in long, colorful blurs.

I almost laugh to myself when I get home—it's completely dark inside, and Dad is nowhere to be found. Not having enough of an appetite, I head straight upstairs. There's a crack of light peeking out into the hallway through the open door of Dad's room. I poke my head inside, my eyes finding the empty, unmade bed first, the white sheets and comforter crumpled into a large heap at the footboard. Dad's sitting at his desk, back to the door, tapping swiftly away on his laptop, his desk light brighter without the shade—which is lying forgotten on the floor beside a full garbage can.

"Hey, Dad," I call softly. "Just wanted to let you know I'm home."

*And I told Mom I don't want to see her anymore. And I meant it at the time. So I don't know why I'm so upset now.*

"Hi, kiddo." He doesn't turn around, doesn't stop typing. His brown locks are standing straight up, and his shoulders are hunched forward.

I close the door.

I make it to my room just before it happens. The tidal wave moves so quickly, with fierce certainty as to its destination, I barely have time to fall onto my bed before it crashes onto the shore, leaving nothing but destruction and despair in its wake. It's all so loud, the noise of it resounding in my head and heart like thunder, but the tears fall in absolute silence, relieved for their long-awaited release.

## *Year Fifteen*

Mr. Worth's eyes snapped to Nana, then to the floor, and quickly back. Charlotte spun around, unnerved to find Nana Rosie pale, her eyes round behind her glasses. Her jaw went slack as she stared at Charlotte's father, who stood just as frozen at the top of the stairs.

"Henry?" Nana whispered, her chest heaving up and down as she gasped. Her knuckles were white around the wooden arms of the chair, and Charlotte was afraid to reach up and touch one.

"Henry?" Mr. Worth questioned, as if saying the name would help him understand. "No. Mom, it's me… *Ben.*"

Charlotte stared at her father, whose eyes remained on his mother. She tried to imagine the man Nana was seeing, the love of her life—the man who had nearly broken her. But she could only see the kind eyes of her father, wide with worry, and chills shot down her spine to think that Nana could see anyone else.

Mr. Worth took a tentative step toward Nana and Charlotte, and when Nana remained silent he took another, his eyes and words imploring her to see him. "Mom. Are…are you okay?"

Some color had returned to Nana's cheeks, much to Charlotte's relief. "Ben?" she asked, her breathing slowing slightly.

"Yes, Mom. Ben." He moved even closer to them now, and Charlotte had to look up at him from her seat on the floor. His eyebrows furrowed as he reached out to touch Nana's shoulder. "Are you alright?"

Nana stared straight over Charlotte's head, her eyes moving quickly back and forth as if she were reading something on the far wall. "Yes," she said on a wisp of breath, and gave her son a tense smile. "I'm fine." She went back to staring at the wall, her eyes now still, and frighteningly vacant.

Mr. Worth lay a hand over Nana's, which had gone slack on the arm of the chair. "Come on, Ma, let's get you downstairs. I'll make you something to eat."

Nana looked back up at her son and smiled. "Oh, thank you. I'm starved."

Mr. Worth helped her stand, and Charlotte stood too, dragging the cardboard box they'd been digging through aside so that Nana could walk to the stairs. Nana looked up at her then, her eyes a light brown in the shadowed attic, and smiled. "You must be hungry, too, Charley."

Her voice sounded normal enough that Charlotte could've believed nothing was amiss. But the first shift had taken place so suddenly that Charlotte knew better. She glanced at her father, who stood just behind Nana, supporting her small frame with his hands on her arms. He smiled at his daughter—not his happy smile, but his encouraging smile—the one he gave her when she jumped into a pool for the first time, and tried crab for the first time, and started high school.

She looked at Nana again. "Um, yeah. I am. I'll just…" She glanced at the box at her feet. "I'll put this stuff away, and meet you downstairs in a minute."

Nana nodded, appeased, and Mr. Worth turned her around. Charlotte stood still until they disappeared down the stairs—couldn't move even if she wanted to, still stunned by what had happened, by the way she'd been ripped out of her imagination, and the way the reality she'd just faced had scared her. But once she couldn't hear them anymore, she knew that moving was the only thing left to do. She stripped out of Nana's dress, removing the pearls with it, and hung it back up knowing that the pulsing ache in her chest meant the time for pretending was over. Then, she put the little statues back in the box, tucking them in between puffs of tissue paper as gently as she could.

That's when she noticed the tiny heap next to the armchair, the small sailor Nana had been telling her about nothing but broken pieces now. His arm had snapped off, his hat had chipped, and several more shards of porcelain surrounded him.

Charlotte carefully picked up the pieces, resolving to glue what she could back together, knowing that, no matter what she did, he would never be the same.

She made her way to the stairs with a glance behind her to make sure everything was exactly as she'd found it, but stood at the top a moment longer, the broken pieces of the sailor cradled in her hands, knowing she'd have to do a whole different kind of pretending when she reached the bottom.

## *Chapter Fourteen*

Bleary-eyed and drowsy, I walk into the theater in a daze, my mind finally asleep after a sleepless night. I almost drifted off on the train, but I've never been good at sleeping in motion. The constant rocking of the train did nothing but give me a bump on the head after hitting it repeatedly against the window.

"Oh, good, you're here," Andrea calls from the stage. "I was just about to set up."

Rehearsal is the last thing I feel like today, especially when Andrea and I start moving the set around, lifting the table and running back and forth for the props we spent a whole two days hunting down last week. But at least Graham won't be here. At least I won't have to face that today, too.

I try not to acknowledge the little bit of disappointment I feel because of it.

"So," Andrea says, sitting in the first row when we're done. The actors will be arriving any minute. "What happened yesterday?"

I sit down next to her with a long sigh. "I finally gave it to my mom."

Andrea's eyes widen. "Good for you, girl. It's about time."

"I know."

"I sense a 'but' coming…" She grins at me, but it doesn't reach her eyes.

My smile barely touches my cheeks. "I don't know, it just…it hurt more than I thought it would."

"She's your mom, Charlotte. Of course it hurt. No one should have to have that kind of conversation with their mother."

Maybe it's a good thing we're interrupted—my eyes are already burning with the suggestion of tears—but when that door opens, I desperately wish we hadn't been.

"Graham?" Andrea stands and turns toward him. "What are you doing here?"

My stomach lurches uncomfortably when he nears, when he smiles at Andrea.

"Couldn't stay away," he says, and I look down when he meets my eye.

"Your rehearsal's not until tomorrow," Andrea says then, as if we haven't already established that he isn't supposed to be here.

"I know." His smile is almost shy now. "I was hoping maybe I could run lines today. When you're not too busy."

Andrea looks flustered, and I know immediately that this is one of the things she hates about actors from when she ranted about how selfish and inconsiderate they could be. When I reminded her that she was also an actor, her response was, "I didn't say *all* actors are that way. Just most."

"Rehearsal is just about to start," Andrea finally says, clearly annoyed. "You're going to have to wait until after. It ends at five. If you want to leave and come back—"

"Charlotte," Graham says, startling me, and Andrea too. "Would you have some time to help?"

Suddenly, I'm not so tired anymore.

Andrea is looking between the two of us with furrowed brows, and I briefly wonder if she can sense my feelings; if she has any idea how drastically they've changed since the last time we spoke about Graham.

"That depends," I finally say, and meet her eye. "Andi, how badly do you need me today?"

She's studying me, jaw ajar, eyes searching mine, and I give her a little nod, hoping she'll see that this is okay, that I'm *more* than okay with it.

"We'll survive," she says after a long, drawn-out sigh. "Can't have my lead stumbling through his lines. But—" she looks right at Graham, "—I need more notice next time, okay?"

Graham nods, a shit-eating grin on his face. "It won't happen again." His eyes meet mine then, smiling at me through them just as much as his lips.

"You guys can work in the dressing room," Andrea says, looking at me and nodding a bit.

"That's fine." I stand, my body stiff and tired, but also completely aware of him, of the way it's moving in front of him.

Graham's grin softens into a more amiable smirk. "Lead on, Sarge."

I can't help my smile, but roll my eyes a little to save face, more pleased than I'd care to admit by his use of the strange nickname. He grins right back at me, and waits while Andrea and I exchange one more long look—hers, questioning, and mine, hopefully reassuring. I feel her eyes on my back as I head for the dressing room anyway, but hers isn't the only presence sending my senses into overdrive.

My limbs are no longer heavy, my vision no longer blurred, but I know this won't be good for me. What I need is time away from him to sort out my muddled emotions, and separate myself from the idea of being with him in any way other than in a rehearsal room with scripts between us. How I've even gotten to this point of wanting him so badly I'm jealous of his co-star is a frustrating, disconcerting puzzle to me, with hundreds of pieces so small, I've given up trying to put them all together.

"So, what happened with Amanda?" I can't keep myself from asking.

Graham opens the door to the dressing room, stepping aside to let me walk through first. "She's busy," is all he says though.

The dressing room is small. One wall is lined with three mirrors and a long counter, seats tucked beneath it. The far corner holds a cabinet, both doors open to accommodate the sheer amount of clothing crammed inside. In the opposite corner stands a clothes rack, lined with even more clothes, and shoes neatly lined up underneath, all likely from the last play.

"Well, it's no Washington Square," Graham says, dropping his bag on the floor before smiling at me. "But it'll have to do."

He pulls a seat out from beneath the counter, and I keep the middle one between us when I sit, aware of how close we'd be otherwise. I'm too nervous to be any closer to him.

"So," I say, focusing on removing my script from my bag. "What did you want to go over?"

Graham's facing me in his seat, and when I look up at him, he looks right down at his rolled-up script, unfurling it and flipping through the pages. "Kind of from the middle on, if you don't mind. I think I've got the beginning down."

I adjust my glasses on my nose and flip through the marked-up pages, determined not to look at him again. "Okay…how about we start from page fiftty-five?"

Despite his coming in today and asking for help, Graham doesn't really seem to need it. He's doing well, barely glancing at the script in his lap. By the time we reach the third scene, I'm confident he could manage in front of an audience tomorrow if he needed to. He doesn't even fumble between lines, doesn't pause to think what might come next, just listens and responds to what I'm saying as Olivia, then as Nick's brother, his eyes locked on me the entire time.

My heart slows as much as it can in his presence, calming with the ease of tossing lines out at him, and waiting for him to catch them and toss them back. It helps that I'm decidedly not looking at him. But after he nails a paragraph-long monologue, detailing how Nick plans to win his wife back—with a fancy dinner and wordy apology and a promise to do better, I pause.

"Are you sure you need my help? Cause it doesn't really seem like you do."

I shouldn't let myself think about why he might've said that he did. Shouldn't consider his reasons for coming all the way here today when he so clearly doesn't need help. And I definitely shouldn't have glanced up when I voiced my question, because the look in his eyes only fuels the fire in my chest.

He smiles, like he's not surprised I'm asking. "I've got most of my lines down. It just helps to have someone run them with me. So I'm not just talking to myself. It's good to hear the responses."

"That…makes perfect sense." I focus on the corner of the page I've been folding and refolding. "Haven't you and Amanda been able to practice together at all?"

I want the question to sound innocent and professional, but it comes out weighted by the emotions I've been working to suppress—the sneaking tone of jealousy, the high squeak of hope, thrumming with way too much interest.

"A few times," Graham says, sounding thoroughly nonchalant. "She's got a lot going on, though, so it's hard to meet up as often as we really need to."

"Yeah. Andrea mentioned her schedule being kind of problematic right from the get-go."

Graham leans forward, curling his script up in his hands again. "What happened yesterday?"

My eyes snap up to his. The question came from out of nowhere, but what he's asking makes my heart start pounding again, as does the darkness in his eyes, only concerned interest hovering there now. But I don't have time to work up a response, because Graham's still staring at me when he speaks again.

"When you left yesterday, you looked…" He doesn't back off, doesn't look away. "Not right."

The rush of emotions left over from yesterday's events slithers around inside, and I take a deep breath, giving Graham a quivering smile so they won't break me again. "I was just tired."

"You looked sad," he says, voice soft.

My heart pulses hard in my throat. "What?"

"I just—I could tell you weren't yourself, and I wanted to know why."

I release a slow breath, easing the tightness in my chest and softening the edge of what feels like a jagged stone in the pit of my stomach. I slump back in my seat, watching him watch me, half afraid he can see right through me, and half wanting him to understand.

It never occurred to me that Graham might be tuned in to me. He's the actor; he has to focus on his character, transforming himself into the broken man he has to portray. I'm just around to help, to create the program artwork, and occasionally run lines with anyone who needs it. I'm supposed to be tuned into *his* needs. The problem is, I've been tuned in to him from the very start, in a way that's had nothing to do with helping him with his role. But Graham has surprised me yet again, noticing more than he should've, and more than I could've possibly hoped he would.

All of this speeds through my mind, none of it making it down to my mouth to form a response.

"Sorry, it's none of my business," Graham says, sitting back in his seat.

This time, an answer forms in my mouth before my brain can catch up. "Graham…are you…*apologizing?*"

His mouth relaxes into a grin, and he breathes laugh. "Don't get used to it."

"Could you say it one more time before we forget this ever happened?"

"No."

"I'll tell you why, if you say you're sorry once more."

"You will?" I don't actually expect him to take the bait, but from his wide-eyed look of hope, I can tell he's willing.

"Two words. That's all you have to say."

Graham grins, settling his feet more firmly on the ground and leaning forward again. "I'm sorry, Charlotte."

I nod. "My name, too. Nice touch."

Graham shrugs. "I like saying your name. Your turn."

Once I've rebounded from him admitting he likes to say my name—what does that even *mean?*—I have to face the reality of what I've promised. I still want to tell him, but a big part of me also wants to pretend it was nothing. My smile wilts and my chest deflates as I consider my options, and then it tightens when I make my choice, enough that I have to force the words out. "It was just…something with my mom. She, uh—we just don't have a very good relationship."

Graham nods, and waits for a moment, then says, "Wait, that's it?"

"We didn't specify how much detail I had to go into, so yes, that's it."

He narrows his eyes, the ghost of a smile on his lips. "Sneaky."

"*Smart,*" I correct.

"Okay." He pats the tops of his legs. "Fine." He unfurls his script, stares at the title page and doesn't look up when he says, "There's uh…there's actually one scene I really wanted to go over."

Relieved to be off the subject of my mother, I nod. "Okay, which one?"

"It's, uh, scene four. In the second act."

The lurch in my stomach isn't from shock or surprise this time, but from nerves. "Oh. Okay. Uh…what about this scene is, um, giving you trouble?"

Graham straightens his spine, reaching forward to grip his knees in a stretch, but he doesn't meet my eye. "It's not giving me trouble exactly." He drums his fingers against his kneecaps. "I know the lines, but I don't feel like I've gotten the emotions right just yet. You know, the extent of them."

"Right," I say over a shaky breath, running through in my mind just what this particular scene entails, knowing just how much it's tortured me before, and nervous to think that the torture now would lie in trying to hide all that I feel. But I can't very well say *no* either. So I summon as much courage as I can, and say, "Okay, well…let's work on it."

## *Year Sixteen*

"Charlotte, start heading home," Nana insisted, the only person truly comfortable to let Charlotte drive so soon after she had gotten her license. "Henry will be getting out of work in a little while. I have to get dinner started."

Fear rose up in Charlotte like a thick, heavy sludge, filling her from the pit of her stomach up to her chest. She squeezed her eyes shut, thankful they were sitting at a red light so that she could focus on how to reply. But she didn't know what to say, and kept driving when the light turned green, selfishly hoping Nana would lose track of her reason for wanting to go home as seamlessly as she lost her grasp on reality.

"Did your mother hear back from that company she applied to?" Nana asked to Charlotte's immense relief. Mrs. Worth had applied for a new job with a small interior design company in Manhattan only a week prior, and the fact that Nana remembered calmed Charlotte's fears.

"Not yet. Hopefully, she'll hear in the next couple of days."

"That's good," Nana said. "She always had an eye for decorating."

Charlotte had always known when redecoration was about to happen. Those were the in-between days, the days when Mrs. Worth was coming out of the bad days and heading into the good. She had usually collected a number of do-it-yourself catalogues, and bought supplies for the process—paint, brushes, and new décor like lampshades, picture frames, small tables, and a bunch of other stuff they didn't need. The pungent smell of cleaning products, or the grinding noise of shifting furniture on hardwood met Charlotte at her bedroom door in the morning. She would follow the sound or smells to find Mrs. Worth in her paint-splattered overalls with the hole in the back of one knee. With a twinge of jealous surprise, Charlotte would watch her for a moment—shifting something here, throwing something else out there, or placing a new object in its potential space, and humming sweetly all the while. If only her mother could put an ounce of that positive energy into her family.

"Yeah, she has," Charlotte responded, flipping her blinker on.

"Maybe it'll be the thing to finally make her happy."

Charlotte knew what Nana meant. Her mother hadn't been truly happy for years, almost as long as Charlotte could remember. She also knew that her parents' marriage was well past the crumbling stage—it was unequivocally broken. But Nana's words hurt her all the same.

"Hurry, Charley. Henry will be home soon," Nana said again, reminding Charlotte of the worry settled deep in her stomach. She still didn't know what to say, so she didn't say anything, too afraid that she might break Nana's heart with the truth—or, at the very least, upset her by pointing out her confusion.

It hadn't happened often at first, and Charlotte let herself be placated by Nana's reassurances every time it did. Nana still seemed like herself, after all, still cheery and energetic as ever. But the small moments of forgetfulness—a word here and there, or someone's name, or the way certain events had taken place—appeared more often, becoming longer periods of complete confusion.

Charlotte could only delude herself so long, and only when Nana Rosie had forgotten who Charlotte was for several of the longest minutes of Charlotte's life—screaming when she found her granddaughter in the kitchen, poking around in the fridge—did Charlotte broach the subject with her parents.

"Have either of you noticed Nana's gotten a little…" Charlotte paused, relieved to find both her mother and father had looked up from collecting their dinner, "…forgetful, lately?"

Mr. Worth sighed and let the serving spoon fall back into the peas with a clank against the bowl. "I have, yes."

"Forgetful?" Mrs. Worth looked between her husband and Charlotte, her plate, only half full with food, forgotten on the counter. "What do you mean?"

"She just… She seems confused a lot now." Charlotte prodded her chicken with her fork, afraid to let on just how bad it had gotten with Nana. "She…she forgot who I was today."

Charlotte couldn't shake that feeling—the hurt, the sadness, and the fear that came when you looked into the eyes of your favorite person in the world and saw no recognition, no love, none of the usual joy. Only wariness, skepticism, and blank curiosity.

Mr. Worth leaned forward, his elbows resting on the counter as he let his chin fall to meet his chest with another long sigh.

"What?" Mrs. Worth spoke in an alarmed whisper, and looked to her husband. "You knew about this, Ben?"

For the third time in a matter of minutes, Mr. Worth sighed, but didn't look up. "Yes."

"She thought he was Grandpa once," Charlotte blurted, sensing an argument brewing. "It was a while ago, and it only happened once, but—"

"It's happened again since then," Mr. Worth admitted, pushing himself up onto his hands and gripping the counter, his eyes still cast down.

Mrs. Worth spoke again, surprising Charlotte. Her voice was soft, and full of concern. "She thought you were your father?"

Mr. Worth looked at his wife then, straight into her eyes, and thought for a brief moment that he knew how Nana Rosie must've felt—knew what it was like to look at someone you loved and only see the ghost of the past in their eyes.

He only nodded, afraid to speak as his eyes filled up.

Mrs. Worth considered that for a moment. "Have you thought about taking her to a doctor?" Her voice was still gentle, comforting, like a hand reaching out to offer support. But her hands stayed flat on the counter.

"Of course I have," Mr. Worth replied. He didn't sound angry, just forceful. He cleared his throat. "I asked her about it, too. She denied it even happening and refuses to go."

"She's still able to take care of herself and get around, though, right?"

"As far as I know," Mr. Worth said with a single, glum nod.

"She goes to the store every Monday like she always has, and still cooks for herself and everything," Charlotte added, even more worried now with talk of doctors. "But…she does look a bit thinner."

"I thought that, too," Mr. Worth agreed, meeting Charlotte's eye with his lips pressed together in a firm line.

Charlotte didn't want to consider all of this, didn't want to think about her grandmother forgetting to eat. But, at the same time, she was relieved to be talking it out, to have both parents on her side, speaking not only to her, but to each other.

"We'll just have to get over there more often, then," Mrs. Worth said after a few moments. "Make sure that she's taking care of herself and eating regularly. But if it gets worse, we're taking her to a doctor. I don't care what she wants if we reach that point. Her well-being is what matters."

"Agreed," Mr. Worth said, and brought his hands up to his eyes.

Normally, things would have escalated by this point, Charlotte thought. Her parents' conversations were no longer a slow burn, snuffed out with the slamming of doors and the following silence, but an explosion set off by a short fuse, leaving a cloud of smoke and debris behind.

Nana Rosie was the one person who they each cared about more than their own problems. She was the only person who could bring them together in this way anymore, and she was probably the only person who had kept them together for this long. Charlotte might never understand why Mrs. Worth seemed to love Nana Rosie so much, but for years, she'd seen that the two had a relationship just as special as her own and Nana's.

The Worth family decided that Mr. Worth would check in on his mother before work, Charlotte could stay with her after school every day, and Mrs. Worth would make it a point to stop in when she picked up Charlotte to make sure that Nana had something for dinner. Though the plan was nothing drastic, they knew Nana wouldn't be thrilled with everyone fussing over her, so they decided they had to be as nonchalant as possible—make it more about seeing and spending time with her as opposed to taking care of her. In truth, it all made Charlotte a little nervous.

It was hard to face the fact that was Nana was fallible—human just like everyone else. Charlotte didn't want to seem selfish, but she *felt* selfish, and she didn't know which was worse. Did feeling selfish—wanting Nana to be healthy because *Charlotte* needed her, because *Charlotte* wanted Nana to see her graduate high school, college, then get married, have kids, and live long enough to remember all of it—equate to actually being selfish? Or did acting selfishly do that? Either way, Charlotte felt it, squandered it as best she could, and beat herself up for feeling it in the first place.

"The food's cold by now." Mrs. Worth's voice was almost back to its emotionless monotone, only a slight edge of her concern left. "Heat it up if you'd like."

She left her full plate on the counter and walked out of the kitchen. Moments later, Charlotte heard sounds from the television.

"Want me to sit with you, kiddo?" Mr. Worth was looking at her, his eyes honey-brown. Charlotte knew he'd probably rather go upstairs and work—it's what he always did at dinnertime.

"That's okay." She gave him her best smile. "I've got homework to finish."

Mr. Worth's smile was strained, but he kissed her forehead, then took his plate of cold food and left Charlotte alone in the kitchen. A few minutes of togetherness was more than enough for everyone, it seemed, and despite the gravity of their conversation, Mr. and Mrs. Worth slipped back into their usual dinnertime routine—eating as far away from one another as possible.

Charlotte scraped her untouched food back into the serving dishes and headed upstairs to her room, passing the closed door of her parents' bedroom—where only Mr. Worth slept now—and chided herself for thinking that tonight might be any different.

## *Chapter Fifteen*

Trying to maintain my professional demeanor feels nearly impossible with all of the nervous energy bubbling through me, so I stand up while flipping to scene four in the second act and pace, hoping movement might expend at least some of it.

Graham sighs behind me, a long, slow exhale, then says the first line of the scene, his voice quiet and pained. “How can you stand it?”

I try to sound disinterested. “What?”

“The constant silence.” He spits the words, reaching his breaking point, “It’s like I’m living with a petulant teenager.”

“Oh, please…”

“I’m serious, Liv.” And he sounds it. After a pause, he goes on. “How did we get like this?”

This is where Olivia goes off, admitting to all of the pent-up emotions and thoughts she’s been letting fester for a year.

Pulse pounding in my throat, I grit my teeth. “You want to know what happened, Nick? You lost your job. I had to take on more shifts at the hospital while you sat here feeling sorry for yourself. The bills piled up—*everything* fucking piled up, and I carried the weight of it for *months* before you lifted a finger to help."

Graham is staring at me, his scruffy jaw clenched, eyes blazing. I recognize that look. It's almost exactly the same as the one he gave me when I asked him the Graham Cracker Question. The only difference? It's not anger boiling there, but sadness. I might have faltered, but my blood is racing in a searing path through my body, urging me forward.

"I could've gotten past that. I really could've. But then, the baby—" I bring a hand to my mouth, letting the weight of the words fall from me like a heavy coat. "If I hadn't been so stressed, with so much constantly on my mind, and the long shifts, maybe…"

Olivia would think of the child they were supposed to have, the child they never had the chance to meet. Tears fill my eyes, my already vulnerable state kicked once more into high gear. I turn around, away from him, resuming my movement around the room, leaving my script on a stray chair. "I couldn't get over that, Nick." I let my voice quiet. "Not without you."

I cross my arms over my chest, feeling like Olivia might've—that I would crack open and fall apart without the support. "But you weren't there for me then, either. It felt like someone had reached inside and yanked out the most precious part of me, squeezing until all the life, the spirit, was gone. And you," I growled. "You watched it happen. You let me disintegrate until what was left of me was gone, too. How could I *not* think that all of it was your fault? You gave me life, and then ripped it away." I stare at him. He stares back. "When you didn't support me through that…what was I left to think?"

Graham stays silent as Nick is supposed to, his wife's words wounding him so deeply he feels completely hollow, the truth scraped out of him.

A breath whooshes out of me, escaping the torment inside. "I don't know what I'm supposed to say anymore, Nick. The silence—it's just easier."

There's a long pause as Nick grapples with his wife's words, trying to make sense of them. A stream of emotions—sadness, confusion, hurt, regret—plays out on Graham's face, in his depthless eyes, before he chokes out, "You're wrong."

"What?" I demand.

"I said…" His voice is thick, and when he looks up at me, I can see why. There are tears in his eyes. "You're wrong."

Graham stands, straightening out his long, lean frame, leaving his script on the counter beside him. "Not about all of it. I should have done more about the job. My ego was wounded, but that's no excuse. I should've realized the kind of pressure it was putting on you." He pauses, and his voice gets lower, with a much more noticeable note of anger in it. "But you're wrong about the baby. I *was* there. And maybe I should've tried harder to get to you, but the more I pushed, the harder you pulled." He takes a shaky breath, bringing his hands up and letting them quickly fall back to his sides. "So I let you." These words come out on a wisp of air, like a weightless leaf picked up by a sharp breeze.

"I was dealing with it, too." He's glaring at me, voice insistent and fraught with emotion. And I *feel* it. "*I was grieving, too*." He sucks his quivering bottom lip into his mouth, the bottom of the ring still visible, before turning away and bringing a hand up to his eyes, letting his cries shake him.

I feel my own eyes burn at the sight of the man falling to pieces in front of me, the emotions so tangible I have to bite my own lip to keep from crying out.

He groans, sniffling to compose himself, nods as if he's resigned to something, and stares at the floor. "I should've been more present for you." Bringing a hand over his mouth, he sniffles again, and clears his throat. His eyes are almost black when he looks at me again, void of anything he might be feeling. "Maybe then you wouldn't have jumped into bed with the next guy who looked your way."

"Fuck you, Nick!" I cry out, clenching my fists. "This is why we're so *damn* dysfunctional. We go for the jugular every time and I'm *sick* of it."

Silence stretches between us, each of us hearing the burdensome words echo in its depths, the ones we've avoided for so long, and both of us pant in exhaustion from having released them. He pulls himself together first, shoulders straightening as he meets my gaze once more, and shakes his head.

"I still *want* you," he says.

The words travel between us like a nerve impulse, zipping across the cord that tethers us and jumping the synapse to reach me. The electrical current sets my body aflame, grounding me, and as he steps closer I'm very much Charlotte Worth again, standing in the shoes I have, for so long, envied.

"I—" I'm struggling to stay in character, and wish I was still holding my script. "I know you want to make things work, Nick." Graham takes another step toward me, eyes black with something else entirely now. "But I don't think I have it in me anymore. We're…" I gulp as he steps forward again, noticing the few wisps of dark hair curling over the v-neck of his black t-shirt. "We're too different now, and—" I have to look up to meet his dark eyes, having backed into the wall behind me, leaving nowhere else to go. "You just…" I'm breathless, dizzy with the smell of him—laundry detergent, a hint of a cologne, and leather. "You make me *hate* you sometimes, like—"

His eyes are lit with amusement now, and something else that disarms me for a moment, causing my breath to hitch in my throat when I recognize it.

Desire.

"Right now," I whisper.

Graham's lips quirk up, drawing my eyes to that tantalizing silver hoop in the corner. His hands find my waist then, thumbs hooking just under my ribcage, which is rising and falling too quickly with my staggered breaths.

"You hate me…" His voice is deep, the words soft as he leans in, speaking the next part right into my ear. "Right now?"

His warm breath gusts over the lobe, tickling the hair around it, and he hangs there, breathing softly until I can't think straight.

"Um," I whisper, scrambling to come up with the line. My hands find his arms, grip the warm, hard muscle until it's all I can focus on.

"You're supposed to say," Graham says just as softly, drawing back to look into my eyes, but not far enough to allow room for sense to return to me. "Yes."

He's smirking at me, and my cheeks warm, but I clear my throat, deciding that if he's planning to continue this, teasing me, I might as well take full advantage.

I draw my hands up his arms, over the soft fabric of his shirt where it covers his shoulders, dragging my fingers down to rest smack in the middle his chest. It takes some effort to keep my surprise from showing on my face. "Yes," I say, looking right into his eyes.

His smirk is gone, and his eyes have grown impossibly darker.

"You, uh…" Graham gulps, the start of a grin returning. "Are you *sure* you haven't acted before?"

I smile, and surprise myself by asking, "Is that what we're doing?"

Graham chuckles, and I feel the rumble of it beneath my fingers. I want to crack another joke; ask if I was so good, he thought I *had* to have acted before. But his thumbs brush along the bottom of my ribcage before his fingers travel further around my waist, up my back, pressing between the ribs like he's trying to fill the gaps. He ignores my sharp intake of breath as he pulls me forward, my hands locked between us, his fingers finding what they're searching for. "Your heart is racing."

My own fingers spread apart on his firm chest, and I flick my eyes down to them for a moment, as mesmerized by the strong, quick thumping of his heart as I was the second I felt it.

"So is yours," I say, looking up at him again, surprised to find the tenderness that Nick reserves for Olivia swimming in his eyes.

The cord I've imagined between us has done its work, and yet I find myself being drawn closer still, my eyes zeroing in on the source of the beckoning force when I glance down at his mouth. All it would take is the added height of tiptoes, and I could fit my lips to his. The thought sends a thrilling zing up from the pit of my stomach to my chest, like a firework lit from below sent to burst into light in the sky. But neither of us moves. We're at a stand-off, it seems, locked in each other's space, our hands on the other's body in a desperate question that I don't have the answer to.

Graham ducks his head to bring my eyes back to his. "What now?" he whispers, his full bottom lip not meeting the top again, small breaths escaping between them.

He's leaving it up to me. His thumbs continue brushing along my sides, and his heart is still pounding into my palms. In all of five minutes, the elusive and strange Graham Hudson, with the dark, questioning eyes, confusing mood swings, and playful teasing, has made himself very real to me; communicated quite clearly without words what he wants. It's surprising to see the desire in his eyes, feel it in the tender touch of his fingers, in the warm, quick beat I'm holding in my hands, but it's all there. And he's leaving it up to me to claim it.

"What now, Charlotte Worth?" he asks, his voice soft and alluring. He lifts a hand from my waist and brings it to the side of my face, tucking a wayward curl behind my ear before running a knuckle against my heated cheek.

It's my choice. But he shouldn't leave it up to me.

Fear beats back my desire, working its way up and around my heart, reinforcing the sturdy walls I had so long ago put in place.

I curl my fingers away from the warmth of his chest, and bring one hand up to cover the one he placed on my cheek. There's another question in his eyes now, and today, he'll get his answer.

"I should go," I murmur, holding his hand in place a moment longer than I should.

A number of emotions flicker in the darkness—surprise, confusion, hurt, and then understanding. His lips press together, shifting the hoop in the corner a bit, but he gives me a small smile. "Right."

With an affectionate swipe of his thumb across my cheek, he lets his hand fall. The one gripping my waist follows, but not before the door flies open.

"Charlotte, do you—?" Andrea stops dead, her eyes immediately going to Graham's hand as it moves away from my body, noting just how narrow the space between us has become.

Cold air rushes between us as I step quickly back, keeping my gaze glued to Andrea, and hoping that it looks innocent.

But Andi's eyes are moving between the two of us now, and I don't dare look at Graham.

"Do I what?" I ask, surprised by the sound of my own voice—how it's fraught with emotion I can't seem to keep hidden.

Andrea looks at me, a question in her eyes that I won't give her the answer to. "Uh… do you, uh—" She squeezes her eyes shut, opens them again as she shakes her head. "—Have the blocking notes for this scene? I can't remember if I told Max to stand stage right or stage left."

I'm too aware of Graham standing mere feet away, too aware of where his hands had been, the way the skin is burning beneath my clothes now, too aware of what I'd done—or *hadn't* done—when he'd given me the choice, and too aware of the fact that I was already sure I'd made the wrong one.

But with Andrea here—she would've walked in. She would've seen us if I'd let myself kiss him. She would've seen just how much I feel for him written all over my face.

"Yeah," I say quickly, determined to seem calm. "Yeah." I grab my script. "I have it right here. We were done anyway, so I'll just come with you."

I grab her arm and don't look back as I drag her through the door, down the hallway, feeling the heat of Graham's gaze on my back the whole way, feeling the cord tugging me back, too.

"What the—?"

"*Shhh,*" I spit at Andi, her too-loud voice echoing in the short hallway. I keep my grip on her arm tight.

"Charlotte," she scolds, and I can't meet her eye. Can only keep moving, and keep her moving, too.

"Nothing happened," I say, eyeing her as we enter the auditorium again. "So, just drop it, okay?"

Andrea scoffs, but she doesn't look mad. "That didn't *look* like nothing."

Max and Tanya are onstage, completely engrossed in their own conversation, but embarrassment slithers around in my stomach, making me feel like they saw, like they know, too.

"Well, it was," I say, already anticipating Graham walking through here to leave, already wondering whether he's mad, whether he was hurt by my choice, whether he'll meet my eye. I stick Andrea in her seat, and try to calm myself down as I slide into the seat beside her, grabbing the pencil I'd left behind on the table to attempt to ease my frayed nerves.

"Charlotte, what—?" Andrea starts to say.

But she goes silent with one look from me.

"It was nothing," I say, already hating myself for not letting it become more.

## *Year Seventeen*

"What about this woman?" Nana tried to whisper, but she was much louder than she realized.

Trains whooshed through the station, shrill whistles signaling their arrival. One stopped every few minutes, and Charlotte and Nana had taken up their usual game—making up stories for the people who disembarked. Now a senior in high school, Charlotte needed the comfort of her grandmother's presence on that brisk fall day.

It was a good day as far as Nana Rosie was concerned, with minimal forgetfulness, and no disconcerting delusions.

Yet.

Charlotte eyed the woman Nana's gaze had fallen on—she was short and rather thick around the middle, dressed in a drab, wrinkled gray business suit. Her salt-and-pepper hair was pulled back with a large clip, and her eyes looked sunken in beneath her brow bone. But what was most distinctive about her was the number of plastic bags she was struggling to carry. There had to be at least eight, not including her purse and laptop bag.

As the woman lumbered past them, Charlotte leaned toward Nana. "She's on her way home to finish preparations for her oldest son's surprise party. Her husband completely forgot about it, and she had to buy all of the supplies last-minute."

Nana laughed. "Typical man."

Charlotte didn't say more, her mind returning to the prospect of all the schoolwork she'd left unfinished back home. But she'd wanted to get Nana out of the house for a little while, and the train station had been their place for as long as she could remember.

As if Nana was reading her mind, she reached for Charlotte's hand. "I see those wheels turning, Charley Worth…and it doesn't look good."

Charlotte grasped Nana's hand in both of hers, and looked into her cloudy green eyes. "Just school stuff."

Nana nodded. "High school can be stressful."

"It *is* stressful." Charlotte waited as another train whipped past them without stopping. Once the roar of it had passed, Charlotte glanced back at Nana to find her grandmother still looking at her, expectant. Charlotte smiled, happy that Nana hadn't lost track of their conversation.

"On top of all the work I have for my classes, I've got to start applying to colleges, and thinking about what I might want to do for the rest of my life."

Nana gave a wave of her free hand. "You'll be fine. You always are."

"I guess." Charlotte wasn't so sure. "It's just a little intimidating."

"But you always do so well in school." Nana sounded confused. Her eyes were fixed on the tracks, which were littered with leaves, stray papers, soda bottles and empty potato chip bags. Charlotte feared she was veering off-track, losing focus on what they were discussing.

"It's not the work I'm worried about," Charlotte said. "It's just…*everything* about the future." She was being sarcastic, trying to earn a chuckle from Nana and ground her focus once more.

But Nana didn't react, didn't respond, only stared at the tracks, a small, dazed smile on her face.

Charlotte tried again, too afraid that Nana would revert into herself, leaving Charlotte alone at the station, a virtual stranger clinging to her hand.

"I guess…I just don't want things to change. It feels like life is catapulting toward me, and I don't know which way to turn—which direction to choose to get out of the way."

Charlotte didn't say that what frightened her most was the possibility of Nana Rosie not being there. Or worse, that she *would* be there, and wouldn't know the difference.

Mr. and Mrs. Worth may as well have been separated. They never spoke to each other anymore, and Charlotte wasn't sure what that would mean for them, or for her. If she went away to college, she could remove herself from the situation in a year's time. But there was still Nana, who had always been there in her corner with a warm smile and loving word.

How could Charlotte leave her?

She just wanted things to go back to the way they were before Nana was sick. While her parents had never seemed to be in love with each other, they were at least able to communicate without it turning into a fight. And Nana was the foundation of their home.

Now, with the foundation falling apart, brick by brick, before their eyes, Charlotte knew things wouldn't last much longer. More change thrust upon her in the form of college was something she wanted to avoid completely.

"Charley Worth," Nana said over a sigh, startling Charlotte from her own thoughts. She whipped her head around to find those green eyes clear and wide. "When did you get to be so negative?"

Charlotte let out a breath, ready to take a gentle scolding if it meant that Nana was still present.

Nana's silver curls fluttered away from her cheeks with the wind. "Things are a little overwhelming at the moment, but for all *good* reasons. No matter what, life will happen. It doesn't speed up, or slow down, or stop for anyone. As long as you're breathing, you have it. And it's always yours to make of it what you will."

Charlotte squeezed Nana's bony hand even tighter, as if the steady pressure would keep her lucid, here in this moment with her granddaughter, indefinitely.

"Change is what makes this life such a gift." Nana reached up and cupped Charlotte's cheek. "It's unavoidable,

Charley. No use trying to hide from it. But I discovered the secret to it a long time ago. Want to hear it?"

Charlotte nodded, feeling like a small girl again, captivated by her grandmother's soothing words.

"You can't let change *happen* to you. You've got to invite it into your life, walk right up to it, and say hello." Nana smiled.

Charlotte considered Nana's words as another train screeched to a stop. People flooded through the open doors onto the platform, and Charlotte searched the faces, looking for one of particular interest, her hand still tucked between Nana's.

"My Charley," Nana murmured, a smile on her lips. "The world's at the tips of your toes."

# *Chapter Sixteen*

"Tech" week isn't what I expected it to be. Between discussing costumes, set changes between scenes, lighting, and who would bring in what props and when, we had full run-throughs of the play where we paid attention to the finer details we'd otherwise overlooked. Like Tanya facing *this* way instead of *that* way so that the light hit her just right, and Amanda shouldn't *throw* the papers, but *toss* them so that they fell in some semblance of neatness to the floor. We had to adjust the placement of a chair to accommodate Max's height so that he wouldn't be too close to the wall and hit it by accident. And Graham, well… I tried not to focus too much on him.

Andrea had tried asking me what had happened between us in the dressing room, but I'd given her variations of the same answer each time: *Nothing. We were rehearsing. Got a little too caught up in the moment. She's lucky she has a stage manager who's willing to go the extra mile, and blah, blah, blah.* Because I couldn't admit to her—out loud—what had really happened. The way my feelings for Graham had changed; intensified.

Thankfully, she'd let it go after several dozen attempts. And after many denials, she also finally picked a sketch to go on the cover of the program, one I wouldn't have expected her to like. It wasn't flashy or bold—it was subtle in black and white, with the two main characters in shadow against a bare white background, their backs to each other, and the wall in between them. I'd modeled the shadowed drawings from life, using Graham and Amanda's profiles to create their silhouettes. Andrea stared at it for a full minute before she said, breathless, "It's perfect."

She regained her full voice to tell me that I'd be in charge of designing and printing out the hundreds of programs we'd need for three shows.

But I don't mind the busy work, just like I didn't mind picking up food to make sure Andrea was eating, or running out mid-rehearsal for duct tape to cover all the wires for Andrea's computer, which she'd be using to control all of the music and sound effects for each show. All of it has been a helpful distraction, and I managed to avoid talking with Graham for almost the entire week because of it.

It isn't that I don't *want* to talk to him. In fact, that's all I've found myself wanting to do, but after what happened between us—or didn't happen—I'm just not sure how to go about it. The whole thing was embarrassing. It's like we both admitted to something, like we were standing at the brink of a steep cliff, daring each other to jump. With him holding me, dark eyes gazing into mine like he could see and understand, I *wanted* to feel the wind whip around me, cradle me in its palm all the way down to a new height, a new perspective. But I was too afraid of the fall, what I might find at the bottom—jagged rocks, or a tumultuous current. So, even with Graham's warm chest rising and falling beneath my hands, his fingers spread open on my waist, and the promise in his soft, dark eyes…I couldn't do it, couldn't step over the edge into nothingness.

More than my own embarrassment, I'm afraid I hurt Graham when I pulled away from him. He hasn't really tried to speak to me since, though I did catch his eye more than once. I smiled each time, sure now that I want him more than ever, and still completely unsure what to do about it.

Busy work seemed like the best way to avoid all of it.

I'm still folding programs when rehearsal ends. It's the last one before opening day tomorrow night, and aside from a few more props to bring in, and the damn programs, we're ready. Andrea practically flew out of the building after a rushed pep talk, and an agitated delivery of a list of things she still needed to get done. The last, echoing sounds of the rest of the cast diminish as the auditorium doors click shut behind them, and the back of my neck prickles with the abrupt appearance of the enveloping silence.

I don't turn as the footsteps grow closer, as the jangling of his keychain rings out through the theater—he didn't leave with the rest of them—only flick my eyes sideways as his beat-up black sneakers slide over the edge of the stage, his legs in faded black jeans settling a respectable distance from mine. There's a moment of booming silence between us, where all I can hear over the crinkle of the paper in my hands is the rush of blood in my ears. Then he reaches between us, grabbing a sheet of paper to fold.

"To answer your question," he says, sliding the paper between his fingers for a neat, crisp fold. "Yes."

I place a newly folded program beside me on the growing stack, each with the title of the play, *What Was Lost,* and my design, face up.

"My question?" I glance sideways again. He's diligently folding another one, bringing each corner to its match, and sliding his fingers over the newly created crease.

"About my nickname."

A thrill shoots through me, and a smile tugs at my lips as I turn my head to fully look at him. "Really? Graham Cracker?"

He meets my gaze with a half-smile. "You didn't actually think you were the first person to come up with it, did you?"

I stifle a laugh, but there's no controlling my smile. "Why are you telling me this?"

Graham sighs, his smile dimming as he faces forward, out into the auditorium. "Billy Ludlow," he says, choosing to ignore my question. "He's the one who figured it out when we were in the second grade. He had the whole class chanting "Graham Cracker" at me by the next day. And it followed me all the way up to high school." He looks at me again. "I was a pretty easy target, not just because of the name."

I can picture it as he describes it to me—a small, scrawny boy with a head of dark brown curls that he refused to cut, glasses with fingerprints all over the lenses, and a distinct lisp. I could see him fumble with the basketball during gym, fall onto his knees during tag at recess, and smile when he got another A on an exam. He wanted to be more like them—play with them, laugh with them, make fun of the teachers with them—but they had the most fun when they were taking aim at him.

"The worst was probably in sixth grade," Graham continues, seeing the world more clearly than I possibly could. "We went to see a play at the local high school. It was the first play I'd ever seen, actually. *Carousel*...the musical?" He looks to me for recognition, but I just shrug. "Anyway...that was the day I decided to try acting. I was so into it, into the characters and their relationships, and the people who played them so well, that I didn't notice the other kids making fun of me for once."

He eyes me with a wry grin. "Until we got on the bus, anyway. This kid, Dominic, leaned over the back of my seat, and goes, 'Hey Graham Cracker, you liked that play, huh?' And me...I was just happy someone was *talking* to me. So I went on and on about how much I enjoyed it before he goes, 'What's that in your hair?'"

I gasp. "No..."

He smiles again. "Gum. A huge wad of it. My mom couldn't get it out without leaving a huge bald spot right on the back of my head. I ended up shaving it all off." He pauses, chuckling a bit. "I don't know why I just told you all of that."

I don't really know why he did, either. "I'm glad you did," I say, relishing the relief in knowing he didn't hate me for what happened. "And I'm glad the curls grew back." In a bold move, I reach out and tug one of them, the silky strands bouncing back into place when I let go.

"Yeah," Graham says with a laugh, reaching up to tousle them himself. "I am, too."

"And I'm sorry," I say before I lose my nerve. "No wonder you seemed so angry that day. Leave it to me to dredge up horrible memories with my big mouth."

He chuckles and brushes his fingers along my arm for just a moment—a moment that ends far too soon. "Don't worry about it. I'm sorry I overreacted. It just took me by surprise. I try not to think about that stuff anymore, so you'd think it wouldn't affect me so much. Guess that's not the case. It totally wasn't your fault."

I nod in response, giving him a weak smile, embarrassed and annoyed with myself for letting my mind go uncensored yet again.

"So, any assholes when you were a kid?" Graham resumes folding, so I take up another program as well. "Anyone call you Charles?"

I laugh. "Plenty. But none of them ever went there."

"No? Did they go for Charley instead?" he asks, chuckling now himself.

And I suddenly understand why he got so upset, why he reacted so strongly. Hearing the nickname—*her* nickname—for me now, falling from his lips…my whole body tenses, and her voice saying it resounds in my head.

"No." The word is cold, hard, unforgiving, and Graham catches it. I see him look up out of the corner of my eye, his hands frozen, suspended above his lap clutching a nearly folded piece of paper. I try to laugh, but even that sounds stiff. "Nothing as bad as all *that*."

I hear the implication in my response with a stab of self-hatred, but it makes me forget my own pain for the moment. Eyes wide, afraid I've offended him again, I quickly glance over to find him focused on the program, expression mostly blank. "At least…not that I know of. I'm sure the other kids had *lots* to say about me."

"Why?" he asks, not sounding angry, as I feared, but curious.

I sigh. "Well, I mostly kept to myself. I played by myself on the playground, didn't talk to anyone but the teacher in class…I raised my hand a lot to answer questions. And just generally preferred to be alone, I guess." I set a newly folded program down. "They definitely thought I was weird, if nothing else."

Graham chuckles again. "Even then."

When he doesn't continue, I look over to find him grinning. "Even then, what?"

Graham meets my gaze, his smile widening. "You're just—you're unapologetically *you*, Charlotte. *All* the time. It's like…" He thinks for a moment, tongue prodding his lip ring. "It's like, you've known who you are all along. And you're not going to be sorry for it."

Incredulous, and slightly defensive, I scramble for a moment. "Well…why should I apologize? I don't owe anyone anything."

"See? *That.*" He shakes his head, still amused. "You're doing it now."

I don't know whether to be offended or flattered, but either way, I remain defensive, accusing. "Well…you're unapologetic, too. Jesus, Graham…you're like a rock. Totally un-budgeable. It took you this long just to apologize to me about the Graham Cracker thing."

Graham laughs. "That's cause that kind of self-assurance doesn't come easy to me. I had to *learn* how to accept myself—that I *shouldn't* apologize, or feel guilty for who I am. No one should. But I didn't know that for a long time. So, when I met you…well, you sort of brought out the insecure side of me."

I'm certainly not flattered now, and I'm not feeling defensive either. Just guilty.

"Acting was something I loved because it allowed me to be someone else—not have to live in my own head for a while. I didn't have to be the person everyone made fun of. Without it, I didn't know how to just *own* who I was. Who I *am*. I still struggle with it. But you…" His eyes stay on mine. "You seem to have known all along. You make it seem so easy."

He picks up another sheet of paper, then gives me a crooked smile. "It scares the hell out of me."

I'm not alone, then. He scares the hell out of me, too. But that's the only comfort I can take from all that he's just said. He was brave enough to be honest with me, admit and own his feelings—the very thing he's praising me for. But it's quickly becoming clear to me that he's wrong, and that my misguided honesty is nothing compared to his well-meaning, genuine, honest admission. Unapologetic I may be, but brave I certainly am not.

"Oh…" is all I can manage in response. My mouth is dry, my palms sweaty as I reach for something, *anything* better to reply with, but Graham doesn't leave me hanging for too long.

"I don't mean it in a bad way," he says. "You scare me in a *good* way."

After my pointed look, he amends, "Okay, that sounded bad…"

I laugh, reaching over without thinking about it. "No, I get it. I think." His forearm is warm beneath my fingers, and the muscles contract before I pull away. His dark eyes hold the same desire I saw the other day.

"So," I say, trying to shake off my own wanting. "You got that much in just a few weeks, huh?"

Graham shrugs. "I'm an actor. It's my job to pay attention to people, notice their characteristics and little quirks, then try to emulate them." He shifts his head slightly, as if taking me in from another angle might help his assessment. "Like, for example, you wrinkle your nose to nudge your glasses up when they're sliding down."

Without thought, I wrinkle my nose, my glasses hitching up just that bit, and I'm aware of their grip behind my ears. I blush, just as embarrassed by this little quirk as I am excited that he's noticed.

"And you doodle in your script almost constantly," Graham says, smiling a little. "Especially when there's a break in the action, but even when we're running through a scene."

My cheeks are full-on burning now. "Hey. It was my job to come up with this." I hold up a folded program, and his eyes flick to the cover. "I needed as much time and inspiration as I could get."

Graham holds up his hands in defense. "I'm not saying it wasn't worth it. The cover is awesome."

"Thank you," I say, placated as I eye the finished creation myself.

"But that couldn't *always* be what you were drawing. A mind like yours?" he says. "It has to be creating constantly. You don't know how not to."

I couldn't respond even if I knew what to say. I'm too stunned by how much he's picked up on, how well he seems to get me.

"And you do this little lip quirk thing." He twists his lips to the side. "When you're putting all of your attention into something, like when you're drawing, or when we're trying to figure out blocking, or when you're trying to think of something to say." His dark eyes skim down to my lips, and his own twitch in a smile. "Like right now."

Feeling that my lips have, in fact, moved of their own volition, I close my eyes, breathing a laugh. "Okay," I say, my cheeks burning even more now. "You really *did* pick up on a lot."

Graham smiles, looking down at his fingers as he taps the stained wood floor of the stage between us. "I may have paid a *little* more attention to a certain someone than was completely necessary." His eyes flick back up to me, and a crooked grin lifts his lip ring. "And by 'certain someone', I mean you."

My heart stutters before regrouping, pounding a quicker rhythm against my ribcage.

We're living in that moment again, breathing each other's air, the dare fresh between us. But I feel closer to him somehow, and I know that if he were to move towards me again, just the few inches more, held me as he did before, beckoned me to him again, I would follow.

But he doesn't.

"Charlotte," he says after several moments, pulling me from my thoughts, away from my nerves.

"Yeah?"

"Would you…would you want to go out some time?"

My heart pounds so hard it hurts.

"After the play, obviously. I think we're both a little too stressed to think about it now."

My chest is burning.

“Charlotte,” he says again, his voice soft. One of his hands comes up, and his eyes lock on mine in question before he brushes the backs of his fingers along my heated cheekbone. I lean into his fingers before I can think too much about it, and his hand turns so that his palm cups my cheek. He’s still looking at me, and he smiles, nervous when he says, “It’s not a marriage proposal, you know. Just dinner. Or a movie. Or dinner *and* a movie if we’re feeling ambitious. But…if that’s too much, coffee works, too. No pressure.”

I was actually just too stunned to answer. But I still don’t know what to say. I’m still not sure what to make of this whole situation.

He leans closer, close enough that I could reach up and touch my fingers to his stubbly chin if I were brave. My breath catches in my throat, and he stops, his eyes falling to my open mouth, then to my neck, where I’m sure he can see the frantic throbbing of my pulse. A moment later, his long lashes lift, his dark eyes light enough that I can just distinguish the deep black of the pupil from the dark brown of the iris.

He smiles again, but this smile holds some disappointment. I’m still trying to understand how and when I became capable of putting it there.

“Did you know,” he murmurs, his eyes shifting quickly while looking into mine, “that your eyes change color?”

I nod, completely breathless.

“They’re green in this light.” He’s studying them like he needs to remember them; commit their hue to memory. “With little flecks of gold.”

Graham glances down at my mouth then, pressing his lips together in a way that makes me want to yank him to me by the hair. But his hand falls from my cheek, and he pulls away completely.

“Sorry,” he mutters, his fists clenching in his lap as he faces the auditorium again.

I don’t want him to apologize. I don’t want him to think I don’t like him. But the fear is lodged in my throat, forcing the words that want to come up straight back down where they came from. And looking at him—I’m sure I can see that little boy again, the one with the lisp and the full head of curls, insecure and desperate for a friend, left disappointed yet again.

"Don't be." My voice is soft, too soft to be convincing, so I reach out and touch his arm, feeling the warm muscle flex in response to the firm press of my hand.

Graham's eyes snap to the point of contact, then to the few programs left to be folded, separating us, before they reach me.

"Don't apologize," I say, needing him to understand that I want him, too. I just can't form those words, can't let the want fall from my lips. He's tried to guide me to the edge, holding my hand the whole way, but what he doesn't realize yet is that I won't jump. I *can't*.

"We should finish these," is what I can say aloud, the fear evident in my whisper. I want to tell him that he's got to force me. That I'll push back. I'll kick, and scream, and punch, and hit and fight him the whole way to the brink. He has to fight harder. But I can't say that either. What I can say is, "But…ask me again."

Graham meets my eye.

So I say it once more.

"Another time. Ask me again."

## *Year Eighteen*

Thirty-four days.

Mr. Worth was torn between thinking she had waited too long, and that she hadn't waited nearly long enough.

It had been thirty-four days since his wife walked out on him and their daughter. Thirty-four days that had seemed an impossibly long time not to see or hear from her, and entirely too short a time once she finally got in touch.

Charlotte remained silent at dinner when he told her, staring at the plate of food in front of her, lips pursed while she prodded her sesame chicken with a fork. Nana Rosie continued dishing the Chinese takeout onto her plate, not acknowledging her son's words.

"She asked how you are…"

Charlotte still didn't answer. She was chewing slowly, as if she was considering whether or not to spit the food back out.

"And she said to—"

"Why'd you even answer the phone?" Charlotte finally looked at him, her brow furrowed, hazel eyes raging with all the intensity of a storm.

He'd asked himself the same question. The truth was, he almost hadn't picked up when he saw her number on the caller I.D. He didn't owe her anything, and wondered what she could possibly have to say to him at this point; how she could justify leaving with nothing left behind but a pitiful note saying no more than that she'd decided to go. He let it ring five times before he answered, each ring a shrill reminder of why he should pick up.

That reason was now staring at him, eyes filled with anger and hurt, freckled cheeks nearly as red as her wild curls.

"You should have left her hanging the way she left us," Charlotte continued, stabbing a piece of chicken. "Radio silence."

"She's still your mother, Charlotte."

"And what kind of mother leaves her family the way she left hers?" Charlotte's voice had risen several octaves, her cheeks stained an even deeper pink. "No mother I want."

"Lindsay *left*?" Nana exclaimed then, eyes wide with shock.

Charlotte winced and stared down at her food, her anger seeming to deflate with each heavy breath she took. Mr. Worth looked into his mother's eyes, still finding himself surprised when she displayed such forgetfulness. He reached a hand over and gripped her shaky one, feeling his chest ache as he admitted to himself once more, "Yeah, Mom. She left."

"But…" Nana's eyes swiveled quickly back and forth behind her glasses. "But *why*?"

Mr. Worth hesitated, then cleared his throat. "I don't know."

But he did know. It had been silent between them for months, the only cause for communication being Nana Rosie, and less often towards the end, their independent daughter. Charlotte was old enough to take care of herself for the most part, and it was like the common thread between them had thinned too much to be sustained. It snapped so easily the day Lindsay left. He knew her leaving hadn't come from out of nowhere, but he also knew that he should have done more to prevent it, or at least prevent it from happening in the way that it did. Maybe he deserved to be abandoned, but their daughter sure as hell didn't.

After a lengthy pause, during which time Nana returned to her meal, the new information perhaps already lost, Mr.

Worth refocused on Charlotte, whose eyes were again fixed on her plate.

"Charlotte," he said softly, hoping she'd look up. She didn't. "Charlotte, your mother mentioned wanting to see you."

He didn't think it was the best idea. He knew Charlotte was angry, too angry to even consider it. But Lindsay had begged him to at least ask, reminding him of the fact that she was still Charlotte's mother, and she deserved the chance to see her daughter and explain.

Charlotte, whose blazing stare had been extinguished by Nana Rosie's interruption, snapped her head up to glare at her father once more. "Is she out of her mind? What makes her think I'd *ever* want to see her again?"

"She just wants the chance to explain…"

"*Explain*…right. She left us to go live with some stuck-up, stuffy artist, who was totally fine with dating a married woman and destroying a family, without a word of explanation—save for a note with a half-assed apology taped to your bathroom mirror." Charlotte smiled, but it was clear she found no amusement in her assessment. "Have I missed anything? What else is there to explain, *damn* it?"

"Language, Charley," Nana scolded before taking another bite of broccoli.

Charlotte sighed, eyes softening at the edges with a different kind of pain. "Sorry, Nana."

The quiet hung among them for several moments, awkward and tenuous. Mr. Worth couldn't blame Charlotte, or begrudge her anger. No matter what he said, no matter how he tried, he couldn't change the fact that her mother had left her, or the fact that his own shortcomings had been the cause. Nothing he did now could make this easier for her. But he knew that things had to get worse before they could get better; disinfecting the wound could sometimes be worse than actually getting hurt. But it had to be done before it scabbed over, trapping the infection underneath. And he knew that Charlotte was old enough to make that decision for herself, when she felt ready.

"Look, kiddo," Mr. Worth sighed. "I'm not going to tell you what to do. You're perfectly capable of making your own decisions. But I will say that your mother loves you, and—"

"*Loves* me?" Charlotte scoffed. "Is *that* why she left?"

Mr. Worth felt a stab of pain, one that surely matched the intensity of the hurt that flashed in his daughter's eyes; hurt he could hear so clearly beneath the stinging bite of her words. He wished with all his might that he could draw it all away from her, let it pummel him instead.

He reached a hand over, knowing it wasn't enough. "And I know that you love her, too." Charlotte gave a bitter laugh despite the tears in her eyes. "If you didn't, this wouldn't be so hard."

It was quiet for a moment, and Charlotte sniffled, no tears finding their way down her cheeks. "If she loved me, she wouldn't have left. Saying she loves me now, now that she's gone…" She bit her lip, and shook her head. "I can count on one hand the number of times I've heard her say it in eighteen years. Saying it now is a complete contradiction, and I don't believe her at all."

She sat back then, crossing her arms tightly over her chest.

Clearly, thirty-four days had proved to be too short a time for her.

"Charlotte," Mr. Worth said again, leaning towards her. "I know I won't change your mind tonight, but…"

Charlotte flicked her eyes up to him, her brow still furrowed. Encouraged, Mr. Worth continued, "People are made of up contradictions. Look at me." He held his hands up as if to display himself to her. "The writer who couldn't find the words to save his marriage. Nana—" he gestured to his mother on his right, "—is the strongest-minded person I know, and she's being conquered by her own mind."

He looked at his daughter with her mane of red curls, round hazel eyes, flushed cheeks and pursed lips, and smiled fondly. "And you, Charlotte. My favorite girl with the big heart—afraid of love."

Charlotte sucked in a breath, but her father went on. "We're all messed up, and we all contradict ourselves. But we're all just trying to figure out life, you know?"

Charlotte stared down at her plate. Mr. Worth hoped he was getting through.

"Maybe the best is yet to come from this. I hope so, anyway," he said, giving her a rueful smile. "Things'll get better, kiddo. You just have to let them."

After a few more moments, Charlotte pushed her chair back and finally met his eye again. "It was a valiant effort, Dad." She grabbed her dish, still half-full. "I'll be in my room finishing up some homework."

Dismayed, Mr. Worth nodded, feeling a little pathetic for trying. He watched Charlotte walk out of the room, seeing the little girl who ran everywhere and slid through doorways in her socks, as the red of her hair disappeared into the kitchen.

"That was good advice, Benny," Nana said. Mr. Worth had almost forgotten his mother was still there.

He smiled a little. "I learned from the best."

Nana's eyes sparkled when she asked in earnest. "Who?"

Mr. Worth slumped in even more disappointment. "*You*, Mom."

"Oh." Nana chuckled, and brushed away his compliment with a wave of her hand. "Thank you, Ben."

He tried to smile again, but it was less than half-hearted. Hers was the saddest contradiction, and it made him sick to see the deterioration of such a strong, colorful mind.

It wasn't fair—any of it. And he had to remind himself of the truth of his words to Charlotte. There was a reason writers didn't focus on the mundane goings-on and routine of life. The contradictions were the source of joy, sadness, anger, surprise, and love, all from which life derived its confused, muddled, elusive meaning.

He just hoped the joy and love would make their appearances soon.

## *Chapter Seventeen*

"God, I'm freaking out." Tanya shakes out her hands as she surveys her appearance in the dressing room mirror. "I almost forgot how nerve-wracking this is. I might throw up."

"Please don't," I say from my seat on the floor beneath her. I remove another safety pin from between my lips and stick it through the folded hem of her pant leg. "Stand up straight."

"Sorry," she says, shuffling a little in her heels with a sigh. "I don't know why I'm so nervous. It's not like I haven't done this before."

I glance around the small room. In one corner, Max is muttering to himself, pacing back and forth in his khakis and plain blue button-down shirt. Amanda is sitting in front of a mirror, her headphones in her ears as she applies her makeup. Jane is next to her, studying her highlighted script and murmuring the words softly to herself. Lou is hunkered down in the far corner, headphones in his ears, eyes closed, and Cam and Mark are talking quietly to each other while Cam stretches on the floor.

Graham hasn't said a word to me today. He arrived in silence, and has been quiet ever since. I look at him now, sitting on the loveseat, head tilted back against the top of the couch, his dark curls poking out from beneath the towel covering his face, and wonder if its because of the way we left off yesterday—an awkward silence while we folded the rest of the programs, peppered with small talk about the play, and the other actors, followed by an even more awkward goodbye. He stuffed his hands into his pockets when I closed and locked the door, smiled, and when it felt like he was waiting for me to say or do something, I thanked him for his help and spun on my heel, leaving him there as I sped down the sidewalk.

He hasn't really looked at me today either. Of course, rather than chalk it up to his own nerves about opening night, I decide he must hate me for the way I've been treating him.

I return my attention to the hem of Tanya's pants when she shifts again, tugging the fabric away from me.

"Stay still," I say.

"Sorry," she says, sighing as she crosses her arms, then lets them fall to her sides. Then her pants move to hug her legs as she looks down at what I'm doing, and I try not to let my frustration show.

"You know…" I glance up at her. "It's good to be nervous. Being nervous means you care. And if you care, the audience will care."

"I guess." Tanya's still studying her reflection, but her fidgeting slows for the moment, and I hope my words—Nana's words—still hold some comfort.

"It's good that you're nervous," she had said when I finished practicing my presentation for Science class in her living room. "It means you care. And if you care, I have no doubt that your classmates will care, too. They don't want to see you fail."

I hadn't been able to help my smirk, then. "I think you're overestimating my classmates."

"Warm-ups in five, guys," Andrea announces, ripping me from the memory as she speed-walks around the small, already cramped space, inspecting the props and each actor. I don't think I've ever seen her so frazzled, so unhinged. She's on an all-out rampage, adjusting Mark's tie more roughly than necessary, barking for Amanda to straighten the back of her hair a bit more, and then she fixes her wild-eyed glare on Graham.

"Graham," she barks. He barely moves in response, leading me to believe he might've dozed off, so she yanks the towel away from his face. He blinks up at her, confirming my suspicion. "Why aren't you dressed? Get a move on!"

Graham stands slowly despite Andrea's frantic insistence, and she tosses the towel onto the couch beside him before turning, her eyes scanning the room for anything else that might need addressing. Graham's expression remains unreadable.

"Okay." She claps three times, rallying her team for a reason this time. "If you're ready, come with me. Less than an hour till curtain, people!" Andrea's out the door before she's finished her thought, with most of the cast following close behind.

In the now quiet room, there's a distinct sound of a buckle, then something—clothes, pooling in a quiet heap on the floor. Locking my eyes on Tanya's pant leg—only two more pins—I try not to think about the state of Graham's undress as the shuffling sounds of his movement fill the room.

"Seriously, Graham?" Tanya cries, and she's holding a hand up between him and her eyes when I glance up at her. "There's a bathroom right outside."

"Get used to it." It sounds like he's smiling. "You're all going to be seeing a lot of me this weekend."

My already flushed cheeks burn more at the mere suggestion.

"You're all set," I say loudly, kneeling back and sucking my finger where I pricked myself with that last one. I keep my stare fixed on Tanya's pants, hoping to change the subject before I implode.

"You're the best! These are perfect." Tanya moves around a little, watching as the hem stays right where I've pinned it. "Alright, well, here goes nothing. Meet you guys outside."

And she's gone. Leaving me alone with a half-naked Graham.

Busying myself with the safety pin clean-up does nothing to help my all-too vivid imagination. I've seen Graham shirtless too many times to not know exactly what he might look like now, but never in a setting where it was just the two of us. It takes all of my willpower just to keep my eyes on my hands.

"Hey, wait, could I get one of those?" Graham says, voice soft.

He has just finished buttoning up his white shirt when I look over. His dark gray pants are in place and zipped, much to my simultaneous relief and dismay.

It takes me a moment to comprehend what he's referring to. "Oh, uh, yeah. Sure."

Walking the few steps over to him makes my heart pound like I've just completed a triathlon in record timing, but I hand him a pin. His fingers brush over mine as he thanks me, and I step back, glancing around the room for anything to do with myself.

But when my eyes land on Graham again, he's fumbling left-handed with the pin and his shirt sleeve. "Here…" I move toward him. "Let me do it."

The button on his sleeve has fallen off, and between wondering how that could have happened already, and trying to keep my cheeks from going completely red, I focus on steadying my hands enough to pin the cuff together. Graham stays perfectly still, his arm held aloft for me to perform the task, and I'm sure I can feel his eyes on my face while I clumsily manage to close the pin. For a second, I consider bringing up these past few days—these past few weeks. Considering the fact that he's been so honest—that he's put himself out there twice now only to receive rejection in return—I feel the need to explain myself, even though I still don't know what to say. I didn't want to hurt him, I didn't expect things to even reach this point, but now that they have, I want him to know—

What?

I still don't know.

But I finish pinning his sleeve anyway, and it feels like the moment for explanations has long passed. Not to mention, we wouldn't have time for all the ways I need to explain myself anyway.

"There," I say, moving away before meeting his eye.

"Thank you," he says from behind me, and I swear I can hear amusement in his voice.

"No problem." To try and calm myself down, I start tidying the counter, where things are already as tidy as they can get. "So, are you excited?"

He lets out a long breath. "If, by excited, you mean so nervous I feel like I'm going to puke, yes."

I can't help but laugh and turn around to face him. "You don't really seem nervous."

"Yeah, well…" He wraps a tie around his neck and begins tying it. "*My* nervous doesn't usually translate into chattering or pacing or anything. It's going into myself. Staying quiet. Internalizing. Probably not the healthiest route."

Either he doesn't know how to tie a tie, or he's so nervous he can't get his fingers to work, because he fumbles and twists the fabric in too many ways that aren't getting him anywhere.

Without thinking about it, I move forward again, grabbing the ends of the dark blue tie, and his hands fall. It's only when I'm right there in front of him, feeling the warmth of his skin reach out and touch my fingers, his cool breath gust across my hands, that my own nerves seem to fire off everywhere all at once.

We're quiet for a few moments as I wrap the fabric around itself in a knot, and I try my best to keep my hands steady. He tilts his chin down to watch me work, and his skin is scratchy on my knuckles. "I also never dress like this."

"Really? I couldn't tell." I smile up at him, stomach fluttering when he returns the smirk. "Head up," I say, taking too much joy in the fact that he sighs, but lifts his chin anyway.

For a brief moment, all I can see is the reflection of my father and me standing side-by-side in his bedroom mirror, both of us tying ties around our necks. He taught me how when I was little because I insisted on 'dressing like Daddy' and wouldn't accept that girls didn't usually wear ties, because it was a 'stupid rule'.

But then I find the small birth mark in the hollow of Graham's throat, usually hidden by a shadow of stubble—stubble that's already appearing again after he shaved this morning per Andrea's request. His Adam's apple is more pronounced than my father's, and I stare, mesmerized by its movement when he swallows.

I push the knot up, my focus not on the tie at all anymore, but I don't let my hands fall away. Instead, they slide slowly down the thin bit of fabric, skimming his chest just enough to feel the dips of it, and his quickening breaths cause it to rise to meet my fingers, which stop just over his heart.

It might just be beating faster than my own.

Glancing up, I only have a second to find the small hole at the corner of his lip where the ring should be, and silently curse Andrea for making him lose that, too. Then I meet his gaze, and my cheeks warm to see the darkness in his eyes again, the fringe of long lashes hovering low as he stares right into mine. His mouth opens a bit, his pink lips allowing a quick, shaky breath to escape between them. And without a word, a sound, a conscious thought, I lean forward and up like a flower unfurling its petals toward the sun, touching my mouth to his with a quiet sigh of relief.

It's the merest brush of lips on lips, but the whisper of a touch makes me want more. Graham's mouth is still beneath mine for a moment, and his sharp intake of breath slides cool between us before I press further, urging him to respond. His hands find the small of my back, pulling me closer still, and mine lay flat on his chest, the strong beat of his heart pounding hot beneath my fingers.

It's the same as all the others, but also profoundly different. I may have taken control as I always do, but I've never relinquished it this quickly. Never trusted that the other person would understand, but somehow, I trust that he does. Never wanted to allow myself to feel this much for someone, but that's all I can do with him. Never wanted to allow myself to think ahead because I was always too busy planning the end, but not with him.

Because I don't want it to end.

His hands grow more insistent, their pressure increasing as they slide up my back, holding me as close as our bodies will allow. Mine clutch at his shirt, his collar, tugging him to me and holding him there. His mouth opens, and I wrap my arms around his neck, finally giving in to what we've both wanted—what I've *always* wanted but never had the courage to let myself have.

Everything is warm, and everything wants him. So, this time, I let myself have him.

"*Graham!*"

The voice startles me out of my hazy bliss, and I stumble back on my heels, Graham's arms the only thing holding me steady.

"Graham! Hurry up!" It's Andrea, sounding angry and anxious all at once.

"Yeah," Graham says, voice cracking. "Yeah, I'm coming!"

Anyone could've walked in. Anyone could've seen.

I'm backing up at the mere thought of what Andrea would say, how she would chew me out for making out with her lead an hour before showtime. How it would confirm for her everything that she already thought she knew. But Graham's hand on my arm stops me, pulls me back. He fits his hands around my waist, hugging the bottom of my ribcage, and holds me in place. His mouth is red, his lips swollen, and I stare at them, the tingling of my own mouth telling me mine probably look the same.

We're panting. My heart hasn't slowed at all, but neither of us speaks. He releases my waist, apparently sure that I won't go anywhere, and brings his hands to either side of my face, swiping his thumbs over my cheeks before leaning in again, his eyes on mine until the very last moment.

It's gentle, tender, not as frantic as the first, and he sucks a bit on my bottom lip as he pulls away, setting my already sensitive mouth tingling like crazy.

I can't open my eyes right away, and I feel another soft kiss at the corner of my lips—a promise of more.

"Wait for me after," he whispers, his breath warm on my ear.

When I don't answer, I feel his fingers on my chin, nudging it up, and I know what he wants. I open my eyes.

His are entirely depthless. "Will you?" he asks, his voice still soft—softer than I've ever heard it. "Please."

Only closing my mouth to swallow makes me realize I'd even had it open. "Yes," I breathe, and his hand tightens on my chin, pulling me closer so that he can press another dizzying kiss to my mouth before he pulls away entirely.

But I still feel him, even as cold air swirls around me, filling the absence he leaves behind, even as the room goes completely quiet—so quiet I can hear the dull thudding of my pulse in my ears—especially when I bring my fingers to my mouth, and the warmth in my chest spreads out, out, out, all the way to my fingers, and all the way down to my toes.

I still feel him.

## *Year Eighteen (and a half)*

"I'm not going in there," Nana insisted, clutching her purse in her lap in the backseat of the car.

Charlotte stood behind her father, watching as he tried to cajole his mother from the car, and scrambled for a way around this, running through all of the possibilities they'd already ruled out, hoping one of them might work now.

The situation had worsened, though, and the truth was, Nana wouldn't get better. The prospect of her getting hurt had become all too real for Charlotte. She could still smell the sharp, pungent odor of gasoline that had wrapped her in a warm embrace upon entering the house. She still remembered the walk into the kitchen, like wading through waves of light-headed humidity, a ringing sense of alarm her only clarity through the thick haze. And Nana, slumped back on the couch in a fitful doze, her mouth hanging open to allow a dribble of saliva to run down her chin, and long, slow breaths of the polluted air to pass her lips—the only indication that she was still alive.

That was when Charlotte and her father decided that Nana couldn't be alone all day, but with neither of them in the position to dedicate the time to take care of her—Mr. Worth wouldn't let Charlotte take time off from school, and had to work himself to support the three of them—a home seemed to be their only viable option.

But that didn't mean Charlotte liked it.

Nana had agreed to it at first, saying she understood and didn't want to burden them. But time had a way of shifting emotions, changing opinions, and for Nana especially, it was a thief as well as a manipulator.

Nana's voice was rising, anger and a frantic urgency making themselves known through her stubbornness. Charlotte felt sick.

"Dad," she called. He didn't hear her. "*Dad,*" she said again, tapping him on the shoulder to finally get his attention.

When he turned, Charlotte noted the crease between his brows, deep with concern, the lines beside his mouth, framing his frown, and she stepped toward him.

"Let me try," she said under her breath, and moved in front of him without waiting for a reply. "Nana," she spoke softly.

Nana Rosie's eyes went wide with hope. "Charley?"

They were honey-brown and familiar, but with a vacant glassiness. Charlotte's chest tightened. "Yep. It's me."

"Oh, thank God you're here," she exclaimed, her shoulders settling back against the seat in relief.

"Of course I'm here." Charlotte wished she, too, could forget that she had been sitting in the front seat for the twenty-minute drive over. "Will you come inside with me?"

Nana dropped her hopeful gaze, looking past Charlotte at the automatic doors of the building. Her mouth opened, then closed before she looked up again. "You'll go in with me?"

The fear in Nana's voice made Charlotte feel like the parent, leaving her kid at school on her very first day, but she was sure this was worse. "Absolutely."

"And you'll stay with me?" Nana pushed. "You won't leave me in there, will you?"

Charlotte reached into the car, grasping for something to say that wouldn't break her grandmother's heart, but only found her knotted hand, shaking in her lap. "I'll stay with you, Nana."

Sunset Living nursing home was well equipped for people like Nana; people who needed consistent care, and constant reminding. The administration had assured Charlotte and her father of that when they'd walked in for the first time. And they certainly knew how to create the feel of a home. With large couches, plush, sprawling carpets, dozens upon dozens of flowers, and cheery staff members, Sunset Living had all the accouterments of a home one would want to live in.

So Charlotte tried to ignore the incessant buzz of the fluorescent lights overhead, the underlying stink of bleach, and the thin layer of dust that had taken up residence on the fabric petals and plastic leaves of the floral arrangements.

Instead, she focused on Nana waddling along beside her, the firm grip of her hand on Charlotte's arm as they headed straight for the dining room. The light fixtures created shadows on the burgundy walls and dark wooden table, but the promise of dinner smelled good, and she and Nana made their way over to the large buffet table, where a wide array of cookies awaited them.

Nana ate her treats in focused silence, taking a bite of each cookie with furrowed brows as she eyed the new surroundings. Charlotte nibbled her own, wishing they were sitting in the kitchen of Nana's old house instead, a freshly-baked batch between them. The open window would allow for the light breeze to mingle with the warm scent of chocolate chip cookies, and Nana would ask her questions about school, her artwork, her parents, friends, boys, and of course, books.

Charlotte watched Nana now, sitting at the large wooden table with cookies toppling over on a plastic plate in front of her, and a mess of crumbs beside it. She could still see that woman sitting comfortably in her kitchen chair with her glasses perched on her straight nose, and still hear her voice firmly insist that Charlotte not worry about whatever was troubling her, or offer a reading suggestion, or laugh in response to one of Charlotte's silly stories.

Charlotte tried to remind herself that the woman she saw now was still Nana, still the woman who had always cared about what Charlotte thought and had to say. The woman who always helped her pick up the scattered pieces when Charlotte felt broken. The woman who was more of a mother to her than her own mother ever had been.

She realized that she had to be that for Nana now. The roles had reversed with the passage of time, and Charlotte, while accepting of the new responsibility, wished desperately that they hadn't.

"Hey, Mom." Mr. Worth brushed a hand along Charlotte's shoulder before kneeling in front of his mother. "I want you to see something."

Having forgotten the tension that existed between them a mere hour before, Nana took her son's arm, and Charlotte followed them out of the room. The other inhabitants of the home were scattered around, some playing board games at a round table in the corner, a few watching a cooking program, and a group of women chattered over a card game. Some of them glanced up as the Worth family passed by, but most seemed content enough in their various activities to remain engrossed. Charlotte took comfort in that.

"Here we are," Mr. Worth announced, allowing Nana to step into her room ahead of him. With the help of a few of the home's volunteers, Mr. Worth had set up Nana's room to what he hoped would be her liking. Almost everything from her room at home made it into the smaller space here. Nana's blue comforter was on the bed, her little clock set up on the night table beside it. Mr. Worth had managed to get her dresser there as well, the cherry wood of it a stark contrast against the cream-colored wall. But he had placed her jewelry box atop it, and the pictures of himself as a baby, his wedding picture, and Charlotte's first grade photo next to it. All of her clothes were tucked away, too. Charlotte stared at all of it and fought the urge to re-pack everything.

"What do you think, Mom?" Mr. Worth prodded, stepping further into the room.

Nana Rosie surveyed the room in silence, and spun around slowly, wringing her hands as she recognized all of her things in such an unfamiliar setting. "But—am I staying here, Ben?"

Mr. Worth swallowed. "Yes, Mom." He placed a hand on her arm. "We talked about this, remember?"

Nana Rosie shook her head, her eyes crinkling at the sides beneath her glasses, and sucked her shaking bottom lip into her mouth. Charlotte wanted to run, to take Nana and go, but her feet felt heavy, and she couldn't move.

"But…I don't live here," Nana said, her breaths coming short. "I don't *want* to stay here."

Mr. Worth's shoulders tightened beneath the plaid of his shirt. "You'll like it here, Mom." He rubbed circles into her back. "They have a baking club, and lots of games, and you'll make some friends, and—"

"I am *not* a child, Benjamin," Nana said, rising to her full five foot four stature, and sounding more like the matriarch she always was than she had in the past two years. "I am your mother, and I am not staying here. Let's go."

Nana Rosie skirted around her son to the door where Charlotte stood, and stopped. Charlotte stared at her grandmother and felt her eyes well up.

"Excuse me," a feminine voice called from behind Charlotte. She glanced back to find a young woman, probably in her twenties, with a name badge that read 'Christine' pinned to her light pink shirt. "Dinner's in a few minutes, so I'm sorry to say that visitors are being asked to leave for the time being."

Mr. Worth called his thanks past his mother and daughter, who still felt unable to utter a word. When the woman left, Charlotte turned to face her grandmother again, whose eyes held all of the recognition and understanding they'd been looking for in the past few years.

"You said you'd stay." Nana's voice had barely risen above a whisper, but it was like the words had been hurled at her, their edges sharp and precise, pinning Charlotte down like the bug she felt she was.

Charlotte tried to speak, but only sucked in air instead.

Nana nodded, her lips pressed together, then turned and walked to her bed, perching herself on the edge, fingers folded in her lap. "You'd better get going," she said after several tense minutes of silence. "I have to get ready for dinner."

Mr. Worth stared at his mother, the crease between his brows even deeper as he searched her stoic face. "Okay," he said finally. "Okay, yeah." His fingers lifted and fell against his thigh several times before he moved to his mother and leaned down, pressing a kiss to her cheek. "I love you, Mom."

He caught Charlotte's eye and motioned to his mother, and they passed one another, he on his way to the door, and Charlotte on her way to Nana. She didn't wait for Nana to look up, only wrapped her in a strong hug, kissing her cheek in the process.

"I love you, Nana. I'm sorry."

Charlotte waited, and when Nana's hands fell from their loose circle around her, she pulled away, still waiting.

Nana didn't reassure her, or return the words.

Charlotte met her father at the door, the guilt filling her like wet cement, solidifying as it rose up from her stomach to her chest. She was sure she would collapse with the weight of it before they reached the car, or at least vomit up the cookies.

Mr. Worth brought an arm around her shoulders, rubbing small circles into her back as he had for Nana, and against all instincts, they started to leave.

That's when Nana finally spoke again.

"Ben," she called, her voice calm, even though her eyes had filled with moisture. "Please don't come back."

# *Chapter Eighteen*

By the end of the play, I'm already sure that the kiss wasn't my best idea.

At least, not the *timing* of it.

The play went well enough, and the applause from the audience at the end had even me feeling giddy. But Graham completely forgot a crucial line, creating a pause so long that Amanda had to jump in even though her character was supposed to remain silent. Then, in an office scene with Max, he knocked the phone off his desk, recovering enough to make it seem like it was just Nick feeling on edge. Then, during the climax of the play, he tripped on the foot of the cot, nearly dropping Amanda onto the mattress.

I'm not confident enough to think that all those mishaps were a direct result of my kissing him, but I've been off-balance since it happened, too—like my brain is no longer in charge of my body. My knees were wobbly for the duration of the hour and forty-five-minute play, and I couldn't hear words, just a jumble of sounds, the clearest of those sounds created by Graham's deep voice. My eyes followed his movements, and only his movements, and I didn't notice the slip in choreography between Jane and Amanda during the "meet the parents" scene. I didn't catch the way Max had to turn around, and slip his zipper up after Andrea had noticed it was down mid-scene either.

Maybe it's cocky of me, and the last thing I wanted was for Graham to mess up on such an important night, but it's nice to think that those little slip-ups were in some way caused by a reaction to me.

Andrea chalks all of it—including Tanya's forgetting to move the desk in a scene change—up to "first show jitters"; the rough patches everyone has to push through once to never allow them to happen again. But from the blush that creeps up Graham's cheeks during Andrea's post-show debrief, and the way he shyly averts his eyes when he catches me looking, I'm pretty sure that first show jitters weren't the only cause for *his* unease and forgetfulness.

The thought has me wired again, as does the way his arm brushes mine when he passes by to get changed. The haze from our kiss has settled over me like a soft blanket, a comforting reminder of what happened, and what might still be to come. But, at the same time, I'm wide awake, like he's stirred something in a part of me that I didn't even know existed.

The clean-up does little for my thoughts, all of it mindless work—putting props back where they belong, moving the table and chairs back to their starting positions for the show tomorrow, then making sure all of the clothes are hung up after the cast leaves the dressing room with only Andrea to keep me company.

"One down." She smiles as she slumps onto the couch.

"Two more to go." I sit beside her and look around, hoping I don't sound too hopeful or disappointed when I ask, "Where'd everyone run off to?"

"I told them to head out and see their families after they finished changing."

"You didn't want to go see yours?" I ask, having spotted the Rollins clan earlier.

"Not yet," she says, rubbing her eyes a bit. "I told them I'd meet them outside. Just need a few minutes to unwind, you know?"

I nod, but don't say anything, wondering if Graham is out there waiting for me, wondering how I can get away without seeming like I'm *trying* to get away…

Andrea eyes the clothes rack, where all of the costumes are now neatly hung by character, looking so relaxed I'm not sure she won't fall asleep. "I'm happy with how it went. What did you think?"

"I thought it was amazing," I say. "It'll be even better tomorrow, now that we have all the kinks worked out."

Andrea leans over to me, letting her head fall onto my shoulder. "Let's hope we do."

I don't know what makes me say it—maybe the guilt in knowing I'd thrown off her lead, or maybe just the fact that I'm happy and want to share it with my best friend—but I find myself saying, "I kissed Graham."

Andrea pulls back, and doesn't look tired anymore. "*What?*"

When all I do is give her a guilty smile, she grins back.

"I *knew* there was something going on between you two! No matter how much you denied it, you bitch." She's smiling when she smacks my arm, but it's with enough force that my hand flies to the stinging spot.

"*Ow*," I say with emphasis.

But Andrea ignores me. "Why didn't you just tell me? Why all the secrecy? I was asking you for *days.*"

"I didn't want you to be mad and possibly hit me," I say pointedly, glancing down at my wounded arm. "And I…I didn't really know what it was anyway."

"But that day in the dressing room…there *was* something going on."

She's not asking. Just confirming.

"I—I guess so."

"You *guess* so," Andrea says sarcastically. "Girl, you two were barely touching and I knew something was up just from the looks on your faces."

I feel myself blush now. But not so much because I'm embarrassed. I'm surprised to find that I'm smiling, too.

I'm…happy.

"So, when did this happen? When did it start?" Andrea's eyes widen. "When did you *kiss?*"

I'm too overwhelmed to answer all of those questions, and I'm also feeling ridiculously eager to think he's out there waiting for me. So, I find myself toying with the hem of my shirt as I prepare to answer her last one. "Um, well…sort of, *right-before-the-show.*"

I know she understood me even though I mumbled the last part quickly through my fingers because she slaps my knee. *Hard.*

*"OW,"* I say again.

"No wonder he was such a mess up there!"

"I'm *sorry*! I just—I didn't *plan* it, it just sort of happened, and I—"

"When did this start?" Andrea asks, sounding less angry and more intrigued now. "You two did *not* get along two months ago."

Was that all it was? "A lot can happen in two months, I guess."

"Apparently," she says, her sarcasm evident again. "What *did* happen?"

But as I think about it, I realize, "I don't know."

Andrea doesn't hide her disbelief. Or her annoyance.

"I mean, I helped him with lines a few times. And we talked." I think of his smile, his expression when I showed him my sketches, the way he listened, so intrigued, the way he laughed, the way he frustrated me like no one else I'd ever met. "I don't know, it just…changed."

"Wow," Andrea breathes. "Now I have an exceptionally clear picture of how the two of you ended up kissing *minutes* before my show."

I giggle, and my chest feels even lighter with the sound. "It was minutes before warm-ups, actually."

"Whatever," she says with a wave of her hand. "So…what now?"

I sigh, because I don't actually know. This part was, and still is, a complete mystery to me. "He told me to wait for him afterwards. But I think he went out to see his family, so—"

"So, what are you still doing in here, girl? Go get your leading man!"

Andrea tugs me up and off the couch, fussing with my hair and pushing up my glasses before her strong hands grip my shoulders. Before she can say anything more, I look at her, and voice the question that's been niggling at me since he walked out of the dressing room earlier.

"I can do this…right?"

Her lips press together, and she lets a breath out through her nose, her grip on my shoulders tightening even more. "You can do anything you want, Charlotte. If you want him, you can have him. If you want it to end with that kiss, you can do that, too. It's all in your power, babe."

For the first time, I'm eager for the former, and I smile, something inside me feeling like it might bubble over. "I better get out there, then."

Andrea turns me toward the door with a wide grin, and slaps me on the ass to get me moving. "That's my girl. Go get 'em."

But I turn around to face her at the door, watching as she settles herself back on the couch.

"Andi." She looks up at me. "I'm really proud of you."

Her smile now is soft. "Thanks. I'm really proud of you, too."

It's one of the more sentimental moments we've shared, so, naturally, Andrea has to ruin it. "Don't go kissing any more of my actors right before a show again."

I smile as I leave the room, calling over my shoulder, "No promises."

The crowd has thinned considerably when I reach the auditorium, with most of the people streaming through the open doors at the back. There's a growing uneasiness tumbling with the tingling desire to find him in the pit of my stomach, but my eyes scan the people left anyway. Max, Jane, Lou and Cameron are nowhere in sight, but Tanya is making her way out the door with a group of smiling people, who I presume are her family. Amanda is on the opposite side of thc room, a large bouquet of flowers in her arms. She's beaming as she talks with two older women, and smiles as a man passing her on his way to the door pauses to say something.

My breath catches when I spot him, and that whole racing heart thing starts up again. Gathering my nerve, I start moving toward him and the small group of people surrounding him.

He changed back into his regular clothes—a gray v-neck, black jeans and, of course, his beat-up Converse sneakers—and his hands are tucked into his pockets as he moves restlessly from foot to foot. From the uneasy smile on his face, it seems he's uncomfortable with all the attention. But he smiles—a genuine one—when the small woman with dark curls just like his reaches up to pat his cheek. He laughs when the guy with the same wide smile gives him a shove, and he reaches out to grab the older woman by the arm as she pulls herself up and out of her seat. His eyes find mine when his brother takes the lady—possibly his grandmother—and starts walking her up the aisle. His mother—he looks just like her—glances between us and smiles as she pats her son on the arm, before following her family. But he stands still, his grin widening in the now bright light of the auditorium.

I've reached this point many times before, when what I've wanted to happen between a guy and me actually comes to pass. I'm well acquainted with the lingering stares, shy smiles, and that final moment before the long-awaited connection of lips; the thrilling lurch in my chest when breaths finally mingle. But that was it. The desire always fizzled with each passing moment of those kisses; faded with each breath shared. That was when my phone was usually inundated with texts and phone calls that I let go unanswered, when I had to duck the object of my fleeting affection in passing, when I was once again left to wonder what was wrong with me, and why I insisted on finding something wrong with everyone, effectively snuffing out the bright, initial flame.

Kissing was always something that was fun for a minute, but only a minute. I'm not accustomed to the strong, nearly painful desire to do it again.

I'm not sure I'll ever get used to it.

Now, even more than before, I want to feel the strong chest beneath the gray shirt, see up close the excited flicker in his eyes when they found me, and I'm taken aback by the fortitude of my own desire, the way it seems to pulsate with each pounding beat of my heart.

That's never happened before, either.

"Charlotte," a voice calls, stopping me cold.

I don't have to turn around to know who it is, but I whirl anyway, the shock of her appearance sliding down my throat like a lump of ice.

"Mom."

She seems to be by herself, standing at the end of a row of seats, clutching her bag to her shoulder with both hands. Her eyes, a deep brown, meet mine, and her perfectly lipsticked mouth opens and closes, no sound escaping her lips.

"Hi," she finally says several moments later, twisting her fingers together in front of her.

I still can't speak.

"The play—it was wonderful," she says when I'm still quiet, and everything that rushed out of my mind at the unexpected sight of her floods back in.

I look past her, determined to catch Graham's eye and figure out what to do. I don't want them to meet—that's not happening. Not because of him. Because of *her*. But that also means I can't go over to him now. I can't let her know there's anything going on between us. She doesn't deserve to know that much. But not being able to stay with him the way I wanted to—the way he'd made me promise I would—hurts. More than I could've anticipated.

And not being able to say goodbye…that was out of the question.

Graham's questioning gaze is already on me, his brows quirked up at the sight of the woman standing in front of me. She glances over her shoulder when I don't say anything more, and for a moment, I'm sure they make eye contact. But Graham looks at me, then, and I'm sure he already understands.

*We just don't have a very good relationship.*

With her auburn curls, pale, freckled skin, and same small nose, the woman standing in front of me looks too much like me to be anyone other than my mother. There's no way he hasn't put that together, and I'm glad I was able to give him that much information last night while we were folding programs. I try to communicate my apology with my eyes—tell him that I can't stay with him now, that I have to deal with her first—but if I had my choice, I wouldn't. If I had my choice,

I'd be walking over to him already. But I'm a lot like my mother in more ways than one. Little did he know, apart from our hair color and freckles, we also shared the same way of avoiding our problems and stifling strong emotions.

I've never had emotions this strong for anyone other than Graham.

I can't be sure he understood all of what I want him to, but I hope he can at least see the regret in my eyes. I hope that he at least can read my goodbye.

His attention is pulled away by a voice—his own mother's—calling him from up the aisle. He glances back at her quickly before meeting my eye again. And when he presses his lips together, disappointment written all over his face before he turns around to join his family, I know he understands.

Disappointment worms it's way through my body, too, as I focus on my mother again. And that disappointment starts morphing, making way for anger I thought I'd gotten rid of after that last phone conversation with her.

"What the hell are you doing here?" I finally ask, trying to keep my voice void of anything except shock. But a good bit of my annoyance bleeds through anyway.

She winces a little, glancing down at the floor before swallowing, and smoothing her hands over her jeans. "Your father told me about it." She meets my eye again. "I think we need to talk."

## *Year Eighteen (and three quarters)*

"What's your name again?" she asked, peering over the top of her glasses.

Sometimes she was smiling. Sometimes she wasn't.

Today, she wasn't.

"Charlotte," her granddaughter said, as she had several times before. When no recognition lit her grandmother's eyes, she clarified. "Charlotte Worth."

Charlotte told herself that Nana's words were meant only for her father, that Nana Rosie would *always* want to see Charlotte, no matter her state of mind. So, she went to the home almost every day after Nana moved in—only to find a different version of her grandmother every time. Sometimes she was in good spirits, eager to talk about her activities and the gossip amongst the women. Other times she stayed mostly quiet, politely answering Charlotte's questions, but not going into detail with her responses. Less and less did she remember who exactly her granddaughter was.

Sometimes Charlotte explained.

Sometimes she didn't.

"Worth," Nana said, seeming surprised and excited. "Do you know Henry?"

Charlotte weighed her options: lie, and hope the questioning wouldn't go any further, or respond with honesty and hope Nana would remember. She sighed, slumping into

Nana's armchair with the well-worn burgundy fabric, her finger finding one of its designs and tracing it like she used to as a young girl in front of the television in Nana's house. No matter how disappointing the results, or how crushing the vacancy in her eyes always was, there was a persistent sliver of hope in Charlotte's chest that prodded her into honesty.

"Uh, yeah, actually." Charlotte paused, watching the hope color Nana's eyes. "He was my grandfather."

Nana's brow furrowed for a moment. "Your…your *grandfather*?" She was trying to make sense of it, tasting the word as if she were checking for truth, waiting for clarity.

"Yes." Charlotte waited, too, watching Nana absorb the new, old information, hoping it would register with her lost memories, and maybe bring them to the surface, if only for a moment.

"Oh," Nana finally said. "Well, when you see him, could you tell him that Rosie was asking for him?"

Nana's smile quivered at the edges, and Charlotte's chest tightened.

"Tell him that she would've forgiven him. Tell him that she *has* forgiven him."

The same sliver of hope that had forced Charlotte's honesty punctured her heart now, so that the only warmth she felt was the life seeping out of her in bubbling rivulets, honesty swept away with it.

"I…" She paused, arranged her features so that she wouldn't alarm her grandmother. A smile pulled at each corner of her mouth, as if some force beyond her control had tethered each side of her lips to a string. But the tug of those strings was met with resistance, too, and Charlotte knew the smile wouldn't last long. "I'll tell him, Rosie."

"Thank you," Nana said, sniffling and regaining her composure. "What was your name, again?"

"Charley," Charlotte said this time, searching Nana's eyes for any glint of realization.

Those eyes went wide, driving the sliver of hope further into its lodging, and it twisted when Nana exclaimed, "Charley?! Isn't that a boy's name?"

Charlotte excused herself shortly afterwards. Nana smiled and thanked her for coming, and even invited her back whenever she had time. But Charlotte wasn't very good at lying.

With one last look at her grandmother, sitting comfortably in her new home with her gray curls smushed to one side of her head, large glasses at the tip of her nose, kind smile, and soft, pink cheeks, Charlotte felt her smile twitch. "I'll try."

*Chapter Nineteen*

My knee won't stop bobbing under the table.

One second, I can calm it, halt its jittering with my hands firmly placed on top, forcing it to stay still. But a minute later it's going again, like its gearing up to run at any given moment. The longer the silence stretches on between us—permeated only by new patrons coming into the diner, waiters taking orders, and utensils clanking against plates in the wide expanse of the dining room—the more eager my knee becomes.

"Thank you," my mother says as our waiter sets two cups of coffee down, only adding to the many things standing between us.

She stirs milk and sugar into hers, I stir just milk into mine, and we set our spoons aside before she finally speaks. "The play really was wonderful, Charlotte."

I sip the hot coffee, scalding my tongue in the process.

Her brown eyes don't shift from her coffee cup, which she's set back down on the table. "That cast was incredible, especially the two leads." A tendril of red hair tickles her cheek, glowing slightly orange in the light hanging directly over us.

I still don't answer, thinking of Graham and trying to arrange my face to keep from revealing anything.

"Did you design the program?" I only nod. "It's beautiful."

There are several moments of silence again, during which time I notice my knee has picked up the pace once more.

"Even the lighting effects were great," she says to slice through the quiet, her eyes finally meeting mine. "They really added to the drama. Tell Andrea for me. I didn't get a chance to see her."

I don't say that that's probably for the best.

She dunks her spoon back into her coffee, stirring again even though she hasn't added anything else. When she sucks in a breath to keep going, I interrupt her.

"What's this about?"

She returns to staring into the depths of her cup, looking as if she hopes it could do her job for her.

"You wanted to talk, right? I'm here. You have my attention." She's still quiet. "So, *talk*."

She sighs, a smile widening on her face as she tucks that stray tendril behind her ear. "Always so straightforward."

"Not always." I wrap my hands around my mug, the warmth filling my hands and moving slowly up my forearms.

She meets my eye again. "I've been wondering where to start. How I should explain…" She draws a deep breath, but doesn't seem to let it out, her sentence hanging unfinished between us.

"Explain why you left," I say for her, taking too much pleasure in the way she flinches. "Why don't you just start at the beginning?"

I cross my arms and stare at her, totally not sure that I want to know everything, but needing to seem like I can handle the truth anyway.

"Okay. Well…" She sits forward, glancing down as she considers her words. "I guess…the first thing you should know is that, me leaving—it was a long time coming."

"That's comforting," I mutter, knowing that I'm not going to like any of what she has to say, abruptly sure it won't change anything anyway.

"Charlotte. I—I know this hard. It's hard for me, too. But it's important to me that you hear me out. And if it doesn't change your mind, if you're still angry, I'll understand. I just—I want you to know everything, so please, I'm explaining, just…*let me* explain."

I want to stomp my feet and allow my jittery knees to carry me out of the diner. I want to plug up my ears and scream so loud the other patrons will think I'm dying. The last thing I want to do is sit in this booth, with its long tear in the uncomfortable red cushion, and listen to her explanation, feign understanding, then give her what she's hoping for, probably even expecting: forgiveness.

But I nod my go-ahead anyway.

Mom lets out a long breath. "Okay. Well…you know your father and I were really young when we got married."

I hold back from commenting that when I said to start from the beginning, I didn't mean before I was born. I suck my lips into my mouth instead, holding them there with my teeth.

"We were fresh out of high school, and neither of us knew what to do when we found out I was pregnant with you. We weren't ready, we were too young, but we were in love. If you take away anything from what I'm about to tell you, let it be that. I *did* love your father."

She pauses, and I don't know if she wants me to respond. I take another sip of my coffee.

"What you *don't* know is that we almost didn't get married." At my carefully blank stare, she goes on, her voice soft. "He didn't want to."

"Who?"

"Your father." She twirls her spoon in her cup again.

"You're lying," I say after a moment, sure this is some kind of ploy to get me to side with her.

But she seems nothing but genuine when she says, "He loved me, he just didn't think we needed to get married. He thought we were too young, and we could take care of you going as we were. He didn't think rings were necessary."

I slump back into my seat, trying to swallow the new information, but it goes down like a large pill, scratching my esophagus the whole way—leaving its mark. Images of my father bringing my mother coffee in bed each morning, toying with her soft curls while she was on the phone, or doing dishes, or even just sitting near him—like he *had* to be touching her in some way just because—come into sharp focus in my mind. I could see the gleam in his eyes that appeared when he looked at her. It hadn't dulled in recent years, despite their hardships, but it had grown smaller, as if it were shrinking away in defeat.

My father loved my mother. I had always known that, because I could see it so clearly, every day. What I couldn't see was the same light in her eyes, the same thoughtfulness in her actions. I was always sure her feelings didn't run as deeply as his did, and part of me pitied him because of it. So this new information, that she loved him, that he didn't want to get married initially, is a lot to process.

I clear my throat and sit up again. "And…what did *you* want?"

She smiles a little, shrugs her shoulders. "I wanted to get married. As soon as I knew I was pregnant, I knew I wanted us to be a real family. Rings and all."

"So…how'd you get Dad to agree?"

"I didn't," she says with another sigh. "Nana Rosie did."

That takes me by surprise. "She did?"

Mom nods. "I guess, looking back, I can't really blame your father. We *were* really young. But at the time, it hurt. No matter how many times he tried to say it wasn't me—that I wasn't the reason why—it *felt* like I was."

I lean forward, resting my elbows on the table, still trying to digest all of this. "Nana talked him into it?"

"I don't know what she said, but he agreed to it almost immediately after their conversation." She pauses, chews her lip, then releases a breathy laugh, speaking more to herself than to me when she says, "I could only get the love of my life to marry me through his mother, and I was too stupidly happy that he'd agreed to let the reason why bother me at the time."

She meets my eye. "But after we had you, I started to resent him…and myself, for being so blind. He spent as much time as possible out of the house, away from me, and you. I grew sadder and angrier each day." She curls both hands around her half-empty mug. "And I knew he had to work—we couldn't ask Nana for help with everything—but he got to go to school and work, and then he spent even more time out of the house. It wasn't fair to me, or to you.

"I was left to take care of you, and he acted like he didn't need to help at all. Like he could just stroll in at ten at night and go to bed. That's what he did, practically walked right by me some nights, ignoring me—*us*—like we didn't exist."

It's hard not to cringe when she lumps us together. Dad and I were "us". *She* was the other. But from what she's describing, my dad didn't want to be part of the "us" when I was a baby. And that's hard to wrap my head around.

"I hated him for it. Every straight-ahead stare, moving past me like I wasn't there, was like he'd twisted a knife into my stomach. But I also loved him so much I could barely breathe." Her grip on the mug relaxes. I didn't notice it tense in the first place. "As I got older, it stopped hurting so much. There's only so many times you can be hurt in the same place before you develop calluses, become numb to it. I chose to live my life rather than resent him for living his. That's when we started moving in different directions. I finally started to grow, change, and feel okay without his attention."

"But…but Dad loved you." My voice sounds more forceful than I intended. "I saw it. He *really* loved you. You were the one who seemed distant. Not him."

She watches me for a moment, her red lips twisting up to the side in a way that makes my eyes widen before she speaks again. "You know how people say that these kinds of things are all about timing?" She doesn't wait for my response. "I believe that. Two people can fall in love with one another at any given point, so what if it's not simultaneously?

"I was blindly in love with him, Charlotte. And he was in love with me, too, in his way. I know he was. But it wasn't enough at the time. I married him anyway, too enamored with the thought of being a family to care that his mother basically forced him to agree. And then the reality of our lives hit me full-force over the next couple of years. We were just kids—two kids playing house with a baby."

A waiter comes over and tops off our coffees, interrupting our conversation like a pin popping a balloon. It takes several minutes for my mother to regroup. She's silent while she stirs more milk and sugar into her fresh cup and takes a sip.

The most troubling thing, I think, is that I believe her. But I don't want to. Hating her is so much easier than understanding her reasons for leaving; than sympathizing with her situation; than choosing to love her anyway.

"Charlotte," she finally says. "The love you saw, what your father felt for me—it just… It came too late. You understand that, don't you?"

"What about me?" I mutter.

"What about you?"

"Did you love me?" I ask, trying to drop the question lightly between us, but it plops with the weight of emotion I can't hide, and I imagine I can hear it thud as it hits the table.

Mom's eyes widen, then narrow with her furrowed brows. "What do you—?"

"You know what I mean." I can't look at her any longer. "You resented me, too. I may've been a kid, but I could feel it, you know."

She sputters for several moments before taking a deep breath and looking straight at me, brow un-creased, eyes wide and bright with tears. "Charlotte…I—I've made a lot of mistakes. So many, it's hard to keep track. Sometimes it feels like all I do is break things, leave a trail of destruction in my wake. But you…" She shakes her head, and reaches tentatively between our coffee cups, nodding awkwardly at me as she touches the top of my hand where it rests on the table.

I let her.

"You were *never* included on that list. Not even for a moment."

I still don't want to, but I believe her.

"I owe you an apology. Lots of them, actually. So, here's the first of many…" She brings her other hand up to hold mine between her palms. Uncomfortable with the contact I'd for so long wanted, then avoided, my hand remains limp between hers.

"I never knew how to be a mom, or even just show affection, really. My mom wasn't around when I was young, and my father wasn't good at…emotions. You know, hanging with Grandpa was about as fun as hanging out in a tomb."

I can't help but smile, and hers widens.

"I've realized recently that I'm a direct product of my upbringing, which is frightening considering I spent so much time thinking I wasn't, after actively trying *not* to be."

Once again, I understand exactly what she's saying. I've tried for so long to avoid becoming her, and in the process, that's exactly what I've done—left my grandmother to suffer with her Alzheimer's in solitude because *I* couldn't handle it. Grew more bitter as I got older, jaded by a world that no longer shone in the same light as it had when I was a little girl. And feared any kind of real feelings for someone because of my parents' miserable relationship—all the while, convincing myself it never affected me at all.

"This is not an excuse, Charlotte." She kneads my hand between her warm fingers. "There could never be a good enough reason for leading you to think I didn't love you. Even for a second. Because I did…" She looks at our hands tangled together, then back up at me. "I *do.*"

"From the moment I met you, and your head was all misshapen from the birth, and your skin was all pink and soft and squishy…" Her brown eyes have filled, but she's smiling. "You were perfect, and mine, and I loved you.

"You weren't the best baby, mind you. So colicky—you screamed your head off for weeks straight. Nana Rosie was my only solace." She smiles, eyes glassy with the memory. "But then your little personality started to take shape, and from the moment you could talk, you had us mesmerized, even more than we already were. You were so honest about everything. So smart. And *so* independent." She leans forward. "You used to scare me to death with some of your antics. Do you remember climbing the tree?"

I smile, remembering being less than impressed with the view of my neighborhood from the branch of the huge oak in our backyard. "I remember."

Mom's laughing now. "I felt like one of those cartoons when something terrifying happens and all the color just drains out of them. You were up there, refusing to come down, and I had no color left. Not until your feet were safely on the ground again."

I remember the fear, but mine was different. The ascent was easy, and the view disappointing, but what I remember most was looking down, seeing the drop. The ground seemed to move farther away the longer I stared at it. I was so scared I started planning how I might survive on the branch. I could eat leaves (they were like vegetables, right?) and make friends with the birds, so they'd bring my letters to my parents and Nana, and I could lie down on the branch to sleep, and the crazy list went on.

I also remember the feeling of being lifted into the large arms of the fireman, the relief of having my feet touch grass again, and have it stay close like it was supposed to, and the unsettling shame of being yelled at by my mother in front of all those people.

She didn't understand, and she didn't want to listen.

"It's always been difficult for me to wrap my mind around you, Charlotte," she says, holding my hand in hers and examining it as if it might disappear. "Not only because of the sometimes life-threatening decisions you made, but because of the way you made them. No fear, no pause for thought, only an insatiable curiosity. You never *really* needed me, not since you were a baby, and I could never understand it."

Even though I've always known all of what she's describing, even though I felt it in nearly every interaction we've ever had, I hang my head, the hurt hitting me in the chest like a curled fist.

"I was too much in awe of you to really understand," she says, gripping my hands and looking me in the eye again. "You were just so different from me, and I often found myself wondering how you were mine. How *you* came from *me*. You were too wonderful, too perfect to have come from me. And instead of loving you the way you deserved, I spent my days worrying about myself, sure that I wouldn't ever be good enough to be your mom. I was *depressed* thinking I'd never be good enough; it sort of became a self-fulfilling prophecy, didn't it? I let all of that get in the way of the relationship we could've had all those years."

Now my eyes are watering, and I sniffle, blinking quickly to try to hide it.

"I'm not looking for pity. But you need to know that I'm grateful you're mine. And, starting now, I'm going to spend every minute showing you that I mean it."

When I realize I'm gripping her hand as hard as she's holding mine, I give her one last squeeze before pulling away completely. The look on her face changes quickly, her features morphing from imploring affection to fearful surprise, then finally to disappointed understanding.

And I bring up the one thing she's so cleanly avoided the entire night.

"Right, so…how does Richard fit into all of this?"

She looks stricken, and I take some satisfaction in that. It isn't that I don't believe all she's saying, but there was so much that happened, so much that was ruined beyond repair when she left. If she thinks she's getting out of this without even attempting to brush away the rubble, then she really doesn't know me at all.

She sits back, blinking several times as she pulls her hands back into her lap. "I—well, I thought I explained that."

"No," I say, feeling the anger brim over. "You told me that Dad didn't want to marry you twenty years ago. But he did marry you. And he loved you. And I…"

I snap my mouth shut, afraid of the words that appeared on my tongue without my mind's permission. She's staring at me with wide-eyed hope, but I won't say them. Not right now.

She can't get them out of me that easily.

"I don't understand what could've been so horrible," I say. "I don't know what could've been so bad that you felt you had to leave the way you did."

The hope in her eyes a moment ago is replaced with fear now. She thought she had me. She thought this would all be over with a few pretty words. She didn't account for the betrayal I've felt for over a year, or the anger I've grown used to—come to expect wedged tight in my chest when I wake up in the morning. All because of her. I knew she didn't understand me, which hurt, but the fact that she never made the effort to *try* made me livid. Then she left us, thinking all the while that I would want to talk to her afterwards, build an entirely new relationship with her and forget the old one. I knew she didn't understand me, but I couldn't understand what would make her want to betray me.

Like she's resigned to something, she folds her hands on the table between us once more. "I met Richard when I started the job with the interior designer—at a holiday party. He was collaborating on a project with Harry, my boss, and I always…noticed him when he came into the office. He's outgoing, and kind, and he always made a point to say hello to everyone.

"One day, I was really swamped with work and calls and behind on my projects. Between that and everything going on at home, I was so overwhelmed and anxious that I broke down at my desk. Just started crying into my hands. I thought I was being quiet, but…Richard came over. And he just…sat with me. Talked to me. Acknowledged my feelings. Then helped me sort out how I could tackle all of the work that was still sitting on my desk."

She's smiling now, and I can see in her eyes the love I looked for for so long—the love that should've been reserved for my father.

"He didn't have to do that. He had his own problems to worry about. But in those few minutes, he made me feel so important, like my emotions and thoughts mattered to someone."

"Is that when you started sleeping with him?" I blurt, taking pleasure in the look of offended shock that registers on her face.

"I…" She's gasping. "I guess I deserve that." Brown meets hazel with a look of fierce determination. "But you asked, Charlotte."

I nod once, and stick my chin out. "Go on, then."

Mom waits a moment, and when she speaks again her voice doesn't have the same breathy quality. She's no longer as taken with her tale of romance. "We started seeing each other a few weeks after that. I left your father four months later."

"And me," I say, glaring at her. "My father and *me.*"

Her eyes soften. "And you." There's another momentary pause. "Well, look, Charlotte, unless you want all the gory details, I think that's all I have to say."

I cross my arms. I didn't want it to, but what she's said has made a difference. There were things I didn't know, factors that contributed to my parents' rocky marriage that I wasn't aware of at all. It's easier to see why she made some of the decisions she did, but it still doesn't make any of it okay. Her explanation doesn't wipe away all of the hurt she's caused me over the course of my life, and I certainly haven't forgotten or forgiven the way she left.

She's my mother. She has the power to hurt me more than anyone else possibly could. And she used it.

"I know an apology isn't enough." She's pleading now. "But I am *so* sorry, Charlotte. You deserve so much more. And…I want to start over."

I sigh, my head still stubbornly refusing to give in to her. Refusing to give her the consideration she's never fully given me. But my heart's shouting otherwise, holding in it the words that my father has learned to live his life by: *Forgiveness is my daily battle.*

My anxiety mounts at the mere thought of what I have to do, her eyes on mine only making it worse. I swallow the bitter taste of coffee that creeps up the back of my throat. "Um, well…thank you, I guess. For explaining. All of it."

Mom starts to smile, but before she gets too eager, I say, "But…it's not—I'm going to need some time. To process everything." I'm sitting ramrod straight, nerves tightening all of my muscles. "It's just…this is a lot to take in."

She looks defeated, head hung so that her curls frame her face like a curtain. I'm surprised by how much I feel the need to reassure her, by how validated I feel now that I've heard all the thoughts and emotions she held too close for so long.

"But I think it'll help me forgive you." Her curls fall back as she lifts her head. "I've always wanted to forgive you, I think. But…you never really gave me the chance. And then, what you did, it…it *really* messed me up, Mom."

"I know, and I'm—"

"You don't have to keep apologizing. But you should know that this won't be easy for me." I lean forward, needing her to hear me, and start to understand. "You *hurt* me, more than anyone else ever has. An apology won't make the hurt go away, only time will do that. Time and hard work—on you, on me—talking more…we have to do all of it, and be honest and upfront with each other."

She's smiling, something like pride shining in her wet eyes. "I want that. I really do."

My voice is so soft for the next part I could be a little girl again. "It's all I've ever wanted."

The tears spill over then, and her hand clamps down over her mouth, but I hear her whispering, "I'm sorry," over and over again into her palm.

I feel the tugging in my chest begging me to revert, pull back, like the beckoning force of a whirlpool that promises to swallow me whole, back to safety. But I fight the pull, gasping and kicking to stay above the surface, and reach across the table, taking her hand in mine—a lifeline for the first time in my twenty years.

"I know you are. Let's move on now." I think of Nana. "Let's do better."

## *Year Nineteen*

The house was too quiet without the constant blare of the television in the living room underlying all other sounds. The days felt longer without Nana waddling to and from the kitchen for breakfast, lunch, then dinner. Charlotte's worries felt much larger without Nana there to lessen her fears.

She hadn't gone back to see her grandmother for a while. At first, she stopped going each day, opting for twice, maybe three times a week. But then twice became once, and once came every few weeks, until it didn't come at all. Mr. Worth understood, and picked up the slack where Charlotte couldn't, grateful, just this once, that the disease had made Nana forget his banishment.

Charlotte felt lost. She wasn't talking to her mother at all, and she didn't think it right to talk to her father about that particular loss. He was grieving it, too, and Charlotte didn't want to infringe on his coming-to-grips with it by bombarding him with her own thoughts. So, she swallowed them back, feeling them lump together with the stresses of school, the guilt over Nana, and the listless sadness that had been dragging her down for weeks, then months, clawing at her to join its depths.

For the most part, Mr. Worth gave his daughter her space. He was used to Nana taking over in such situations—when Charlotte seemed troubled, or down, or, in this case, both. As much as he wanted to help, he didn't think he knew how.

He tried in his way—attempting to sneak it out of her at dinner with pointed questions, which she deftly deflected. Or trying to ease her into it by putting on a movie and making popcorn, but she always had homework or studying to do up in her room. So, Mr. Worth let himself feel helpless, as useless as he'd felt when he and Lindsay had first gotten married. He loved her, he loved their daughter, but he didn't have a clue how to care or provide for them.

As much as was possible, he and Charlotte avoided each other, only making small talk in the mornings before school, and during the twenty minutes they spent together for dinner before Mr. Worth headed up to his room to wallow by himself. Allowing the communication to go silent between them was easier, in both of their minds, than disturbing it with the clanging sounds of their thoughts, clamoring for escape.

But that's when Charlotte decided she needed an escape herself.

"I want to go to London in the spring," she announced when they were rushing around early one fall morning. "There's a class I can take over there with school, and it's not terribly expensive. I've saved enough money over the years through babysitting, and birthdays, and Christmas gifts that I should be able to cover most, if not all of the plane fare."

It wasn't the first time his daughter had rendered him speechless, and Mr. Worth recovered with a clear of his throat. "Um, don't you think…? Are you…? What, uh, what brought this on?"

Charlotte wrapped her hands around her coffee mug. "Oh, I don't know. The fact that mom left without even saying goodbye to live a whole new life might have had something to do with it. Or maybe because the one person I can actually talk to no longer remembers who I am. Or maybe just because I can't seem to do anything that takes the least bit of focus, and have generally become disenchanted with the current state of my life. Or maybe all of the above."

Mr. Worth stared at her, felt his mouth hanging open, but couldn't figure out how to close it. Charlotte stared back, unsure now that her little tirade was the best plan of action.

When she spoke again, she kept her voice as steady and clear as possible. "I *have* to get out of here, Dad."

It was funny, he thought, and strange to see a child—*your* child—become an adult before your eyes. How had the tiny body he'd helped to make grown into the woman standing before him, her eyes blazing as bright as her red hair? How could he see the echoes of himself in those eyes? Not just because they were the same color as his own, but because he recognized the feeling in them, the same pleading certainty that he'd once known so well. How could he just as easily see his mother, hear her voice in Charlotte's, and see her determination in the firm set of Charlotte's jaw? And if he turned his head, just so, there was Lindsay—the same beauty, the same fire.

He wouldn't put this one out.

"Okay," he finally said, and the shock that registered in the quick lift of Charlotte's eyebrows was his own.

"Okay?" She set her mug down, and let her shoulders relax.

He shrugged, already feeling the pangs of missing her. "Okay. As long as you're sure this is what you want…"

"I'm positive." She met his eye. "I *need* this, Dad."

"You remind me so much of your grandmother." He had to say it.

Charlotte winced, and Mr. Worth resisted the urge to reach out and hold her, cradle her like the child she no longer was.

"She used to say," he went on, turning to pack his bag for the day, "that it's a rare thing. To feel so certain of something." He zipped his bag. "So when you are…" He turned to look at his daughter. "You have to trust it."

Charlotte stared back at him, wide-eyed, and he saw himself again, reflected in her hope.

"Don't worry, kiddo." He grabbed the strap of his messenger bag, and lifted it onto his shoulder. "I'll take care of everything."

The smile she gave him then was unequivocally her own.

## *Chapter Twenty*

"I'd just like to thank you all for being so dedicated, and really giving every rehearsal, every run-through, and every show your all." Andrea is smiling so wide, I'm sure I can count all of her teeth. "This whole experience never would've been this amazing without each of you, and I'm proud to say that I had the pleasure of working with you. Cheers!"

She raises her plastic cup, and Tanya lets out a loud *whoop!*, which causes us all to laugh.

"Hold on…" Graham jumps in before anyone sips their champagne. "None of this would have been possible without you, Andi. Your talent, your eye, your dedication to not only making the show great, but to each of us in the process. You helped us surpass our potential every night, so, for that, we thank you."

"Here, here," Max says, his cup almost touching the ceiling when he lifts it.

The champagne bubbles salty-sweet against my tongue, and I meet Graham's dark eyes over the rim of my cup. My cheeks heat before I glance away.

We're at Tanya's apartment, a cramped two-bedroom that she shares with two other girls, who have made themselves scarce for the night. But there are a few more people here I don't recognize—Tanya's friends, I'm assuming—and Andrea is now under the arm of one of them, a tall guy who's smiling down at her like she might disappear if he glances away.

"This is sad," Tanya says, looking around at each of us. "I've lived and breathed this play for the last two months. And just like that..." she snaps her fingers. "How am I supposed to just move on from it?"

"If you figure that out, let me know," Andrea says before tossing back the rest of her drink, still tucked under the guy's arm. "I've done how many plays, and I still sink into a post-show depression when the end comes."

"Don't cry because it's over." Max curls a long arm around Tanya so that her braids are tucked into his armpit. "Smile because it happened."

"Get out of here with that cliché crap." Tanya whacks him gently, her hand just reaching his breastbone, and she tries not to grin when she pulls herself away.

"What?" Max is fighting a smile of his own. "I'm just trying to help. Baby, come back!" He sings when she walks over to the stereo.

I laugh as he continues the song and spins her around when she turns up the music.

Everyone seems to have paired off, and when Graham gets caught up talking to Lou, I scoot into the kitchen, the only empty space left in the house, to fill my drink and get a bit of a breather.

"Hey."

Andrea comes up beside me, fixing herself another drink. "How are you doing?"

She knows this kind of party isn't exactly my thing. I really only came because she asked me to, and because I would miss everyone (and because Graham would be here). While the play had turned into something much more time-consuming, and frustrating, and stressful than I initially thought it would be, it was also something that turned out to mean a lot to me. It was a distraction from missing London, but, like London, it was also a distraction from my life. It gave me the chance to pour my creativity into something; to do what I'd gone to London to do all those months ago—escape.

"Just wondering who thought it was a good idea to smoke on the fire escape." I watch the pungent smoke curl away from the window, then a hand pass the joint to another hand, and wrinkle my nose at the stench.

"I meant, are you having fun?" Andrea says with a laugh. She takes a sip of her drink.

"Yeah," I say, and I mean it. "I actually am."

"Good!" She lifts her cup and gestures for me to raise mine. "For keeping me sane, for creating the most beautiful program I ever could've hoped for, and for being my best friend. To you, Charlotte."

I clink my plastic cup against hers. "To both of us."

"Am I interrupting?" says a voice from doorway, and I almost spit out the sip I've taken when I turn to find Graham watching us.

Lucky for me, Andrea isn't so easily shaken. "No, not at all."

I face the open window again, and try to convince my lungs to keep breathing.

"I was just leaving, actually," Andrea says, giving my arm a soft squeeze, and it only takes her three steps to get out of the kitchen, leaving me alone with him for the first time since we kissed.

I feel him step up beside me and keep my eyes fixed on the window, even though they're not seeing anything that's going on out there anymore.

"Keeping an eye on things, Sarge?

I grin. "Someone has to."

Graham breathes a laugh, and out of the corner of my eye I see him pour soda into his cup. "They're lucky it's you."

My heart thumps hard in my chest, and heat floods my cheeks, but I don't know what to say to that. He lifts his cup to his lips.

"Not drinking tonight?" I ask, and glance up in time to catch his smirk.

"I had one earlier, but that's my limit." His smile widens when he meets my eye. "I got this—" he points to his lip ring, "—one really drunken night in high school. And I had alcohol poisoning when I was nineteen. Just a couple of my many failed attempts to fit in. Let's just say I learned my lesson." He takes a sip of his soda to prove his point.

I don't say what I'm thinking—*thank God for the lip ring*—but I don't know what to say to the other thing either. I don't know where we stand, to be honest. We haven't said a word to each other since the kiss. Two days have passed since then, and he hasn't tried to talk to me until now. I've been trying not to dwell on what that silence does or doesn't mean.

"So," Graham says after a few moments. "Did your family like the show?"

Happy for a distraction from my thoughts, I smile up at him. "Yeah. My dad was there tonight. He said he wanted to see the last show so that he knew, without a doubt, that the actors would leave everything on stage."

"That's fair," Graham says. "What's the verdict?"

"He really seemed to like it." I smirk. "Of course, he did mention that the lead actor was shit."

Graham grins and rakes his hands through his hair, his curls still stiff from the gel he used as Nick. "Couldn't agree more. That guy didn't have a clue what he was doing."

"Actual disaster. A real damper on an otherwise brilliant performance.

Graham's eyes spark with amusement, and his lips press together in a smile he's trying to suppress.

I can't keep it up any longer.

Laughter bubbles up my throat, cheats its way past my lips, but Graham's laughing too. Suddenly, the air between us—only moments before charged with nerves—is tremulous with possibility, with excitement, with relief.

"What did he *really* think?" Graham asks, turning towards me, leaning his hip against the counter.

"He really did like it." I see my father's face—the smile that tried to be happy, his hazel eyes, brown in the dim theater, shining with pride but something else, too. "But I think… I think it hit a little too close to home for him, actually."

The people on the fire escape—two girls, Tanya's roommates—clamber back through the window then. Alarmed, I grab each of their arms as they pass through. The first girl thanks me with a slow smile, the whites of her eyes lined with red, but the second just walks through the kitchen, eyes glassed over, back into the living room without a word.

Graham looks between me and the window, then holds a hand up, gesturing to the fire escape. "Want to?"

I look from him to the window, feel the cool breeze on my face, and smile. "We're the only sober people in this apartment, so we probably should before someone else does."

Graham chuckles and gestures for me to go first. But as soon as I lift myself through the window and look down, I'm second guessing my decision. "Oh, um…this is high."

Graham pokes his head through, glances down at the four-story drop, and pulls himself up. "This is nothing."

"Speak for yourself." I sit cross-legged, my back against the building. It's still not far enough away from the edge.

He settles down next to me, both of us sitting close on the small, cramped grate, and when he slides his legs through the bars so that his feet are dangling over empty air, I can't hide my alarm. "What are you doing?"

Graham looks at me. "What?"

I stare pointedly at his knees.

He chuckles, and I'm surprised when his warm hand finds my knee. "Come on."

"Are you crazy?"

"Just crazy enough, I think," he says, and taps my knee. "Come on. There are bars here, you're not going to fall."

I stare at the black bars, like just looking at them will reveal if they're sturdy enough.

"I'm right here, nothing's going to happen." He holds his hand out then, and I surprise myself by taking it. He holds it tight while I scoot forward, while I slide my legs through the bars next to his. When he lets go, it's only so that he can put his hand on my back. "Alright?"

I'm looking down at the ground, which seems to get farther and farther away the longer I stare at it, putting me back in that tree in my backyard. "Not yet."

He chuckles, rubbing warm circles into my back. "Don't look down."

It's good advice. Between looking up at the sky, and feeling his hand on my back, everything is calming inside of me: my breath, my heart, my nerves… And then his hand is gone.

"So…" Graham says, propping both arms up on the bar in front of him. He turns his head to look at me. "You were saying?"

"What?"

"About your dad. Why'd it hit too close to home?"

I forgot. Why couldn't he? It still amazes me that he's so interested. He's asked me more questions about myself—the things that really matter to me—than any other guy ever has. And while I know I like that about him, it also terrifies me. But before I start overthinking it, I blurt out, "My mother left him." *Left us,* I mentally correct. "A little over a year ago."

It's the first time I've said it aloud to anyone other than my father, or Nana, or Andrea—the first time I've felt comfortable enough to reveal it, and, once I say it, I can't stop there. "We never really got along."

Without understanding why or how, I tell him about my relationship with my mother before she left, the way it always felt like she was holding me at an arm's length. How she seemed happier at her new job, but now, looking back, that happiness had more to do with Richard than anything else. She was cheating on my father. She was cheating on me, too, but she was happier than I'd ever seen her. I relive how she left—the crippling fear that came with not knowing what had happened to her, the way her note felt like it had punched me in the stomach, ripping my innards out in a closed fist, and how all she'd left me with was the anger, the emptiness I've had to endure every day since.

"So…the other night…" Graham glances at me, looking for clarification.

I feel stretched thin, like the truth has worn down a path on its way out of me. "That was the first time we talked about any of it. Like, *really* talked about it." I rest my chin on my arms, now propped up just like Graham's. "It was the first time she showed any kind of remorse for what she did."

Graham is quiet for several moments afterwards; moments that open a sinking feeling in my gut. I've revealed too much. I've opened up too much of myself, too quickly…

"I could use another drink," I say with a laugh when he's still quiet.

I hear him breathe a chuckle, but his voice is serious when he asks, "Have you forgiven her?"

My lips press together. It's so hard, especially having laid everything out the way I just did, to even *want* to forgive. The pain will always be there, a constant reminder of what she did; how she left—an urgency not to forget. And how could I forgive without forgetting?

"I'm trying," I say, giving him a tight smile that feels like it might crack my face in half. "It's not like saying the words wipes the slate clean, you know?"

"Of course not," he says, and a jolt shoots through me like a fuse catching when he reaches over and tucks a wind-whipped strand of hair behind my ear, his fingers sliding away too soon. "But, in time, you'll have new memories to tamp down the old ones. A new relationship with your mom to replace the old one with the woman who hurt you."

I don't say anything.

"You deserve that, Charlotte."

I close my eyes and smile then, feeling like the cool breeze might just pick me up and whisk me away if he keeps looking at me like that, his dark eyes earnest and sincere and locked on mine.

"Thanks, Graham Cracker."

He grimaces a little before his mouth turns up in a grin, his lip ring catching the little bit of light out here. "I never should've told you that story."

"Nope. Definitely not." I giggle, staring over at him, recognizing the shift in his eyes. I've gotten good at it, noticing the subtle changes in them, and linking those changes with what causes them. He's amused now, so they're crinkled up at the edges, the darkness lighting with laughter. But when he's listening intently, eyes totally focused on me, I can see the lighter brown around the black pupil, even lighter flecks of gold shimmering within.

And when he's flirting, well…that's when they appear depthless.

"I probably don't have to say this…" His hand finds my knee again, and he watches his index finger as it toys with the hole in my jeans, skimming over the skin there. "But knowledge of that name is strictly confidential."

"Of course." My thoughts are a little fuzzy at the edges, but not because of anything I've had to drink. "I realize it's privileged information."

Graham's smile widens when he looks up at me. "Only those with the highest security clearance have access to it."

"Well, then…" I break off because he's leaning closer, his hand coming up to play with the ends of my hair. "I promise to handle it with care."

He breathes a laugh through his nose and glances down when I reach up to take his hand in mine, grinning like a kid who's snuck dessert before dinner. His fingers close around mine, pulling them to his lips. He doesn't kiss them, just runs his mouth over the knuckles, the rough stubble against my skin sending my heart racing. I can't stop myself: I unfurl my fingers, touch his chin, let them slide up his cheek. He looks at me again, lips parted.

"I *really* want to kiss you now," he says, and it sounds like he's asking for permission.

I'm breathless and excited as I lean toward him. "Well, what are you waiting for?"

I only have time to catch the quick widening of his smile before his lips are on mine. Both of his hands come up, holding my head steady by the jaw, and I don't know if it's just the cool night air swirling around us in stark comparison, but everything is searing hot between us—his mouth on mine, his hands on my neck, his chest beneath my closed fists, clutching handfuls of his shirt—all of it ignites something deep within me, in a place I've fought hard to keep protected. Something that's pulsing and warm and *alive.*

All sense of time dissipates as we sit there, locked together. The sounds of Manhattan and the party surely haven't quieted around us, but they're lost on me. All I know, and all I *want* to know is the firm, insistent pressure of Graham's mouth, the cool hardness of his lip ring between my lips, and the reassuring, gentle feel of his fingers on my neck, guiding and steadying me.

Loud whoops and peals of laughter sound behind us, separating us, and I feel myself blush to find almost the entire cast peering out the window, smiles on all of their faces. Max is the one making the most noise, but it's Tanya I hear most clearly.

"Get it, girl!" she shouts, and she and Andrea high-five, laughing together like they had something to do with Graham and me making out on the fire escape.

I turn my face away, pressing my burning cheek into Graham's shoulder, and his hand tightens around my wrist.

"Alright, alright," he says, his voice colored with amusement as it rumbles against my hand. "Show's over."

"Looks like it's just getting started to me!" Max calls, and everyone starts laughing once more. Even me and Graham.

Everything quiets down again after a few more jokes at our expense, settling to a normal level of loud with only the music and low thrum of voices drifting out the window.

Graham's hand comes up, rubs my back again, and I feel the press of his mouth, the warmth of his breath on my hair. "Coast is clear."

I lift my head and glance into the kitchen behind us, a relieved smile stretching onto my mouth. "Well, that was embarrassing."

His hand is still on my back, and I stay close enough so that it won't go anywhere else.

"I've had weirder moments," he says. When he leans in before I can ask for specifics, I don't stop him despite the very real possibility of being caught again.

It's a much softer kiss, and he laughs into it after a moment.

"What?" I ask, pulling back just enough to look into his eyes.

"Nothing, it's just…" His smile gets bigger. "I've been wanting to do this for a while."

I grin.

"But, until the other day…" His smile softens, and he reaches up, touching just beneath my chin, rubbing the skin slowly with a knuckle. "I didn't know if you wanted me to."

I don't say anything, just acknowledge the tightness in my chest and hope it'll go away.

"It kind of felt like…maybe you were holding *me* at arm's length."

I blink up at him, realizing what he's said—that he used my explanation of my mother to explain me—and I'm embarrassed to think it was that obvious. "Look, Graham, I—"

His mouth is on mine again, capturing my explanation before it can ruin the moment.

Graham presses another peck to my lips before pulling away, looking right at me, his eyes moving quickly between my own. "It doesn't matter," he says, and his hands curl my hair back behind my ears before resting on my cheeks. "Not now."

The cold grip of fear wraps itself around my heart, but Graham's eyes are locked on mine, the sincerity like a fiery warmth within them. His fingers touch my temples, brushing back the doubt, the anxiety. And his kisses linger on my lips, sending a pleasant buzz down to the tips of my toes—all of it sending an echoing crack racing down that icy wall.

Someone makes a loud, wet kissing noise, and we turn to find Max with his head out the window, waggling his brows. "Join the party, lovebirds. We're just about to play a rousing game of Cards Against Humanity."

He doesn't wait for us to answer, just ducks back into the kitchen.

Graham surprises me by asking, "Want to get out of here?"

My stomach feels like it's flipped over. "Yes."

I would have been sidetracked by the crooked tilt of his lips if he didn't take me by the hand and help me stand up. I had forgotten about the drop until now, and my grip tightens on his arms.

"Don't look, just go right through. I'm right behind you."

I bend down before I can get too wobbly, and slide one leg, then the other, through the window. A long breath flows out of me when my feet land on solid ground. Graham hops down beside me a moment later, takes me by the hand, and leads me through to the living room.

"We're going to head out," he announces. And once everyone gets over their disappointment, he lets go of my hand so we can make the rounds to say goodbye.

Andrea quirks a brow when I reach her. "You want this, right?"

I smile—I'm not sure I've stopped. "Definitely."

She nods. "As long as you're sure. And remember, you can always change," she hiccups, "your mind."

"I'll remember." I eye the guy waiting in the wings beside her. "Be careful, okay?"

"You too," she says, and pulls me into a hug. "Text me."

Graham's fingers lace with mine, and I'm happy for it, afraid that if he lets go again I might float away, or worse…walk away all on my own.

It's nearly one in the morning when we make it out of the apartment.

"Think they'll miss us?" Graham asks as we head toward the elevator.

"Definitely not," I say with a nervous giggle.

We're quiet as we wait for the elevator, quiet still when we step inside, and we smile at one another when it begins its descent, but Graham's voice breaks through the silence halfway down. "Do you want to go to my place?"

I bite my lip, my doubts weighing more than my newfound certainty for a moment, but all I say is, "Okay."

Graham smiles, pulling our joined hands up to his mouth, and pressing a long, warm kiss to the top of mine.

The elevator dings on the ground floor, the doors open wide, and I follow his lead.

## *Year Twenty (During London)*

Mr. Worth was comfortable in silence; it was the only time he could truly hear his thoughts. But it had been a week since Charlotte had gone, leaving him for another country—a week of silence, a week of only his thoughts for company. While he knew it was irrational, the silence dredged up old feelings of abandonment and readjustment—making coffee for one in the morning; coming out of the shower to not only an empty bedroom, but an empty house; waiting for the sound of the front door to open and close, followed by footsteps echoing up the stairs…then realizing that none of it would happen.

Now, he didn't even have the comforting sound of bare feet padding down the wooden stairs in the morning, no flashes of red hair skidding around corners, and no warm smile from Charlotte to make his loneliness feel less painful.

It was the first time he'd ever felt that silence was too much.

"Ben!" his mother exclaimed when he entered her room at the home. "It's so nice to see you!"

There was an element of guilt in his relief; he wanted an escape from his resounding thoughts, and had been hoping she would remember him today. Not for her own sake, but for his.

"I've missed you, Mom," he admitted, his words holding more meaning than she could ever really know. He felt like a boy again when he leaned down to kiss her withered cheek.

She laughed. "You need a shave, Ben."

He smiled and moved to sit. "I'll get right on that."

"Do you want something to eat? I can have that young fellow bring something in for you." Nana's large eyes were magnified almost comically by her thick glasses.

"No, thanks. I'm okay for now."

He was happy to see the recognition in her eyes, but even happier that she seemed to have found some semblance of herself today. The woman he knew couldn't rest if her family, or anyone, for that matter, wasn't well fed in her home.

"Well, you let me know if you change your mind." She settled back into her armchair, a pleased smile on her face. "How are you, Ben?"

Mr. Worth shrugged. "I'm alright. Just trying to keep busy."

"How's work?"

"Going well." He thought of the papers he had yet to read and grade for his next class.

"Good. Have they promoted you yet?" She leaned forward, an eagerness in her eyes. "That store wasn't the same before you showed up."

Mr. Worth chuckled, nervous now. "Uh, Mom, I work at the college now. Remember? I'm teaching English."

Nana's eyes flicked back and forth, waiting for the memory to come to her. But it didn't. He saw the plain confusion in her eyes, and squelched the dismay he felt when she tried to cover it up with an unconvincing, "Oh…right."

She leaned forward again. "Have *they* promoted you?"

His laughter shook up the tightness of fear in his chest, loosening it. "No, not yet. But I'm pretty happy where I am."

"Remember—" she crooked a finger his way, "—always work with dignity, no matter the job, because when you do that—"

"The rest will come," he finished for her, smiling. "I know, Ma."

Nana was beaming. "That's right." Her breaths were escaping loud from her mouth, and after a few quiet moments, her brows furrowed. "Where's Charley?"

Mr. Worth felt his own good spirits plummet with the casual mention of his daughter. The sting of missing her was back despite his relief in knowing that Nana remembered her today.

"She's in London, Mom, remember? She's studying there for the semester."

Nana's eyes grew to an impossible size, and her voice quivered with a note of outrage when she asked, "By herself?!"

"With her school," he said, hoping she'd remember before her mind went into a complete tailspin.

Nana's large eyes moved swiftly back and forth behind her glasses as she considered his words. If Mr. Worth wasn't so upset by the turn of their conversation, he might've laughed at the sight.

"How old is she?" Nana asked after several moments, seeming to realize that her own memories and thoughts didn't match up with what her son was telling her.

"Twenty."

"Oh." Nana looked thrown off, but pulled her shoulders back as if to collect herself. "Right. Well, that's alright then, I suppose." She eyed her son again. "How long has she been there?"

"About a week now," he said, already dreading the next three and half months.

Nana nodded satisfied, then glanced up at him again. "Have you talked with her? How does she like it?"

Mr. Worth nodded. "She checks in every day. She seems to be having a good time so far."

As happy as he was that Charlotte was loving her experience—it would've been much harder for him to deal with if she were miserable—he also worried that if she liked it *too* much, if she were *too* happy there…

He scolded himself.

"I miss her," he admitted, more to himself than to his mother, but she smiled sympathetically.

"It's so hard," she said. "Seeing them grow up. I wanted to keep you small for as long as I could." She smiled. "Thinking that if I continued treating you like a boy, you might never grow up."

Mr. Worth nodded. He'd been having flashes of little Charlotte padding around the house in her nightgown, hair flying wild around her, a wide-eyed little girl whose chief enjoyment was making the people around her smile.

"But you figured it out despite me, Ben." Nana gave a shake of her head. "You were a parent before I even had time to adjust to you being an adult."

She was laughing, so he chuckled, too, recalling a time when so much was thrust upon him, so many responsibilities and worries and obligations. He fiddled with his fingers, touching the band he still wore on the ring finger of his left hand.

"It was hard," Nana said. "But seeing you now, a man so committed to his daughter…" She shook her head, pride set in her smile. "It's also rewarding."

He chewed at his bottom lip. "I just… I don't want that for Charlotte. My life, I mean. She's the best thing that could've happened to me, and I love her more than anything, but…"

His mother was staring at him, and he was sure that she knew what he was going to say, but felt he had to get the words out, as if saying them might make them less true; might make the fear weigh less in his heart. "I'm afraid she'll grow up too soon, like I did. She's already had to deal with so much. I just don't want her to make any rash decisions, and with her so far from me, I feel helpless."

Nana smiled, a familiar, knowing look in her eye. "Even if she were here, you couldn't control her, Ben. She's a young woman now, right? Her choices are her own, just like your choices were yours." She paused, thinking further. "But we raised her—you, me, your wife—and none of us wanted that for her. She saw what it was like for you two. She felt the strain of it even if she, or you, didn't realize it. And she's stronger for it, believe me."

Mr. Worth felt the twist of guilt in his gut, so like a knife tearing through him that he nearly doubled over. "So, what? I'm just...not supposed to worry?"

"It's not a matter of whether you should or not." Nana sounded exasperated now. "You *will* worry. You *do* want what's best for her. It *will* be scary. But you have to let her live."

Mr. Worth bit his lip. He wanted to. Really, he did. But at the same time...

"You're doing that, Ben. Without even realizing it."

He nodded. He wanted Charlotte to live her life—that's why he'd said yes to this whole study abroad thing to begin with—but the instinct to protect, to shelter her from the world and all its evils, rose up in him, fierce in its need.

"Will it always feel like this?" he asked, hoping that the suffocating grip of anxiety and fear, and the ache in the gaping hole created when she left, would subside.

Nana smiled grimly, knowing exactly what he was talking about without asking him to elaborate. It rose up in her now, the same need. She wanted to reach over and pull him close, hold him like the little boy she still saw. But he wasn't that little boy anymore. He hadn't been for some time. He was a man; a father—a role he had no frame of reference for, yet he was still ten times the father his ever was. So a greater need rose up in her: the need to tell him the truth.

"Every day of your life."

## *Chapter Twenty-One*

"And this is my room."

It's the smallest of the rooms in the already tiny apartment, made to feel even smaller by the mess of clothes scattered around. He has nothing more than a twin bed and tall dresser. An open window allows for the cool night air to whisper inside, and the walls are white and bare like the rest of the apartment. We've only walked by his roommate's room, but I didn't have to go in to tell that both guys have no use for interior design.

I feel Graham's eyes on me as I step inside and glance around, my eyes finding the only pop of color in the tiny space.

"Is that your dad?" I ask, trying my best to feel settled in spite of the nervous energy buzzing around inside.

Graham glances at the photo for only a second before tossing the shirts and pants he's quickly collected into a heap by the door. "Uh…yeah."

The handsome face is so like his, but more severe somehow. The jaw has a sharper edge to it; the brow is more pronounced, drawn further down over the same dark eyes, filled with a hardness that even Graham hasn't managed. But the long lashes are the same, so is the straight nose, and the bow-shaped lips pressed into a firm line—all of it made more handsome by the military uniform he wore.

"You look a lot like him," I say, eyeing Graham as he nabs a stray pair of boxers he missed, his back to me. "He's in the Army?"

Graham scoots around me, dropping the last few items of clothing on top of the pile. "Used to be."

"Oh, he's out now?"

"He's dead now," he says, so casually he could've been telling me it was his birthday.

Shocked, I stay quiet for a moment, both because of the news and the offhand way he delivered it, then mutter a pathetic, "I'm so sorry."

Graham shrugs, giving me a half-hearted smile before staring at the picture himself.

Hating that I feel like I've already overstepped my bounds, but unable to stop myself, I ask, "How…how did he—?"

"In Iraq. An IED. Hidden explosive. I was fourteen." The words are punctuated with little emotion, as if he's said them too many times, had too much practice explaining, and doesn't want to have to do it again.

I'm no longer sure why I needed to know in the first place.

"I…" Graham starts, his eyes swiveling to me, a firm look of decision settling in them after a momentary flash of fear. "I don't really talk about him. Ever. With anyone."

"That's totally fine. You don't have to." I mean it, but wish I could figure out why what he's said is so disappointing. If there's anything I understand, it's wanting to keep things—personal, having-to-do-with-family things—private.

But Graham moves to the bed and sits, folding his hands in his lap. "He, uh…he was a Sergeant First Class. I lost track of how many times he was deployed. He was always leaving."

I sit beside him, but don't say anything.

"That's actually how I started cooking. My mom worked all day, so when my brother and I got home from school, I'd start dinner. I learned to love it when I was older, but then I was just trying to make her life a little easier. When my Dad was home, though, he was in charge. It didn't matter that we had established our own routines, or whatever. We worked around him. When I was little, I didn't mind that, but as I got older it bothered me."

The relationship Graham describes sounds all too familiar. His father spoke his mind with little discretion or care for how his loud opinions might be received, and his mostly internal son was a mystery to him, one that he was determined to crack. Graham recalls all of the sports he'd had to play as a kid, his father shouting at games, getting kicked out by referees, or into verbal altercations with fathers of the opposing team. He had to practice when his father was home, and Mr. Hudson's army training became apparent in the way he drilled his son, keeping him out for hours at a time. A young Graham was eager to please, but also more than relieved when his father wasn't around, no matter how much he missed him.

"I know now that he only did all that stuff because he cared." Graham twists his fingers in his lap. "But I didn't understand that when I was little. I just felt inadequate. So, when I got older, I quit everything, and that's when we really started butting heads. He didn't understand the whole acting thing, but he didn't make the effort to try, either. So, I stopped trying to impress him.

"He didn't like to talk about what went on over there, either, so we didn't have much common ground at all at that point." He looks thoughtful, and gives his head a shake a moment later, as if to knock the memory from the forefront of his mind. "He was…pretty different each time he came home, drawing more and more into himself. Becoming more and more short-fused with us." Graham clears his throat. "It would've made sense for him to stop, retire, live his life for himself, and for us. But…he only wanted to go back."

Graham's focus stays on his hands, tangled together in his lap. I remain quiet, sensing that there's more, that maybe he just can't say it yet.

Sure enough, a few moments later, he says, "We moved here after he died. My mom's mom lives out on Long Island, so we moved into a house not far from her. We've been here ever since."

Graham reaches over, then, picks up my hand and unfurls my fingers. "I was mad at him for a while, even after…" He traces the lines of my palm with the tip of his index finger, and I pull in a quiet breath, hold it, realizing the proximity of him and where we're sitting for the first time since we came into his room.

"But then," Graham says softly, his eyes fixed on his fingers as they travel up, skimming over the pulse point on my wrist, and circling the erratic beat. "One day…it just wasn't worth it to be angry anymore. That's when the real missing him started."

I've been fighting the urge to squirm the whole time his finger moved in soft circles on my wrist, and my voice is no more than a whisper, betraying just how affected I am by his touch when I say, "Did you—could you forgive him?"

Graham's eyes flick up to mine, and the suggestion of a smile touches his mouth as he curls his hand around my wrist, his long fingers meeting each other around the circle of it. "He was only doing what he thought was right, and trying to relate to me at the same time. He cared, maybe too much, and he was just trying to show it. I can't fault him for that."

I'm not sure that answers my question, but I don't say that.

"It still hurts sometimes," Graham admits after several moments, the pad of his thumb now skimming the width of my wrist. "And it took a while to get to this point, but I regret not opening up to him more. I spent so much time angry with him and the fact that all he seemed to want was to change me, and I wish I tried harder to understand him, build a relationship with him. Knowing that I'll never have that chance? That's what hurts the most."

His eyes are a glassy black, and the longer I stare into them, the more clearly I see myself reflected back.

I turn my head.

We're quiet for several moments, and I try focusing on Graham's fingers in mine rather than the sharp turn my thoughts have taken. But his touch, the warmth of him beside me, only makes me realize again where we're sitting, and what it might mean to him. Fear slides like ice through my veins—

ice that somehow sets ablaze the entire surface of my skin in a hot-cold prickle of goosebumps.

"Want some coffee?" Graham asks then, squeezing my fingers a bit.

I can't help but laugh, the simple question knocking me right off the frightening track of my thoughts. It's well after one in the morning, but, "I'd actually love some," is what I find myself saying.

Graham leads me back through the small apartment and sits me down on the couch, where I have a perfect view of him in the teeny-tiny kitchen. His long limbs move almost gracefully, probably the result of having people watch his every move on stage. The muscles of his broad back shift beneath his plaid shirt as he opens the cabinet for mugs, and his curls are still slick with gel in the back, where his hands don't usually reach when he runs his fingers through them. All of the things I love to notice about him, the things that make my heart thump unevenly, are only intimidating me now, here in this small, private space—his *apartment.*

"So, where's your roommate?" I ask, hoping my level of discomfort might ease with more conversation.

"Working," he says, his back to the now-percolating pot of coffee. "He's a bartender at some night club on the West Side."

I nod, afraid to ask if that means he'll be out all night.

But secretly hoping it does.

Perhaps sensing my nerves, or maybe dealing with some of his own, Graham busies himself with pouring the coffee, getting the milk out of the fridge, and he smirks when he holds the sugar up. "Still no?"

I shake my head, grinning. "Too sweet."

Graham shakes his head, smiling as he pours milk into both mugs, and two heaping spoonfuls of sugar into only one. "See, my logic is: never sweet enough."

"Guess we just have to agree to disagree," I say, smiling up at him as he hands me a steaming mug. "Thanks."

"You're welcome," he says, and sits beside me, taking a sip of his coffee.

I take a sip of mine, glancing around the room at the flat-screen TV, the well-stocked DVD collection, the coffee table in front of me with all the rings on the surface. My mother would cringe.

"Your apartment's nice," I say, mostly just to interrupt the silence, but it's true. It may be small, but it's surprisingly clean for two twenty-something guys living alone.

"Thanks," he says with an amused smile. "It works for us."

I want him to say more, but he doesn't. And I want to come up with something else, something more stimulating to get the conversation going, but I can't. It's like my nerves have frozen, leaving my muscles stiff, my vocal chords numb and useless in my throat. I turn over thought after thought, deeming nothing important enough to mention, but I also keep coming back to one thought—a question that *is* worth posing, but too terrifying to actually consider voicing.

"Are you okay?"

I meet Graham's eye, and try to laugh. "What? Yeah." He sees right through it. "Well…not exactly."

"What's wrong?" His brows draw together in concern.

"No, nothing like that. Nothing bad," I say, seeing the way he's looking me over, searching for the source of discomfort. "I just… I'm a little nervous."

"Why?" he asks, looking just as worried.

I wrap my fingers around my mug, feeling sweat bead in my palms. "Cause of *this.* This whole situation."

His eyebrows shoot up. "Because of me?"

I quirk a brow back at him. "You're surprised?"

"Well…" Graham breathes a laugh. "Yeah, a little." He shakes his head, and his brows furrow again like he really doesn't understand.

I'm even more uncomfortable now, and I don't want to hurt him, but at the same time…he needs to know.

"I just, I don't know what you expect…from tonight. From me being here." I feel his eyes on me, but can't meet that stare—those eyes that challenge me, break me down, and put me back together with a single look.

"Hey," he whispers after several quiet moments, and his hand touches my arm. "I don't expect anything from you. Nothing. I'm just… I'm just happy you're here. That's it."

I stare at him, watching as he sets his mug down on the table sans coaster, and slides closer to me. I set mine down too, bringing a leg up on the couch so that I can fully face him.

"Now I'm the one who's nervous," he says, releasing a breathless chuckle. I grab his hand, glad I'm not alone. "Okay, look…this is going to sound ridiculous, but…" He bites his lip, then sighs. "That very first rehearsal, when I saw you…I don't know why, but I assumed you would be playing Olivia."

I almost laugh, and my surprise eases my nerves. "What?"

Graham shrugs. "You were the first girl I saw when I walked into the room. Sue me." We're both chuckling now, but Graham quiets before I do. "Your head was down, and you were so focused on whatever you were drawing, and you did that little nose-wrinkle thing to push your glasses up, and…I was already attracted to you." He wrinkles his own nose and smiles. "Then you looked up. All wild hair and big eyes."

I giggle a little, bringing a hand up to cover my eyes in embarrassment—I nearly knock my glasses off in the process and start laughing even more. My first impression of him was so completely, totally wrong—stoic leather-jacket guy, who could've made a nice mannequin in a store near you.

"You were quiet at first," he says. "But you looked around at everyone, all curious and cute. Then you started talking, and you were funny and smart, and you took no nonsense. None of my shit."

All I can remember is how uncomfortable I felt giving it right back to him after he yelled at me.

"It was hard to keep from staring at you," he admits, toying with my fingers in his hand. "I was disappointed you wouldn't be playing Olivia, and pissed that you already had me so enthralled. I was supposed to focus. Save my attention for Amanda. But you became a constant distraction."

It's strange, seeing it all from his perspective, but thrilling, too. His presence felt like a black hole to me from day one. All of the energy in the room swirled toward him, beckoning me to get closer, but I stubbornly refused to get sucked in, and was exhausted for the effort. Being near him now still feels like too much, like I'm staring into the eye of a supernova—the very point of explosion—his presence outshining everything else, even the blinding light of the sun. But I don't want to be scared anymore. No matter how short a time he might stick around, I don't want to miss a second.

He chuckles. "I must've seemed like such a dick when you zeroed in on 'Graham Cracker'. But you just smiled, defiance in your eyes…and despite my reaction, all I could think was, 'You *have* to get to know this one.'"

I giggle and smack his arm. "No, you didn't."

"Well, not *right* then." He meets my gaze. "But it didn't take long."

My heart hammers unevenly, and I'm overwhelmed with the urge to launch myself at him, curl around him, hold him close. But my hands stay locked together in my lap, and my heart stays right where it is despite its efforts, trapped in its cage.

"I guess my weird, roundabout point is that I don't want to ruin this. I do that enough, and I don't want to do it with you." He reaches over, touches the end of a long curl. "I like you, Charlotte. A *lot*. And I won't push you away by pressuring you into anything you don't want to do."

I didn't realize I was holding my breath until all of it whooshes out of me.

"Okay?" he asks.

I nod, smiling at him. "Yeah." He grins back, and pulls the hand he's still holding up to his mouth, pressing a kiss to it. "Okay, well…now I feel like I should, um—"

"Hey." Graham ducks his head to meet my eye. "No pressure, remember?"

"It's okay. I want to, uh…explain." But I'm not sure where to start…how to say it. "I, uh, I'm not very good at *this*." I motion between the two of us. "Which is probably why I've never had a real relationship before."

"Never?" His eyes are wide, incredulous, but not judgmental.

"Well...not *never*," I say, completely embarrassed. "But it was in freshman year of high school. It didn't mean much and ended quickly."

"Why?"

I'm a confusing mix of *happy* he's so interested, and *nervous* because he's so interested.

"I don't know. We were kids. It just didn't last." Images of Adam with other girls flicker into focus, and the echo of my jealousy pangs like a bell tolling, the vibrations rocking through me, and passing just as quickly as they came.

"Well, okay, that's not exactly true." I take a deep breath. "I'm just not very good at this stuff. Relationships—starting them, maintaining them...ending them. I have a bad habit of running from every almost, sabotaging it somehow. But I don't usually regret it because I've always known that I don't need anyone else to be happy."

He's still looking at me, still listening carefully, and he's still holding my hand.

"That's uh...started to change recently." My chest gets inordinately tight, making it difficult to take a sufficient breath. "I'd regret you if I ran now. I know it. Even just thinking about it..."

He squeezes my hand. It feels like treading deep waters, pressure coming down on me from all sides, but I swim further down, further than I ever have, fearing the cold, watery darkness, but needing to conquer it.

"I don't need you, Graham. That hasn't changed." I make myself look him right in the eye. "But I do want you, and the two don't feel that different, and, to be completely honest, it *terrifies* me."

I try to laugh it off, make light of the truth I've just lobbed, heavy and wet between us, but Graham barely smiles, just stares.

"So...that's me," I say, feeling awkward and shy with his gaze on me now, aware of every inch of my body the way I always am when he looks at me. "What about you? Any girlfriends, Graham Cracker?"

He gives me a pointed glare, but smiles. "Not until well into high school. Then...there were a few."

"A *few*? Do tell."

Graham shakes his head, grinning at me. "None of them are really worth mentioning."

"Uh-oh. Was Graham Cracker scorned by love?"

"Who isn't?"

He says it with a laugh, like it's a joke, but the rhetorical question cuts to the core of me with all the sharp edges of a blade. It's what I've lived my life trying to avoid.

"And please," he goes on, oblivious to my train of thought. He brings a hand to my jaw, his knuckles grazing it in a way that sends my blood tearing through my vessels. "Stop calling me Graham Cracker."

I smirk at him, feeling my cheeks heat under his touch. "But there are so few pleasures in life."

Graham's eyes flash with a devious glint. "I can think of *many* things more pleasurable than that."

I suck in a breath, his words stirring up the dust of my fears, but something else too—something that's lain dormant within me for a long time, and hums eagerly at the thought of…

"Like eating ice cream," Graham says, finishing his thought.

I blink at him, my staggered breaths halting.

"I have some if you want it." His lips quiver then, and when I smile, he can't keep from laughing.

"Speaking of eating," I say. "Doesn't now seem like a *wonderful* time to make that meal you promised me?"

"One, I promised nothing of the sort. But, two, if you stick around until breakfast, there might be something I can do about that."

"Can I put in an order for pancakes now?"

"Only if you like them with chocolate chips and a side of bacon. Otherwise, no deal."

My eyes widen, and I gasp, holding a hand to my heart. I say it as sarcastically as I can manage, but there's no denying how right it feels.

"I think I might love you."

## *Year Twenty (Post London)*

Charlotte Worth was never afraid to be on her own, doing things for herself, in her own time. Mr. Worth knew that about her, saw it even when she was a little girl, burrowing herself into her closet with a night-light, blankets, toys, and snacks she'd swiped from the kitchen when her mother wasn't looking. She would talk and sing to herself then, giving her dolls different voices and opinions, all while he stifled his laughter just outside the closet door.

Nana told him how Charlotte relied on herself for fun at the playground, too, seeming not to care about what her classmates might think. But, even so, he couldn't help feeling surprised when he discovered that, as a teenager, his daughter spent a good chunk of her time at the local park by herself, reading.

He had to admit there was a little bit of worry mixed in with his surprise. Was it normal for a young girl to spend so much time by herself? Did it mean there was something wrong with her? He knew her to be talkative, personable, and kind, someone who made him smile on a daily basis—but was he just biased? Was she different around other people?

He had to remind himself that he shouldn't care. Charlotte didn't seem to, and she was learning to rely on herself. Besides, finding comfort in solitude wasn't strange to him. She had to have gotten it from somewhere—or *someone*, he thought with pride. Every father hoped that his daughter would grow to be independent and self-sufficient. He was lucky.

Charlotte never knew how to be anything else.

So, it didn't come as a surprise to him that she loved her time in London, three thousand miles away from all she had ever known. Charlotte thrived by herself. She always had. He'd known she would be fine, that she wouldn't shy away from any opportunities over there, or get homesick. And it certainly wasn't surprising to him that she'd made friends. Her spirit was too kind, too gentle and bright, for people not to gravitate toward her.

The surprise came when she returned home. It wasn't that she looked different to him—same unkempt curls, same freckled cheeks, same smile—but her eyes…was it possible they were wider? Somehow brighter with all they'd seen? There was a distance in them now, a faraway look that he was desperate to understand.

But she held back, even when he asked for specifics. He knew from that distant look that she had seen and done more than her skim-the-surface responses revealed.

The difference between him and his daughter now, he realized, was that she *chose* to be alone, while the people he loved chose to leave him. He could almost see Charlotte making the decision when that faraway look came over her at dinner, when she stared out the car window on their way to the train station, when she returned, exhausted after a long day of rehearsal.

Unlike Charlotte, Mr. Worth didn't want to be alone.

Not really. Not anymore.

## *Chapter Twenty-Two*

I'm being taken away in an ambulance, lying prostrate on a gurney while a faceless EMT works tirelessly above me, poking and prodding me with needles, the constant beep of my heart on the machine next to me signaling that I am, in fact, still alive. But there's no pain anywhere that I can tell, and I try to ignore the fact that I can't feel anything at all.

I want to tell him—*her?*—that I'm fine, this is unnecessary, but I can't find my voice. My mouth opens, but only a soundless breath comes out. So I lie helpless, the bright light in the back of the van hurting my eyes, and the swerving motion of the vehicle making me nauseous. The sound of the siren resounds painfully in my head, and I want to bring my hands up to cover my ears, but my arms lay limp beside me, no matter how hard I try to move.

That's when I wake up, startled to hear the same blaring ring from somewhere around me, and find that I really *can't* feel my arms. Once I manage to get both eyes open, I realize why—I've been sleeping on them. And they feel like slabs of lifeless meat. With a groan of exhaustion and frustration, I roll over and try to shake some blood back into them.

"You okay?"

I gasp, a tingling hand coming up and clamping over my mouth so that my yelp of surprise is muffled.

"Sorry!" A head of dark curls pops up from the other end of the couch, and I let out a nervous giggle, partially embarrassed, but mostly giddy at the sight of him, hair pressed to one side, scruff covering his cheeks, and long eyelashes blinking heavily at me.

We didn't make the decision to fall asleep, but staying up talking until at least four a.m. after a stressful weekend of performances took its toll. The last thing I remember talking about is, for whatever reason, getting lost in a department store when I was little.

It was getting close to Halloween, and the store had a whole aisle of costumes. My mom wouldn't take me to look at them—we'd already gotten my hot dog costume—so when she wasn't looking, I went to look myself. But when I tried to find her again, I couldn't. A lady saw me, and I must've looked afraid, because she offered to help me find my mom.

Next thing I knew, a man's voice sounded over the loudspeaker, asking Lindsay Worth to come to the customer service desk.

"I was so embarrassed," I said. "Even at four years old."

Graham was snickering, and he sounded sleepy when he said, "Could've been worse. You could've asked a pedophile for help."

I smiled. "Or my mom could've left me."

Graham had already fallen asleep by the time it hit me, the foreshadowing of it all: I was *always* losing her, never finding her. I fell asleep not long later.

He's smiling at me now, rubbing the sleep out of his eyes. "Didn't mean to scare you," he says, his voice raspy, thick with sleep, and I feel my mouth open a bit when he lifts an arm over his head to stretch, the muscles rippling as he moves.

"Well, you did." I don't mention that scaring me is *all* he's been doing.

"And you—" he tickles my feet, and I draw them up with a yelp of surprise, "—were kicking me all night."

"You had your own bed," I say with a smirk, more than happy to know he stayed right here on the couch. With me.

Maybe he's just tired, but he stumbles for a moment. Searching for a response. Very unlike Graham.

"Well, I—I couldn't leave you all by yourself. That would've been rude."

"If you were worried about being hospitable, wouldn't offering me the bed have been the right thing to do? Or at the very least, letting me have the couch to myself?"

I'm enjoying watching him blink the sleep from his eyes. Enjoying the way my questions are catching him off guard.

Finally, he meets my eye. "Are you always this *awake* in the morning?"

I start to giggle, and would've replied with a snide remark, something about *most* people being awake in the morning—that's what mornings are *for*, but the ringing starts again, and belatedly I realize it's my phone.

"That's you," Graham says, setting his head back down on the pillow.

"Thanks, Captain."

I reach for my bag, unwilling to get up just yet, and rummage through it for my phone, straightening my glasses in the process.

"Oh, shit." I mutter when I see my Dad's name on the screen.

I forgot to text him.

Graham's head pops up again. "What is it?"

"Charlotte?" comes my father's frantic voice over the line.

"Dad," I say and sit up, upset to think how much I probably worried him. "I'm *so* sorry, I completely forgot to tell you that I wouldn't be home. I'm sorry, I—"

"Charlotte," he says, cutting me off. But he doesn't continue, just sighs. It's not a good sigh.

"Look," I say. "I know you're upset with me, and I know I was wrong. I should've at least texted, and I—"

"Charlotte," Dad says again. It's the first time I realize his voice is strained. "Something's happened."

Graham has either heard my father's voice, or seen the look on my face, because he sits up and swings his legs over the side of the couch, sidling close enough to put his hand on my back while he eyes me.

My heart must've known before my father says the words, because it slows, pounding carefully to prepare itself for the shock, to slow down the world around me. But when he speaks again, voices the words I never could have been prepared for, my heart and my world stop dead.

"Nana passed away."

## *Chapter Twenty-Three*

It's funny how things come back to you after a death—*when* things come back to you.

I can hear her, voice loud but worn through with age, as she says, "Charley, the world's at the tips of your toes."

All that's at the tips of my toes now is a freshly dug grave.

The words "thank you" feel like cotton in my mouth, only growing thicker each time I have to say them. My somber smile is strained, weary, as if the two invisible strings holding it up are about to snap. Their stories are hard to hear, and the fact that they think I want to hear them makes it harder to listen. What I really want is to not have to talk, not have to listen, not have to be around people at all any longer.

I just want to get out of here.

But my heels have sunken into the damp grass, and I can't move. The crowd of people starts to dissipate from around me, taking their polite frowns, and kind words, and solemn head nods with them as they move toward their separate cars, lined up one behind the other, too similar to the headstones just beside them. And the image of my father crying—tears streaming gently enough down his face, like he was trying to be strong as he held my hand—will stay with me no matter where I am or where I go.

"Charlotte," my mother's voice says.

I turn away from the coffin to face her and Richard, yanking my heels out of the holes they created, only to set them down and sink once more.

"Come here," she says softly before pulling me into her arms.

It's still strange, awkward…as much as neither of us wants it to be.

When she pulls away, she fusses with my hair. Because the hug wasn't uncomfortable enough.

"Are you going to be okay?" she asks.

Of course I'm not.

I nod, hoping that will be the end of it, wanting to squirm away, not only from her attention, but from Richard's pitying gaze as well.

Someone walks up behind me, and when my father's hand settles on my shoulder I feel myself go even stiffer.

"Thanks for coming, Linds," he says, and his voice is still thick enough that I know he's still crying. I don't want to look at him, I don't want to feel that strange, unpleasant quiver in my stomach—the jolt to do something to comfort him, even though I don't know how. But I don't want my mother to look at him either. I don't want her to see him cry. I don't want her to imagine it's how he might've looked after she left.

But as she takes him in, Mom surprises me. Everything about her is gentle, kind, worried as she smiles, her red-lipsticked lip quivering just slightly. "Of course. I loved her, too."

He tries really hard to control it, but when Dad's face crumples, she reaches for him before I can, and I'm surprised when he reaches back. I watch as she hugs him, as he tries to muffle his sobs into her shoulder. And I'm stunned when she lets him, when she holds his head there, letting him soil her black blazer with tears.

It's only a few moments, but it feels like a lifetime later when Dad pulls away, when Mom holds his face, looks into his teary eyes with tears in her own beneath furrowed brows, and gives him a small, encouraging smile.

Dad's the one to step back first, but he does it gently, takes her hands in his and gives them a soft squeeze before letting go. As if he's thanking her once more.

Mom's smile doesn't budge, only becomes a bit more pained. And the light I've always looked for in her eyes when she's with my father is blazing bright. She does love him, I realize with a start. Just not the way he needed her to. Not the way I *wanted* her to.

We're all still quiet as Richard's hand comes up to her shoulder, and she leans into him, her head turning slightly towards him for a moment, before she turns back to face us.

"I didn't get a chance to ask on the phone," she says, and looks at my father. "But how…how did she—?"

"In her sleep," Dad says, still trying to collect himself. I hear him swallow. "The doctors said it was peaceful, and that's all I really wanted to know."

Mom nods, giving him that solemn smile everyone seems to be wearing today. I glance at Richard, who is watching the exchange with a serious expression, and his eyes go wide while looking at my father, as if he's just realized it's his turn to speak and everyone's waiting on him.

We're not.

"So very sorry." He shakes my father's hand. Dad pulls his away quicker than he might normally have. "From what Lindsay's told me about her, your mom sounds like quite the woman."

"She was," Dad says, voice strained, not so much with grief now, but something else. Something that makes me glance up at him. His mouth is drawn down at the corners. "Thanks."

We all stare at each other for several uncomfortable moments; moments during which I'm sure I can see all of my mother's misdeeds flash through her eyes, all of Richard's guilt flash in his, and all of my father's well-meaning forgiveness bleed out of him through the hand clenched too tightly around my shoulder.

"Well," my mother says, and reaches for my hands, "I guess we'll head out now." She kisses my cheek, and gathers me in for a long hug. "But if you need anything, don't hesitate to call."

"Thanks," I say, because I'm supposed to.

She looks right at my father, then.

"That goes for you, too, Ben," she says, and her gaze doesn't move from his face.

Dad nods, and his face softens again as he meets her stare. "Thank you. Means a lot."

My mother nods, presses her lips together in a smile, and leans into me again, forcing another hug that I'm not sure I want or need.

"I love you," she says, giving me a shake. The words sound persuasive, like she's afraid I still won't believe her. "Remember, if you need anything—"

"I'll call," I say, and wave an awkward goodbye to Richard, who backs away with a smile, but mercifully, without a hug.

Dad sighs, a long release of breath that makes me look up at him, and his eyes widen as if to say, *"Glad that's over with."*

"Ready?" he asks, his voice still thick. His nose still congested.

I haven't forgotten where we are, or why we're here, but I was distracted for five minutes. I still can't believe that after everything, *today* of all days, I just witnessed my parents *hug*. But it makes sense in a weird way, too. Almost as if my parents have come full circle. Nana was the one to bring them together all those years ago. It's only right that she's the reason that after everything they've been through, they can still love and respect each other now. And though it was strange to see them so emotional together after so many years of nothing but long silences and distance between them, it doesn't feel like a bad thing. In fact, in a weird way, it's made me feel just marginally lighter.

But that feeling rushes away when I glance down at the grave, over at the men readying to lower her casket into the ground, and feel like my lungs might cave in on themselves.

I nod, afraid any unnecessary loss of air might deflate them sooner, might make me collapse right here in the middle of the cemetery.

Perhaps sensing my distress, my father wraps his arm around my shoulders, strong once again as he guides me toward the exit, holding onto me through each sinking step.

"Charlotte," someone calls once we reach the road, and I turn to find Andrea walking towards me, dressed in black from head to toe.

Behind her, not moving, stands the one person I never expected to see here.

"Hey," I say, swallowing quickly and trying to keep myself calm. My lungs are burning for an entirely different reason now.

"Come here, babe," she says, and my father's arm disappears from around my shoulder so that Andrea can wrap me up instead. But, as always, our size difference makes it seem more like I'm wrapping *her* up.

"I'll be in the car, Charlotte," my dad says, and I nod my head over Andrea's shoulder.

She rubs my back, and I close my eyes, waiting for the tears that still haven't come. They have stay locked inside, shocked into submission.

Andrea pulls away, but keeps her hands in mine, and she stares up at me with big, soulful eyes. "I'm so sorry, girl."

I pull the corners of my lips up once more, and try to ignore the weight of those eyes on me, but I feel them like a touch.

"I know. Thanks," I say, forbidding myself to meet the gaze.

"She was special to me, too," Andrea says with a smile, and I'm confronted with another memory—the billionth for the day. Andrea and I sitting at Nana's dining room table, laughing and talking instead of doing homework, and Nana, a tray of pigs-in-a-blanket in hand, coming in, never scolding us for not actually doing our work—just dropping in with different snacks every so often, and joking that we were "eating her out of house and home".

I nod, afraid more talk will open up the vault of emotions that I've otherwise managed to keep shut tight. It can't happen here, now, in front of him.

Andrea releases a breath. "I, uh, brought someone with me." She gestures subtly behind her with a tilt of her head. He's leaning on her car, but that's all I let myself see. "I knew you wouldn't want him to come, but he was insisting, and I just…didn't know how to say no."

When I look again, he's staring right at me, and his gaze doesn't falter.

"It's okay," I say, even though I'm so nervous now I think I could puke. "I should probably talk to him anyway."

Andrea nods. "I'll come over tonight if you're up to it. Netflix and junk food?"

I try to smile. It still doesn't quite work. "Okay, I'll text you."

She hugs me once more. "I'll send him over."

I watch as she walks towards him; as he looks at her, waiting for the permission he wasn't sure I'd give. It only makes me more nervous, so I glance behind me at my father's car, which is idling by the curb.

But he isn't looking for me, and when I turn around again, Graham is striding my way. He's all dressed up for the occasion, and very little of him looks like the Graham Hudson I've come to know. In fact, it's like he's all Nick today. His curls are tamped neatly down, his scruff gone, and he's wearing a white shirt and a long, skinny black tie, loosely tied at the collar under a slightly-too-tight black blazer. But the pants he's trying to pass off as dress pants are black jeans, and even though the key chain usually dangling from his belt loop is conspicuously missing, I love him for that little bit of himself he's left.

"Hey," I say as he approaches, my voice quaking slightly as I stare at the black Converse sneakers he's not even trying to pass off for dress shoes.

Then I'm in his arms, completely surrounded by him, and he holds me so tight, for a moment, I'm sure I could never fall apart. When I breathe him in, we're back in his apartment, curled up on the couch, giggling and talking and feeling like the world could go to complete shit around us, but if we were still there, having enlightening thoughts about bagels, or Shakespeare, or the always Uncertain Future, it wouldn't really matter.

When I hung up the phone with my Dad that morning, Graham had taken me by the shoulders, asked me repeatedly what was wrong. But the words refused to come out. They were stuck in my airway, choking me. He'd cupped my jaw, ran his thumbs repeatedly along my lips, my cheeks, coaxing them up, up, up, until almost every agonizing syllable was forced out.

He held me then just like he's holding me now, but I couldn't say that last word, that *final* word. Couldn't admit out loud what I was still grappling to understand. But I didn't have to. He knew.

I didn't cry. Just heaved, panicking because I couldn't get a full breath of air, hearing my father's voice saying the words over, and over again, no closer to accepting them than I'd been when he said them. If Graham hadn't been holding me up, I surely would've collapsed onto the floor.

When it was over, when my chest accepted oxygen again, I'd gathered my things, and Graham was asking me questions, but I can't even remember what. I just needed to leave, and I told him as much. And when he didn't let me—that part I remember a little too clearly.

"*Just*," I'd said, my voice too loud. "I can't do this right now. Okay?"

It was a wonder I was able to get all of that out, but I had to force it, and my voice came out yelling. Graham backed off then, albeit reluctantly. He walked me to the door, turned me around, looked right into my eyes, and said, "Call me when you get home."

I nodded, even though I had no intention of doing so.

"Hey," he said when I tried to turn, catching me by the elbow. "*Please* call me."

He was pleading, as if he somehow knew I wouldn't, and could convince me otherwise.

He couldn't.

Now, he kisses my cheek before pulling back completely, and I close my eyes, regretting the way I treated him three days ago, regretting the fact that I hadn't called, or answered any of his texts, or even let myself *think* about him since I left.

"Look," he says, and his hands are still on my arms. "I know saying I'm sorry is probably the last thing you want to hear right now. But I have to say it… I'm *so* sorry."

"Thank you."

"And I know everyone has probably said this to you today, but I really mean it when I say I know what you're going through, and I wish more than anything that you didn't have to go through it, and if I can help in any way, I want to."

I smile, knowing not even he could understand.

"Anything. Just say the word. I'll do it."

Now I sigh, because while there's nothing he can do, I don't *want* him to do anything.

"I think I just…need some space."

His grip on my shoulders loosens.

"Space," he says after a moment, letting the word hang between us. He drops his arms. "Okay."

I don't know if it's because he looks so disappointed, or because *I'm* disappointed, but I feel the need to clarify. "It's just, I…"

Graham tilts his head, waiting for an explanation I'm afraid to give. Because wording what he deserves to hear would be admitting to everything I've been feeling since my Dad's phone call—all the guilt, all the anger, all of it directed at only one person.

Me.

"It's been almost a year since I've seen her. A *year*. All because I couldn't handle it. And I justified it by telling myself that she wouldn't remember anyway. How fucked up is that?"

Graham doesn't answer.

"And now she's…" I *still* can't say it. "I won't ever get the chance to see her again. And what's worse is, she *did* remember."

I don't tell him how I know that. How I went to the nursing home with my father to clean out her room, to take her things back home. How I found her paintings; how they were neatly stacked in a trunk at the foot of her bed. How I sat on the edge of the bed and leafed through them. There were scenic paintings of trees passing and changing through the seasons—bare, save for little buds of life yet to blossom, then leaves in the richest shades of green, then those same leaves in every hue of orange and yellow and red, then just the tree, dark and naked as bones against a gray sky. There were incredible paintings of sunsets, pinks, purples, and yellows blending out to the horizon over a body of water she'd imagined. There were still-life images of flowers, fruits, a lamp, a chair—anything she could find, really.

Only a few depicted people.

One person.

I recognized the girl immediately. In one, she was dancing, spinning around with her curls spread out around her like a mane. In another, she was picking a flower, in another she was sitting in a sandbox, and in another, she was sitting under a tree, her hair the color of the autumn leaves above her, glasses on her nose, a book in her lap, and her eyes on the sky.

"All that time…wasted. All that time I could've been spending with her, I just…" I don't want the tears to come now, but they're there, and I do my best to keep them at bay.

"Charlotte," Graham says, and he reaches a hand out, but I back up a step.

"I mean, what kind of granddaughter *does* that? She was there for me through *everything*, especially when my parents weren't, and I let her go through that alone. I let her think that I didn't want to see her because I was too scared of how it would feel if she forgot me while I was there in front of her. Not for a moment thinking of how *she* might feel if she remembered. If that isn't disgraceful, I don't know what is."

The anger burns hot in my chest, like a red-hot coal just beneath my heart, making it pound faster and faster until I'm sure I'll have another anxiety attack, right here in the middle of the cemetery. The thought makes me hope that the ground beneath me will open up and swallow me whole before it happens. It's where I belong anyway.

"Charlotte," Graham says again, and this time, he does touch me. His hands are on my shoulders again. "Don't you see what you're doing? You're punishing yourself for things that are out of your control."

"No, I'm punishing myself for the things I *could* control, and chose to avoid instead."

"Either way. It's over. Done. And this may sound harsh, but you can stop punishing yourself now. Wherever she is, she knows how much you love her. I truly believe that."

I feel a tear fall, and swipe it away.

"Want to know what the last thing I said to my father was?"

His hands are warm on the curves of my shoulders, and they don't loosen their grip when I shrug.

"I told him that he was selfish, that he only cared about himself. I told him that I didn't need him anymore. That I never would. Over *video chat*, Charlotte. While he was in Iraq. I hung up before he could even answer me."

I want to feel sympathy for him; want to fully grasp what he's telling me and relate to it. But I just can't.

"When we heard what happened, the guilt ate me up. And I let it, because I told myself I deserved it. But no one deserves to live like that. And it took a while before I realized that it's not what he would've wanted for me. He gave his life so that I could live freely, and I was chaining myself down with grief."

I look away, the tendrils of connection reaching out seeming more like accusatory fingers. You *should've* done this. You *should* do that. You *can't* do this.

"It's what you're doing to yourself now."

I shake my head. "It's different."

"How?"

"Your father knew you still loved him. Nana didn't know I still loved her. How could she? She lived every day for a year in a strange place, a place that wasn't home, and never saw me. Not once. *Everything* was wiped clean. Every memory, happy or sad…gone. How could she possibly know?"

"So, what, you're just going to hang onto this guilt as some sort of penance, or something?"

I stare at him, into his dark eyes, and for the first time in three days, my anger rears its ugly head outward.

"I have to go."

"What?"

"It's none of your business anyway."

"Charlotte, don't—"

"*Don't* tell me what to do," I snap at him. "You don't get it. There's no way you could understand."

"Charlotte, please…" His fingers wrap themselves around my arm, but I wrench myself away.

"No. Just…just leave me alone."

"Charlotte," he says, almost desperate now. I don't know why I stop, but I do, and I keep my back to him. "The other night…you said you were scared. You need to know that I'm scared, too. But please…don't end it this way. Don't run this time."

I walk away without looking back. He doesn't call after me again.

Dad stares at me as I slam the car door shut, but I don't look at him, just buckle my seat belt and try to get a grip. When I'm done with that, I still don't look at him, just say, "Don't ask."

"Later, then," Dad says, and when we drive away, I close my eyes, trying not to think about what I've just done. Because if I think too much about it, I'll start to regret it, and I've got enough on my plate to regret.

***

Days pass in a blur of exhaustion dotted with restless wakefulness. I spend most of my time in my room, watching Netflix, mostly. Reading or sketching leaves too much room for my mind to wander, but watching senseless TV shows seems to keep and hold my attention.

My only interruptions are dinners with Dad and whenever Andrea comes over, demanding that I eat something, demanding that I shower, change my clothes, sit downstairs on the couch for a while. But when she tries to talk to me about Nana, I shut her down. I'm just not ready. I can't do it yet. She understands, thankfully, though I know that understanding will only go so far.

"The theater gave me the go-ahead for another play this spring," she says after one such attempt, during her longest visit. It lasts all of two hours.

"Really?" I ask, trying to drum up enough enthusiasm to sound genuine. "That's awesome."

"Yeah," she says, and curls her legs up on the couch beside me. "I've got a couple in mind, and I'll need your help to decide when you feel like it."

I smile at her. "Am I going to have a choice this time about whether or not I want to be involved? Or are you going to trick me into it again?"

Andrea smiles back, but it doesn't hold the offense, or the mischief I'm expecting. "No, not if you don't want to. I appreciated the help so much on this last one, but I don't want to make you do anything you don't want to."

As much as I complained, and made a fuss about being tricked into being pseudo-stage manager for the play, was as much as I enjoyed the experience. I needed a distraction—from my life, from missing London, from missing Nana… It gave me another excuse not to go see her, but it also gave me an excuse to live; to broaden my horizons here at home. For that, at least, I would always be grateful.

"No, I want to," I say, and Andrea's head kicks back in surprise. "We make a good team."

She smiles. "That, we do."

I feel better when she's here, but she's always been like a tumbleweed, blowing in whichever direction the wind is taking her, so she doesn't stay long. I know that's partly because of me. My company these days is not what it used to be.

So I end up back in my room, tucked into bed between sheets I should've washed two weeks ago, but I don't care. It's cozy and warm, and lulling me back into another fitful sleep—until my door creaks open.

"Dad?" I say when he pokes his head through, wondering why he's home so early. He's supposed to be teaching until five today.

He steps into my room with something like a smile, but it turns into more of a grimace.

"What is it?" I ask, turning over on my back to see him more clearly.

He sighs, and the sound makes me suck in a breath because it reminds me of Nana. It's the way his shoulders fall, the way his bottom lip juts out—the way he's looking at me. His gaze is firm. Focused. His eyes are the same color and shape as hers. "It's time to get up, Charlotte."

"What?" I ask, trying to ignore the slash of fear right in the middle of my torso. I can't handle any more bad news.

"It's been over two weeks. I've let you wallow long enough, I think. You're starting to make me nervous."

I'm so startled by what he's saying, by the way it makes me feel—a mix of shame and embarrassment poorly disguised by anger—that I pull my blankets further up, under my chin, as if they can shield me from the truth.

"No," is all I can think to say, and I'm embarrassed by the way it comes out, like a child refusing just because she's learned how to say the word.

But he doesn't get it. It's safe here. It's—it's where life doesn't make any demands. It's where no one's asking me to talk about it. It's where Graham can't get to me, even if there's a big part of me that wouldn't mind if he did. It's where I can push away every thought and memory of Nana by turning on the TV and losing myself in a senseless show.

"Charlotte," he says, and he sits on the bed by my feet, pity in his eyes. "I miss her, too. But that doesn't excuse me from living my life, and it doesn't excuse you, either. Come on."

"But it's not like I have anything to do," I say, feeling the suggestion of tears burn behind my eyes now. "School doesn't start for another week. It's not like I'm neglecting responsibilities."

"No, but holing yourself up in here is keeping you suspended in the grief, and it's enough now. You can't keep doing this. You haven't been outside since the funeral."

"I don't want to go outside."

He sighs again, his eyes closing and opening slowly as he tries to measure his words. "I know that you're angry. I'm angry, too. The way Nana died…"

Now I squeeze my eyes shut.

"It shouldn't have been that way. I hated that she had to go through that. But you know as well as I do that she wouldn't want you to do this. She would've hauled your ass out of this bed after the first day."

He smiles. I almost do.

The movement of my mouth quickly turns into a quiver, one I can't seem to still.

"I can't," I whisper.

I see my pain reflected in his eyes, and wish I could explain how much I hate myself; how much I hate that she died not knowing that I loved her; how much it hurts me to think that she had no idea who I was when she passed, all because of my own selfishness, my own fears. But voicing all of that would only bring all of that guilt right to the surface, where I'm sure it will do the most damage. I can control it while it's buried deep, but digging it up, letting my father see just how screwed up and warped it is—I can't do it.

"Come on," he says, patting my legs with a hand. "I have to show you something. You don't have to get dressed or anything, we're only going into my room. You just have to get up."

He holds his hand out, and I consider not taking it, consider keeping myself here, the shame a weight I don't want to carry, even the few steps to his bedroom. But then, something inside lurches toward him, and I grab hold.

## *Year One*

His mother was humming, and the sound stopped Mr. Worth in his tracks. It was the same tuneless sound he'd heard so many times as a child. The same tone-deaf kind of melody. But still, it made him want to stop and listen.

He was exhausted. After two long shifts at the grocery store, he just wanted to crawl into bed. Maybe sleep for the rest of his life.

*In a minute,* he thought to himself. He just wanted to be a child again for a minute.

Mr. Worth stayed just out of sight of the only bedroom in his apartment, and peered around the corner to look inside.

Lindsay was curled up on the bed in her regular clothes, auburn curls in a bun, fast asleep. Mr. Worth touched the wedding band on his finger with his thumb, smiling a little to himself when he noted the sparkle of hers on the hand curled beneath her chin. They were going on two years together in love.

And Charlotte—he heard her gurgling as his mother hummed, and his heart swelled. She was only going on four months.

Three months old.

Mr. Worth had been a father for three months. And he didn't know if it would get easier—he certainly hoped it wouldn't get harder—but he almost didn't care. He loved that baby—his daughter—more than he'd ever loved anything else in his life. And he would take care of her, no matter the cost. He would provide for her, no matter how much time he had to spend away from her to do it. He would do everything in his power to make her happy.

To make her proud.

He'd never felt drive like this. The need to better himself so that he could take care of Lindsay and Charlotte. His little family. But he was doing his best to put it to good use. He woke up every morning at the crack of dawn, and went to work, taking as many shifts as they would give him. Every day, over, and over, and over again.

But coming home to this—to see his beautiful wife asleep in their bed after a full day of her own, to hear his daughter cooing in his mother's arms as she sang—all the hard work, all the exhaustion, was well worth it.

"You are wide awake," Nana murmured then, his mother's voice so familiar, so soothing to him, even now, he leaned his head against the wall beside him. "Aren't you, Charley?"

Mr. Worth would've shaken his head at the nickname if he'd had any energy left to spare. Instead, he just chuckled to himself.

"That's right," Nana said as Charlotte gurgled. "You're wide awake."

It was just past eleven at night, and Charlotte had been a little difficult to put down to sleep right along—as if she already knew that all the good stuff happened while she was awake.

"You look just like your father did when he was a baby," Nana said, keeping her loud voice low enough so as not to wake Lindsay. Mr. Worth could still hear every word, and pictured his mother holding his daughter in her arms, smiling down at her, glasses perched on the end of her nose as she rocked the baby in their rocking chair, set up just beside Charlotte's crib.

"You have the same cute little nose. And the same big hazel eyes." Nana laughed when Charlotte made a noise, then—as if the baby could understand and was trying to respond. “You’re more talkative though. I can already tell.”

Charlotte made more noises in response, and Nana laughed some more. Mr. Worth loved that sound—his mother’s laughter. She didn’t do it often enough. At least, not up until Charlotte had been born. She’d done a lot of laughing since.

“You’re just a bundle of personality, aren’t you?” Nana asked, and it sounded as if her question was to the baby’s delight. “Yes, you are. And why wouldn’t you be? You’ve got two wonderful parents who love you, a cozy home, and an old grandma who just can’t get enough of you.” Charlotte cooed. “That’s right, I can’t. Hope you don’t mind.”

It was quiet for a beat.

“You’ve got such a wonderful life ahead of you, little one. And that personality will serve you well in it. I hope you never lose that spark.”

Nana’s words had softened, lost the edge of amusement, and it made Mr. Worth think back to their life together. It was a wonderful life—his mother had always been strong and determined and had loved him fiercely enough to pick him up when he was down, to share in his happiness and make it even better, to prod him forward when he didn’t have the courage to do something himself. All without his father by her side.

“Between you and me,” she went on now, after several long, quiet moments. “It’s a hard thing—holding onto yourself.”

Mr. Worth held his breath, wondering what was bringing this on—why she sounded abruptly sad. But he didn’t interrupt. He wanted to hear the rest.

“As you walk through life, you’ll meet lots of people. Different kinds of people. Some who stay for a while, others who don’t. Some who make you laugh, others who make you cry.” Charlotte made a soft noise then, and as far as Mr. Worth could tell, his mother ignored it. “The really important ones will make you do both.”

He didn’t need to wonder what Nana was thinking about anymore—he knew. And he knew she’d never say any of this aloud if she thought anyone who could understand was listening.

"I've met lots of people over the course of my life, Charley Worth, but only two of them changed me irrevocably. Only two of them made me feel...alive."

Two. Only two. His father was one. Mr. Worth was certain of that, and he'd nearly broken her. But the other—who was the other?

Charlotte fussed a little, then, and Nana hushed her, soothed her. Mr. Worth stayed right where he was, watching Lindsay through the crack in the door. She didn't move.

Nana calmed Charley again, and it sounded like she was on her feet now, moving back and forth, back and forth—the baby in her arms. Mr. Worth waited with bated breath for her to go on, to add more to her thoughts. The thoughts she'd kept to herself, determined to be strong, for his entire life.

It took long enough that he was sure that was it, sure that she'd lost her train of thought. He almost started backing away when he heard his mother's voice again, even quieter now.

"Wait for it, Charley," she murmured, and the baby stayed quiet. "Wait for the ones who make you feel alive."

It was only many years later, when Charlotte was an adult, when Lindsay had left him, when his mother was gone—it was only then that he understood.

His mother had given him life, and that would always be a huge part of his love for her, but it didn't count for this. He hadn't had to wait for her—she was *there*. Always. So, Mr. Worth could say with certainty that he only had two as well. And because he had two, he knew who his mother's second was.

For the brief time they were together and in love, Lindsay had brought fire into his life. Fire and passion he'd never known again. Charlotte had given him love—an inordinate amount of love. But more than that, she'd given him something to live for.

That was how he knew—what he'd perhaps always known since that night standing outside his bedroom door.

His father was Nana's first, and he'd blazed so brightly, he'd burnt himself out.

But he—Benjamin Worth—was her second.

*Wait for it*, she'd said, and Mr. Worth promised himself he would never forget it or take his two for granted as long as he lived.

## *Chapter Twenty-Four*

Dad closes the door behind us.

I don't know why. We're the only people living in this house anymore.

He loosens his tie, walks straight over to his desk, and sits down in his chair, right in the slant of late afternoon light streaming through his window. He hasn't shaved in a few days, and his beard is coming in dark and patchy. His short locks look like he's run his fingers through them too many times. He takes off his glasses, sets them down on the desk, and his eyes—I've never thought my father looked old. He's a good-looking guy, with a boyish charm, even now. But his eyes look sunken and dull, surrounded by lines. He rubs them now, bringing weary hands up and letting them fall after a moment with a long sigh.

"Dad," I say, abruptly nervous. "I—"

"I'm going to talk first, okay?" His eyebrows rise fractionally, and despite the fact that he's asking, I know better than to think it's a question I have the choice to answer. "Why don't you sit down?"

That's not really a question either.

I walk over to his unmade bed, sit down at the edge, facing him, and wait.

He leans forward to rest his elbows on his knees. "Your mother told me you two had a chance to talk."

I wait a moment, wondering where this is going; why he's brought this up. "I thought you wanted to show me something."

"I do. But, I just… I want to talk to you about this first."

I'd be lying if I said the conversation with my mother didn't change the way I viewed my parents' entire relationship. I used to think Mom just had good or bad days, but now I realize that the kind of day she had may have been dependent on the kind of day my father had. Were the good days good because he was around more? Were the bad days bad because he was doing well in school or work, while she was stuck home with me, while she worked office jobs for too many years? Was my father aware of any of it?

"I think I owe you an apology," he says. "For not being honest with you about your mother and me."

"Dad, you don't have to."

"No. I want to." He stares at the floor between his knees, then looks up at me. "I'm sure she told you about before you were born. How I didn't want to get married."

"Yeah, but it doesn't change any—"

"I was young and stupid and scared," he says. "Those are the only reasons I didn't want to get married. Not because I didn't want to be with your mother. I was eighteen, we'd just found out she was pregnant with you, my whole world turned upside down, and then…marriage was just another thing I had to confront, another thing that I wasn't ready for. Your mom didn't understand that then, and I guess I can see why. But as your grandmother so aptly put it, I made my bed, and had to lie in it."

He looks down at his hands again, folding and refolding them between his knees. "So we got married. But we weren't ever the same. Especially after we had you. Life just sort of pulled us apart."

I understand being young and scared better than he might realize, and I can't imagine the pressure of an impending baby to put all of the confusion, all the decisions to be made, under time constraints. What I can't understand is why he hid it for so long.

"Why didn't you tell me?"

He looks right into my eyes, which I'm sure are as green as his in the setting sunlight. "I loved your mother, Charlotte."

"I know. I could always see that."

He smiles a little. "I spent most of our marriage trying to prove it to her—working non-stop when you were born, going to night school, making a career for myself, all so that I could make a life for us. I worked myself into the ground to be the man you both deserved." He bites his lip for a moment. "She never saw it that way, though."

He isn't looking at me now. "I was ashamed. There are so many things I'd change if I could. More than anything, I wish I'd been around, really present for you over the years. It's taken losing Nana for me to admit to it, but—" he shrugs, "—I don't want to live with those regrets anymore. I don't want to live in the shame anymore. And I want to be here for you, all the time, starting now, if you can forgive me."

I nod, swallowing back the emotion that's welled up in my throat, behind my eyes. "Forgiven."

He smiles—a quick, pained one. "You have to let this go, Charlotte."

I feel the confusion form on my face. "What?"

"The anger," he says. "The regret. You can't hold onto it like this."

There it is. It's ears prick up first, then it lifts its head. "You don't understand..."

"I understand better than you think..."

I shake my head. It's standing up now, flexing its muscles. My voice quakes with it. "I *left* her."

He only stares at me.

"I wasted an entire *year*. The last year of her life." It's stretching, trying to release the tension in its limbs. But there's so much of it, my anger only becomes angrier. "I don't know what's worse. Wishing she'd completely forgotten me in the last year, or knowing that she didn't. She *remembered*, Dad. You saw the paintings."

I say it like an accusation, and Dad absorbs the blow by closing his eyes, sighing through his nose.

"She must've been wondering where I was. Why I wasn't there with her. Why I never came to see her…"

"You were living your life, Charlotte."

"While she lost track of hers!" My voice is loud and frantic, trying to make him understand. "I traveled three thousand miles away to avoid watching it happen because I couldn't take it. I couldn't watch her forget me. And *you* let me do it. Why? How could you *let* me do that?!"

"Because I couldn't stand to see my daughter wither away, too!"

My anger falls for the moment, taken aback by his blow. But it's already getting up again, waiting for the next opening to attack.

"Every day, you were drawing more and more into yourself. Your mother used to get the same look in her eye—this closed-off, hard look. She numbed herself to everything. I couldn't sit back and watch you do the same thing."

It's pacing, glaring at him, surprised by the turn of our conversation, but waiting, watching, looking for a chink in his armor.

"Nana's disease…it poked a lot of holes in her mind. She could only remember pieces of things, of memories, and they weren't always the same pieces. But one thing she always knew, without a shadow of a doubt, was that she loved us. She knew she loved you, Charlotte."

That's it. My father's words hit their target, straight and true, sharp as an arrow, and my anger falls, crashing to the ground with the force of a boulder, cracking clean through to reveal the shaking form of my grief hidden within, trembling in fear.

Dad's at my side a moment later, pulling me to his chest, and I let him hold me as my body convulses with the sobs I've fought so hard to keep contained. I clutch at his chest, pull fistfuls of his shirt, and his arms tighten around me, squeezing, as if he can keep each broken piece together by sheer force of will. I'm desperate for it to end, the pain—it's clawing at me, pulling me down, down, down into the oppressive weight of nothingness, until I can't see anything but black—but there's another part of me that's relieved, that knows I need to let myself be taken; let myself feel every inch of the descent before I can start to climb back up.

I'm exhausted when it's over. My head aches, and I can't breathe through my nose, and only when I've stopped gasping, when I'm no longer crying out from the terror of it all, does my father pull away.

He doesn't say anything, just removes my glasses and wipes away the last of the tears; brushes back my hair, and kisses my forehead, eyes full of concern and pain.

"Sorry about your shirt," I say, noticing the large wet spot on his light blue button-down. My voice is almost unrecognizable.

When Dad smiles, I feel my own lips twitch up, and it's the first time in weeks it doesn't take any effort.

"What, this old thing?" he says.

I run my fingers over the wet spot as if I can wipe it away, but he grabs my hand, and holds it.

"Let this be the end of your punishment, Charley. You've had enough."

My eyes burn again at the use of Nana's nickname for me, and when the tears threaten to spill over, I let them, the slow trickle of each one down my cheeks drawing with them a little bit of the pain.

"I miss her," I say, and Dad thumbs away the tracks of my tears, even as more rush down. His eyes are filled with them, too.

"I do, too. But she wouldn't want you to do this to yourself. You know that."

I nod. "I just… I hope she didn't forget how much I loved her. How much I *still* love her."

Dad looks thoughtful for a moment, but his eyes—so like hers—don't stray from mine. "Her heart was always strong, even when her mind wasn't. That's where she knew, kiddo. That's where she kept it."

He hugs me close when I break again; when the thought of Nana passing in the night, letting out one last breath in her strange room at the home, is all I can see. But I calm faster this time, the pull of the pain not as strong, the fear of the darkness not as sharp, the climb back up not as exhausting.

It's not going to be easy—going forward without her. Forgiving myself every day like she'd want me to. Or forgiving my mother. Or my father. It's going to take work, and strength, and a whole lot of love. Because I can't forget, not in this case.

But that's okay, because, for the first time, I don't want to forget a thing. For the first time, I'm certain that remembering every moment will make forgiveness all the more worth it.

I sniffle, my stuffed nose not allowing any air through, and Dad's brushing back my hair again, swiping away the moisture on my cheeks, but before he can say anything more that'll make me cry again, I ask, "What did you want to show me?"

He pulls away and smiles, the kind of grin I haven't seen him wear in years. "I almost forgot." He stands, and moves toward his desk, opens the bottom drawer. "I wasn't around much when you were younger. Even now—now that I've got a much more steady job and pretty much make my own hours—I'm not really around when I *am* around. My mind was always somewhere else." He pulls a large, bound bundle of pages from the depths of the drawer. "At least I finally have something to show for it."

I gasp as he hands it to me, glancing from the manuscript to him in amazed disbelief. "You *finished* it?!"

He's grinning even wider now, and sits beside me, staring at the stack of pages when he says, "Well, it's kind of an ongoing project. I've only just finished the first revision, but I don't think I'll ever publish it."

"What? Why not? That's all you've ever wanted, all you've ever worked for! Why wouldn't you at least *try*?"

Dad just smiles at me, eyes a light golden brown. "No. It's not all I've ever wanted."

"But…" He's being ridiculous. Stupid, even. I'm already plotting ways to send it out without him knowing.

"I love to write, Charlotte," he says, putting an end to my inspirational rant before I can even get started. "But there are other things I will always love more." He spreads his palm out on top of the manuscript, still gripped tight in my hands. "This was an even mix of the two."

I scrunch my nose up, a little surprised not to feel my glasses slide up, only to remember that he removed them when I was crying. "I don't understand."

"I want you to read it, kiddo."

"Well, *of course* I'm going to read it. If you thought I wasn't, you've got another thing—"

He's laughing when he interrupts me. "I just mean it'll explain everything."

I stare down at the bound book sitting in my lap, imagination running wild with concepts, what he could possibly mean. I don't have a clue what it's about. He never wanted to talk about it. But here it is, in my hands. And he's finally trusting me with it.

"It doesn't have to be now, if you have something to—"

"Nope, I don't have anything!" I exclaim, holding the manuscript now as if it holds all the answers to life's greatest mysteries. And, in a way, for me, it does.

Dad chuckles, and it's a nervous sound. "Alright, well…I'll leave you to it." He gives my curls one last tug before I stand, heading for the door. "Oh, uh…before I forget."

I turn back around, and he presses his lips together, bringing a hand up to rub the back of his head.

"I, uh, wrote a letter for you, too. It's tucked in there."

I flip the front page open to find folded sheets of looseleaf, thoroughly wrinkled with ink.

"Read that first, okay?"

I look from the scribbled over pages to him, and run back, wrapping my arms around him, unable to contain my smile, my excitement.

"I love you, Dad."

His arms tighten around me. "Love you more, kiddo."

The door to my room slams shut in my excitement to start reading, and I launch myself onto my bed, tuck myself back under the covers, and turn on my lamp.

I don't let myself look at the title of the book yet—just take a breath and unfold Dad's letter, letting myself smile at the scrawl of his handwriting before I begin to read.

*To my favorite girl,*

*You know better than anyone how much this book means to me. You've lived twenty years with the quiet, obsessive man who created it, after all. You know how much effort, time, and thought went into its creation—mainly because it was effort, time, and thought that should've been put into loving and caring for you. What you don't know is that it has been a labor of the utmost, selfless love I can manage, because it is a book all about you.*

*Kiddo, I have not lived an adventurous life, or a brave life, or a valiant life, either. Mine is a life full of mistakes, hurt, self-pity, and regret. I've played it safe, kept to myself, and taken as few risks as possible. My rashest decisions are the ones I made with your mother, because I was in love, and nothing about love makes sense. But those decisions are the ones I most treasure; the ones I keep at the center of my heart, and the forefront of my mind, because those decisions brought me you.*

*You weren't part of the plan, Charlotte Worth, but by God, you were the best decision I've ever made. From the day you were born, I watched you, fascinated by your emerging facial features, and quirks, the things that reminded me of myself, or of your mother, taking note of the changes in you from the very beginning. You amazed me, Charlotte, with your unfiltered honesty, your innocent curiosity, your wide-eyed independence, and your forceful will to see the good in the world, despite all that's wrong with it. Amazed me, and inspired me—to the point that I found myself scribbling down things you would say, just so I wouldn't forget them. Jotting down stories of you, just to keep them around in my head for a little bit longer.*

*I've always wanted to be a writer, Charlotte, but I've never found anything as compelling as you, and your many stories helped me find the writer within myself.*

*This book is full of them: your stories. Your triumphs, your failures, your smiles, your tears, your shortcomings, and your growth—all of it seen through my eyes. I've had the honor and pleasure of watching you grow, kiddo, and I thought it might be nice for you to see it all yourself now.*

*Many of the stories, I embellished—I couldn't get all of the details from Nana. (Don't be angry with her for revealing them. She wanted to read Charlotte Worth's story in its entirety, too.) And some of the things I've included are conversations overheard, things you might've purposely kept from me. And I'm sorry for that.*

*But, Charlotte, please know (I think you already do) that nothing you could ever do would make me angry enough to stop loving you. It's impossible. Never going to happen. Not even if you tried. I can no longer imagine a world where I don't love Charlotte Worth. If it were possible, it wouldn't be a happy place.*

*I know you're young, and it's natural to keep some things from your parents, but I hope you know now that you can always come to me—the crazy Dad who spent twenty years of his life documenting his daughter's. (Promise I won't document anything you don't want me to...anymore.)*

*It's hard for me to let anyone read it. It feels kind of like letting strangers into the deepest, darkest recesses of my mind—the parts where my heart is so vulnerably beating, breathing life into me, that all I really want to do is shield it from the outside. But then I remind myself that this is you, Charlotte, my favorite girl with the big heart. And I know that you have to see it. You have to know just how much I love you, admire you, and how inspired I am every day by your warm heart, gentle spirit, and smart mouth.*

*I may not have lived an adventurous life, or a brave life, or a valiant one...but that's all I want for you, Charley*

*Worth. And you should know that you're already doing it. You always have been.*

*With that said, there's not much I can say by way of parental wisdom. You're already living life far more fully than I ever did (it must be because you're so much smarter). But in all these years of watching you, kiddo, I have noticed one thing in particular that troubles me. You are brave, beautiful, strong in your convictions, and passionate about what you want. But, Charlotte Worth, you are scared to let yourself love. Being the tortured artist that I am, I blame myself. Maybe if I had given you a better example of love—what it is, what it means, how to fight for it, and how to maintain it—things would be different for you. But I can't take all the credit on this one. Fear only stretches its claws as far as you allow it to, and Charlotte, you are giving it a lot of room to sprawl.*

*Nana said something once that's always stuck with me, even though I wasn't meant to hear it. She said it to you, Charlotte. When you were a baby. She said to wait for it. To wait for the ones who make you feel alive.*

*I don't know if that'll mean anything to you now, but if it does, here's my measly bit of fatherly advice (which probably goes against the Dad Code, decreeing all fathers must despise their daughter's love interests...it says it, I swear):*

*Let love in.*

*Let love in, and give love back.*

*Because you deserve love, Charlotte, all that the world has to offer. Remember that, always.*

*Love,*
*Dad*

## *Chapter Twenty-Five*

Only when I lift my hand, feel the hard metal of the door beneath my knuckles as I rap against it, and hear the knocks echo down the short hallway, do I let myself think.

This isn't a good idea.

This is the *worst* idea I've ever had.

If I run now, I can still get out of here.

But I want to see him.

I hope he wants to see me, too.

Once I let myself cry (again) over Dad's letter, and finally collected myself enough to see through the blur of my tears to the title page of his book, it started all over again.

"About a Girl," by Benjamin Worth, it read.

I still can't believe it.

It took another five minutes to collect myself enough to flip the page, to keep myself together as I read the first one, his words—all about me.

And Nana.

*She turned her face toward the light, determined to find the glittering outline of the golden orb pressed against a blue sky. Her eyes watered, so she squeezed them shut, just for a moment, before blinking them open, and searching again.*

*"Charley Worth." Nana's hand closed around her granddaughter's. "I'm starting to think you* want *to blind yourself."*

I laughed through my tears, remembering every moment, wondering how he knew; how he could capture that moment even though he wasn't there. Nana must've been more of a help than he let on.

It was so clear, so vivid, it felt like I was standing right there again, my hand in Nana's as she dragged me away, toward her car. I remember the confusion, the disappointment—wondering how something so bright, something that lit up my days, could bring about that kind of darkness. How something so beautiful could bring about that kind of pain.

Every sunny day for years, I searched for it—the source of the light—my eyes burning and watering with the effort, and I stubbornly refused to close them, choosing to work through the pain of it. It was a wonder I *didn't* go blind. But I remember the satisfaction I felt in finding it, in seeing the outline of the sun, just for a second, and it made the tears worth it.

The door creaks open, and my heart feels like it's being dribbled against my ribcage, trying to get out, to get to him.

"Uh…can I help you?"

My breath whooshes out of me, and my racing heart stops, kicks back into a slower gear. He's several inches taller than me, and he's got long blonde hair tied up in a bun. His light blue eyes are looking me up and down, his brow furrowed in confusion, and it takes me longer than it should to regroup.

"Uh, is Graham here?" I ask, still nervous, still anxious to see him, still desperate to know I didn't totally screw everything up.

The guy's eyebrows furrow. "Who are you?"

"Oh, right. Charlotte. I'm Charlotte." I reach my hand out for him to shake. He stares at it like it might bite him before taking it. "I'm Graham's, uh…friend."

"Oh," the guy says, nodding now, and I can almost see pieces fitting together in his eyes. "Cool. I'm Jack. Graham's roommate."

As great as that is… "Is he here, by any chance?"

"Oh, yeah. Graham!" he calls into the apartment behind him.

It takes a moment, but when I hear his voice, his annoyed, "*What?*" coming from somewhere within, my heart picks up its pace again.

"You've got a visitor," Jack calls, nodding for me to come in.

Last chance to run…

I step over the threshold.

But I stay by the door, still afraid that this won't go my way. My heart is pounding so hard, I feel everything go red, and I clasp my hands together in front of me, surprised by how cold they are; by how much they're shaking as I hear shuffling movements coming from the direction of his room, then the distinct creak of a door opening.

It all seems like such a bad idea now, standing here in his apartment, hoping he'll forgive me, hoping he'll still want me. But I couldn't shake my father's words, couldn't shake the feeling that I had to try. I didn't even make it through the first chapter of Dad's book before I made my decision.

I *had* to try.

I suck in a breath when I hear his footsteps, and let it out when he rounds the corner, when those dark eyes land on me.

Everything calms in an instant—my heart, my nerves, my panting breaths. My hands stop shaking, and I let go, letting them fall to my sides, opening myself to him for the first time since we met.

"Hi," I say, and my voice is strong, sure, just as certain as I feel.

He continues to stare at me, lips parted, curly hair a mess, like he's just woken up and hasn't had a chance to look in a mirror. He's wearing basketball shorts and an undershirt, and his fingers are loosely curled into his palms as if he wants to reach out, but isn't sure if he should.

He's beautiful. So beautiful it hurts, and I almost want to look away.

But I don't. I *can't.*

"Hi," he says back, and the relief in seeing his smile widen is almost painful, but I keep staring, taking in every twist and curve of his colors.

I smile back, glad for the pain, because, in spite of it, I can't help but feel like I can finally see.

## *Acknowledgements*

When I sat down to write this book over three years ago, I hadn't yet written a story longer than ten pages. And I'd only written something that long because it was required of me for my writing classes in college. So, when my father walked into the house to find me sitting at the kitchen counter, furiously scribbling away on a legal notepad, naturally his first question was: "What are you doing?"

I could only look up at him, heart aflutter, still sort of unsure myself, and say, "I'm writing a book."

I don't know what I expected. A scoff? A roll of his eyes? A bark of laughter?

Because what I received was a great big smile and a, "Good. Keep going."

If not for my parents' support and their unending faith in me, this book might not have been written, so to Mom and Dad: THANK YOU from the bottom of my heart.

Thank you also to Bryony Magee, the lovely editor from across the pond who believed in Charlotte Worth and her story as much as I did from the very start. There are no words to express how grateful I am to you. This book would not be what it is today without your insight. Thank you for your kindness, your support, your passion, and your love for this story!

And another HUGE thank you to one of my dearest friends, Alyssa Perfetto, for the stunning cover of Trace the Edges! It truly captures the essence of Charlotte's story, and I couldn't ask for much more than that. Thank you for sharing your talent not only with me, but with the world.

And lastly, to my Wattpad and Radish readers—over the last three years, writing for you has given me the confidence I needed to reach this point. Thank you for being so wonderfully supportive, and for believing in me all along.

Made in the USA
Middletown, DE
10 January 2018